Praise for

RUINATION

"Anthony Reynolds weaves a propulsive tale of love, loss, and war. Those familiar with *League of Legends* know where this story must leave us, but *Ruination*'s power is that knowing how it ends is just the beginning."

—Evan Winter, author of *The Rage of Dragons*

"*Ruination* is a rousing, intrigue- and action-rich tale sure to delight fans of fantasy."

—Anthony Ryan, author of *The Pariah*

"Fast-paced and entertaining epic fantasy—thoroughly enjoyable. Recommended for fans and newcomers alike."

—James Islington, author of *The Shadow of What Was Lost*

"Reynolds has crafted an engaging fantasy novel full of memorable characters in *Ruination*.... The characters alone are enough reason for any fantasy lover to pick up this book, but *League of Legends* fans will especially love it."

—*Cosmic Circus*

"A novel that I could recommend to someone who just likes fantasy books, even if they've never played *League* [*of Legends*]."

—*Polygon*

By Anthony Reynolds

League of Legends

Ruination
Garen: First Shield

By Riot Games

League of Legends: Realms of Runeterra

RUINATION

A LEAGUE OF LEGENDS NOVEL

ANTHONY REYNOLDS

orbitbooks.net

Cover design by Lauren Panepinto
Cover illustration by Mike Heath | Magnus Creative
Cover copyright © 2022 by Hachette Book Group, Inc.
Maps by Tim Paul
Icons and graphics by Greg Ghielmetti
Interior character illustrations by Kudos Productions
Author photograph by Riot Games

Orbit
Hachette Book Group
1290 Avenue of the Americas
New York, NY 10104
orbitbooks.net

First Paperback Edition: January 2024
Originally published in hardcover and ebook by Orbit in September 2022

Orbit is an imprint of Hachette Book Group.
The Orbit name and logo are registered trademarks of Little, Brown Book Group Limited.

The publisher is not responsible for websites (or their content) that are not owned by the publisher.

The Hachette Speakers Bureau provides a wide range of authors for speaking events. To find out more, go to hachettespeakersbureau.com or email HachetteSpeakers@hbgusa.com.

Orbit books may be purchased in bulk for business, educational, or promotional use. For information, please contact your local bookseller or the Hachette Book Group Special Markets Department at special.markets@hbgusa.com.

Library of Congress Control Number: 2022935455

ISBNs: 9780316469159 (trade paperback), 9780316469258 (ebook)

Printed in the United States of America

LSC-C

Printing 1, 2023

For Beth, my love and my life.

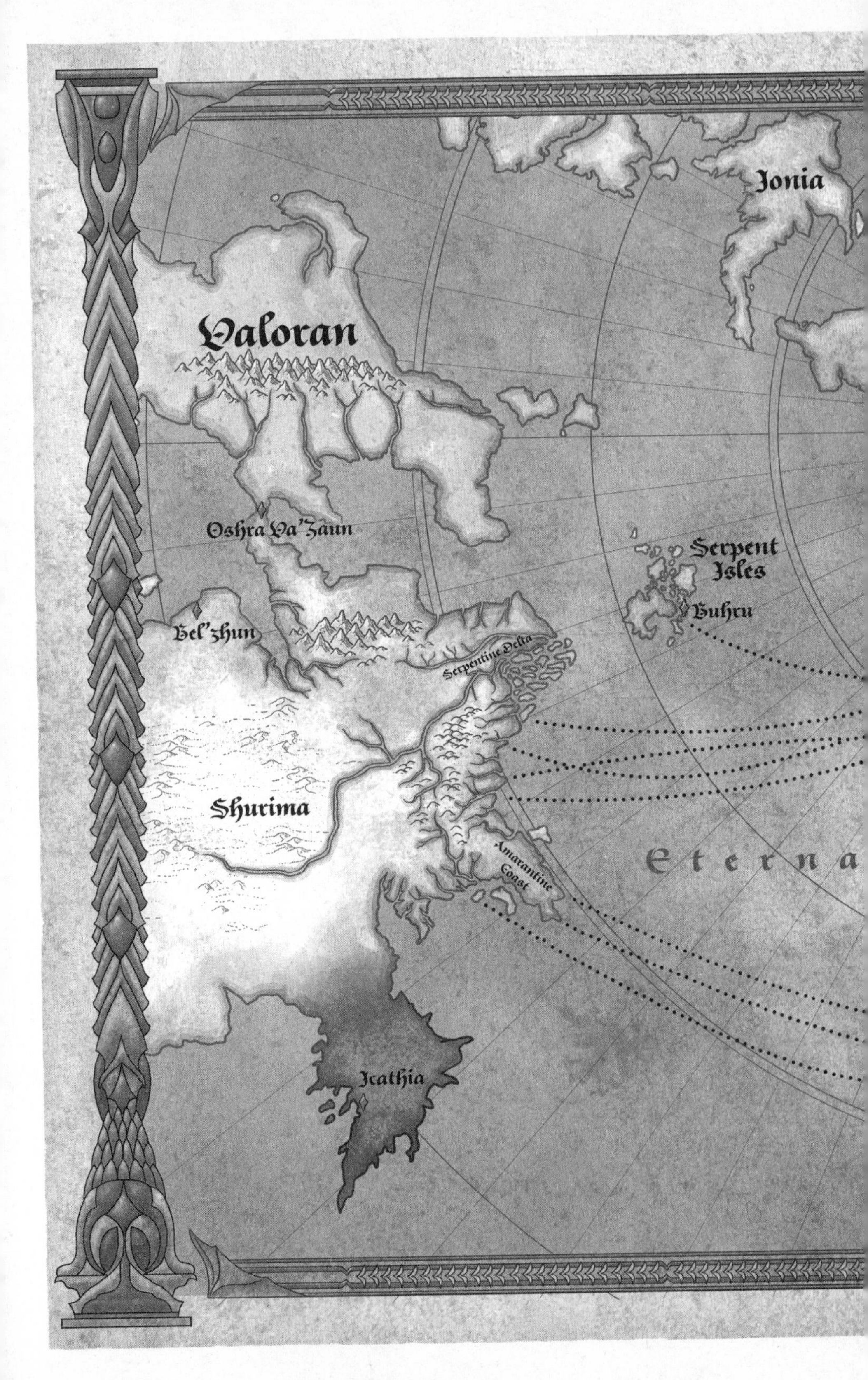
Jonia
Valoran
Oshra Va'Zaun
Serpent Isles
Buhru
Bel'zhun
Serpentine Delta
Shurima
Amarantine Coast
Eterna
Icathia

N
nw
ne
W
E
sw
se
S
Camavor
Alovédra
Independent Lands
cean

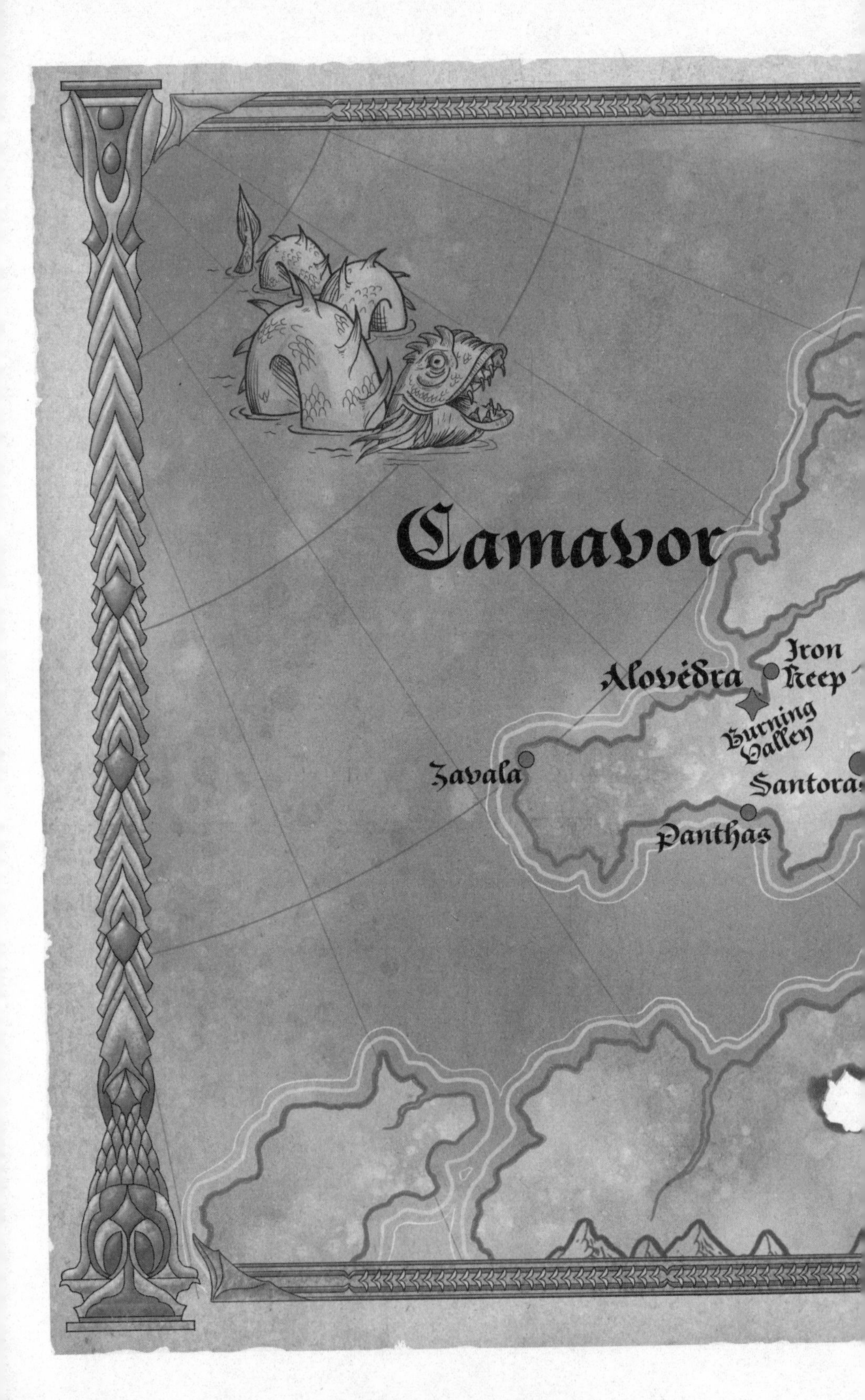
Camavor
Iron Keep
Alovédra
Burning Valley
Zavala
Santora
Panthas

askaros
olemia
Alshalaya
Port Takan

THE ROYAL LINE OF

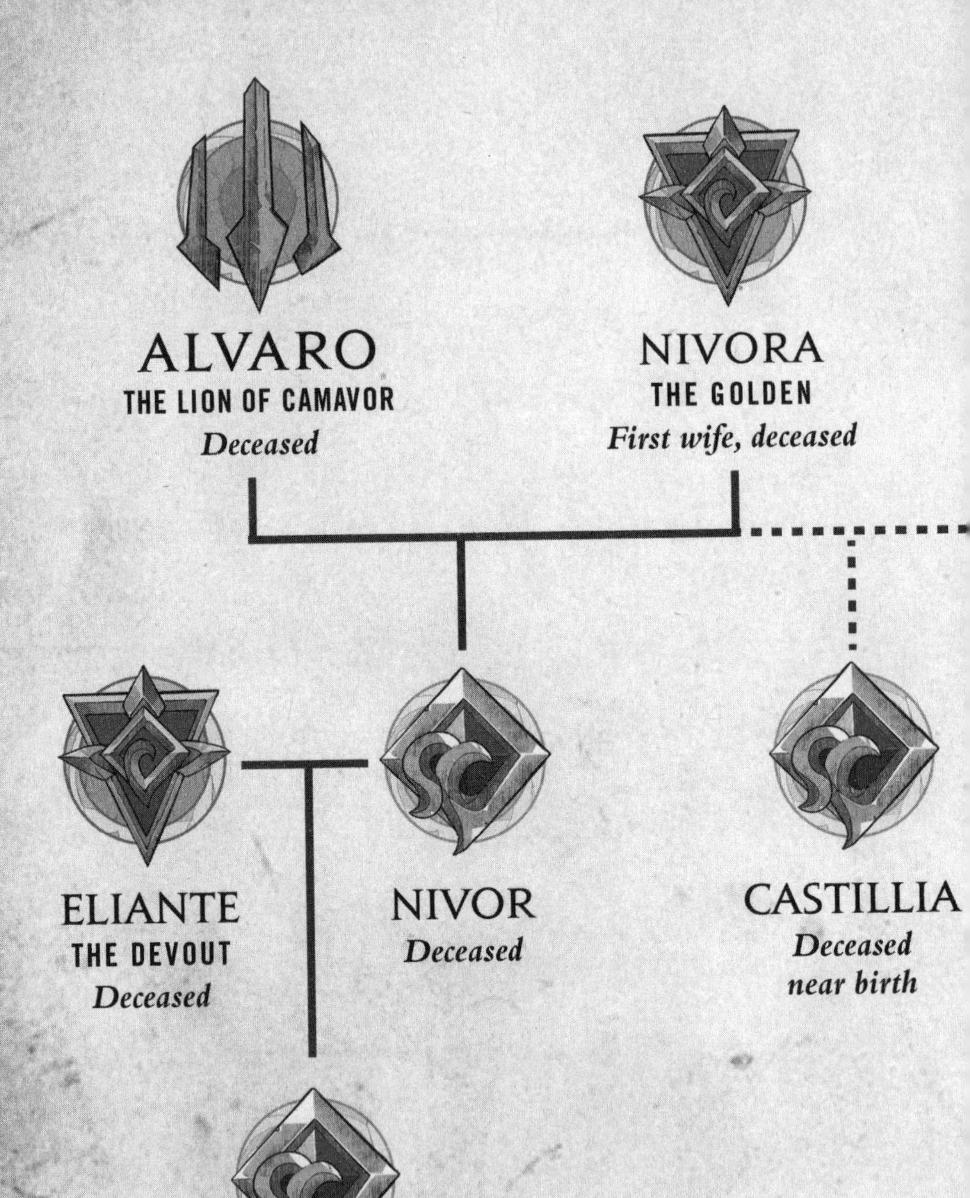

VOL KALAH HEIGAARI

CAMAVILLA
OF PANTHAS
Second wife, deceased

LIANOR
OF ZAVALA
Third wife, deceased

BASTILLON
Deceased near birth

VIEGO

ISOLDE

RUINATION

Invariably, all nations crumble, fall, and are forgotten. And in their final death throes, they often drag others down with them.

—*The Histories of Empire, volume VI*,
by Tyrus of Helia

Prologue

Helia, the Blessed Isles

Erlok Grael stood separate from his peers, awaiting the Choosing.

They waited within a small open-air amphitheater, the architecture all gleaming white marble and gold-encased capstones. Helia wore its opulence proudly, as if in defiance of the brutalities of life beyond the shores of the Blessed Isles.

The others joked and laughed together, their collective nervousness drawing them closer, yet Grael stood silent and alone, his gaze intense. No one spoke to him or included him in any of the whispered japes. Few even registered his presence; their gazes slipped over and around him as if he didn't exist. To most of them, he didn't.

Grael did not care. He had no desire to swap inane small talk with them, and he felt no jealousy at their juvenile comradery. Today would be his moment of triumph. Today he would be embraced into the inner circle, apprenticed within the secretive upper echelons of the Fellowship of Light. He had more than earned his place there. No other student present came close. They might hail from wealth and nobility, while he came from a line of illiterate pig farmers, but none were as gifted or as worthy as he.

The masters arrived, filing down the central stairs one by one, silencing the gaggle of hopefuls. Grael watched them, eyes burning with a hungry light. He licked his lips, savoring the prestige and glory that were soon to be heaped upon him, anticipating all the secrets that he would soon be privy to.

The masters shuffled into place upon the lower tiers of the amphitheater, their expressions solemn, staring down at the cluster of adepts on the floor below them. Finally, after an overlong pause to build suspense, a pompous, toadlike master, his skin pale and wet-looking—Elder Bartek—cleared his throat and welcomed the graduating students. His verbose speech was heavy with gravitas and self-congratulatory asides, and Grael's eyes glazed over.

Finally, the time came for the masters to choose which of the graduates would be taken under their wing as apprentices. There were leaders here from all the major disciplines and denominations of the Fellowship. They represented the Arcanic Sciences, the various schools of logic and metaphysics, the Blessed Archives, the Astro-Scryers, Hermetic Oratory, Esoteric Geometry, the Seekers, and other branches of study. All served, in one way or another, the greater purpose of the Fellowship—the gathering, study, cataloging, and securing of the most powerful arcane artifacts in existence.

It was an auspicious gathering of some of the world's most brilliant minds, yet Erlok Grael focused on only one of their number: Hierarch Malgurza, Master of the Key. Her dark skin was heavily lined, and her once-ebony hair was now mostly gray. Malgurza was a legend among the adepts of Helia. She didn't appear at every year's Choosing ceremony, but when she did, it was always to embrace a new apprentice into the inner circle.

The Baton of Choosing was brought forth. It was passed first to Hierarch Malgurza, the most honored master present. She took it in one gnarled hand, causing a ripple of murmurs among the students. Malgurza would indeed choose an apprentice this day, and the ghost of a smile curled Grael's thin lips. The elderly woman cast her hawkish gaze across the gathered hopefuls, who held their breaths as one.

Whoever was named would be marked for greatness, joining a hallowed, elite cadre, their future assured. Erlok Grael's fingers twitched in anticipation. This was his moment. He was already half stepping forward when the hierarch finally spoke, her voice husky, like oak-aged spirits.

"Tyrus of Hellesmor."

Grael blinked. For a second, he thought there must have been some mistake, before the cold reality of his rejection washed over him, like a bucket of frigid water to the face.

There was a delighted whoop from the chosen student, along with a burst of whispers and gasps. The newly named apprentice stepped forward amid a flurry of slaps on the back and ran up the steps of the amphitheater to take his place behind Hierarch Malgurza, a broad smile on his smug face.

Grael made no outward reaction, though he had gone dangerously still.

The rest of the ceremony went by in a dull, surreal blur. The Baton of Choosing passed from master to master, each choosing a new apprentice. Name by name, the crowd of hopefuls around Grael dwindled, until he stood alone. The sea of masters and former peers stared down at him, like a jury ready to announce his execution.

His hands did not twitch now. Shame and hatred writhed within him, like a pair of serpents locked in a death struggle. With a click of finality, the Baton of Choosing was sealed back within its ceremonial case and borne away by golden-robed attendants.

"Erlok Grael," announced Bartek, his eyes smiling. "No master has spoken for you, yet the Fellowship is nothing if not benevolent. A place has been secured for you, one that will, it is hoped, teach you some much-needed humility, and at least a modicum of empathy. In time, perhaps, one of the masters may deign to take you on—"

"Where?" interrupted Grael, eliciting murmurs and tuts, but he did not care.

Bartek looked down his bulbous nose at him. His expression was that of a man who had inadvertently stepped upon something distasteful. "You will serve as a minor assistant to the Wardens of Thresholds," he declared, malice gleaming in his eyes.

There were smirks and stifled laughter among his former peers. The *Threshers*, as the student body derisively called them, were the lowest of the low, both literally and figuratively, those who guarded and patrolled the lowest depths of the vaults beneath Helia. Their ranks consisted of those who had earned the ire of the masters, whether through gross political misstep or misdemeanor, and any others whom the Fellowship wished out of the way. Down in the darkness, they could be forgotten. They were a joke. An embarrassment.

Bartek's patronizing voice droned on, but Grael barely heard his words.

In that moment, he swore that this was not the end. He would serve among the wardens and ensure that his worth was noticed, such that none of these pompous, sniveling masters or his snobbish peers could deny him. He would serve a year, maybe two, and then he would take his rightful place within the inner circle.

They would not break him.

And he would remember this insult.

Alovédra, Camavor

It was dark and cool within the hallowed Sanctum of Judgment, and Kalista appreciated the reprieve from the scorching Camavoran summer outside. Standing at attention, bedecked in form-fitting armor and a high-plumed helm, she waited for judgment to be rendered.

Despite being out of the sun, the slender young heir to the Argent Throne, kneeling at her side, was sweating, and his breath was shallow and quick.

His name was Viego Santiarul Molach vol Kalah Heigaari, and he waited to see if he would be crowned king, or if this day would be his last.

Absolute rulership, or death. There could be no middle ground.

He was Kalista's uncle, but she was more like an older sister to him. They had been raised together, and he had always looked up to her. He was never meant to be the next king. That should have been Kalista's father, the firstborn, but his unexpected death had placed Viego, his younger brother, next in line.

The sound of the massed crowds outside was muted within the cold walls of the sanctum. Hooded priests, their faces obscured by shadow and blank porcelain masks, stood anonymous in the gloom, forming a circle. The incense from their censers was cloying and acrid, their whispering chant monotonous and sibilant.

"Kal?" breathed Viego.

"I am here," Kalista replied, standing at his side, her voice low.

He glanced up at her. His patrician face was long and handsome, yet in that moment he seemed younger than his twenty-one years. His eyes were panicked, like those of an animal caught between fleeing and fighting. Upon his forehead, three lines had been drawn in blood, coming together to a point just between his eyebrows. The blood trident was traditionally drawn only upon the dead, to help speed them on their way to the Beyond and ensure that the Revered Ancestors recognized them. It spoke of the lethality of what lay ahead.

"Tell me again of my father's last words," whispered Viego.

Kalista stiffened. The old king had been the Lion of Camavor, with a fearsome reputation in battle—and on the political stage. But as he lay dying in bed, he hadn't looked anything like the robust warrior-king who had so terrorized his enemies. In those final moments, his body was wasted and thin, all his vaunted power and vitality sapped from him. His eyes had still radiated a small measure of the power he'd had in his prime, but it was like the last glow of a fire's embers, one final glimmer before the darkness claimed him.

He clutched at her with the last of his strength, with hands that more closely resembled a vulture's talons than anything belonging to a man. "Promise me," he croaked, burning with a desperate fire. "The boy does not have the temperament to rule. I blame myself, but it is you who must bear the weight, granddaughter. Promise me you will guide him. Counsel him. Control *him, if needed.* Protect Camavor. *That is now your duty."*

"I promise, Grandfather," Kalista said. "I promise."

Viego waited expectantly, looking up at her. The faint roar of the crowd outside rose and fell like the crashing of distant waves.

"He said you'd be a great king," Kalista lied. "That you'd eclipse even his great deeds."

Viego nodded, trying to take comfort in her words.

"There is nothing wrong with being afraid," she assured him, her stern demeanor softening. "You'd be a fool if you weren't." She gave him a wink. "*More* of a fool, I mean."

Viego laughed, though the sound had an edge of hysteria to it and was too loud in the cavernous space. Priests glared, and the heir to the throne gathered himself. He pushed a wayward strand of his wavy hair behind one ear, and was still once more, staring into the darkness.

"You cannot let fear control you," said Kalista.

"If the blade claims me, it will be *you* kneeling here next, Kal," Viego whispered. He reflected on that for a moment. "You *would* make a far better ruler than I."

"Do not speak of such things," hissed Kalista. "You are blessed of the Ancestors, with power flowing through your veins that your father did not have. You are worthy. By nightfall you will be crowned king, and all of this will be just a memory. The blade will not claim you."

"Yet if—"

"*The blade will not claim you.*"

Viego gave a slow nod. "The blade will not claim me," he repeated.

There was a change in the air, and the priests' incessant chanting quickened. Their censers swayed from side to side. Light speared down into the sanctum through a crystal lens set in the center of the dome high above, as the sun finally moved into position directly overhead. Motes of dust and ribbons of cloying scented smoke drifted in the beam of light, revealing... nothing.

Then the Blade of the King appeared.

Its name was Sanctity, and Kalista's breath caught in her throat as she looked upon it. Hovering suspended in midair, the immense sword existed only in the spiritual Halls of the Ancestors, except when called forth by the rightful ruler of Camavor, or when summoned by the priests for the judgment of a new sovereign.

Every monarch of Camavor wore the Argent Crown, a belligerent tri-spiked circlet perfectly befitting the long line of belligerent rulers, but Sanctity was the true symbol of the throne. The primacy of whoever held Sanctity was undisputed, and to possess the Blade of the King was to be soul-bound to it—although not every heir to the Camavoran throne survived the ritual of binding.

Kalista knew that was not some vague, mythical threat, either. Down through the line of history, dozens of heirs had perished here in the Sanctum of Judgment. There was a good reason some called the blade Soulrender, and it was rightly feared by Camavor's heirs and enemies alike.

The crowd outside had fallen silent. They waited in hushed anticipation, ready to welcome a new monarch or mourn his passing. Either the doors would be thrown open and Viego would stride forth in glory, blade in hand, or the bell atop the sanctum would toll one singular, mournful note, signaling his end.

"Viego," Kalista said. "It is time."

The crown prince nodded and pushed himself to his feet. The blade hung before him, waiting for him to take it. And yet, still he hesitated. He stared at it, transfixed, terrified. The priests glared, eyes wide behind their expressionless masks, silently urging him to do what they had instructed.

"Viego..." hissed Kalista.

"You'll be with me, won't you?" he whispered urgently. "I don't think I can do this alone. Rule, I mean."

"I'll be with you," said Kalista. "I'll stand with you, as I always have. I promise."

Viego gave her a nod and turned back to Sanctity, hanging

motionless in the shaft of light. In seconds, the moment would be lost. The time of judgment was now.

The priests' chanting reached a fevered pitch. Smoke coiled around the sacred blade, like so many serpents, writhing and twisting. Without further pause, Viego stepped forward and grasped the sword, closing both hands around its hilt.

His eyes widened, and his pupils contracted sharply.

Then he opened his mouth and began to scream.

Part One

How different the world might have been had that blade found its mark...

—Sentinel-Artificer Jenda'kaya

Dearest Isolde, sister of my heart,

By the time you receive this, you will have left Alovédra and be only days from Santoras.

It disappoints me that our efforts to find a diplomatic solution fell short, but don't be disheartened—the idea of a bloodless negotiation would never have been even considered during my grandfather's rule. This is progress, and your impassioned pleas for Camavor to avoid creating more enemies and to preserve the economy of our ally were compelling. Were Viego not so keen to cement his rule with a victory on the field, he might not have listened to the arguments of the priesthood and the Knightly Orders at all.

Viego holds your counsel in the highest regard, and your positive influence on him will rein in the Knightly Orders' worst excesses. He's come so far, just in the short time you've been married! Already he has enacted changes that I never would have dreamed of. The nightly opening of the East Barracks kitchens to feed the poor and needy—which I know was at your urging—has earned him much goodwill among the less fortunate of Alovédra, and I am still in awe that you were able to convince Viego to give a council seat to an elected representative from the lower classes.

I still worry about you traveling here to Santoras and being in such close proximity to the coming conflict, but I understand your reasoning. Indeed, if the rest of Viego's court had even a fraction of your wisdom, empathy, and compassion, the world would be a far brighter place. There is no doubt Santoras will fall, as so many other city-states and nations have before, but I believe you are correct: Your presence will ensure that Santoras is not put to the sword after the battle.

The Grand Masters will balk at being ordered not to sack the city—they have grown wealthy filling their coffers with ill-gotten riches stolen from conquered foes—but they will not dare go against Viego. There will still be some violence and looting, of course. It would be unrealistic to believe otherwise. But I do believe this is the dawn of a new era for Camavor, one built upon bolstering trade with allies and improving the lives of average Camavorans, and not fixated upon brutal conquest and bloodshed hidden behind the veneer of the "noble quest."

It will take time to change the outdated and savage questing culture of the Knightly Orders, but with your help, I am confident that we can guide Viego toward ending it once and for all. What perhaps began as a noble endeavor has become corrupted by greed, and it is long past time for this vile practice to end. Your people witnessed the worst of it firsthand; no one should have to see their homeland ravaged and their loved ones butchered like they did. Nothing can be done to atone for that atrocity, but we can ensure that it never happens again.

The histories will record your influence on the future greatness of Camavor, I have no doubt. You bring out the best in Viego. It gives me such hope for the future.

Your dearest friend and ally,
Kalista

Chapter One

The Scouring Plains, Santoras
Eighteen Months After Viego's Coronation

Kalista vol Kalah Heigaari, General of the Host, Spear of the Argent Throne, and niece to the king, ripped the helmet from her head. She sucked in a deep breath and ran a hand through her long, sweat-damp hair.

The sun beat down upon her, relentless and unforgiving. The heat was searing, burning her lungs, but slowly, her heart rate began to steady. Only then, with the fury of battle dissipating, did she feel the ache and sting of wounds she didn't remember taking. Her head felt heavy, and there was a ringing in her ears. Had she taken a head blow? It was possible, yet the battle had been so chaotic, she couldn't be certain.

Her arms were leaden, her back sore. All she wanted to do was sink to the ground and close her eyes, but she did not. No soldier wanted to see their commander giving in to exhaustion. And so she remained on her feet, praying to the Ancestors that her legs did not collapse beneath her.

Thousands of bodies were strewn across the dusty plain. Where the fighting had been thickest, they were piled high, in lines where the soldiers had clashed and died. Most were motionless, but not all. Survivors on both sides twitched and moaned. But the Camavorans were the victors, and so while their wounded would be borne away, their injuries tended, the Santorassians were already being finished off.

Beyond the battlefield, the wives and daughters, husbands and sons of those soldiers watched from atop the sloping sandstone walls of their city. Kalista imagined she could hear their wails. There would be panic within those walls. Their king had gambled all by standing against Camavor, but he was dead, and his city would be claimed.

Far behind Kalista, upon a rise overlooking the battlefield, was the covered pavilion where her king watched, his queen at his side. Viego had wanted to be down here, fighting, leading from the front, the mighty blade Sanctity in hand. He came from a lineage of warrior-kings, and his father was the legendary Lion of Camavor, after all. Viego had been king for a year and a half now, and wanted to prove his might to his allies and his detractors alike.

Before the battle, he had dismissed the counsel of his advisors and generals who urged him to watch from afar, out of harm's way. Once they had gone, Kalista had confronted him.

"You are the king, and you do not yet have an heir," Kalista had said through gritted teeth, starting to lose her patience.

"I am sick of living in my father's shadow," Viego had snapped. He was garbed for battle, wearing gleaming black plate edged in gold. "I am every bit the warrior he was. I want this victory to be mine."

"It will be yours whether you take the field or not," Kalista shot back. "The histories will record it as a victory for King Viego. It doesn't matter if you fight."

"It matters to me," he had returned hotly.

No one else would dare speak to him in the tone she had used, but as a child, he had always sought her approval, and in many ways still did.

Even so, Viego was not to be convinced. He had opened his

mouth to argue, until Queen Isolde placed a hand on his arm. "Kalista is wise, my love," she had said. "Stay by my side. Please. You have nothing to prove."

As gently spoken as she was, there was a formidable strength in Isolde. Viego had sighed, and finally relented. "I guess it is just pride that makes me want to fight," he had said, placing a hand over his queen's. "I will do as you wish, my love."

On the dusty, hot battlefield, surrounded by the dead and dying, Kalista raised her spear high, in salute to the royal couple in the distance.

"Best get that seen to, General," said a voice, a deep baritone rumble. Kalista turned to see Ledros, her most trusted and capable captain. He was a giant of a man, standing head and shoulders above the next tallest soldier in the Camavoran ranks, and his deeply tanned face was crisscrossed with pale scars. As with all the lowborn infantry of the Host, his armor consisted of little more than a baked-leather breastplate, a humble bronze helm, and leather greaves. His large wooden shield was splintered, and it fell to pieces as he unhooked it from one arm. Those arms were massive, as big as any other man's thighs. He was splattered with blood, but little of it was his own.

Kalista stared at him, trying to understand what he meant. He gestured to the side of her head, and she reached up to her temple. She frowned as her fingertips came away bloody. Glancing down at her helmet, held loosely in numb fingers, she saw the rent gouged in its side. Axe strike. It must have been a glancing blow, else she would have been lying in the dust with the other corpses. She'd been lucky, and Ledros knew it.

"It's nothing, Captain," she said.

Ledros was carrying a severed head, holding the grisly trophy by its hair. The Santorassian king. It had been the death of that warrior-monarch that broke the enemy. And as always, once the rout began, the end had been inevitable. Fear was contagious on the battlefield, and the resolve of soldiers could be fragile. The death of one man could cause an entire battle line to shatter, just as a single pebble could cause an avalanche.

"That was a fine kill," Kalista said.

The enemy king had a reputation as a consummate swordsman, and from what Kalista had seen of him fighting, that reputation wasn't exaggerated. He'd carved into their right flank at the head of his elite guard, fighting like a demigod, slaughtering everything in his path. The Camavoran line had buckled, threatening to break, until Ledros had shouldered his way through the fray to face him.

There was no doubt the king had been a gifted warrior... He'd just never faced the likes of Ledros before.

"Bastard put up a good fight," Ledros grunted.

"Not good enough, it seems," Kalista observed. "The Knightly Orders will be furious you denied them the chance to claim that glory themselves."

Ledros grinned. His features were too broad and thick for him to be regarded as handsome, but he had an honest face. He had absolutely no guile in him, which was far too rare a trait. "That just makes this victory all the sweeter," he said, a wicked gleam in his dark eyes.

Kalista snorted. It was an undignified sound, but there was no one near to hear it but Ledros and her other loyal soldiers of the Host. She may have been highborn, but she had always felt more comfortable among the common rank and file than among other nobles, with all their flattery, lies, and backstabbing. Camavoran court politics were as dangerous as any battlefield, full of feints, sudden assaults, and desperate last stands, but Kalista would much rather face her enemies across the field. At least there you could see who was holding a blade.

Dust clouds in the distance showed where the scattered

remnants of the enemy army had fled. They wouldn't last long. Three major Knightly Orders had marshaled for battle alongside the Host to defeat Santoras—the Knights of the Azure Flame, the Horns of Ebon, and the Iron Order—along with a handful of minor orders. They had been denied the glory of a decisive, victorious charge, for the enemy had broken before any of them had fully committed themselves to the battle, and so those knights would satisfy themselves by running down the survivors.

Pushing aside her exhaustion, Kalista walked among the Host, Ledros at her side. She wanted them to see their general. She stopped frequently to compliment individual soldiers, to joke with some, and commiserate with others. She knelt beside the injured, and held the hands of the dying, and drew the blood trident upon the foreheads of those who had already passed, speaking words of thanks for their bravery—it sounded empty to her but seemed to give solace to those still living to hear it. She told the younger soldiers they were veterans now, and nodded to the real veterans, with their haunted eyes. Porcelain-masked priests picked their way across the field, tapping at the taut surface of their finger-drums to help guide the spirits of the dead to the Revered Ancestors.

Everywhere they went, soldiers slapped Ledros on the shoulder. Even those who had not seen him kill the enemy king knew of it. Every soldier in the Host regarded him with awe and reverence. He was their talisman. Kalista dreaded what would happen should he ever fall in battle, for he truly was the heart and soul of the Host.

The sun had dipped low as Kalista and Ledros made their way through the gathered knots of soldiers. Her throat was parched and dust-coated, and she gratefully accepted a waterskin from one of her officers.

Now that the shock of combat was fading, there was a jubilant mood among the Host. They had survived the day and were victorious. They would see their wives, husbands, and children once more, and the next dawn would seem glorious for that.

A great cheer went up for Ledros, and he obligingly lifted his bloody trophy high for all to see. Kalista saw the blush on his broad cheeks and smiled. As big as he was, indomitable in battle and able to face charging heavy cavalry without a hint of fear, this kind of adoration made him nervous. She found it endearing.

Ledros caught her eye. *Help me*, his eyes begged, but that merely goaded her on. She placed a hand on his massive shoulder—well above her own head—and lifted up her spear.

"Ledros!" she roared. "Slayer of Kings!"

He stared down at her, aghast, and she laughed at his embarrassment.

The Host roared their approval and chanted his name. Everyone was on their feet now, thrusting dented and bloodied weapons in the air. Only when it began to die down did Kalista notice the heavily armored horseman nearby, watching silently. Sitting astride a steel-encased warhorse of titanic proportions, the knight was resplendent in his ornate armor, a rich purple cloak of the finest velvet draped over his shoulders.

Hecarim, Grand Master of the Iron Order. *My betrothed.*

She hurriedly removed her hand from Ledros's shoulder. The jubilation of moments before was gone, leaving only silence. The big captain turned toward Hecarim and lowered his gaze in dutiful deference, as did every member of the Host. Kalista did not follow suit. She was of royal blood and lowered her gaze to no one but the king.

Hecarim's features were proud and noble, refined and aristocratic, and he cast his imperious gaze across the soldiers. It lingered on Ledros for a moment before settling on Kalista. His wavy shoulder-length hair was dark, his olive skin unmarred by flaw or blemish. His eyes were the deep green of ocean depths, and they had an intensity that was at once alluring and dangerous.

He dismounted, sliding smoothly to the ground with a rattle of armor. He was tall and broad-shouldered. *Not Ledros-tall, but who is?* A squire rushed forward—the daughter of some nobleman wealthy enough to buy her place at Hecarim's side—and took the warhorse by the bridle. The beast snorted and stamped one iron-shod hoof, eyes flashing. For a moment it seemed it would bite the girl, but a sharp word from its master settled it.

"Lady Kalista," Hecarim said, bowing his head, though his eyes never left her own.

"My lord Hecarim," Kalista returned, with a subtle inclination of her chin.

The silence lengthened as she waited for him to speak. A bead of sweat ran down her taut, muscled back, beneath her armor. They were set to be wed before the year was out, yet this was only the third time they had spoken. There was an understandable awkwardness between them, for they were barely more than strangers. Dozens nearby watched and listened, but if she was being honest with herself, she was mainly conscious of Ledros, standing statue-still at her side.

As if sensing her thoughts, Hecarim glanced again at Ledros, lingering on the severed head still clasped in the captain's hand. Kalista wondered if he was going to say something about a lowborn bondsman denying him the honor of that kill. Instead, he smiled. It was warm and lit up his face.

"Will you walk a moment with me, lady?" Hecarim said.

"Of course," she answered.

He turned and held out his arm. Kalista passed her spear to an attendant and stepped beside him, placing her hand lightly upon his ornate vambrace.

We must make a strange sight. A leisurely afternoon stroll through a garden would perhaps have been more fitting for a betrothed couple, but here they were, walking among the dead and dying. Hecarim's appearance was spotless, and Kalista was acutely conscious of the fact that she was covered in blood, dust, and sweat.

"Don't ever say I don't take you to the nicest of places," Hecarim murmured, a smile in his voice. "If you're lucky, next time I may take you to a charnel pit. Or a swamp. Chaperoned, of course."

Kalista was pleased to see he had some wit about him. She felt the tension between them ease a little, and she looked up at him. How were his teeth so perfect? she wondered idly.

"It is good to see you smile, lady," he said softly.

She glanced around them. "It surprises me that I am able," she admitted, "given the circumstances."

"You have won a convincing victory this day. A victory for the ages."

"In the king's name, glory be upon him."

"Of course."

The ranks of the Host stood at attention as they walked by, saluting sharply.

"They really do adore you, don't they?" remarked Hecarim.

"They appreciate a general who doesn't treat them as chaff."

Hecarim grunted. Kalista wasn't sure whether he was amused or he'd never really considered the notion. In truth, few nobles had.

"There are those who worry you hold too much sway with the common masses," he mused.

"Because I don't lead them to slaughter, like cattle?"

"Because there are *a lot* of them," replied Hecarim, scratching his chin. "Populist monarchs have come to power in the past through lowborn uprisings."

Kalista laughed. "Anyone who thinks I am plotting to take the Argent Throne is an abject fool," she said. "I have no desire to rule, and I detest court politics. I'll stick to the battlefield."

Hecarim smiled. *Ancestors, but he is a good-looking man.*

"And you lead your soldiers well," he said. "But in a void of decent gossip, there are plenty who feel the need to manufacture it. Though declaring your best bondsman soldier *Kingslayer*, well, that is perhaps not going to do much to quell such talk."

Kalista frowned. "I really don't care what they whisper behind my back," she declared. "The court is a mass of vipers."

Hecarim's expression became more serious, and it was like the sun dipping behind a cloud. He stopped and turned to face Kalista, taking her hands in his own. It was the first time they had ever really touched.

"My apologies, noble lady," he said earnestly. "It was not my intention to cause you upset. I had merely come to ensure that you were unharmed, and to offer congratulations for your strategic mastery today."

Kalista felt her cheeks blush. "Thank you," she murmured.

Hecarim released her hands, and they continued in silence until they came full circle, returning to where they had started. The knight's squire still held his angry ebony steed, and she looked relieved to hand back the reins.

"I must leave you, dear lady. The king has ordered that the city not be sacked, and I want to ensure that that decree is followed," said Hecarim. "There will be a triumphal feast held within the walls. Will you do me the honor of being seated at my side?"

"The honor would be mine, my lord."

Flashing a final smile, Lord Hecarim remounted his immense steed. He wheeled once, then rode off, attendants following in his wake, like leaves in the wind. He rode like one born to the saddle, as if he and his furious warhorse were one.

His knights cheered as their Grand Master rejoined them. With a blare of a horn, the one known as the Iron Harbinger signaled their advance, and the order rode for the conquered city.

Dust rose behind them, and Kalista's expression darkened. The city of Santoras would not be sacked, but there would still be some degree of looting and plundering, despite what Hecarim said; there always was in the aftermath of battle. And she knew that any who resisted would be slaughtered.

Ledros spat onto the ground.

"He rides well enough," he said. "I'll give him that."

Chapter Two

Santoras

As arranged marriages went, Kalista had little to complain about.

She had always known the choice of her husband would not be her own, as the old king's granddaughter, and niece to the new king, Viego. Hers was always going to be a marriage of political gain. She had never felt any bitterness about it. It was just the way of things. She had long resigned herself to being married off to some fat old nobleman, so when Viego had informed her that he wished her wed to Hecarim, she was pleasantly surprised.

She was under no misunderstanding, of course. Hers was a betrothal orchestrated purely to consolidate power...but as she sat beside Hecarim at the triumphal feast, in the central square of the conquered city of Santoras, she felt the Ancestors had not been unkind.

Hecarim was only a few years her senior, and his rise within the Iron Order had been swift. He was its youngest-ever Grand Master and had already earned a swathe of victories and honors. The Iron Order was the most powerful Knightly Order in the realm, in terms of both political weight and military strength...and that was not even accounting for its wealth.

Hundreds of years of conquest had ensured that the coffers of the Iron Order's impenetrable fortress were overflowing with gold, precious jewels, and magical artifacts.

It was several hours after nightfall. The tables were laden with food, and the ale and wine were flowing freely. It was clear that the feast was already being prepared even as the two armies had clashed on the plain before the city. Doubtless this was meant to be a victory banquet for the Santorassian king. Kalista noted the fear among the servants, though they tried to hide it. Their masters had been slaughtered by those they now served.

"Thank you," she said to a young servant as a plate of food was placed before her, but he looked startled to have been addressed and practically fled.

Already it was a raucous affair. The Camavoran revelers shouted across the tables, laughing loudly as they toasted the victory. Musicians played, and a troupe of feline vastayan dancers performed, trailing magical swirls of iridescent light as they spun, somersaulted, and backflipped with inhuman grace.

Viego and his young queen had not yet joined the feast but had sent word for it to begin without them, and the nobles were embracing that command with vigor. Kalista felt it was obscene to drink and dine while the city's inhabitants cowered in their homes, fearing for their lives, and she made only a pretense at eating. She would stay as long as etiquette demanded but not a moment longer. Of course, things would have been much, much worse for the city had Viego not ordered restraint, but that would be little comfort to the many people who had lost their loved ones this day.

She was still bedecked in her armor, though it had been cleaned. She had not had time to bathe, but her hands and face were washed, and servants had combed and oiled her long ebony hair. She wore it unbound and free-flowing, as she would until the day of her marriage, whereafter it would be bound into braids, symbolizing the tying of her life to Hecarim's. Her spear leaned against the table at her side, never far from reach.

There were close to a hundred present, all of noble birth. Most were knights, though a few were aristocrats serving as her officers in the Host. Those had been shunted to the tables on the edges of the gathering, of course. There was little honor to be had serving in the Host, and even less gold; it was within the Knightly Orders where real wealth and prestige were made. Kalista was well aware of the privilege afforded her through being part of the royal bloodline, but she liked to think she would have served in the Host regardless. She would certainly have rather been feasting with her soldiers outside the walls than sitting among the warrior elite of Camavor, but this was where Viego wanted her, and so this was where she was.

Hecarim sat at her left. He was an attentive and charming suitor, and his conversation was easy and light. Immediately around them were the other leaders of the Knightly Orders who had accompanied Viego and the Host to Santoras: Lord Ordono of the Knights of the Azure Flame—tall and severe—and the statuesque Lady Aurora, Grand Master of the Horns of Ebon. The latter was a loud and forthright woman with a fearsome reputation. Kalista had instantly warmed to her.

Across the table sat the Grand Master of the Golden Shield, one of the lesser Knightly Orders. He was of middling years and heavyset, with small, piggish eyes and an ugly scar across his pale face. He was also well into his cups.

"It seems you have achieved the unachievable, Lady Kalista," he drawled.

Kalista sighed inwardly, having no desire to engage him in small talk, but graced him with a smile that did not reach her eyes. "How so, Grand Master Siodona?"

"You have forged the lowborn rabble into a passably decent

army," he said. He raised his goblet unsteadily, spilling some of its contents. "I'll drink to that, for I never thought such a thing possible. Nor that anyone would bother. Particularly one of the royal bloodline."

"It pleases me to defy expectations."

Most at court were aghast that she led the Host. She didn't feel it arrogant to acknowledge her gift for military strategy, and stepping into the role of general of Camavor's immense standing army was, she believed, the best way she could serve her nation. Aristocrats saw little honor in leading lowborn soldiers, but what did she care of what the feckless nobility thought of her?

"But why the Host?" continued Siodona. "Any noble order would be honored to have you ride with them. Why lead that rabble?"

"That *rabble* won the day today," Kalista noted. "Besides, I am where I can serve Camavor best. *All* of Camavor. Too often in the past the Host has been used to simply soak up arrows and blunt the enemy's charge."

"They *are* lowborn," said Siodona, wiping his mouth.

"They are Camavoran and deserve more than to be treated as expendable. It is my belief the Host can be far more than that. And a strong Host can help ensure that we have a strong Camavor."

Grand Master Siodona grunted as his goblet was refilled. "The *Knightly Orders* ensure a strong Camavor," he said. "*That's* where the true power lies. As it always has."

Kalista barely concealed her dislike for Siodona. "The Knightly Orders are *not* Camavor," she stated. "There have been times when various orders have reneged on their promises or refused to pledge themselves to a newly crowned monarch. I believe the knights of the Golden Shield fought *against* the crown during the reign of my ancestor King Seuro, did they not?"

"She's got you there," Lady Aurora said, grinning.

Siodona glowered. "That was three hundred years ago," he snarled. "My order has bled for the Argent Throne, more than most. We swore ourselves to the new king on the day of his coronation. More than can be said for others." He glanced pointedly at Hecarim.

The Iron Order had not pledged itself to Viego right away. That was not unusual, but it was also not a sign of confidence in the new king, particularly since the Iron Order had always been the throne's most stalwart defender. It had taken them a full week—and the promise of Kalista's betrothal to Hecarim—before the Iron Order offered its oath.

Necks strained as the nobles seated nearby waited to see if Hecarim would rise to the bait, but he merely laughed under his breath, dabbing at his mouth with a silk napkin.

Kalista raised a hand placatingly. Goading Siodona further would serve no one, even if it was amusing. "No one is besmirching the honor of the Golden Shield," she said. "My point is merely that it's wise for Camavor to have a strong, loyal military force of its own, independent of and in *addition* to the honorable Knightly Orders, long may they serve."

Siodona grunted at Hecarim. "And you agree with this?"

Hecarim shrugged. "If a strong Host means less of my own will die, then why would I be opposed?"

Siodona waved his hand dismissively. "If you weren't marrying her, you'd say otherwise. And the king's order not to sack the city? Bah! Makes this war hardly worth the effort!"

Hecarim's smile became cold, though his tone remained light. "Drink some water, Grand Master Siodona," he said in a loud voice, "else you'll be waking tomorrow with a sore head and a handful of honor duels from everyone you've offended tonight."

There was soft laughter from those within earshot. They had gathered something of an audience, as the nobility were always hungry for court drama. Two Grand Masters flexing their muscles was a delicacy few of them could resist. Siodona snorted and took another drink, ignoring Hecarim's suggestion of switching to water.

Kalista appreciated how Hecarim had deftly turned the attention from her. He gave her a wink only she saw. *He's far better at these games of politics than I.* Clearly it was more than just his strength of arm that had seen him rise to lead his order so quickly, when the previous Grand Master had fallen in battle.

Tying the Iron Order to the throne through marriage was a smart move. She had suspected initially that the idea had come from the king's shrewd chief advisor, but now she wondered if it had been put forward by Hecarim himself. He was certainly bold enough to have approached the king directly with the proposition. And if it *was* him who had proposed the marriage, she wasn't sure if she should be impressed with the scale of his ambition, or wary of it. Something of both, she decided.

Before she had a chance to puzzle on that notion further, a crier raised his voice above the din of the feast. "King Viego of Camavor, and Queen Isolde! Long may they reign!"

As one, the gathered nobles rose to greet them.

Flanked by the royal guard, and with the ever-present figure of the king's bodyguard, Vaask, close behind, Viego and Isolde swept into the courtyard amid a fanfare of trumpets. The young king strode forward eagerly, a broad, winning smile on his face, while his wife seemed to glide along elegantly on his arm. They were utterly besotted with each other, and Kalista couldn't be anything but happy for them. Viego had not known a lot of love in his life.

As a child, he was given everything he demanded... except for the love of a parent. His mother had died in childbirth, and his father—already an old man when Viego was born—had completely ignored him until his elder heir was dead, and even then, his attention was cold, stifling, and overbearing. The old king had died only months later, so Viego was given little preparation for ruling.

Kalista loved Viego as a brother and was fiercely protective of him, but even she acknowledged he'd been a spoiled boy and had grown into an entitled young man, unused to being denied much. Nevertheless, she knew him better than anyone. He had a good heart and felt things deeply, for better and worse. With the right guidance, she believed he could become a good king, once he matured a little.

At first, Kalista was as shocked by Viego's impulsive marriage as any of the nobles, and more than a little concerned. Isolde was not from a long and proud lineage, and the union didn't bring Camavor political power or wealth—she was not even Camavoran, but merely a lowborn seamstress from a conquered nation. Yet Kalista had quickly adjusted her assessment after seeing them together.

Viego doted on Isolde like he had doted on nothing and no one his entire life. For the first time he put someone else above his own wants and needs. He listened to her, valuing her opinions far more than those of his advisors or even Kalista. And while the new queen was not formally schooled, she was fiercely intelligent and had an instinctive understanding of people and court politics. More importantly, perhaps, she was kind and considerate, and she tempered Viego's more impulsive and ego-led decisions. Kalista finally had an ally—someone who could help rein in Viego and help ensure stability for Camavor.

Now he was finally growing into his role as Camavor's monarch, and tonight's performance—for it *was* a performance, one that was masterfully constructed—showed a glimpse of the powerful and beloved ruler he could become. He oozed charisma and confidence, and he had timed their appearance perfectly. The crowd was already well oiled, on both wine and victory, but other than the red-faced Siodona, none were yet so drunk as to be sloppy or belligerent.

Viego was dressed regally but not overly ostentatiously—that might suit the court back in Alovédra, but not here, in the aftermath of battle. He wore his gleaming black cuirass over his chest to assure them that he was a warrior, even if he hadn't taken part in the battle. The jagged crown of kings sat upon his brow, but his sword, the immense blade that was the true symbol of kingship—Sanctity—was conspicuous in its absence.

For her part, Viego's queen, Isolde, was a vision of demure beauty. Her face was a perfect oval, her blue eyes large and soulful. Her dress, which she had made herself, was formed of innumerable layers of silk and velvet. It flowed around her like the petals of a blossom. Rather than trying to conceal her foreignness in traditional Camavoran garb, Isolde had taken the bold stance of crafting a dress that *enhanced* it. The effect was magnified by the queen's artful choice of jewelry—a web of delicate silver chains bedecked with sapphires, unlike anything worn by the ladies of the court, though Kalista suspected many would soon be mimicking the style.

Isolde looked every inch the captivating foreign queen. Among the mass of rowdy knights and nobles, clad in plate and chain, she seemed as delicate as a flower, as precious as a jewel. Yet even so, Kalista could see the contempt and disapproval behind the smiles of many of those around her. They hated that Isolde was lowborn; they hated that she was foreign.

Oblivious, Viego and Isolde made their way to the table set aside for them at the head of the courtyard. Viego helped his queen into her chair, giving her a kiss upon her hand, then turned to the gathering.

"Brothers and sisters of Camavor," he declared, his voice

as smooth as velvet and loud enough to be heard by every ear, "today you make your kingdom proud! You make the Revered Ancestors proud! And you make me proud!" A goblet was in Viego's hand, and he hefted it high. "Tonight I drink to *you*!" A wholehearted cheer rose from the gathering, and hundreds of goblets lifted into the air, sloshing wine. Viego drained his own cup and hurled it aside, to the delight of the crowd. "Bring me another!" he roared, laughing.

Viego began to sit, but Isolde leaned over and said something to him, placing a hand on his chest. "Ah yes, thank you, my love. I almost forgot!" he said, though Kalista knew he had done no such thing. "The entire reason we came here to Santoras!"

He clapped his hands, and an awed hush descended on the courtyard as a coterie of priests came forward, their heads low, their faces hidden behind their blank porcelain masks. Behind them, four bondsmen bore a golden box upon their shoulders, straining beneath its weight. They lowered it to the stone ground and dragged free the poles used to bear it, before bowing and slipping away. Viego stepped forward, smiling, and ran his slender hands over the intricate surface. He paused theatrically before releasing the catches with a solid pair of clicks, and slowly opened the box. The entire gathering leaned forward, straining to see.

Kalista silently applauded. He knew how to manipulate a crowd, and she didn't think that a bad thing, not in the slightest. It was a necessary trait in a successful monarch.

Viego's eyes widened as he drew the moment out, and he whistled through his teeth. "For this, we're going to need some more light," he announced. His smooth voice was low, but everyone heard him clearly. They hung on his words.

Queen Isolde produced a glass sphere, small enough to fit comfortably in the palm of a hand. Viego took it from her with a flourish and held it to his lips. He breathed a word upon it, then tossed it lightly into the air. It hovered some ten arm-spans above him and began to glow from within, casting its pale light down upon the king and the golden box.

Viego squinted up at it, frowning. "Well, that is clearly not bright enough." He scanned the faces in the crowd. "Where's my most trusted advisor? Nunyo Necrit, come forward, please, if you are not already too deep in your cups! Your king has need of your talents!"

Laughter followed the advisor as he picked his way through the crowd. His face was heavily lined, like well-worn leather, and his eyes were sunk deep in shadowy sockets. Old he might be, but a fierce intelligence still burned brightly within him. He was unsmiling and severe at the best of times, but his perennial frown was even deeper as he made his way toward his king. It was obvious he did not approve of his singular talent being used as a parlor trick to entertain drunken nobles, but he shuffled dutifully forward regardless.

Viego leaned down and spoke in the advisor's ear. Nunyo scowled and said something sharp in reply. Then he turned his gaze up toward the glowing sphere. His mouth moved in a whisper, forming silent, unknowable words, and a fey light appeared in his eyes. He extended one hand, and the sphere was sent hurtling high into the night sky, like a shooting star reversing its course and returning to the heavens. As it did, the light it emitted intensified, such that everyone in the courtyard was forced to turn away for fear of their eyes burning out.

Within a matter of heartbeats, it was as if a new sun had been born, burning coldly above Santoras, casting everything for leagues around in brilliant, pale light.

"Bravo! Bravo!" cried Viego, as his queen clapped her hands in delight. "My thanks, revered Nunyo, that is *much* better! Much better indeed."

Still scowling, the old advisor slunk away.

"Today, my friends, we make the founders of our great nation proud!" Viego continued. He paced before the nobles, his eyes burning with passion and belief. "Our founding Ancestors, the twins Camor and noble Avora, smile upon us! They smile upon all of Camavor!" He was standing once more before the golden chest. "And now, without further ado," he said, reaching within, "I give you, my friends, *Mikael's Chalice*!"

With that, he lifted the revered artifact high. The chalice was lidded, inscribed with runes and ancient symbols. The air around it seemed to shimmer faintly, as if surrounded by a haze of heat. Murmurs of appreciation and awe erupted from the gathered knights.

"Our noble quest to liberate this sacred artifact has been completed! When revered Camor lay dying, pierced through the heart by the Black Arrow of Astor, his sister Avora saved him. We all know the story. But what I did not know until recently was that she saved him using this! She held this chalice to his lips, and his wounds were healed! And now, after many centuries, it is returned to us!"

This was met with yet more cheers, louder than before. Glancing around at the sea of faces, Kalista was disturbed to see a rapacious hunger in the eyes of the gathered aristocrats.

How long has our noble questing culture been corrupted? How long did it take for our quests to become little more than convenient and transparent excuses to plunder and raid? To kill, claim fertile lands, and steal from our neighbors? How long before they were used to justify invading any city-state and nation that would add wealth and esteem to the kingdom of Camavor?

At her most generous, Kalista guessed it had taken a handful of generations for Camor's questing ideal to be tainted irrevocably. At her most cynical, she wondered if it had started with Camor himself. He *was* a warlord, after all, and with Sanctity in hand, he had built their beloved nation upon the corpses of defeated enemies.

Today's battle had been no different. Santoras had long been an independent city-state to the southeast of Alovédra, just outside Camavor's ever-expanding borders. They had fought together as allies on numerous occasions through their shared history, and trade between the two had benefited them both. Yet all it had taken to sever those ties was for one priest to declare it the will of the Ancestors to reclaim—*protect*, in their words—some ancient heirloom of arcane power that resided within Santoras's walls.

Any satisfaction she had felt from the day's victory was soured, and she did not join in the greed-fueled cheering. *This has to end.* That would be no easy task, of course. Yet for all his juvenile failings, she knew Viego to be a good man at heart. She had faith that he would do the right thing...with the right guidance.

While everyone else cheered, Kalista watched Isolde. The queen was smiling and laughing, but Kalista could see that it was forced. Quietly, she thanked the Ancestors. With Isolde's influence, change might actually be possible. While she was now queen of Camavor, the kingdom had crushed Isolde's own nation before she was born. That invasion had been declared a holy quest by the priesthood, just as this one had. If it were Kalista alone seeking to guide Camavor past its questing culture, she did not think she would have much success. But with Isolde's help, she was confident Viego would be swayed.

Nevertheless, Kalista was also deeply pragmatic. She knew today had nothing to do with claiming Mikael's Chalice. Who beyond the priests had even *heard* of that artifact before this invasion was announced? It had little to do with claiming Santoras, either, though its wealth was a welcome addition to Camavor's coffers—even if peaceful trade alliances would be more lucrative in the long run.

No, today had been about giving Viego a victory in the

field. He needed to send a message to those beyond their borders. It announced that while the Lion, the fabled battle-king of Camavor, was indeed dead, his son carried his bloodline. It declared Viego as someone not to be treated lightly, a timely reminder that Camavor was still a force to be reckoned with, and that to deny it would lead to slaughter.

And besides, the Knightly Orders had been getting unruly. Giving them this victory would keep them content, at least for a time.

Kalista forced herself to smile and clap her hands. Today had been necessary.

And yet, as she looked around her, the knights and nobles hardly looked like people at all. The unnatural glare from above leached their faces of color, making everyone appear as vile specters and ghouls.

A cold shiver of dread ran through her.

Chapter Three

It was their studied calm that gave them away.

All the other servants were jittery and scared, as if expecting the Camavorans to turn on them at any moment. Kalista couldn't blame them. The Santorassian army had been slaughtered on the field just hours ago. They served their conquerors with shaking hands, unwilling to meet their eyes.

In contrast, the two servants who approached the king's table, bearing fresh jugs and platters of food, were neutral in their demeanor. A man and a woman, they were unremarkable in all ways, their faces instantly forgettable. In other circumstances their disguises would have been perfect, but in this situation, it was their training that revealed them to Kalista. If they had appeared nervous, she might not have noticed them until the deed had been done.

Ignoring the questioning looks from those around her, Kalista rose to her feet and snatched up her spear. Hecarim said something behind her, but she didn't hear it, her focus narrowed on those two false servants. She did not call out, for she had not yet ruled out that she was mistaken.

She strode toward the royal table. The guards surrounding it were vigilant. They patted down the two servants, checking their sleeves and sides for concealed weapons. Finding nothing, the guards allowed them to proceed.

Maybe I'm wrong, Kalista thought. But something about those two still didn't sit right with her, and she picked up her pace.

The pair split, the woman heading around to the king's side of the table, jug in hand, head demurely downcast, while the man headed in the other direction with his platter of freshly cooked delicacies. He placed the heaping dishes of food upon the table, then began collecting empty and discarded plates, moving toward the king.

Kalista was halfway to the king's table. Viego was doting on Isolde, oblivious to anything else, and had not yet noticed her approach. Still she did not cry out. Still she was uncertain.

Vaask, the king's bodyguard, stood in the shadows nearby, one hand resting lightly on his sword hilt, scanning for threats. He turned his attention to the approaching serving-woman. He was known as the king's hawk, and it was an apt description. If there was a threat, he'd see it.

Wouldn't he?

The woman's lips moved, and Viego half turned his head. Without looking up, he nodded in thanks, gesturing to his goblet. She leaned over and began filling it, turning her body so that her other hand was concealed from Vaask's unblinking gaze.

A coiling ribbon of dark smoke, resembling a swirl of ink in water, extended from the woman's hidden, clenched fist. *Sorcery!* A fraction of a second later it solidified into a blade of pure darkness. This was magic of a kind Kalista had never seen. Neither Vaask nor any of the king's guard had yet noticed anything amiss. Only Kalista.

The assassin readied for the fatal thrust. Even then, her face was blank, evincing no hint of emotion, giving away nothing of her lethal intent. Even then, Kalista did not shout, knowing the king would be dead before anyone was able to react.

With a grunt, she hurled her spear. She put all her years of training and strength into that throw, praying to the Ancestors it would be enough. It flew straight and true, hissing through the air, past the king's guards.

Too late, the assassin looked up. She tried to spin away but was too slow. The spear took her square in the chest, hurling her violently backward.

For a moment, there was stunned silence. Then the courtyard erupted. Shouts filled the air. Knights and nobles launched to their feet, sending benches and stools crashing to the flagstones. Viego rose, staring wide-eyed at the skewered figure of the would-be assassin behind him.

Kalista drew the short-bladed sword at her hip as she sprinted forward. In the confusion, several guards tried to intercept her, but she deftly sidestepped them, straining not to lose sight of the dead assassin's partner amid the chaos. He had dropped the plates he'd been collecting and knelt by the table, as if cowering in fear and shock. It was a ploy. Darkness coiled as a pair of blades formed from nothing in his hands.

Vaask saw Kalista coming. His sword was drawn.

"There, there!" she shouted, stabbing a finger at the second assassin.

Vaask nodded, seeing the threat. He dragged Viego back, none too gently, and interposed himself between the assassin and his king. Isolde was crouching low, having slipped from her chair. With a roar, Vaask flipped the king's table onto its side, forming a makeshift barricade. Earthenware plates and jugs shattered on the flagstones.

The assassin snarled, the mask of unnatural calm discarded. Two guards attacked. Moving like liquid, the assassin slipped around their blade thrusts, making the soldiers look clumsy and slow. He was unnaturally fast, and his movements left a blur of motion in his wake. Only once he was past the guards did they fall. Kalista had not even seen the strikes.

Then she was there, her blade hissing for the assassin's neck. He turned her short sword aside and slashed at her with his other blade, savagely fast. His weapon seemed to drip with black shadow. Kalista swayed back from the vicious slash, which missed her by a hairsbreadth. His foot connected with her sternum, driving the air from her, and she stumbled back.

Two more of the king's guard fell to the scything dark blades. Then the assassin brought the table barricade crashing down onto its top, clearing the way to his target. Vaask was there, darting forward like a striking snake. Kalista had seen few swordsmen as quick as the king's hawk, but even he seemed slow compared to the assassin, like he was moving in water. The killer wove around Vaask's strikes, getting closer with every step.

Kalista pushed back to her feet, scarce able to breathe but desperate to protect Viego.

Vaask knew he was outmatched. Kalista could see it in his eyes. He offered an uncharacteristically clumsy attack of his own, which gave the assassin the opening he needed. He darted in close and plunged both dark blades into Vaask's chest.

The king's bodyguard was looking over his killer's shoulder, his eyes locked to Kalista's. *He intentionally opened himself up for the killing blow*, she realized. The assassin realized it as well, but too late. The king's hawk grabbed him, gripping him tightly. The man fought to free himself, but he could not. Kalista drove her sword tip into the base of his neck, killing him instantly.

She did not have a chance to offer Vaask thanks for his noble sacrifice. He was already on the ground, twitching in his death throes. Blackness was seeping through his veins, visible through the pale skin of his neck, and filling his eyes.

She yanked her spear from the body of the first assassin and moved to the king's side. Viego was comforting Isolde and guiding her back to her chair, his arm around her shoulders.

"Are you hurt?" Kalista asked.

"I'm fine," Viego replied.

"And you, my queen?"

Isolde looked up, eyes wide and frightened. She nodded, shock rendering her mute.

"Who are they?" snarled Viego.

"A better question might be who sent them," Kalista murmured. She cursed herself for a fool. *I should not have killed that second one.* The secret of who hired them had died with him. She nudged the female assassin's dropped blade with the butt of her spear. It disintegrated, like it was made of ash, leaving nothing but a black smear on the stone.

More guards were around the king and queen now, weapons at the ready. Nevertheless, Kalista did not lower her guard. She scanned the sea of faces for any further threat. It was difficult, as there was so much movement and noise, but her eyes were drawn to a servant edging through the crowd, head down.

"Stop that man!" Kalista yelled, pointing at him. "Take him!"

Onlookers swiftly backed away, and guards rushed toward the servant. The man instantly threw off any further pretense and danced nimbly up onto a table, a blade of darkness forming in his hand. He flipped the now-solid knife around, catching it deftly by the point, then hurled it.

It spun, end over end, toward Viego.

"No!" Kalista shouted, leaping forward, desperately swinging her spear into the knife's path. She made contact, but only just. It was the slightest of touches, not a true deflection, but it was enough to make the spinning blade wobble in the air.

For a sickening heartbeat, Kalista believed she had failed. She followed the course of the blade, certain it would kill Viego.

The blade embedded itself in the high-backed chair where

Isolde sat. The queen flinched away from the hateful weapon, which was quivering just beside her.

Kalista allowed herself to breathe. She had done enough. *Just.* Knights and guards encircled the assassin in a ring of steel. There was no escape, even for one of such talent. "Alive!" she ordered. "We need him alive!" Three guards fell, but the assassin was brought down beneath an avalanche of shields, mailed fists, and pommel strikes.

Viego was not satisfied. Seeing his queen so nearly struck by the assassin's blade drove him past the point of reason—and the assassins were not the only ones who were able to form weapons out of nowhere. He thrust out one hand, and with an almost imperceptible displacement of air, Sanctity materialized in his fist. Soul-bound with the Blade of the King, he was able to summon and dismiss it at will. Face flushed, eyes flashing dangerously, he strode toward the assassin, now pinned to the ground.

"Lord king," Kalista cautioned, hurrying to match Viego's pace.

"Get out of my way!"

"Viego," she hissed. "We must—"

"*Back!*" He made a sweeping motion as if to shove Kalista aside, though his hand never touched her. Nevertheless, she was pushed away, sliding and staggering, by a force that was impossible to resist.

There were more than a few gasps from the onlookers. Viego was the first Camavoran monarch in the kingdom's history to have magical aptitude—it was generally believed he must have inherited it from his mother's lineage—and few outside the palace had ever seen him manifest it. It was one of the reasons Viego had wanted to fight on the field—to show his subjects and allies the power he wielded.

When Kalista regained her footing, she was easily fifteen feet away.

"*Back!*" the king bellowed again, his face murderous, and all the soldiers pinning the assassin to the ground were hurled away, blasted by the invisible force of his fury.

"We need him!" Kalista cried, but Viego did not even register her words. She had seen him like this before. He'd been more controlled since taking the throne, but his rages were common when he was a child. While the blood boiled in him, he heard nothing. And the arcane power that flowed through his veins seemed to become more potent when his emotions ran hot.

He stood over the bloody and broken assassin, Sanctity clasped in both hands like an executioner's blade. He was breathing hard, and his eyes were narrowed in hatred. "You *dare* threaten my queen?" he hissed. "You dare attempt to kill *me*?"

The assassin pushed himself unsteadily to a sitting position. Blood trickled from one of his ears, and his eyes were swollen almost shut. One of his arms was bent at an odd angle. It was a wonder he was not unconscious. Numbly, he blinked up at Viego.

"I am the king of Camavor, the greatest nation this world has ever seen," snarled Viego. "And you are *nothing*."

"Viego! Keep him alive!" Kalista shouted, straining against his power, but it was like pushing against an invisible wall.

Viego reversed his grip, so that he held the Blade of the King in both hands with the point down, and drove it down into the assassin.

The pressure holding Kalista back was suddenly released, and she staggered forward. Viego slid his blade free, and the assassin fell face-first to the ground. His flesh was already desiccating, like a piece of fruit left too long in the sun.

The courtyard was quiet. Everyone was on their feet, transfixed.

The queen's voice broke the silence. "Viego," she breathed. There was blood on her fingertips.

In horror, Kalista realized the assassin's thrown blade had grazed her, slicing through the delicate fabric of her dress and scoring a shallow wound on her shoulder. Kalista thought of the king's bodyguard thrashing on the ground, black veins throbbing beneath his flesh, and her heart dropped. "Ancestors have mercy," she whispered.

The blade, still embedded in the wood of the high-backed chair, turned to ash and was borne away on the gentle evening breeze.

The queen's eyes rolled back in their sockets, and an anguished, strangled cry tore from Viego's throat.

With a sigh, Isolde collapsed to the ground.

Chapter Four

Helia, the Blessed Isles
Eighteen Months After Viego's Coronation

Erlok Grael scowled as he walked the vault halls, deep below Helia.

Chains and keys rattled at his belt, and the flickering light of his lantern cast a dancing array of shadows around him, like so many cavorting spirits and demons. Far from being unnerved by them, he felt a measure of comfort in their presence. For nearly fifteen years they had been his companions, his cohort, his cadre. They were his silent witnesses, his confidants. His co-conspirators.

Sometimes the shadows seemed to judge him. And in the darkness, there were times when they whispered to him, filling him with hateful urges and ever-more violent thoughts.

He paused to rattle a heavy wooden door on its hinges, checking that it was locked. Holding his lantern aloft, he peered through the door's barred window. All the cell contained was a padlocked iron chest, placed in the center of the floor. Grael cast his lantern back and forth, banishing the gloom lingering in the corners of the cell, ensuring that nothing untoward lurked there. Satisfied, he moved on.

This was his life as a lowly Warden of Thresholds. He was

tasked to walk the dark halls and passages below the city of Helia, ensuring that artifacts deemed important or dangerous enough to be hidden from the world remained so. Insultingly, it was not even the most potent of these artifacts that he guarded, only the lesser ones. He'd been given no opportunity to distinguish himself, and his petty direct superior, Prefect Maksim, took delight in undermining and belittling him at every turn.

The masters had lied. They had not sent him here for a short year or two in order to learn humility or empathy. There would never be an opportunity for him to prove he had grown from this experience. He'd long since acknowledged that he'd been sent here to *disappear.* They had brushed him out of sight and wanted to forget he even existed.

He continued on his lonely patrol, checking that doors were locked, ensuring that seals remained unbroken. It was possible to go weeks at a time without seeing another living soul down here in the darkness. In shifts, each vault warden patrolled their own assigned section. There were hundreds of leagues of tunnels in the sunless depths, spread across dozens of levels, so it was uncommon for one to encounter another, unless by intent. Grael preferred to avoid the others. He despised them.

On its surface, Helia was a wondrous place of beauty and learning, where fresh-faced young scholars and robed masters pursued and preserved knowledge, an intellectual utopia of peace and plenty. Scratch beneath, however, and the fetid nepotism and hypocrisy of the Fellowship were revealed.

While maintaining the pretense that the Fellowship of Light was one of egalitarian learning, the inner circle labored hard to keep its deepest mysteries buried. Grael had made it his mission to claim these secrets for himself. And the deeper he delved, the more he discovered.

Grael would exhume these secrets, like corpses. Anything the masters put so much effort into hiding was surely of immense power. Who were they to decide what knowledge ought to be shared, and what was concealed? The hubris was profound. The masters of the inner circle were hoarding this power for themselves, guarding it jealously.

He should have been part of that coterie. *He* should have been embraced into its fold fifteen years ago, but they had instead decided to grant that honor to Tyrus of Hellesmor. Tyrus! The man was an idiot! He did come from wealth and standing, however, whereas Grael had come from nothing. And while Grael had once believed that his superior intellect and scholarly acumen would see him rise to the top, he had become convinced that the masters would never have embraced him into their number. He didn't have the right connections, wealth, or heritage, and people like him were excluded.

The humiliation still gnawed at him.

The tunnels Grael patrolled extended far, worming their way beneath the surface. It was a warren, and for all his explorations, there was still so much that remained hidden. Helia was like a rotten stump riddled with termites. It was decaying from the inside out, built upon a foundation of cronyism and complacency. It was only a matter of time before it collapsed.

Grael was in no way a devout man. He paid fealty to no god. He saw piety as a desperate fear of what came after death, a desire for false comfort in the face of the truth: that there was no grand purpose to life, that the world was an uncaring, cold place, and that whether one lived or died meant nothing. And yet Grael nonetheless prayed he would be there when the Blessed Isles fell.

He continued on his route, walking the silent hallways, accompanied only by his entourage of shadows and his bitterness. The endless tunnels were a twisting, confusing labyrinth, though after all these years, he knew them well. When he'd first joined the ranks of the wardens, he had frequently become lost. On one occasion, he'd been stuck in the dark for three days after his lantern had run out of oil. He'd felt his way forward with his hands, and it was only thanks to luck that he'd eventually found his way out. It was not uncommon for wardens to perish down here, particularly those new to the calling.

In those first years, he'd relied on maps, chalk markings on walls and floors, and spools of thread to guide him. Now he didn't need them. He knew his patrol routes by rote, and had even, on occasion, taken to walking the way in pitch darkness, to challenge himself. He knew every uneven step, every misaligned stone, and even without his sight, he did not so much as trip. In his spare time, when he wasn't feverishly flicking through forbidden tomes and scrolls he'd secreted from locked vaults, searching for the secrets the masters hid, he delved deep into the labyrinth, well beyond his own assigned levels, exploring and testing the boundaries.

It was impossible to gauge the passage of time down in the depths, nor even to know whether it was night or day. No light reached any but the uppermost levels, through cunningly crafted shafts that speared up to the surface. A handful of hallways had narrow window slits looking out across the sea, and while one could see little through them, the fresh breeze, laden with salt and spray, was a welcome reprieve from the stagnant, dry air of the vaults. Of course, those locations were highly favored, and guarded only by the highest-ranking wardens…those who through bribes and favors had wormed their way to the top.

Even the cell where he slept and kept his meager possessions was in the all-consuming darkness. When he snuffed out his lantern, he could not even see his hand waving before his face. Too long in the blackness, and the mind started to play tricks on you. Deprived of visual stimulation, it would create images of its own, drawn from the depths of memory and the deepest corners of the soul. It was not uncommon for wardens to lose themselves to madness.

Finishing his long, winding patrol, his fingertips absently brushing the cold stone, he began heading back toward his cell. Other wardens would go straight to the communal mess halls when their shifts ended. Those meals were generally the only time they came into contact with living beings, but Grael only subjected himself to the presence of others when necessary. He had jugs of water and several weeks' worth of dried foodstuffs in his room. He would take his meal alone. And besides, he was eager to continue scouring the latest tomes he had purloined from a vault of the lower east levels just a few days back.

He was descending a narrow, spiraling staircase cut through solid stone when he heard something below. He paused, hastily shuttering his lantern, hiding its light. He stood there for long minutes, listening.

Nothing.

Had he been mistaken? It was certainly possible. Sound traveled strangely in the tunnels, making it hard to gauge the distance and direction of a noise. There were also plenty of unexplainable knocks, creaks, groans, and footsteps that echoed through the darkness.

He waited a moment longer and was ready to continue on his way when he heard it again. This time there could be no doubt. Someone was speaking in a low voice.

Keeping his lantern shuttered, Erlok Grael crept down the stairs as silently as he was able, then turned down the corridor toward his cell. He heard muttering, and there was a crack of breaking wood. His face twisted in anger as he rounded the last corner and saw light spilling from his room. He'd locked the door before commencing his rounds, some nine hours earlier. The heavy padlock securing it lay broken on the stone.

There was another crash from within, and Grael picked up his pace, striding furiously. His eyes were wild and full of hate as he stepped over the threshold of his cell. It had been ransacked. His desk drawers had been pulled out, their contents upended onto the floor. His heavy chest had been dragged out from under his bed, its lock smashed, and the clothes and books inside scattered. The bed itself had been violently yanked away from the wall, his bedsheets and blankets ripped from the hard mattress.

He saw instantly that the secret compartment at the bottom of the chest had been found. The flagstone concealing the carved niche behind his bed had also been discovered.

That wasn't good.

Wardens like him were tasked with *guarding* the artifacts and tomes locked away in the vaults. Banishment awaited any who removed anything from the vaults without the express written permission of the masters...and he'd been doing it for years. And here, in his cell, all the evidence of his crimes had been laid bare.

His face red, his eyes bulging, Grael stared at the muttering, bald figure of the warden who had uncovered his wrongdoings. The man was on his knees, rifling through his notebooks. He looked up.

It was Prefect Maksim. His face was fleshy and pale, and he wore an expression of undisguised glee. Long had he made Grael's life a misery, seeking to break him. And long had Grael resisted, enduring every petty torment the prefect had inflicted upon him.

Maksim licked his lips, as if savoring a delightful morsel. "This is the end for you, Grael," he declared.

Chapter Five

The Burning Valley, Camavor

Kalista strode down the length of the marching column, walking against the flow of soldiers. The Host marched in serried ranks, sandaled feet striking the hard, cracked earth in perfect unison, making a great dust cloud rise in their wake. There had been no rain for almost two seasons now, and there was already talk of the drought's impact on the kingdom's granaries. A hungry army was of great concern to Kalista, but that was a problem for another day.

The soldiers lifted their spears into the air as she passed, but she did not return the salute. Her expression was grim, and her gaze fixed on the huge, enclosed litter.

The royal palanquin was massive, larger than most lowborn homes, and it was carried on the shoulders of fifty sweating soldiers of the Host. They had been marching for three days through the unrelenting heat. The soldiers bearing the palanquin were rotated every two hours, so that their progress did not slow. They began their march before dawn, trudging on without interruption until stopping for a brief break in the middle of the day, then continuing until after sunset. It was a grueling pace, but it would see them back in the capital city of Alovédra in two days.

The queen still lived, and Kalista thanked the Ancestors for that mercy. Isolde might well have died at the banquet if not for Mikael's Chalice. There was a dark irony in that—their attack on Santoras might have precipitated the assassination attempt, yet it had also delivered them the magical artifact that kept the queen alive. In truth, Kalista was somewhat surprised the artifact actually worked and was not merely a trinket used as an excuse for the attack against Santoras.

That sacred chalice had divine healing properties, and so after the queen collapsed, water was hastily poured into it, and it was held to her lips. However, its power—even magnified by the innate talent of the king's advisor Nunyo—was unable to halt the spread of the poison. It slowed it, however, which at least bought them time to find a cure.

While the queen yet lived, there remained hope. But as Kalista headed toward the dusty palanquin, she shook her head bitterly. It should never have come to this. She cursed herself for acting too slowly. She cursed herself for not seeing the assassins earlier, for not shouting out sooner. She cursed herself for not being fast enough, or strong enough, or clever enough to have forestalled this tragedy.

She was lauded for saving the king's life, but she didn't feel like a hero; she felt like a *failure*. Her spear might have deflected the assassin's blade from its true target, but that deflection had caused the queen's affliction. It haunted her, and she kept going over the assassination attempt in her mind, thinking about what she could have done differently, how she could have better protected Viego and Isolde.

Kalista pushed aside her regret and self-recrimination as she approached the litter. The guards surrounding it allowed her through with a nod. A golden staircase extended from the front of the litter, reaching down almost to the ground. Kalista stepped onto it, somewhat uncomfortable in the knowledge that her weight was now borne upon the backs of her soldiers.

She removed her helmet as she climbed the stairs, tucking it under one arm. The heavy canvas sides of the litter had been tied back, allowing air flow and light within, but the sheer silk curtains were lowered for privacy. A guard opened the way, sweeping the silk aside.

The interior was fully furnished and opulent, as befitted the royal couple. It was so luxurious, and the movement of the litter so steady, that Kalista had to remind herself that they were not in the palace. The queen lay upon the massive bed, unconscious, which was certainly better than when she was racked with pain and delirium.

Viego sat at her side, holding one of her limp hands. He looked up as Kalista entered. His eyes were red and hollow, with deep rings below them. Kalista didn't think he had slept since his queen had been struck down.

The royal physician, Ramon, was dressing Isolde's wound, applying fresh bandages after completing his inspection. He had arrived several hours earlier, after riding from the city to meet them. Kalista knew him well, for he'd served the royal family for decades. He'd tended her when she broke her arm as a child after trying to ride an unbroken stallion bareback, and again when she almost drowned after jumping off the headland of Camor's End, which rose almost a hundred feet from the sea.

"Well?" said Viego, his voice hoarse.

Ramon sighed and wiped the sweat from his brow. "It's unlike anything I've seen before," he said. "I will need to see how it responds to the healing poultice, but I am not confident that I will be able to do more than ease her pain. The darkness is spreading beneath her skin. It's slow, but I fear that it will, in time, reach her heart. I'm truly sorry, Your Majesty. Short of a miracle, I am not sure what more I will be able to do."

Kalista's heart wrenched. Viego didn't react, and didn't take his gaze off Isolde.

Ramon turned and looked at Kalista. There was genuine sadness in his eyes, and his shoulders slumped. She gave him a tired smile and patted him on the back. His diagnosis wasn't a surprise, at least to her.

"So you can't do *anything*?" asked Viego. The king hadn't spoken aggressively, and hadn't so much as looked up from Isolde, but Kalista knew him well enough to recognize the warning signs.

"Viego..." she cautioned.

"My lord king," began Ramon, but Viego silenced him, turning toward him with one slender finger leveled.

"No," he hissed. "If you don't have anything to say that can help my queen, don't say another word."

"I might be able to help her if I knew what the poison was."

Kalista winced inwardly. If Viego had not killed that last assassin, they might have gleaned that information.

Viego surged upright, grabbing the physician by the front of his tunic. Like Kalista, the king was tall and wolf-lean, with an iron strength in his limbs. Ramon gaped like a landed fish.

"What good is a healer who can't heal?" Viego snarled.

"Viego, leave him be," Kalista said, placing a hand on his shoulder, but he ignored her.

He marched Ramon backward. The old physician's sandals scuffed and slid, struggling for purchase, as he was pushed toward the exit.

"If you cannot help, then do something useful and find someone who can!" With a savage grunt, Viego shoved Ramon out of the pavilion. He tumbled down the stairs with a cry, before hitting the dusty earth with a dull thud.

Breathing heavily, Viego returned to his vigil at Isolde's side and took her hand back in his own. Through the sheer silk curtains, Kalista saw the physician struggling to regain his feet.

"I can't lose her, Kal," whispered Viego. "I don't care what it costs. I *can't* lose her."

Kalista pursed her lips and said nothing. Without further word, she turned and strode from the royal pavilion. Descending the golden stairway, she slipped her plumed helm back in place and dropped lightly to the ground.

"Forgive him," she said, as she helped Ramon stand. The old man was covered in orange dust, and doubtless had a few bruises, but it seemed only his pride had been hurt in his fall. "He is suffering. The queen is his world."

The physician looked grim as he made a vain attempt to brush the worst of the dust from his robe. "Then I fear what is to come," he said, "for it is my belief that the queen will *not* recover. He was always unpredictable and willful, even as a child. What will he do when his world dies?"

Kalista had no good answer to that.

"I grieve for the queen, and feel for the king, I truly do," Ramon continued. "But Camavor needs a strong and stable ruler. Is he that?"

"Careful, old man," Kalista said in a low voice. She did not like the way this conversation was turning. "He is young, and he is in pain, but he is also your sworn king, remember."

He shrugged. "There's a lot more of the old king in you than in Viego, Kalista. Would that *you* sat on the Argent Throne."

"Never voice that sentiment again," Kalista snapped.

Ramon looked her in the eye, then grunted. "I'm not sure my presence will be welcome, if the worst comes to pass," he said. He bowed his head and gave her a sad smile. "It has been an honor serving your family. But I think it is time that I take my leave."

Kalista watched him go, feeling like she was slowly drowning. "You made a promise," she reminded herself, a promise sworn to a dying king. He stood among the pantheon of Ancestors now, watching and judging.

Protect Viego. Protect Camavor.

"I'm trying," she whispered.

The leaders of the various Knightly Orders and their senior captains were gathered in Hecarim's lavish command tent, standing around a map laid out across a table. Kalista stood among them, arms folded across her chest, a deep frown on her face. Ledros was with her, though he remained in shadows behind the nobles, as befitted one of low birth.

"We cannot allow such an attack to go unpunished!" declared Lord Siodona, Grand Master of the Golden Shield. "We would look like weak fools!"

"And who do you propose we retaliate *against*?" asked Lady Aurora of the Horns of Ebon. "We do not know who sent them!"

Siodona jabbed a gloved finger at the map. "Half the world's assassins hail from Port Takan. For too long the highlords have harbored them. I say we strike there and make an example of them. Show what happens to those who dare threaten Camavor."

"Port Takan is an ally!" protested Aurora.

"So was Santoras!" Siodona sneered. "And now it is part of Camavor!"

"That was a holy war, ordained by the priesthood," growled Lord Ordono. The Knights of the Azure Flame were renowned for their piety, and Kalista knew that their Grand Master was particularly devout.

Siodona smirked. "I'm sure we can find a priest who will proclaim it the will of the Ancestors to see Port Takan burned to the ground, if that is what you need."

Ordono scowled, his face flushing. "The Revered Ancestors are not tools to be cynically wielded in games of war and politics, Siodona. They will not be mocked."

"Oh, come now! The priests play a more ruthless game of politics than anyone at court! Even you can't think otherwise, surely!"

Ordono looked set to argue further, but Kalista interjected. "Even if the assassins did come from Port Takan, it is unlikely the highlords had anything to do with it," she said. "Anyone could have hired them. It is not as if we are short of enemies."

"And with the killers dead, it is unlikely we will *ever* know who was behind it," added Hecarim.

"Doing nothing will merely embolden others!" snapped Siodona.

"So you would have us attack an ally, knowing they were likely not responsible, just for a show of strength?" Kalista shot back.

"If it would put some fear into others who might wish to strike against us? Then yes, I would. In a heartbeat."

Kalista was shocked at the brazenness of this admission. The thought of starting another unjustified war against an ally merely to appear strong made her feel sick. How many more innocents would die? *There must be another way.*

"The jackals are circling," Siodona continued. "They feared the Lion, but the Lion is dead, and his young cub is still largely untested. Santoras was a good start, but a further demonstration of power and ruthlessness is necessary. If our enemies do not learn to fear him, we will be picked apart, piece by piece."

Kalista struggled to maintain her composure. "Did you really just call your king an untested *cub*?"

"I meant no disrespect, but we must speak plainly," said Siodona. "Your grandfather would have agreed with this course of action. He'd have leveled Port Takan already!"

"Does it not occur to you that my grandfather's brutal conquests likely *created* the enemies we now face? That our victory over Santoras simply ensures that we have more enemies tomorrow? And that striking against Port Takan will make our other allies wonder if they are next, and plan accordingly? We created this cycle of violence, war, and retribution. It is time to *break* it, not continue it."

"This is Camavor!" declared Siodona. "If we create more enemies, then so be it! We will destroy them as well!"

Kalista's expression darkened. "Your intentions are clumsy and obvious, Siodona," she hissed. "Long have you coveted the wealth of Port Takan, which lies conveniently near the stronghold of the Golden Shield. You seek to use the assassination attempt to justify a new war for your own gain, a war Camavor can ill afford."

"How dare you?" Siodona bristled, hand closing around the hilt of his sword.

Kalista felt more than heard the low warning rumble from Ledros. It was the sound of a war dog rising to meet a challenge. Of course, if the giant captain made a move against the Grand Master, his life would be forfeit, no matter the mitigating circumstances. She raised her hand, calming him.

"Enough!" Hecarim boomed. "The queen lies grievously wounded not fifty paces away! Now is not the time to turn on one another."

Siodona wheeled on him. "She dishonors the legacy of the Lion by—"

Hecarim's sword hissed from its scabbard. "Lady Kalista does not need anyone to fight her battles for her, least of all me," he growled, blade pointed at Siodona. "But if you say one more disrespectful word, I *will* call you out."

Siodona's face was red. "You want to take Port Takan just as much as I do," he snapped.

"Not like this," said Hecarim, "and not behind the king's back while he tends to the queen. If we ever move against Takan, it will be only at the express order of the Argent Throne."

Siodona stared at Hecarim, then nodded. "My apologies, good lady," he offered, with the slightest bow toward Kalista, though he didn't look her in the eye. "I spoke in haste."

Hecarim sheathed his blade, and Lord Siodona made an excuse to leave. One by one, the other knights followed him out.

"Entertaining, as always," remarked Lady Aurora, with a wry grin. "Though I would have paid good money to see you *or* Lady Kalista beat him down."

She filed out with her own knights, leaving Kalista and Ledros alone with Hecarim and a few senior members of the Iron Order.

"Your captain here needs to learn to control himself," said Hecarim.

"I'd say he did," replied Kalista. "Siodona still has his arms."

Hecarim smirked and glanced up at Ledros. Hecarim was half a head shorter than the lowborn captain, but Ledros's bulk made him seem even larger. "Fair point," Hecarim conceded.

"Siodona said you want to take Port Takan as much as he does," Kalista said, eyes narrowing. "I was not aware of that. Is the king?"

Hecarim sighed and rubbed a hand across his face, suddenly looking tired. "Talk of conquest and legacy feels inappropriate right now, given the situation," he said. "But for some of the orders, the promise of glory is what keeps them loyal."

"But not the Iron Order?"

Hecarim smiled again, but this time it seemed more honest, more real. "In the past?" he said. "Of course it was. But with our betrothal, the fates of the Iron Order and Camavor are intertwined. It is time to move beyond the endless quest for glory, and look to a better future. For all of Camavor. And for all Camavorans."

Kalista frowned, unable to hide her surprise. This was not what she had expected from him.

He rubbed his eyes again. It seemed like he was allowing his mask to drop, and she would be lying if she said she was not pleased by what she saw.

"Get some rest, my lady," Hecarim said. "It's still two days' hard march before we arrive in Alovédra."

Kalista was silent as she walked through the darkened camp, back to her tent, Ledros her equally silent shadow.

"Do you trust him?" Ledros asked, when they were back in the Host-assigned section.

"I don't know," admitted Kalista. "But I would like to."

Chapter Six

Helia, the Blessed Isles

They came for him in the hours before dawn.

A fist hammered against his door, jolting Grael awake. He was on his feet in an instant, heart thumping. Flickering orange lamplight seeped under the door from outside. Someone stood just outside his room. The hammering came again, making him flinch.

Dropping to the ground, he slipped a hand underneath his hard pallet, searching blindly. His fingers brushed what he was seeking—the flensing knife he'd stolen from the kitchens a few days earlier. He pulled it free, licking his lips.

The pounding sounded again, and Grael moved toward the door, clutching his knife. Steeling himself, he slid the bolt aside and eased the door open, blinking against the light. He kept his blade hidden from view.

"Erlok Grael," said a deep voice.

"Yes?" he answered, squinting as he tried to make out the features of the dark silhouettes. There were two of them, a man and a woman. They were big, considerably larger than he was. That didn't concern him. If it came to it, a blade in the neck would drop anyone, no matter how much stronger they were. They were both carrying heavy-bladed halberds, however, and wore the ornate white breastplates and fluted helms marking them as custodians. That didn't bode well. Helia didn't have a city guard, but the custodians were about as close as it got.

"You are summoned," growled the woman. "Magister Nizana wants to speak with you."

The magister.

Grael had never spoken with her directly, but knew of her, of course—she was the overseer of the Thresholds, and all the wardens reported to her through the various prefects and administrators who served her. She had a reputation for being cold, ruthless, and uncaring toward those who fell underneath her authority.

"What does she want?" Grael said.

The big man looked over at the other custodian, smirking and shaking his head.

"I forgot to ask," the woman snapped. "She wants to see you. *Now.* That's all you need to know."

Grael was still tightly gripping the flensing knife, held out of sight. Indecision tore at him. This summons likely had to do with Prefect Maksim's discovery of the books he had been secreting from the vaults. *How much does she know?*

"Let me dress," he said, finally.

The man glanced down at Grael's night-robe, a look of disdain on his face. "Fine," he snarled. "But be quick."

Grael nodded and slammed the door in the custodians' faces. He stood there for a moment, running through every possible outcome. He then moved to his desk, put down his knife, and lit his lantern. He washed his face in his hand basin and dressed himself in his ornate warden's robes. He took his time, refusing to be rushed, despite the growled threats from the custodians outside his room. With a snap he clicked his belt in place and looped his chains around it. The chains were hung with the many keys under his purview, and they rattled as he finished getting ready. He combed back his thinning hair and snipped a few errant whiskers with a tiny pair of silver scissors.

He stared at the flensing knife for a heartbeat before sliding it into one of the many pockets in his robes.

The custodians were glowering at him when he opened his door.

"Ready?" said the man. "Or do you need me to give you a foot scrub, first? Oh, perhaps you'd like me to run on up to the masters' bathhouse, get you some of those scented oils for your perfect hair? Hmm? What do you think?"

"That will not be necessary," said Grael, ignoring the man's insolence.

"Move," the other custodian ordered.

In silence they climbed up through the warren of tunnels, spiraling staircases, vaults, and passages toward the surface. The custodians walked with one in front and one behind him, like he was a prisoner. Perhaps he was. Grael did not know.

He considered trying to make a break for it. If he could get away from them, he was certain he could lose them in the darkness below. He could probably remain hidden down there for months, but without access to the wardens' kitchens, he'd surely starve.

The sun was rising when they arrived at their destination. One of the custodians rapped sharply on the door—though not with the same aggression as when they'd woken him—and a voice inside ordered them in.

Grael walked in first, and the custodians followed. Magister Nizana sat at her desk, a magnifying monocle strapped over one eye as she carefully pruned a tiny tree growing within a square, lacquered pot. Behind her was a lead-lined window looking out across the sea. The glare of the morning light made Grael squint. He couldn't remember the last time he'd seen a sunrise.

There was no spare chair in the room, and so Erlok Grael stood, and waited. The magister didn't acknowledge his presence in any way. She was a severe-looking woman, with hair as pale as spider silk, pulled back in a tight bun. She could have been forty, or she could have been seventy. She remained intent on her pruning, clipping away the odd shoot or leaf with deft snips of her tiny shears.

Grael glanced at the custodians, standing just behind him, but they stared resolutely forward, like the magister's dutiful guard dogs. Turning back toward the magister, he watched as she continued her work.

"You wanted to see me?" said Grael.

Magister Nizana didn't look up. "This tree may be small, but it is over three hundred years old. Remarkable, isn't it? And do you know what the key to its longevity is?"

Grael stared at her, brow furrowed. "I...do not," he said.

"Cutting away the weaknesses," she declared. "A tree has only so much energy to spend. Of course, sunlight, water, and nutrients help, but if left untended, the tree will waste precious energy producing leaves and branches that will weaken its integrity. Weaken its aesthetic."

"As decided by you," said Grael.

"What?" Nizana looked up for the first time. Her monocle lens made her right eye appear gigantic.

"You say it weakens the aesthetic, but that's only to your eye. Your opinion. What does the tree care?"

She sniffed and turned her gaze back to the tree to continue her work. "I ensure its roots get the water they need. I ensure it receives the sunlight it craves. It lives, or dies, by my whim. To this tree, I am god. I would say my opinion is the only one that matters."

Erlok Grael frowned, seeing multiple weaknesses in the magister's argument, but he thought better of pointing them out. It would not serve to antagonize her.

"The Wardens of Thresholds are like this tree," the magister mused. "I tend to them, nurturing them, feeding them. And sometimes, I need to prune a leaf here, a branch there. For the health of the whole." She removed her monocle, carefully set it into a leather-bound case, and clipped it shut. Then she moved the miniature tree to the side and turned her full attention to him. She steepled her fingers and leaned toward him, elbows on the desk. "Do you know why you are here?"

Grael licked his lips. His hands found the pockets in his robes. Without conscious thought, his fingers closed around the handle of his flensing knife.

The magister arched her eyebrows. "Well?"

"I do not, Magister," Grael said, without blinking.

Magister Nizana made no reaction, and her cold demeanor gave away nothing. "Do you know what the punishment is for taking things from the vaults without permission?" Grael tensed. "Books, for instance?" she added pointedly.

"Banishment," said Grael, not breaking eye contact.

"Banishment," agreed the magister. "One little snip, and the offending leaf is gone. In the past, some magisters were more lenient than I. They preferred to reserve banishment only for the worst offenses. But I believe that attitude, that *laxness*, is too ambiguous. It does little to dissuade people. Worse, it encourages them."

Grael stared at her, unmoving. His fist tightened around the blade.

"When did you last see Prefect Maksim?" said the magister.

"A week ago," Grael said smoothly.

The magister watched him closely, saying nothing. After a moment, she stood and moved to her window, gazing out across the ocean. "Prefect Maksim is missing," she said. "Do you know anything about that?"

"Missing?" said Grael, brow furrowing. "I don't understand. Is he sick?"

"No, he is not sick. He is missing. Gone."

"Gone where?"

"A number of forbidden tomes, stolen from sealed vaults, have been found within his cell. I take it you don't know anything about those either?"

"No, Magister," he said, shaking his head.

She turned back to face him, and he tensed again. Was this the moment? Was this when she would finally tire of toying with him and order him seized?

"Perhaps he knew his indiscretions would be discovered, and he fled rather than facing the consequences," said Magister Nizana. She gave a shrug. "Sometimes the leaf falls before it can be cut."

Grael released his grasp on the knife. His eyes lit with hunger as the magister produced a large iron ring from a pocket in her robes. Dozens of keys hung from it.

"These keys belonged to Prefect Maksim. Now they are yours."

"Mine?" breathed Grael, not taking his eyes off them.

"Of those under Maksim's command, you have served the longest. Therefore, his duties are now yours. Congratulations, *Warden-Prefect* Grael."

With new keys hanging from his chains, Warden-Prefect Grael made his way through the darkness, a satisfied smile twisting his lips. He hummed as he walked down through undercrofts, the forgotten tunnels, the rarely used passages, deeper into one of the oldest parts of the vaults, where he doubted anyone other than he had been for years.

At the entrance to one long, narrow corridor, he knelt, holding his lantern to the floor. He had sprinkled salt here a few days earlier, and was pleased to see that it remained undisturbed. No one had come through here. Satisfied, Grael continued down the passage, crunching over the scattered salt. There was a jaunty spring in his step. Things were finally starting to go his way.

At the end of the corridor, he came to a locked door. He produced a large key, and the mechanism clicked as he turned it in the lock. Still humming, Erlok Grael stepped into the cell. The stink of blood and foulness washed over him, its intensity stinging his eyes.

A sturdy wooden bench was situated on one of the cell's walls. All manner of butcher's knives, cleavers, and blacksmith pincers were carefully laid out upon the bench in order of size. Grael picked up one of them. It was his favorite: a cruel, curving sickle, its edge razor-sharp.

There was a whimper from the shadows on the far side of the cell. Grael smiled at the wretched, broken figure chained to the wall, waving the curved sickle before him.

"Good morning, Prefect Maksim," he said.

Chapter Seven

Alovédra, Camavor

The mood was subdued as the king and his soldiers returned to Alovédra. To Kalista, it felt like a funeral procession.

Word had reached the capital of the queen's condition, and crowds had gathered—indeed, it looked like the entire city had turned out to witness their return.

The Host escorted the curtained litter bearing the royal couple through the towering sandstone city gates and down the main thoroughfare toward the palace. The citizens who witnessed their passing were somber and silent, lining the boulevards and streets, packing into squares and atop flat rooftops. Orange blooms were strewn before the royal litter. Such flowers were traditionally offered to the sick and injured, an entreaty to the Ancestors to protect and heal them. So many petals lined the way that the stonework became slick underfoot. The shock of color was breathtaking, a solid line that led all the way from the main gate to the palace. Kalista knew the queen was beloved by the common folk, but this outpouring of love took her breath away. The crowd seemed even larger than was present for Viego's coronation, or her grandfather's funeral.

Each of the Knightly Orders that had accompanied the king

to Santoras had peeled off from the Host before they reached the city, offering unheard words of condolence to the king before riding back to their fortresses and strongholds. Last to leave had been the Iron Order, whose impenetrable Iron Keep was carved into the top of a giant rocky bluff, located just half a day from Alovédra. Its proximity had helped ensure that the city had never been successfully besieged in all the centuries since its founding. It was also a good part of why the alliance between the order and the Argent Throne was so important.

Kalista had watched Hecarim ride away. They were to be wed within the year, and while he was no longer a *complete* stranger, she still did not feel she knew him. He seemed honorable, and was certainly charming and capable. He also clearly knew how to play at politics, which was undeniably important... but it made her wary.

Through the city they escorted the royal litter, until the palace's towering spiked gates slammed shut behind them.

"Orders, General?" Ledros's tone was subservient and neutral, the same one he used when speaking to other highborn nobles. There was a distance between them, one that hadn't been there just days earlier.

"I want the Host bolstering the palace guard," she said. She could hear the coldness in her own voice—the tone of a highborn speaking to a bondsman—and she hated it. Nevertheless, she pushed the feeling aside, as she always did. Now was the time for duty, and she would not be distracted by feelings she didn't wish to acknowledge.

"As you will it, General," said Ledros, saluting and swinging away.

Kalista paced outside the royal bedchamber, as she had done for several days. Sometimes she sat, staring into the distance, her thoughts a tangled mess, anxiety and guilt gnawing at her. Sometimes she dozed fitfully in one of the uncomfortable golden chairs outside the door. But mostly she paced.

Guards were posted at the doors, watchful and vigilant. The hours rolled by. The guards changed, and changed, and changed, but Kalista remained, holding her vigil. A steady procession of servants came and went, heads bowed, taking in meals, fresh bowls of water, and towels, then bearing sweat-soaked bedsheets and uneaten plates of food back out.

Scores of healers, physicians, leechers, herbalists, sorcerers, and priests arrived. The lucky ones walked out, scratching their heads and muttering under their breath. Others were hurled from the room, chased by the king's curses. None had proved able to do anything to halt the poison slowly claiming the queen, and with every passing hour the chance of finding a cure grew slimmer.

None of the many magical relics that the rulers of Camavor had acquired over the centuries had been able to help, either. For hours each day, Viego ransacked the vaults while Isolde slept, desperately trawling through the spoils won by previous monarchs, searching for anything that might aid his queen, but to no avail.

The whole of Alovédra prayed for Isolde. The city's temples and shrines were flooded with well-wishers, begging the Ancestors to return the queen to health. Flowers and wreaths were laid daily at the gates of the palace. Letters of condolence and hope that the queen would make a full recovery were delivered from all the noble families of Camavor, as well as the Knightly Orders, but those lacked the raw emotional outpouring of the common people. The lowborn masses loved her far more than the nobility ever had.

Inside the royal bedchamber, the queen cried out, and Kalista paused in her pacing. The sound was soul-wrenching. She wondered if it would have been less cruel if Isolde had taken the cursed blade to the heart. At least then it would have been quicker, and her suffering less.

It was dark outside, a few hours before dawn. If the end was near, she prayed that Isolde's passing would be peaceful and painless. She deserved that much.

The great gilt doors clicked open, and the hunched advisor, Nunyo, peeked out, neck craning. If the situation were not so dire, Kalista might have found the image amusing, for he looked not unlike a tortoise peering from its shell. He saw her and ushered her over with one wrinkled hand.

"Does she worsen?" Kalista asked in a hushed voice.

The old man sighed, seeming to deflate. He tended to give the impression of being perennially unhappy, scowling and muttering under his breath, but Kalista knew it was mostly bluster. He had served the royal line for decades, and he loved Viego dearly, like the grandson he never had. Seeing the queen laid low, and witnessing the depths of Viego's grief, was taking its toll on him. As it was on them all.

"She does, my lady," Nunyo admitted. "The healing properties of Mikael's Chalice, even enhanced, are still unable to cure her. It has slowed the poison's spread considerably but hasn't stopped it. Nothing else has been effective. I fear the end is inevitable."

"Viego won't accept that, not until every possible avenue is exhausted."

"The *king* is exhausted," he said. "He hasn't slept in days. He barely eats. He is fading away before my eyes, just as his queen is."

Kalista nodded grimly. "I'll try to speak with him again."

"I think that would be best," Nunyo said, pushing the door open enough to allow her entrance. "He won't hear me, or the advice of the healers, but he'll listen to you."

Kalista paused in the doorway. "How long do you think she has?" she asked, keeping her voice low.

"An hour? A week? It's impossible to say."

It was stiflingly hot inside, and heady with the stink of sickness and sweat. All was silent but for the sound of a plinking music box. It had been a wedding present for the royal couple, one that Isolde particularly loved. In the gloom, it sounded eerie and forlorn.

"We may be losing the queen," Nunyo said, as Kalista passed him. "We cannot afford to lose the king as well." Then the old advisor left, closing the door behind him.

The tall windows were shuttered, and the bedchamber was dim. The jewels set into the pillars around the room could be brightened with a spoken word, but now they were dark. It took a moment for her eyes to adjust. When they did, she made her way toward Viego. He was little more than a shadow, slumped by the immense bed, holding one of the queen's slender hands. Isolde was pale and motionless, her eyes closed. If not for the almost imperceptible rise and fall of her chest, Kalista would have believed she was already with the Ancestors.

"I'm so sorry, Viego," Kalista breathed, dropping to one knee beside him.

He looked haggard, his eyes sunken and hollow. He wore exhaustion and grief like a shroud. "I can't lose her, Kalista," he croaked, fresh tears filling his eyes.

There was nothing Kalista could say. Feeling helpless, she put her arms around him. He clung to her, weeping softly. She just held him, sharing in his pain.

"Not very kingly, is it?" he said, pulling away and wiping at his tears. "I don't think I ever saw my father cry."

"Grandfather was a cold bastard," Kalista said. "I'd rather have a king who shows some real emotion than one who doesn't so much as shed a tear when he loses a child."

"I never liked him, but I do envy him," admitted Viego. "I don't think anything could have broken him. How was he so strong?"

"He never had the kind of love you have with Isolde," Kalista said. "Pity him for that, rather than envy his coldness."

"He loved Camavor," Viego said.

"He did." Kalista nodded. "Far more than he loved any of his own family."

A ghost of a smile appeared on his face. "That's the truth," he agreed. "What was it he always said? *The kingdom above all.* That is what it meant to be king, he said. He'd have never allowed me to wed Isolde. Marry for love? I don't think he would have understood that."

"It is possible to be a good man *and* a good king, Viego," said Kalista.

Viego's hollow smile faded. "Without her, I'm not sure I can be either," he whispered. "I cannot live without her, Kalista. And I don't think I would want to."

Kalista stared at Viego with a mix of horror and pity. He had always been somewhat obsessive, but there was a darkness in him that she had not seen before. *This is just his grief talking*, she told herself. *He'll recover.*

But what if he didn't?

"Isolde would not like to hear you speaking like that," she said.

Viego nodded, chastised. "She wouldn't." He took a deep, shuddering breath and made an attempt to compose himself. "For her, I must be strong. Isolde will come back to me. She has to."

As if hearing her name, Isolde moaned in her sleep, and her eyes flickered. "Viego?" she whispered. Now that Kalista was better attuned to the darkness, she could see how bad the queen looked. She was gray and clammy, as if all color had been leached from her. She lived, but already looked like a ghost.

"I'm here, my love," said Viego, holding her hands.

Kalista stood and moved back a few steps, feeling like an intruder during such an intimate moment.

"I thought I was drowning," Isolde breathed, her voice vague and distant. "I was slipping under the water. Couldn't breathe. Men in robes stood nearby, but they didn't help me. They just... watched."

"Just a dream, my love," Viego said gently. "Just a bad dream."

Her gaze was unfocused, but her face lit up as she saw Kalista, hanging back in the shadows. "Kal!"

Kalista came forward, smiling down at her. "My queen."

"I'm glad you are here," Isolde said. "You've always been kind to me."

"And I always will," said Kalista.

Isolde closed her eyes, and her breathing deepened. It seemed she was falling into a deep sleep once more, but then she started awake and leaned toward Viego. "Will you do something for me, my love?"

"Anything," replied Viego.

"Will you get Gwen for me? Whenever I was sick as a child, she was with me."

"Of course, my love. I will have one of the servants—"

"Could you get her yourself?" asked Isolde, eyes wide. "She's dear to me."

Viego looked uneasy at the notion of leaving Isolde's side.

"Kal is with me," she added. "She will keep me safe. I'll be fine."

Viego glanced at Kalista, who shrugged and smiled at him reassuringly. He nodded and stood. "I will be back shortly, then," he said, kissing his wife upon her forehead.

"Gwen?" said Kalista, after he had gone. "A friend of yours?"

"An excuse to speak with you alone," said Isolde, struggling to sit up. "But he won't be gone long. I must be brief."

Kalista helped her up and propped a pillow behind her. "What is it?"

Isolde took a deep breath. "Viego doesn't accept it, but I am dying, Kal."

"There still might be a chance—"

Isolde took hold of Kalista's hand. Her skin was feverishly hot. "I am at peace with it," she said. Then she sighed and shook her head. "But Viego..."

"You're worried about him," said Kalista.

"I'm worried what he will *do*," Isolde whispered. "When the time comes, you need to help him accept that I am gone. Help him move on. Please. I cannot bear thinking about what he might do otherwise..."

Isolde's fear was valid, and Kalista shared it. Viego had a good heart, but he was unpredictable, driven by his whim and ego. *I can help guide him, but it is Isolde who brings him balance.* She tempered the worst of his arrogance and impulsiveness. With her gone, Kalista feared what would become of Viego, and Camavor. She could imagine him spiraling dangerously out of control, flailing blindly like a drowning man, dragging everything he clung to down with him.

"I will do what I can," said Kalista.

"I wish we had more time together, Kal," Isolde said. "We would have been sisters, I know it."

"We already *are* sisters."

Isolde's smile faded. "The man I fell in love with is still in there, but he's...changed," she said in a low voice. "His rages are getting worse."

Kalista felt her blood run cold. "Grief affects us all differently."

"It's not just since I was wounded," said Isolde, casting a wary glance toward the door. "It's been like this for months. He hides it from you—from everyone but me. He's controlling, obsessive. He tells me he needs me, that he couldn't exist without me. That scares me."

Isolde produced a thin leather-bound book from under the bedcovers and thrust it out to Kalista.

"Here," Isolde urged. "Quickly, before he returns!"

Kalista took the proffered book, brow creasing. "What's this?"

"My thoughts, my hopes, and my fears," said Isolde. "Read it when you're alone. It will help you understand him."

Kalista nodded, her brow still furrowed.

"I worry about what will happen when I am gone, Kal. But it gives me hope knowing you will be here. He'll need your guidance. And your love."

Kalista had a dozen questions she wanted to ask, but before she could voice them, Viego returned, breathless and sweating. It was clear he had been running. Under his arm he clutched a cloth-stitched doll with brightly colored hair.

"I brought Gwen!" he declared, brandishing it triumphantly as Kalista slipped Isolde's journal out of sight. "What are you doing sitting up, my love? You need to rest!"

Isolde allowed herself to be eased back down upon the bed, clutching the doll to her chest. *Thank you*, she mouthed to Kalista over Viego's shoulder.

Kalista mulled over Isolde's words as she walked out of the royal suite and took up her vigil once more. The changes the queen spoke of in Viego disturbed her, and she cursed herself for not having seen them earlier. She felt the weight of responsibility pushing down on her. Another promise to another dying member of the royal family. The burden was becoming increasingly heavy.

She prayed she was strong enough to bear it.

"My lady."

Kalista was up instantly, surging to her feet and reaching for her spear. The serving girl recoiled with a yelp.

"My apologies, you startled me," said Kalista. She blinked her bleary eyes, still not yet fully awake, and glanced around.

She was in her own room, and still wearing her armor. It

was three days since she had spoken with Isolde. She'd spent most of that time outside the royal chambers but had finally relented to Nunyo's urging to get some sleep in her own bed, with promises that he'd send someone if the queen's condition changed.

Her blood ran cold as she focused on the serving girl. "What is it?" Kalista asked, expecting the news she had been dreading.

"The king begs your presence," the girl said. "He asks that you hurry."

Kalista sprinted through the palace. She knew all the shortcuts, all the routes through the servants' back corridors. She and Viego had run these same halls as children, barefoot and wild. She'd always been faster and more agile, and he quickly frustrated unless she allowed him to catch her or held herself back, letting him get away.

She skidded on the smooth marble as she rounded a corner, making a startled servant gasp and press himself against the wall. She bolted through antechambers and drawing rooms, past bewildered guards, heading for the royal bedchamber.

Heart hammering, she arrived. The guards ushered her in, and she darted into the darkened room. She found Viego sitting at the desk beside Isolde's bed, surrounded by books, tomes, and rolls of parchment. Kalista's gaze was drawn to Isolde, lying in repose, hands crossed over her chest.

"The queen," Kalista panted. "Is she...?"

"Unchanged," said Viego. "Did you...Oh! I'm sorry, I didn't mean to scare you."

"She's...still with us?"

"She is." Viego's eyes lit with excitement. "What's more, I think I have found it!"

"Found what?"

"Salvation!"

Chapter Eight

"The Blessed Isles," said Kalista flatly.

"Yes!" declared Viego, pacing back and forth, gravel crunching under his slippered feet. "They're real! I am convinced of it!"

They were in one of the many cloistered gardens within the palace. Kalista had ushered Viego out of the royal bedchamber, fearing he would wake the queen with his sudden exuberance. It was called the Queen's Garden, and it was a place of serenity and privacy, a hidden oasis that Kalista had always loved. Surrounded by walls and columns, with a gently bubbling fountain in its center, it had lovingly tended flower beds replete with blooms from all across the known world. Brightly colored flit-dragons fed on their nectar with long tongues, tiny wings humming, as clouds rolled lazily across the blue sky.

Kalista watched Viego in growing alarm. He looked like a madman, dressed in little more than a night-robe, his hair disheveled, and gesturing wildly as he raved on about the Blessed Isles.

"And you say this came to you *in a dream*?" she said, trying to keep the skepticism from her voice.

"Not a dream! A *vision*! Sent to me by the Revered Ancestors!"

"Viego," said Kalista gently.

"No, Kal, it *was* a vision! I have spoken to the high priests, and they have confirmed it as such!"

Kalista's brow creased. *Why is the priesthood indulging and feeding Viego's fantasies? That won't help him move on.* "But the Blessed Isles are just a myth," she said.

"Yes! I mean no!" Viego declared, stopping his pacing and pointing at her in excitement. "I thought so, too. But I've been reading everything I could find in the archives, and it is my belief that the adepts of the isles propagated the myth themselves to keep outsiders away. They're real, and that is where a cure for Isolde will be found."

Kalista sighed. "I know the story, Viego. It is said that upon the Blessed Isles there is a wellspring where life-giving waters flow, able to cure any mortal wound. But that is all it is. *A story*. It's a tale told to children, nothing more."

"Ah, but I've found *proof* the Blessed Isles are real, Kal!" said Viego, clasping her shoulders. His eyes were wild, and he was shaking with frenzied belief. "Isolde will be saved!"

Kalista took a deep breath. She could see that there would be no arguing with him. "Show me," she said.

The king's research had been moved into the drawing room next to the royal bedchamber, laid out across desks and side tables. Viego stood in the doorway, looking back and forth between his sleeping wife, in the royal bedchamber, and Kalista and Nunyo, who were studying the various accounts, maps, diaries, and histories spread out before them.

"Well?" Viego said. "You see it, don't you?"

Kalista glanced at Nunyo, who gave an almost imperceptible shrug.

"I don't know," said Kalista. "There are a lot of contradictions..."

"But too many details line up for it to be a coincidence!"

declared Viego. He strode over to a side table, gesturing emphatically. "Look here, in the account of this fellow. Zhulan? Zilean? Whatever. This is translated from the original Icathian script. He speaks of visiting the city of Helia. He writes of his time among its scholars, libraries, and secrets. And that name, Helia, comes up again and again, here, and here, and here," he added, pointing at different open books and scrolls. "And, look! Helia appears on this map, over a hundred years after these other mentions! It's only a fragment, but correlate that with our own maps, and it places the Blessed Isles somewhere around here."

Kalista and Nunyo squinted at the location that Viego had indicated on a contemporary map.

"In the middle of the Eternal Ocean?" she asked.

"Yes! They're out there! And they have the secret that will cure Isolde!"

It was the most energized Kalista had seen Viego in some time, and it reminded her of when he was a child, getting deeply enthused about one thing or another, then turning his focus onto something else. She'd always found his boundless enthusiasm for his latest obsession somewhat contagious, but this theory reeked of desperation. She had no desire to take the wind out of his sails, however, particularly when this was the first break from his dark despair.

"Our ships have plied those waters for a long time, Viego," she said softly. "I'm sorry, but I think we would have heard if they'd come across the fabled Blessed Isles."

Viego looked at her with frustration and gave an exasperated growl before turning to his advisor. "Nunyo, tell me all these connections are not convincing!"

Nunyo rubbed his wrinkled forehead. "It isn't *beyond* the realm of possibility," he offered, pawing through the leaves of an ancient text.

"See!" Viego exclaimed. "Even old Nunyo agrees with me!"

"Well, young king, I wouldn't say I agree with your hypothesis *just* yet," he clarified. "But if you take out the more fanciful aspects of these tales—the stories of undersea empires, of fights with demigods that fell from the heavens, and such—then it *could* point toward an island chain out there, where this Helia might be."

"It does!" said Viego, his voice rising in excitement. He glanced back to see if he had woken Isolde, then continued more quietly. "And the more I research, the more convinced I am that they are there!"

"But, my king, if this is true," said Nunyo, gently, "then it appears that no one has seen the Blessed Isles, or at least written of them, in centuries. It's like they just...dropped off the map."

"Or sank beneath the waves," muttered Kalista.

"Which is why I had the shipmaster's office bring me the logs and navigational charts of all the vessels crossing the Eternal Ocean for the last fifty years," said Viego, gesturing to a pallet stacked high with wooden boxes, each meticulously labeled. "Amazing what records are kept!"

Nunyo hissed through his teeth, clearly impressed. "That's why you requested the assistance of the temple disciples?"

"To help scour through these records and charts, yes," said Viego. "And, from the information they gleaned, I had the royal cartographer draft *this*." With a flourish, he rolled out a new map, hand-drawn onto fresh vellum. "Who knew we even *had* a royal cartographer?"

"I knew," said Nunyo, dryly.

"Anyway, I scared the man half to death when I knocked on his door in the early hours this morning," said Viego. "But he does good work. Look."

The map showed Camavor to the east, as well as the roughly sketched-out archipelago of Ionia to the north, and to the west, the eastern edge of Valoran. In its northern reaches, that land was icy and wild, with no real civilization, while the rest of it was a mass of squabbling tribes and barbarians. To the south was Shurima, dominated by sand, and with largely impenetrable, savage jungles to its east. The Eternal Ocean stretched between Camavor and those distant lands, a great, unbroken expanse that took weeks of sailing to traverse. Few islands offered any respite during that voyage, other than the small chain known as the Serpent Isles.

All the major trade routes and sea lanes trafficked by Camavor's fleet were marked on the map. It was a spiderweb of intersecting lines, scores of them. And in their center, where a spider would have crouched, there was... nothing.

"Why is there that gap there?" Kalista asked.

"Why indeed?" said Viego.

"It interrupts the most direct route to several of these locations." Kalista frowned, tracing the lines with her finger. "Is there some danger that our ships avoid? A maelstrom, perhaps?"

"The logs of those who have found themselves in that region speak of getting turned around in an unnatural fog, their navigation tools failing. Here, look," he said, moving to the stack of boxes. He opened a crate, rifled through it, then produced a tiny leather-bound logbook. He flicked to a page that he'd marked earlier, and cleared his throat. "*We found ourselves adrift, becalmed, and confused, and visibility was poor. When we were finally again able to see the stars, we were many leagues north of where we should have been, and sailing in a different direction, though there was no noticeable current or wind.*"

He looked at his audience, eyebrows raised expectantly.

"So that is where you think the Blessed Isles are hidden?" said Kalista.

"That's where I am *convinced* they are," said Viego.

Kalista stared down at the map, considering. "Let's say

they do exist," she said. "What makes you think Isolde's cure will be found there?"

Viego rolled his eyes and gave another growl of frustration.

"There *is* usually a measure of truth in even the most fanciful tales," admitted Nunyo. "If we were to accept the possibility that these mythic islands are hidden where our king suggests, then it is not an overlarge leap to venture that the stories of how they're a place of healing might hold a grain of truth as well."

Kalista wasn't convinced. "This feels like false hope, Viego. I don't think it wise to believe there is any salvation to be found on these mythical isles."

Viego sighed, and the feverish enthusiasm that had been fueling him began to dissipate. He sat down on an ornate desk chair, the seat cushioned with plush burgundy velvet, and motioned at the books, maps, and charts. "It might be the only chance she has," he said, in a subdued voice. "Nothing else is working."

Again, guilt struck Kalista, like a twisting knife to the guts. *This is my fault.* She glanced over at the old advisor.

"It can't make anything worse by trying to find them," Nunyo said, shrugging.

Kalista shot him an angry glare. What was he thinking? As tragic as it was, Viego needed to accept the way things were, not pin his hopes on some desperate quest that would likely lead to failure.

"Viego, this is folly!" she said. "I love Isolde like a sister, and would do anything to see her recover, but we have to face the truth, and that is that she is unlikely to be healed. I know it is hard, but if these are truly her final days, as the physicians believe, then your place is at her side, not delving through the archives seeking some desperate secret cure."

Viego looked hurt, and Kalista sighed. She didn't want to upset him, but he needed to accept the way things were. She placed her hand upon his arm, hoping to soften her words and help him understand that she only had his best interests at heart.

"I'm sorry, Viego."

He shrugged her hand away, anger blazing in his eyes. "I thought you of all people would have understood," he hissed.

"Viego—"

He pointed a finger at her face. "No," he said. "I have heard your counsel, and I reject it."

"But if you—"

"Enough!" he snapped. "I have made up my mind. The cure is there, I know it. I want our fastest ship sailing on the next tide. Nunyo, see it done."

The advisor bowed, even as Kalista's face burned. "It will be as you order, my king," he said.

Viego looked back at Kalista. His anger had already disappeared. "It is likely that there will be those at court who will speak against this decision. But I can rely on your support, can't I, Kal?"

She sighed. "Of course. But if this really is the course of action you are set upon, whom will you send?"

"It has to be someone I trust," Viego said. "Most of the nobles think I was a fool for marrying Isolde in the first place, so I have no faith in them. And the loyalty of the Knightly Orders can be fickle."

"Who, then?" asked Nunyo.

"Lord Hecarim," declared Viego. "The Iron Order's loyalty is bound to the throne with Kalista's betrothal."

"We are not married yet," murmured Kalista.

"No, but we could bring that forward, as Hecarim has been urging," said Viego, waving his hand.

"He has?" said Kalista, raising her eyebrows. "That is the first I have heard of it!"

"You could be wed tomorrow, if needed," Viego continued, ignoring her. "It could be arranged, could it not, Nunyo?"

"It could, lord king," the old advisor said, casting a sidelong glance at Kalista.

Viego and his chief advisor began speaking of the logistics that would be involved, but Kalista hardly heard them. She thought of how conquered nations had burned, pillaged and brutalized by the Knightly Orders. In the past, the Iron Order had been a part of that savagery, and it was only the express order of Viego, and the presence of Isolde, that had restrained them at Santoras. But now... If even a quarter of what was written about the Blessed Isles was true, then it was a place of tremendous wealth. She could almost hear the screams already...

"Do not send the Iron Order," she said. "Their place is here, protecting the kingdom."

"Then...?" prompted Nunyo.

"I will go," declared Kalista.

Helia, the Blessed Isles

Erlok Grael could not remember the last time he'd truly laughed. But discovering the long-dead corpse of a master of Helia, in one of the deeper vaults below the city, made him laugh until he cried.

The body was little more than a desiccated husk, bedecked in robes slowly turning to dust. Strings of hair still clung to the master's scalp. One of the man's ankles was broken, wrenched at an awkward angle. A lantern lay nearby, all of its oil burned away. He surmised the old fool had tripped and broken his leg, and was unable to get back out before his light gave out. How long would he have lasted before madness and thirst claimed him? The masters despised and looked down upon Threshers like Grael, so to think of one of them spending their last days crawling around in the darkness was sublime.

It was hard to gauge how long the corpse had been down here. Twenty years? Fifty, perhaps? The dryness of this particular section of the vaults would have slowed the decomposition, so it could have been closer to a century.

The fact that the man was a master was instantly apparent, as evidenced by the intricate, corroded sigil hung around his neck. It came apart in Grael's hand, and the pale stone set within slipped loose. "A *keystone*," he murmured. It was roughly a handspan long, inscribed with runes, and curiously warm to the touch. Only the masters of the Scintillant Tower were given these stones. He cradled it, relishing its feel, before slipping it into his robes.

This section of the vaults had clearly not been entered in decades. His newly acquired prefect's keys granted him a far wider hunting ground than he'd had before, and access to some of the deepest, oldest vaults beneath Helia.

"What were you doing down here, all alone, away from prying eyes?" Grael asked the skeleton.

It was only then that he realized there was something clutched in the corpse's hand. He had to break the fingers to peel them loose. They snapped like dry twigs to reveal a tarnished old key, greened with verdigris, its bow in the shape of a staring eye. It quickly found its way onto one of Grael's chains.

It took him several hours to find the lock that was the key's match. And behind that door, he found the book that would change everything.

Chapter Nine

Alovédra, Camavor

"You're leaving Camavor?" Ledros lowered his blade. "Now? Is that wise?"

Kalista attacked, jabbing with her spear in a flurry of strikes. The spear tip flickered like the tongue of a serpent, but he turned it aside. She stepped back and circled around him, looking for another opening.

"I don't know," she admitted. "But it's something I have to do."

Now it was Ledros's turn to attack. For his size, he moved well, with far more speed and balance than expected. He feinted low, then came in with a scything blow toward her neck. Moving lightly, she ducked and stabbed toward his exposed ribs. He knocked the spear aside with his shield and slashed at her again. He didn't hold back, and she would have been furious if he did. Moving like a dancer, she swayed away from the hissing blade and the follow-up strikes, countering each with a blow of her own, none of which landed.

They separated again, both sweating, and continued to circle each other.

"When you say it's something you need to do, do you mean for the queen? Out of duty to the king?" Ledros asked. "Or for *you*?"

He has me there. She might try to convince herself otherwise, but there *was* a good measure of guilt in her decision to go herself. "If there's a chance to save the queen, however small, I have to try," Kalista said. "And besides, if this comes to nothing, then perhaps it will give the king a measure of closure."

"It wasn't your fault," he said.

"I have to do this."

Ledros did not press her further.

They continued to train in silence, each lost in their own thoughts. Only once they were done, sporting more than a few bruises and welts from their blunted blades, did they speak.

"So when do we leave?" Ledros said.

Kalista took a deep breath. She had not been looking forward to this. "*I* will be leaving tomorrow at dawn," she said. Ledros went very still. Looking away, Kalista plowed on. "The king has requested that you stay in Alovédra."

"Since when does he know I exist?"

"Since you took the head of the Santorassian king."

He looked wary. As well he might, Kalista thought. She sighed. It would be her preference to keep Ledros as far out of the court and its nest of vipers as possible, but Viego had been insistent.

"What is this about?" asked Ledros.

Lord Hecarim was speaking with Viego as Kalista and Ledros arrived in the anteroom outside the king's audience chamber. The doors were wide open, and the Grand Master's voice carried to them clearly, probably more than he realized.

"With the greatest of respect, my lord, I am... unsure this is the wisest course of action," Hecarim said.

The king—disheveled and dressed only in his nightgown—was seated on the grand Argent Throne, distractedly tapping on a silver armrest. Hecarim stood one step down from the top of the dais, while Nunyo lurked nearby.

"This goes against traditions that have been in place since the founding of Camavor," he continued. His tone was respectful, but there was an exasperated edge to his words.

Ledros's eyes were wide. Kalista had been around the throne since childhood—she'd gotten into trouble dozens of times, clambering onto it with Viego as adolescents. It was easy to forget how intimidating it was. It was gleaming and massive, dominating the room in such a way that anyone who saw it knew the wealth and power of the one sitting upon it, just as intended.

"Breathe," she said quietly. "It's just a hunk of polished metal, and he is just a man."

"Just a man, she says," Ledros muttered. "Just a man who could have me executed for not bowing low enough or, or, I don't know, using the wrong fork at dinner."

Kalista looked at him evenly, trying to keep the smile from her face. "So don't use the wrong fork."

"Who needs more than one? It makes no sense."

She placed her hand on his chest, holding his gaze. "You'll be fine."

"I don't understand," said Ledros. "My place is in the line, shoulder to shoulder with the men and women of the Host. What does he want with me?"

Kalista sighed. "He didn't want me to speak of it until he saw you."

She felt far more anxiety than she was letting on. Viego was unpredictable at the best of times, and right now was far from the best of times. Lack of sleep, despair, and now this feverish, desperate hope were fraying him at the edges. It made her uneasy.

"All will be well," she said, as much to convince herself as Ledros.

The big man nodded but looked unconvinced.

"What do I even wear?" he had asked her earlier, his eyes revealing more concern than she'd ever seen him show in battle. "I don't have anything that looks, well, *good*. Certainly nothing to meet the king in."

Kalista had laughed at his unease. He'd bathed and shaved and, with her repeated assurance that it was fine, garbed himself in his field armor, though he had made an effort to ensure that it was spotless and freshly oiled.

"He's lowborn!" Hecarim said. "The orders will not be impressed."

Viego waved Kalista and Ledros in through the doors. "I really don't care if the orders are impressed or not," he declared. "I want someone I can trust. Someone not wrapped up in politics and intrigue. I have not ruled out the attempted assassination as being ordered from within my own court. I need someone with no connections to any of the nobility."

Only once Kalista and Ledros were halfway across the room did Hecarim register their presence. Knowing they must have heard him, he had the good grace to look abashed. At the foot of the stairs leading up to the throne, Kalista and Ledros both dropped to one knee, placing their hands on the floor and lowering their heads in deference.

"Yes, yes, enough of that," Viego said, ushering them closer. "I do not want to be long away from the queen, so let's get this done quickly. Bring him here—I want to look at him up close."

Kalista advanced up the steps, stopping one from the top. "Lord Hecarim," she said, inclining her head toward him.

"My lady," he returned, bowing his head.

Ledros stopped a step below Kalista. He was lowborn, and that was as high as his station allowed.

Viego pushed himself from the throne and brushed past Kalista and Hecarim, the tails of his open robe trailing in his wake. Ledros stood motionless, eyes dutifully downcast, as the king walked around him, assessing him like a prize bull.

Kalista traded a glance with Nunyo. The advisor gave a very slight shrug of the shoulders.

"Well, he's certainly big enough," said Viego, "and he has an intimidating air about him, while also appearing respectful. I like that."

"Captain Ledros is the best warrior in the Host," Kalista said, feeling her hackles starting to rise, but also very conscious of Hecarim, her betrothed, standing nearby. "He has served loyally through many campaigns, and he is my finest officer."

"He's the one who slew Agripos, yes?" Viego was standing before Ledros again. "That's impressive. The king of Santoras was no slouch with the blade."

"He did," said Kalista. "And it is not the first honor he has earned in battle."

"And he's loyal?"

"Yes, he's loyal." Kalista scowled. "But you can ask him yourself, King Viego. He's right here."

Viego looked over at Hecarim, raising his eyebrows, which only irritated Kalista further, but she held her tongue. It would not serve anyone for her to lose her temper.

"Lift your gaze, soldier," Viego said, addressing Ledros.

When the captain hesitated, Hecarim spoke up. "Look up, man," he said, with a roll of his eyes. "Your king has given you an order."

Ledros slowly lifted his gaze, as if this command were a trick. Though he stood two steps below the king, his eyes were nonetheless on a level with Viego's.

"Are you loyal, Captain?" Viego asked softly.

"I am, lord king," Ledros said, his voice low and booming. "My life is yours."

Viego held his gaze for a moment, then nodded. "I like

him," he said to Kalista, before turning back to Ledros. "You will be my new bodyguard and champion."

Ledros blinked. "My...my lord king?"

"I have found myself in need of a new one," Viego said, as if he were speaking to a child. "I would like you to fill the role."

Ledros gaped, and glanced at Kalista in confusion. She gave him an encouraging nod.

"It would be my honor, lord king!" he said.

"No offense to the good captain, but he *is* lowborn, my lord," purred Hecarim. "The role has traditionally been assigned to a knight from one of the orders. But even putting that aside, the role *must* be filled by a noble. That is the law."

"But I am king," said Viego, sitting back down upon his throne. "I can change the law, can I not? Nunyo? Can I not?"

The old advisor sighed. "It is not quite as simple as that, my lord," he said. "These things *can* be changed, but they do take time. There are...protocols that must be followed."

"But I don't *want* to take any more time. What if there is another assassination attempt? I want him protecting us *now*."

"There is another option, I believe," offered Nunyo.

"Spit it out, then."

"If he were a noble, you could assign him the role right now," he said. "So...make him a noble."

"We can do that?" said Viego.

"*You* can do that, my lord king," said Nunyo. "Several nobles without next of kin have died in recent months, leaving their estates with no master. In such situations, those lands and titles default to the Argent Throne. It is within your power to assign them to a new master. Give Captain Ledros an estate and a title, and he becomes a nobleman."

"Huh," said Viego. "And that's all it takes."

"That's all it takes," said Nunyo. "I can have the paperwork readied immediately."

"Do that."

"I would suggest Panthas, my lord king," said Nunyo. "It is a humble estate, on the southern coastline. Has a fine vineyard. Makes good wine. And as for title...perhaps baronet would suffice. And he will need a more suitable military rank to stand as your protector, of course. I would suggest commander."

"*Commander* Ledros," Viego said, testing it out. "Yes, it has a good ring to it. And Panthas sounds like a fine choice." He turned to Ledros. "You have no objections, I take it?"

Ledros's mouth was still agape. His entire world had just changed, in the space of a heartbeat. "I...have no objection," he managed.

"Nunyo, see it done." Viego waved his hand. "Now, I must return to the queen."

The king rose from his throne, and everyone else dropped to one knee, head bowed. Surrounded by guards, he strode from the room.

After he was gone, the others stood, with the elderly advisor using Kalista's proffered arm to help him up. Without speaking, they made their way from the room. Ledros looked stunned, Hecarim pensive. Nunyo shuffled off, muttering about seeing to the paperwork, leaving Kalista, Ledros, and Hecarim standing awkwardly in the anteroom.

Hecarim broke the silence. "Well, I guess congratulations are in order, *Commander*." He flashed a winning smile, his polished veneer back in place. Ledros reflexively dropped his gaze. "No more of that," the Grand Master said, wagging a finger. "You're a noble now. The only man you need to bow to is the king."

Ledros lifted his gaze, warily, and Kalista smiled. "Commander," she said, dipping in a slight curtsy.

"This...is going to take some getting used to," said Ledros.

Kalista did not sleep well. She had been up late reading Isolde's journal, and when she finally did sleep, it was fitful. She kept waking through the night, anxious it was already dawn and she had missed her ship. Her stomach churned. Doubts plagued her, whispering that seeking the Blessed Isles was a fool's errand, and that no good would come of it.

She also couldn't stop her mind from replaying Hecarim's vociferous reaction to Ledros's sudden elevation. And thinking of that just made her thoughts turn to Ledros, which in turn made her stomach churn further...

Kalista threw off her sheet and swung her legs over the side of her bed. The night was warm and she had her windows open, casting the chamber in pale moonlight. This had been her room since childhood, though she rarely slept in the palace any longer, more often sleeping on a simple soldier's cot in a tent while out on campaign. Her armor and helmet hung from the rack on the other side of the room, and her spear and scabbarded short sword leaned nearby. The rucksack she had packed and repacked a dozen times sat at the foot of the armor stand.

Sighing, she rose. She wore a long nightgown, which was a rare luxury, for in the field she generally slept in her armor. She stretched, then padded toward the balcony. The stone underfoot was pleasantly cool. Pushing the shuttered doors open, she stepped out into the darkness.

Her room was high in the palace, and the waves crashed against the cliffs far below. It was still several hours before dawn. Closing her eyes, she listened to the sound of the breakers, breathing deeply of the sea air and calming her mind.

A gentle knock on the door interrupted her, and she frowned. Who would be coming to see her at this time? She silently went back into her room and drew her short sword from its scabbard. The knock came again, quiet but insistent. Blade at the ready, Kalista eased the door open.

A big hooded figure stood there, but even with his face shadowed, Kalista recognized him instantly.

"Ledros?" He hastily looked away, and Kalista rolled her eyes. "Get in here before someone sees you," she hissed, grabbing hold of his arm and dragging him into her room. She glanced each way, ensuring that no one was observing, before closing the door behind her. She rounded on Ledros, who was standing awkwardly, still conspicuously looking away. "What are you doing here?"

"Can you...put the blade away?"

Kalista glanced down at her short sword. "I don't know, *Commander*," she teased, a hint of a smile in her voice. "I might still have need of it."

"Kalista." Ledros looked at her in earnest. "I would never harm you. *Never.* You know that."

Now it was Kalista's turn to avert her gaze. She felt a blush rising to her cheeks and turned away to sheathe her sword. "I know you wouldn't," she said. Her back was to him, but she could still feel his eyes on her. "It was a poor jest."

"I wanted to see you before you left," Ledros said.

Kalista's heart was thumping, her stomach churning again. She took a measured breath, trying to reclaim her calm. It wasn't working. She turned and looked up at Ledros. There was caution in her eyes, but also something else, something deeper, something that she had long sought to bury. He was close enough that she could smell him, the mix of worked leathers and oiled steel, with a hint of sweat. It was a comforting, familiar scent, but its presence in her room was... confusing.

And yet she did not want him to leave.

"I have something for you." From around his neck, Ledros removed a delicate chain. A silver pendant hung from it, engraved with two entwined roses, their stems and leaves wrapped around each other, like lovers.

"It's beautiful," Kalista breathed. She reached for it but pulled back before taking it. A piece of this quality was not cheap. Ledros was a man of wealth now, with land and title, but there was no way he had bought this in the hours since receiving that news. Something like this would have taken years of saving on the meager wage of a lowborn soldier, even a captain. "Ledros—"

"I don't expect anything," he said. "But it was either give this to you now, or throw it in the harbor."

Kalista swallowed heavily, feeling a tumult of emotions roiling within her. Duty won out. "I can't take this," she said.

Ledros nodded stoically. It felt like someone was clenching Kalista's heart and squeezing hard. The big man closed one massive, scarred fist around the delicate pendant, making it disappear. "Guess the harbor would have been the better choice," he murmured. "I'm sorry, I don't know what I was thinking."

"No, I am the one who is sorry," said Kalista. "The betrothal—"

"You do not need to explain anything," he said, his voice low. "Least of all to me."

Kalista's face was impassive, but she felt like she was breaking inside.

"You are a princess of the royal blood," he continued, "and yet you are a slave to duty, as much as I. More, probably. It's fine. I'm a soldier. Duty is something I understand." He attempted a smile, though it looked more like a grimace of pain. "Least we'll avoid any awkwardness at training tomorrow, with you sailing at first light."

It seemed like he was going to say more, but he evidently thought better of it, and turned to leave. Kalista ghosted along behind him, wanting to say something but unable to conjure the words.

At the threshold of her door, he glanced back. "Be safe,

Kalista," he said, in a hoarse whisper. "My heart is with you, now and always."

Then he turned, and was gone.

She was alone.

Hecarim stood in the shadows of the corridor as the lowborn captain emerged from Kalista's bedchamber. His eyes narrowed as he watched the big man pull a hood over his shaved, scarred head, then lope off into the darkness.

His hands turned to fists at his sides.

Helia, the Blessed Isles

Erlok Grael pored over the open tome, eyes burning with feverish light. It was an ancient book, its pages cracked and faded, but it was mostly legible. He'd found it in the sealed vault unlocked by the key belonging to the dead master. No, Grael corrected himself. It belonged to *him*.

Licking his lips, he turned the page, and his eyes widened at what he saw. It was a sketch, precise and detailed, of a room located far beneath Helia, dominated by a massive pool, with steps leading down to it. Dimensions, measurements, and calculations were scribbled around the illustration, and Grael realized this was an architectural plan of a place that had yet to be built.

He flicked through the next pages, scarce daring to believe what he was looking at. Every inch of the room, and its adjoining chambers, had been drawn in painstaking detail, from the geometric columns to the intricate arches that formed mathematically perfect patterns across the ceiling. There were instructions on how the room would be lit, and calculations of how the natural spring beneath it would fill the central pool.

"The Waters of Life," Grael breathed. The rumors were true.

The secret of eternal life was in the hands of the masters... and they had kept it for themselves.

Bitterness and fury surged within him, solidifying his purpose. He *deserved* access to those waters. And he would find a way to have it.

Part Two

Better to act and risk a mistake than do nothing, trapped by indecision.

—Ancient Camavoran proverb

From the journal of Queen Isolde

I have come to realize that mine is a liminal existence.

I was born of low station but am now a noble—a queen, no less. I float between those two realms, like a shadow, belonging to both, and to neither.

Viego and I are newly married, yet already I seem to have worn out my welcome at court. The courtiers and aristocrats despise me for my humble bloodline and foreign bearing, and ignore me whenever not required to do otherwise. The Grand Masters of the Knightly Orders speak only to Viego when in my presence. Even the servants look down when I am near, fearful and suspicious, for in their eyes I am no longer like them but one of the nobles, and no doubt as untrustworthy and cruel as the rest.

The only person other than Viego who makes me feel like I exist is Kalista. She hears me. She sees me. sees *me. And what a wonder it is to learn that she shares my vision for a more benevolent Camavor! But everyone else? They'd all rather I disappeared, or better yet, that Viego had picked a more suitable wife in the first place.*

There was a time when this hurt me, and I felt adrift and lost. But I have come to realize that the space I occupy, this uncomfortable, awkward, unique in-between place, is right where I need to be, and that it's a place of utmost privilege. For here I can act as a bridge across the gulf between those who have nothing and those who have everything. It is from this place alone that I can bring these two sides together, for the betterment of all.

Viego's love and his willingness to listen give me such hope. He is imperfect—aren't we all?—but he wants to be better. More importantly, he wants Camavor *to be better. He gets so impassioned when we speak late into the night of all the improvements we will enact! With him at my side, and with Kalista guarding our backs, I know that we will succeed, despite the misgivings and machinations of the court.*

So yes, I live between two worlds, a part of both, but accepted by neither, and I give thanks for being here. I welcome it. And the future I see unfurling before me is one filled with light and with hope.

Chapter Ten

The Eternal Ocean

Kalista sprinted across the deck of the sleek Camavoran ship, spear in hand.

The vessel was named the *Daggerhawk*, and Kalista ran straight for its port railing, as if to launch herself over the side—but as she stepped up onto the ornate carved edge, she twisted, pushing off hard to reverse her direction. She hurled her spear midleap, and it sliced across the aftercastle deck to impale a hanging sack of sand ballast.

She landed lightly, before straightening and rolling her shoulders. As she moved to retrieve her weapon from the wildly spinning target, someone nearby clapped their hands in applause.

Kalista tore her spear free from the ballast sack, spilling sand, and glanced over to see the stocky figure of the ship's captain watching her. A no-nonsense vastayan woman named Vennix, she was leaning casually against the rearmost mast. Her features were broad, her eyes dark and intense. Her fur was feltlike and pale on her face and the underside of her arms, but elsewhere it was thicker, and as dark as mahogany. She had round, furry ears resembling an otter's, pierced with a score of rings, and her hands ended in stubby claws painted vivid pink.

"My crew were taking bets on how long it would take for

you to lose your spear overboard," the captain said. "Some bet an hour. Others a day. It's now been more than ten days, and you've not missed a single throw."

"Sorry to disappoint," said Kalista.

"Oh, don't apologize to me." Vennix smiled, exposing small pointed teeth and pronounced canines. "I was the only one who put coin on you *not* losing your spear. Keep this up, and you'll make me a tidy little profit."

Kalista gave a mocking bow. "I do what I can," she said.

The sun beat down upon them mercilessly. It had been two weeks since they had departed Alovédra—two weeks since Kalista had last seen any hint of land. The Eternal Ocean lived up to its name, stretching as far as the eye could see in every direction. But the winds had been favorable, allowing them to make good time.

Though Kalista grew up by the coast, she rarely spent time on the water. She had imagined the ocean to be teeming with life and activity, but it seemed more like a wasteland. While in the first few days they had seen an abundance of birdlife and great schools of leaping dragon-fish, and even glimpsed the immense shape of a breaching scythe-whale off the bow, there had been virtually no sign of other life for days.

The novelty of being on the open ocean kept Kalista occupied at first. Sitting with her legs hanging over the side, she had watched in rapture as porpoises joyously leaped and spun in the *Daggerhawk*'s bow wave. At other times she simply lay on her back, enjoying the sun, the creak of wood, and the rhythmic movement of the ship beneath her.

Soon monotony had set in. To keep herself occupied, she'd taken up residence on the deck of the aftercastle, turning the area into a training ground. Every day, she pushed herself through hours of punishing exercises and drills, from push-ups and climbing up the rigging to endless repetitions of spear thrusts, steps, turns, and blocks.

"Thought you might be getting hungry, princess." Captain Vennix tossed Kalista a bread roll.

She caught it deftly. "Please stop calling me that," she said.

"Whatever you say, princess."

Kalista shook her head, snorting in exasperation. She tapped her roll against the railing and grimaced. It was as hard as a stone.

"There's soup down below," Vennix said. "Makes these almost palatable."

"Thank you, Captain." Kalista only now realized how hungry she was. The sun was almost directly overhead, and she'd been training since dawn. For once, she hadn't noticed the time passing.

"We're nearing the supposed location of your mythical islands," the captain said. "If they're out there, we should be passing them in the next day or two."

"You really don't think they exist?"

Vennix sniffed, making her whiskers twitch. "Never said I don't believe in 'em," she said. "I've seen enough strangeness out on the open ocean not to dismiss things out of hand. And legendary islands where folks live forever? That's a long way from the most far-fetched thing I've seen. Don't mean we'll find 'em, mind, if they don't want to be found."

Kalista stared toward the distant horizon. If no one had been able to locate the Blessed Isles for hundreds of years, what made her think she would? *This very well may be a complete waste of time.* "Perhaps I should never have come," she muttered.

"And miss all this?" said the captain with a chuckle, gesturing around her. The *Daggerhawk* wasn't the largest of vessels in the Camavoran fleet, but she was one of the swiftest. When becalmed, she was able to be powered by oars, but if there was even the slightest of winds, her multiple sails took full advantage, and she sliced through the water like a knife.

Nevertheless, the immense scale of the Eternal Ocean made the ship feel like a tiny, insignificant leaf being carried at the whim of the current and the wind. And if they sank? The ocean wouldn't care. The sun would rise the next day, and the world would keep turning. It was a humbling thought.

"Look," said Vennix, "if you'd stayed back in Alovédra, you'd be doing what? Moping around the palace, waiting for the queen to breathe her last? Sorry to be blunt, but you're better off out here. At least you're *doing* something. And if it doesn't come to anything, then so be it."

After the captain headed back to the quarterdeck, Kalista mulled over her words. She didn't mind being spoken to so directly; in truth, it was refreshing, and she appreciated it. The captain's advice would have appealed to her grandfather as well. The Lion of Camavor was an advocate of taking decisive action, even in the face of uncertainty and doubt.

She was just about to go find some soup when there was a shout from the ship's lookout, high upon the mainmast. He was pointing straight ahead. Kalista leaped down the stairs onto the main deck in one bound. Dodging lightly around sailors, she darted to the starboard side.

"Hold this," she said, handing her spear to a startled cabin girl. Kalista climbed up the rigging, hand over hand. The wind up here whipped at her, and every movement of the ship was far more pronounced, making her stomach lurch as the swell rose and fell. Finally, she reached the meager platform that served as the lookout's post. The sailor looked more than a little surprised to see her.

"What do you see?" she asked.

"Take a look for yourself," he replied, offering her a slender silver tube.

There wasn't enough room on the platform for both of them, so Kalista looped the rigging around her leg to lock her in place and carefully took the seeing glass in her hands. She placed it to one eye and squinted, adjusting the focus with a twist of the tube's end. "Where am I looking?"

"Look to the horizon, straight ahead."

Kalista adjusted and readjusted the lenses, frowning. "I can't see the horizon."

"Exactly," said the sailor.

A white mist stood before them like an immense fortress wall. It rose up hundreds of feet, though it was impossible to see exactly where it ended and the sky began, so it could have been higher still.

No fog or mist Kalista had ever heard of began so abruptly. There was something deeply unnatural about it. It seemed unaffected by the wind that propelled the *Daggerhawk*, the mist refusing to disperse, like it was solid.

And the *Daggerhawk* was sailing directly toward it.

"A hundred yards, Captain!" called the ship's first mate.

Kalista glanced at Vennix. The vastayan captain stood with arms crossed, staring straight ahead. There was a slight smile on her face.

She's enjoying this.

"Ever seen anything like it?" Kalista asked.

The captain flashed her canines. "Never. This should be fun."

"Fifty yards!"

They'd lowered several of the sails, slowing their progress while not completely giving up their forward momentum. Vennix's eyes kept flicking down to the ornate brass compass in her hand. "Keep her steady on this heading!"

"Yes, Captain!"

"Twenty yards!"

The wall of mist was all they could see now. It felt surreal, like they were sailing into nothingness. Kalista held her breath, her knuckles white from clutching the railing so tightly. She almost expected the ship to smash against the vast whiteness…but then they passed into it.

It was cooler here, and dampness surrounded them, like they were sailing through a rain cloud. They could no longer see the sun, and the *Daggerhawk*'s sails wilted, for there was no hint of a breeze. Kalista saw that the water was flat and still, like a lake, and the only sounds she could hear came from the ship itself: the creak of timbers and ropes, the nervous shuffling of sailors' feet.

Captain Vennix sucked in a deep breath, closing her eyes. "There's old magic in this mist," she said. "It feels… *wonderful*."

Kalista wasn't surprised that the mist was arcane in nature. It was the only logical explanation. The vastayan captain gave a long, contented sigh and opened her eyes. They radiated fey light, and a soft aura surrounded her.

"You're…glowing," said Kalista.

Vennix grinned. "My kind were born of magic, in an age long past. This is like a…rekindling of sorts."

Kalista glanced over Vennix's shoulder at the ornate compass. The needle was steady. "Still on course?"

"Still on course." The captain nodded. "Though we're not going anywhere fast," she added, looking up at the listless sails. She shouted her orders. "All right, girls and boys, time to break out the oars! Get to it!"

The crew diligently went about their tasks, unplugging oar-holes and extending long golden oars into the unnaturally still water. Then, at the shout of the first mate, the oars were dipped in unison, and the *Daggerhawk* began to glide forward.

They traveled through the eerily silent mist for what seemed like hours, though without the sun, it was impossible to track how long it had been. The captain's compass said they were maintaining their heading, but it was starting to feel like they'd never find anything in here. It was easy to imagine that nothing beyond the mist existed. Or perhaps that they'd been caught within some magical entrapment, and no matter how long they rowed, they'd never go anywhere.

Kalista was relieved when she saw movement overhead. "Birds!" she cried out, pointing.

"Well, would you look at that!" exclaimed Vennix. "If birds are here, that means land is here as well." The captain turned to Kalista, nodding in grudging acknowledgment. "Looks like these mythical islands of yours ain't so mythical after all, princess."

"So where are they?" said Kalista.

"Good question."

They continued on for some time, until a shout came from the forecastle. "Think I see something up ahead, Captain!"

After a few moments, Kalista could see it too—what looked like a darkening of the mist. Her breath caught in her chest. Had they found the legendary Blessed Isles?

Then they were out of the mist, and the *Daggerhawk* was rocked by the sudden return of the wind and ocean swell. But there were no islands before them, just open water.

The captain swore. "We got turned around!" she snarled, and swore again, louder and more colorfully than the first time.

"But your compass?" said Kalista.

The captain held it out to show her. The needle was spinning wildly, but gradually began to slow, until it was pointing... back the way they'd come.

"We're back where we started?" said Kalista.

"Almost exactly," said the captain. "Guess those islands don't want unexpected visitors."

Three more times the *Daggerhawk* entered the mist. Three more times it was repelled. During each attempt, they tried something different, but with no success.

One time, they swung to starboard as soon as they breached the mist, rowing just within its perimeter, to map its extent. But they somehow found themselves turned around and rowing in the *opposite* direction, before abruptly leaving the mist again, back where they had started. During their next try, they tacked back and forth once through the veil, hoping it might increase their chance of running across the isles. But again, the mist rejected them. In a final attempt, they entered the mist, then swung completely around and rowed back the way they had come. It seemed absurd, but they didn't exit the mist immediately. They remained within it even longer, and Kalista began to think they had outfoxed whatever magic had pushed them out the other times.

At one point, a handful of sea otters with glowing iridescent fur popped their heads up out of the glass-still water to watch them slide by. Kalista had been struck by their similarity to the captain's appearance.

"Don't say it," Vennix had growled.

"Say what?"

"Whatever you were thinking. Just don't."

The presence of such creatures reinforced the notion that there were islands tantalizingly close, but again they proved unwilling to reveal themselves. The mist thinned before the *Daggerhawk*, and try as they might to alter course and avoid leaving, the Camavorans soon found themselves back out on the open ocean.

They were instantly engulfed in darkness and lashed with wind and rain. While the mist had seemed to radiate its own pale light, night had descended while they were ensconced within. It was a few hours before dawn when the clouds and driving rain cleared, allowing the captain to gauge their position from the stars.

They were days to the west of where they had expected to be.

"We're closer to the Serpentine Delta than Camavor," Vennix said. "To get home, we either need to spend several days skirting around this infuriating mist, or we try to cut back through it, though the Ancestors know where we'll end up."

"We can't go home yet. Viego was right. The islands are right there!" Kalista said, gesturing at the wall of mist.

"They might as well be on the silver moon," said Vennix. "We'd be as likely to find 'em there."

Kalista clenched her fists. Knowing the islands were so close, yet so frustratingly out of reach, was worse than finding nothing at all. "I can't go back empty-handed," she said.

"Who even knows if the queen has lasted this long?" said Vennix.

That was certainly a fear that had been plaguing Kalista, but she pushed it aside. "There has to be a way through."

"Well, I'm gonna get some sleep, princess," declared the captain. "Wake me when you decide what you want to do."

Kalista retired to her cramped cabin. The captain had tried to give up her own quarters for her, "on account of you being a princess and all," but Kalista had refused. Most of the sailors were already snoring in hammocks belowdecks, but she could not fathom the idea of sleep. Lighting a lantern and hanging it from a hook in the curved ribs of the hull, she dug out her oiled leather satchel and clambered into her hammock.

Swaying gently with the roll of the *Daggerhawk*, with the sound of waves lapping at the hull, Kalista flicked through the handwritten notes and sheaves of paper Nunyo had given her. The old advisor had worked through the night with a small team of scholars before she left, copying anything from Viego's research that might be of use. She scoured the pages, desperately seeking something, *anything*, that might help, but found nothing but vagaries and flights of fancy.

Dawn had already risen when she noticed a tiny note

scrawled on the side of one page. She'd read it before but never really paid attention to it. Blinking her tired eyes, she turned the sheaf sideways, holding it up to the lantern light. It was written in Nunyo's precise, flowing hand.

Cross-referencing astral charts with the constellations at the start and end of his final leg indicates this voyage took roughly ten days.

She reread the section that Nunyo was commenting on. It was an extract from the painfully verbose translations of the Icathian, Zilean, about a visit to the Blessed Isles. It went into detail about such things as what he ate for breakfast and his clear fascination with the passage of time, as well as descriptions of the constellations he saw. There was nothing to give her practical information about getting to the isles, but maybe that didn't matter. Maybe Nunyo had been on to something...

Kalista scrambled from her hammock and ran from her cabin, ignoring the muttered groans and protests of the sailors she passed. She ran straight to the captain's cabin and burst in unannounced.

The captain had been sleeping, and she blinked up at her intruder, squinting against the early-morning light. Her bedsheets only partially covered her, and it was obvious she was not wearing anything at all.

"You wanting to join me, princess?" Vennix said with a sleepy, wicked smile, making no effort to conceal her nakedness.

It was clearly a joke meant to make her feel uncomfortable... and it worked. Kalista felt her face burning, and she looked away.

"Thank you, no," Kalista said. "How many ports lie about ten days from here? Ones that have been around for many hundreds of years."

"You've interrupted my beauty sleep to ask that?"

"It's important," said Kalista.

Vennix rose from the bed, again making no effort to cover

herself, and Kalista turned to face the wall. She shook her head at the captain's confidence and complete lack of shame, yet she also admired it. She was free in a way that Kalista, as a princess of the royal line, felt she could never be.

"Ten days? Well, that might get you to the Amarantine Coast, but not to any notable port. Wouldn't get you up to Harelport, either, and certainly not around the coast to White Spire. Nah, the only place of note close to ten days from here would be Buhru, and that would be a stretch."

"Buhru," said Kalista. "That's... on the Serpent Isles?"

"That's the one," said Vennix. "Interesting folk. They've been there a long time. Damn good sailors. Damn good navigators, too. Don't have any fear, either. Most folk go out of their way to avoid the things that dwell in the darkness down below, but those ones go searching for them. They *hunt* them, the crazy bastards, every damn night. You can turn around now, princess."

The captain was dressed in an ostentatious mishmash of styles, including tight leather trousers and thigh-high boots, a garish shirt overflowing with ruffles, and a velvet coat that hung almost to the floor. "How do I look?" she said, striking a dramatic pose.

"Like you are ready to sail me to the Serpent Isles to find a guide," Kalista said wryly.

Vennix laughed. "Come on, then, princess," she said, opening the door and ushering Kalista out. "You can tell me more about why we're going there while I think of how to break it to the crew that we're not heading home just yet."

Chapter Eleven

Buhru, the Serpent Isles

Kalista stormed out through the stone doorway, sweeping aside a curtain of hanging amber beads. Her face was thunderous. A domesticated, partially feathered creature the size of a dog waddled past, and she resisted the urge to kick at it.

From a balcony carved into the rock above, a heavyset Buhru man clad in a dark red chitinous shell watched her go, massive tattooed arms folded across his chest. Captain Vennix followed in Kalista's wake, hurrying to keep up. Both were unarmed—the Buhru demanded that all outsiders leave their weapons aboard their ships before coming ashore, and they were rigorous in enforcing that decree.

"That didn't go as well as I'd hoped," Vennix admitted.

"It was a complete waste of time!" Kalista snapped.

"The Buhru are insular, but I didn't expect him to refuse to aid us quite so . . . loudly."

Vennix had acted as interpreter for Kalista since they'd arrived, four days earlier.

"I thought you'd only been here once or twice," Kalista had said, astonished at Vennix's fluency in the native tongue.

"We vastaya pick up languages easily," Vennix had replied with a shrug.

Nevertheless, every attempt they'd made to get information about navigating the strange mists, or to hire a guide, had been met with vague answers and polite but pointed deflections. When pressed, everyone had deferred to the patriarch... but getting a meeting with the priest had taken endless hours of negotiation, all for an audience that lasted just minutes. He'd heard their plea but cut them off abruptly, refusing them any aid.

Kalista was fuming. "It's clear the crab-priest knows more than he's letting on," she said. "Why won't they help us?"

Vennix shook her head. "I don't know. Perhaps some religious taboo? I'm sorry, princess, I feel like I've let you down."

The two made their way down the precarious stone steps chiseled into the rock spire that housed the patriarch's temple and domicile. They passed several guards, all bedecked in jagged, crimson-red crab armor, and walked by walls brightly painted with depictions of the priest's deity—a crab the size of an island, with a vast volcano upon its back. Vennix had explained that the god's worshippers believed it had made the Serpent Isles at the very dawn of time, though it was not altogether benevolent; from the fiery depictions of its deeds, it seemed simultaneously a force of great destruction and creation.

It was not the only god the Buhru appeared to venerate, but just one in a rich and varied pantheon. One of the other important gods was a young woman with flaming hair who stood upon the backs of a pair of flying sharks—a sun-deity, perhaps—while another was far more monstrous, depicted with a mass of coiling tentacles that both rose from below the waves and descended from the sky. It was a world away from the Ancestor worship of Camavor, and Kalista found it fascinating.

Brilliantly colored parrots swooped past her and Vennix as they headed closer to the base of the rock. They glimpsed six-limbed monkeys swinging through the jungle canopy below, and the humid air was filled with raucous calls and hoots from other unseen beasts. It was so utterly unlike the more arid lands of Camavor. Under other circumstances she would have been overjoyed to explore and learn about these islands...but the pressure of her task was a constant burden on her heart. And the Buhru had made it clear that outsiders were allowed to stay for only brief visits. Kalista was already pushing the limits of their hospitality.

In the distance, she could see the *Daggerhawk* anchored just beyond the protected harbor. The harbor itself was too shallow for the Camavoran ship, though not for the scores of Buhru vessels tied up at the stone docks jutting into the water. There were a few other foreign vessels moored out near the *Daggerhawk*: an elegant Ionian sloop, which had what looked like a living tree forming its mast; a galley with a giant golden statue of an eagle-headed warrior at its stern, which Kalista figured came from the sandlands to the west; and several ships of a design she did not recognize.

A dozen or so rock spires rose from the jungle, each carved with coiling tentacles and riddled with doorways and windows. The rest of the Buhru settlement spread out below them, half-hidden by the greenery.

"It's a damn shame," Vennix said as she led the way back to ground level. "Buhru navigators know their way around the ocean like no one else. It's like it speaks to them. Make me and my crew look like amateurs, and we're the best in the Camavoran fleet."

"Modest too," remarked Kalista.

"Just the plain truth, is what it is," said Vennix. "So what now?"

Kalista slapped a biting insect off her neck. Buhru locals watched them from windows and doorways. The people were not hostile, but they were intimidating. Even the weavers, artists, and priests among them had the look of warriors.

"I don't know," she said. "This all feels like a wasted venture. I'm not sure where to turn."

"Well, for some good news," said Vennix as they reached the base of the spire, "the *Daggerhawk* is re-provisioned, and my crew content. Amazing what a good hot meal does for morale."

It was busier down on ground level, with Buhru moving about on their daily routines. Fishermen hawked their catches, and a group of giggling children ran past. The settlement was far larger than Kalista had realized, and easily as bustling as any Camavoran fishing town.

"I also managed to haggle down the price on a couple of kegs of this local brew," Vennix said, pulling out a flask and unstoppering it. She took a long swig and gave a satisfied sigh. "This'll make the crew *very* happy."

Kalista took a sniff as Vennix held the flask out to her, and her eyes watered. "What in the name of the Ancestors is *that*?"

Vennix laughed. "A local specialty," she said. "It'll put hair on your chest, that will."

"Why would I want—" Kalista stopped herself after seeing the look on the furred vastaya's face. "Never mind."

Vennix grunted and knocked back the last of her acrid drink. "Come," she said, slapping Kalista on the shoulder. "There's a place I know down by the dock, serves the best crab I've ever tasted. Let's head there, and we can at least fill our bellies while you consider our next move."

The captain was right—the crab was exquisite. But it did little to temper Kalista's dark mood.

They sat overlooking the ocean as the sun went down and the fishing fleets of the Buhru readied to set off for their night's work. The fishermen looked like they were going to war, grimly hauling harpoons and barbed spears aboard their vessels and kissing their loved ones goodbye on the stone docks. That made sense, since as Kalista understood it, they were heading out to hunt the various serpents and monsters that rose from the depths under the cover of darkness. Curiously, they all tossed something into the ocean as they clambered onto their ships.

"What are they doing?" Kalista asked. She and the captain were seated at a long table, the remnants of their meal before them. They'd been joined by several of the *Daggerhawk*'s crew. The rest of the table was made up of various locals and sailors from the other ships anchored out in the bay, making for a diverse group, with easily half a dozen different languages being spoken. It was a busy place that seemed as popular with the Buhru as with the visitors.

"Offerings to the Mother Serpent," said Vennix, throwing back another cup of the potent local brew. "It's a respect thing."

Kalista looked at her own half-empty cup, contemplating whether she should finish it. It had a foul taste, but the sensation of warmth it gave her was not unpleasant. Before she could make up her mind, Vennix reached over, grabbed it, and knocked it back in one gulp.

"What?" she said, seeing Kalista's surprise. "You've been staring at that for over an hour!"

Kalista smirked, shaking her head.

"At last!" the captain crowed. "That's the first time you've stopped scowling all evening!"

Her expression clouded once more. What right did she have to enjoy herself while the queen lay dying, dying of a poison from a blade she should have stopped? "Maybe I should head back to the *Daggerhawk* and leave you and the crew to it," she suggested. "I fear I am not the best of company right now."

"Give it just a little longer, and we'll head back together," said Vennix, leaning back in her chair and casting her gaze around the tables.

While the locals were paying them no mind, more than a few of the foreign sailors were giving them dark looks, and Kalista had heard several of them muttering under their breath when they'd arrived. Camavor's reputation reached even as far as this, it seemed. Perhaps they thought the *Daggerhawk* was a scouting ship, assessing new lands to conquer. She had enough of a warrior's intuition to know that the mood could easily turn ugly, and was suddenly thankful for the Buhru law that ensured that no outsider could come ashore with a weapon.

"It might be best if we all went back now," she cautioned in a low voice.

"Nah," said Vennix, with a smile. "I'd say things are just about to get interesting."

As if on cue, a foreign sailor bumped into one of Vennix's crew, hard enough to make him spill his drink. The two were instantly nose-to-nose, and others were rising, waiting to see if anything escalated. A pair of massive local bruisers moved in, but Vennix intervened first.

"Gentlemen, gentlemen, I'm sure this can be resolved amicably," she said, hands raised placatingly. Her tone was jovial, but the dangerous glint in her eyes told Kalista exactly what was going to happen, and she slowly rose to her feet.

One of the sailors from the western sandlands glanced down at the captain, who came barely to his chest height, and said something dismissive before looking away again. Kalista winced. *That wasn't smart.*

Without missing a beat, Vennix hit the man square in the throat, twisting her hips to put all her weight behind the blow. He crumpled backward, and the room erupted. More sailors were on their feet, roaring in anger and throwing punches. A chair got smashed over one sailor, and a hurled plate took another in the side of the head, felling him instantly. Vennix laughed uproariously, ducking under a wild roundhouse before lifting her attacker off the ground with a perfectly weighted uppercut to the chin.

Kalista watched the melee, arms folded across her chest. For their part, most of the locals were standing back, letting the foreigners beat one another. The two big bruisers were smirking.

A sailor turned toward her, unsteadily wielding a broken chair leg.

"Don't do it," she warned, but he came at her in a rush. She caught the blow and with a deft twist forced her attacker to his knees. He dropped his makeshift weapon and cried out in pain as his shoulder was wrenched out of its socket. As a general, Kalista didn't approve of off-duty brawling, but she did take some satisfaction as she received a respectful nod from the locals after she kicked her howling opponent away.

A tiny old woman emerged from the kitchen, shouting, and the two big bruisers finally moved in to break things up. One of them pulled apart two scuffling combatants, lifting them off their feet, one in each massive hand, while the other grabbed a fighting sailor by her pants and shirt back and hurled her straight into the ocean.

"We're done! We're done!" laughed Vennix, as one of the big Buhru turned toward her. The captain pulled the last of her crew from the brawl and escaped into the night, leaving destruction behind her.

Kalista was last to leave.

"The Argent Throne sends its apologies," she announced, with a slight bow, but it was clear no one had any idea what she was saying. All eyes were on her now, and many of the expressions spoke of the potential for more violence.

Knowing there was one language everyone spoke, Kalista pulled out a handful of Camavoran coins—enough to pay for the damages twice over. She held them up for all to see, then placed them in a neat pile on one of the tables remaining upright. Seeing that everyone's eyes were now on the coins, Kalista swiftly made her exit, hurrying to join Vennix and her crew.

More than a few of the crew were sporting injuries—though nothing more serious than a few broken ribs and black eyes—but all were chuckling and chatting happily as they headed toward the docks.

"So what was that all about?" said Kalista, falling in beside the captain.

"Figured we could all do with letting off some steam," Vennix replied. "Fun, wasn't it?"

Kalista shook her head but couldn't help smiling.

Still comparing wounds and exploits, the sailors piled into their rowboat, and Kalista was about to step aboard herself when she saw a man approaching. Frowning, she turned toward him. It was dark, but it was clear he wasn't local. She tensed, wondering if it was someone looking for payback from the brawl, though taking on all of the Camavorans alone would have been foolish in anyone's book.

He said something Kalista did not understand, his words sounding guttural. Vennix barked back at him in the same harsh language.

"You speak his tongue as well?" said Kalista.

"Like I said, languages come easy."

"What does he want?"

Vennix and the man spoke. It sounded like they were arguing, practically shouting at each other, but Vennix didn't seem angry. The vastaya turned back to her. "He says he knows you didn't get the answers you were looking for from the Buhru elder. Says he knows someone who could give you those answers, though. And he offers to lead us there. For the right price, of course. Oh, and he also knows you're a princess, which I imagine has doubled his price, at a minimum."

Kalista assessed the stranger. She didn't particularly like the way he smiled at her. His teeth were made of steel, and they glinted in the moonlight.

But what other option do I have?

"You sure about this?" said Vennix.

The *Daggerhawk* was anchored in a wide bay near the largest of the Serpent Isles, the better part of a day's sail from the Buhru port where they had met their newfound guide. Kalista stood at the very rear of the Camavoran ship, poised to clamber into the rowboat hanging off the stern, held in place by a series of ropes and pulleys.

"No," she said. "But I don't have a better idea right now."

Through Vennix, Kalista had learned that the man who'd approached her the night before was Rhazu Ferros, a "trader, explorer, and sometime purveyor of information and hard-to-find things," as he described himself. He hailed from a port city called Oshra Va'Zaun, on a narrow isthmus to the west. Kalista vaguely remembered the name and believed that a delegation from that city had come to Camavor years earlier, seeking trade relations. They'd been rejected, from what she could remember.

"All he sees when he looks at you is coin."

"Oh, I know," said Kalista. "Doesn't mean I won't get the answers I seek, however."

Ferros's ship, anchored nearby, was unlike anything Kalista had ever seen. Her name was *Progress*, and she was a wide vessel of sturdy construction, with what looked like fortified manors built into the bow and stern, complete with shingled roofs, glass windows, and chimneys. The one at the rear even had a giant clock built into its front, and when the hour chimed, an array of tiny doors opened and tiny figures paraded out.

"What's wrong with telling the time by the sun?" Vennix had remarked when they first glimpsed the ship.

"And there is no magic involved?" Kalista had asked Ferros. He flashed his steel grin and spoke with passion.

"No magic," Vennix had translated. "Gears, hidden mechanisms, and Oshra Va'Zaun craftsmanship is what he says. I'm not going to bother translating everything else. He's bragging, saying how expensive it was to build and such. I think he's trying to impress us. Seems like a total waste of money, if you ask me."

Vennix might be disdainful of the ship's practicality, but Kalista was impressed with the ingenuity on display.

"I really don't think this is a good idea," Vennix said as Kalista climbed into the rowboat. "But I'm coming with you." She clicked her fingers, getting the attention of her cabin girl. "Go get Jada for me, would you, love?"

"Jada?" said Kalista as the youngster shot off below deck.

"My best girl, and I've known a few," said Vennix. "Not countin' the *Daggerhawk*, of course. She'll always have my heart."

Jada, Kalista discovered, was a massive two-handed, curved scimitar with an ornate crossguard shaped like a coiled serpent.

"It's almost as big as you," she said as Vennix strapped the scabbarded blade over her shoulders.

"She ain't ever let me down," said Vennix. "Best relationship I've ever had." She turned to a sailor on the deck. "Take us down!"

Ropes were untied and slack given out, lowering the rowboat to the glassy sea. There were four of the *Daggerhawk*'s crew on board in addition to Kalista and Vennix, and they took up the oars, rowing toward shore. It was an isolated, untouched part of the island, with no evidence of habitation. Immense rock formations rose up before them, bursting with waterfalls and greenery.

"Why would this seer be out *here* of all places?" said Vennix, staring at the dense, hot jungle. "It seems very impractical for visitors to find her."

"Perhaps that's the point," said Kalista.

"Or perhaps the point is merely to lure you to a quiet location and take all your gold?"

"Not beyond the realm of possibility," she agreed. "Perhaps just view it as another way to blow off some steam?"

Vennix grimaced. "I'd sooner stick to barroom brawls with drunk sailors."

"Noted."

They neared the beach, and Kalista jumped into the waist-deep water to help haul the boat onto the sand. The water was warm and inviting, but the number of fins and scaled things she'd seen between the *Daggerhawk* and the shore meant she had no desire to linger any longer than necessary.

Rhazu Ferros stood alone, smiling broadly as they approached, his teeth glinting. He bowed to Kalista and then spoke to Vennix. Vennix scoffed.

"What is he saying?" asked Kalista.

"Unsurprisingly, he wants to talk about payment."

"Where is this proclaimed seer of his?"

Vennix spoke with Ferros again, who nodded toward the trees. "He says the seer is a ways into the jungle, but he's being purposely unclear. Says we can be there by sunset if we get moving. I don't think he wants to give too much away before we pay him."

Ferros spoke again, gesturing to himself, then to Kalista and her companions.

"He's again saying how he is a man of his word. That he is leading us in there alone, without any of his guards, as an act of good faith. But he really wants to be paid."

"Fine," said Kalista, producing a pouch and holding it up. "This is a third of your payment. You'll get the rest after we see the seer and are back safely." She tossed the pouch over to him, and he caught it deftly. "Do not betray me, Ferros," she added, leveling a finger at him. "You will come to regret it if you do."

Vennix translated, and the man laughed, shaking his head. Among his words, Kalista recognized one—*Camavoran.*

"What's so funny?" she asked.

"We are, apparently." Vennix sniffed. "He says not everyone is as ruthless and driven by greed as Camavorans. I really don't like this man."

"Let's just get going, shall we?" said Kalista.

Ferros gave her another bow and gestured up at the jungle.

Once they were on their way, Kalista stepped close to Vennix. "Keep an eye behind us. Make sure no one follows us."

Chapter Twelve

They began their trek into the jungle under a blazing sun, but dark clouds quickly formed above the immense cliffs and spires overhead. Lightning crackled out to sea, and thunder rolled in booming waves. Rain soon followed, coming down in a relentless, hammering assault, hard enough that it was near impossible to hear anything above the deluge.

Drenched to the skin, they trudged single file along ever more treacherous paths, slipping and sliding in the mud. Kalista used her spear as a walking stick to maintain her footing. Alone among the group, Vennix seemed unbothered by the weather. The rain ran off her fur like it was an oiled coat, and she hummed a haunting vastayan melody while she marched, her eyes unwaveringly fixed on the back of Rhazu Ferros.

"We've had more rain in the last hour than Camavor gets in a year!" said Kalista, looking up at the towering cliff face before them.

"What?" bellowed Vennix.

"Oh, it doesn't matter," replied Kalista.

"What?"

"I said, it doesn't matter!"

"I'm looking fatter?" replied Vennix, outraged.

"No, I said—" Kalista began, before noticing the wicked

gleam in Vennix's eyes. The captain laughed as Kalista shook her head in exasperation.

"I heard you the first time!" shouted Vennix. "And for the record, I would have taken that as a compliment!"

It was dark in the chasms and cracks between the rocks. In some places, they were forced to squeeze through, while elsewhere they had to wade through deepening pools of gushing rainwater. By the time they neared their destination, the rain had ceased and the clouds had given way to a glorious crimson sunset, glimpsed in the narrow ravine openings overhead and the occasional view across the bay.

A dull roaring announced their arrival at a massive, plunging waterfall that descended into a great, gaping sinkhole in the jungle floor. An immense rainbow could be seen in the spray as the last beams of sunlight disappeared.

Kalista gazed down into the depths of the sinkhole. "I'm guessing she's down there, isn't she?" Ferros nodded, and she sighed. "Of course she would be," she muttered.

It was night by the time Kalista reached the bottom of the sinkhole. She'd left the others at the top and climbed down by herself—apparently, the seer would see her only if she was alone.

Stars glimmered in the sky, mirrored in the large, deep pool formed by the waterfall. The ground was covered in broad-leafed plants, creepers, and vivid flowers. The crashing of the waterfall echoed around her, and the air was filled with swirling vapor. The area was cavernous, far larger than it had looked from above, and the pool extended back beneath the overhanging rim of the sinkhole, delving farther than Kalista could see.

A narrow strip of land, hugging the sheer wall, led behind the waterfall. Guessing the seer would likely be there, Kalista walked along the path, carefully picking her way across water-slick rocks and through dense foliage.

A tall, slender figure waited for her atop one of the rocks. At first, she thought it was a statue, so still was it, but its head turned toward her as she came closer. The being was obscured by the billowing water vapor, so she could not see it clearly, but it was obvious that this was a creature unlike any Kalista had seen before.

"It's beautiful, is it not?" said the creature.

The strangely ethereal voice was feminine and curiously devoid of accent. Kalista was not actually sure *what* language it was speaking, though she understood every word. She approached warily, trying to see the speaker more clearly.

"This bay, these jungles, this waterfall," the creature continued, gesturing with languid movements. "It's all so untouched. So unspoiled. Pure. But it will not remain so forever. A city will grow here, like a canker sore. A place of lies and murder. It...saddens me."

"You speak of things to come as if you have seen them already," Kalista said.

"I have, Kalista vol Kalah Heigaari of Camavor," said the creature. "I have been waiting for you."

"Who are you?"

A gust cleared the mist between them, and Kalista's eyes widened. The seer's skin was the pale purple of dusk, and she stood upon long, reverse-jointed legs that ended in hooves. From the center of her forehead extended a curving horn that shimmered like moonlight.

"I have been called many things, by many beings," said the seer. "But I am a child of the stars. You may call me Soraka."

Soraka led Kalista behind the waterfall to a shallow natural cavern. Pinpricks of light covered the ceiling like stars, and clusters of fungi radiated a gentle glow, bathing the cave in soft blue illumination.

The seer moved with subtle, unhurried grace, and Kalista felt a profound sense of calm in her presence. Soraka folded her legs neatly beneath her and lowered herself onto a low stone shelf, gesturing for Kalista to sit as well. A tall staff, topped with a crescent moon, leaned nearby, and a small teapot and pair of cups sat upon a flat rock. There was little else within the cavern to indicate this was the seer's home, but Kalista felt certain that it was.

"Tea?" Soraka said.

Kalista nodded her thanks and took one of the cups. She was surprised to find it was hot, and aromatic herbs rose on its steam. "How did you know to expect me?" she asked. "And how did you know my name?"

The strange being's eyes were captivating, seeming to reflect stars and distant cosmic bodies within their depths. "I do not believe those are the questions you came all this way to ask, but I will answer them nonetheless," she said. "The answer to both those questions is the same: The stars told me."

"I see," said Kalista, not seeing at all. *Such is the way with seers.*

Soraka laughed gently. "I take no offense at your skepticism."

Kalista pressed on. "If you speak the truth, then you already know why I am here."

Soraka smiled, though there was something sad in it, as if it were filled with regret. "I know why you came, and I will answer as best I can," she said, "but you could ask a *different* question. You could ask what would happen if you just... left. You could ask what would happen if you threw off your burdens and left your homeland with the true love of your heart."

Kalista did not move, suddenly guarded. Could this creature read her innermost thoughts and desires? "And what would be your answer, if that were the question I asked?"

"You would be happy. You'd live a long, fulfilling life. You'd have children, and they would have children, and those who love you would be at your side when your time finally came, as gently as a breeze." Soraka's smile faded. "But even knowing what that path would bring, it is unlikely that you will take it."

"Why are you telling me this?"

Soraka sighed. "Perhaps I would simply like to see you avoid a long and mournful path. Perhaps I would wish you to have a little happiness in your life. A mortal span is so short."

"Are our fates decided for us, then?" asked Kalista. "Are they already set in stone, and what we do merely an illusion of choice?"

"Oh, no," said Soraka, shaking her head, "your future is your own. What path you take is yours to choose. What I see are *possibilities*. Myriad possible futures are spread before you, but the choice is *always* yours."

Kalista took a sip of her tea. "And what have you seen in these futures of mine?"

"Darkness," Soraka whispered, a shadow falling over her. It might have been a trick of the light, but it seemed like the glowing mushrooms and glimmering constellations had dimmed.

"Well, that's encouraging," Kalista muttered.

Soraka laughed softly, and the shadows lifted. "Even when a flame is smothered, and all seems lost, a single ember may be hidden beneath the ashes. As long as that one ember remains burning, all the darkness in the world can be banished. And while it glows, there is hope."

"I don't understand."

"I know," said Soraka sadly. "And you may never need to. As I said, the future is not fixed."

"This is all... fascinating," said Kalista, "but I came here to get the answer to a specific question, and I do not have the luxury of time."

"You are a pragmatic soul, Kalista vol Kalah Heigaari of Camavor. You are wise not to put much trust in those who claim to know the future. Most who would describe themselves in such terms *are* false."

"And now is when you tell me that *your* prophecies are real?" said Kalista. "How all those others are liars, but not you?"

"It does not matter if you believe me," said Soraka. "The sun will continue to rise and fall each day, until the end. Truth does not need belief in order for it to be true. It just... *is*."

"Give me something solid and provable, and I'll believe it," said Kalista.

Soraka smiled. "I do not need to prove myself to you, but I will tell you this. You seek the isles hidden in the mists. I say you will be better off not finding them. But if you will go anyway—as you and I both know you will—I can tell you that the golden maiden of the sea will take you there."

"The golden maiden of the sea," Kalista repeated flatly. "And who's she, then?"

Soraka sipped her tea, making it clear that her prophecy had been spoken and that she would speak no more. Kalista rolled her eyes. Pushing herself to her feet, she paced back and forth.

"Why speak in riddles and vagaries?" she said. "Why not tell me directly?"

"I can only tell you what I see," said Soraka. "I am sorry I can do no more."

"So that's it? That's my prophecy? Find a golden maiden who will take me there?"

Soraka's face was full of regret and empathy. "I can say no more."

Kalista stared at the seer, frustrated at her riddles and angry at herself for coming here in the first place. There was much the creature was not saying, but she realized she would never get a straight answer. "Thank you for the tea," she said, placing her cup down upon the stone shelf. Then she bowed her head and turned to leave.

"The pool is deep," Soraka said. "And it leads back to the bay."

Kalista frowned and glanced over her shoulder at the strange creature. The seer was staring wistfully toward the moonlight reflecting through the waterfall and didn't meet her gaze.

Is she mad?

Kalista shook her head and left.

Kalista kept going over the seer's words as she climbed back up toward the rim of the sinkhole. None of it made sense.

Her expression was dark as she reached the top of the narrow ledge, and her heart was hammering from the exertion when she saw the crossbows leveled at her.

"Easy now," said a heavily accented voice. "Drop that spear of yours over the edge, please. Unless, that is, you fancy getting filled with bolts, and your captain's throat slit."

Kalista swore under her breath. *Ferros. The swine speaks Camavoran after all.* She could see him up ahead, knife held to the throat of Vennix, who had been forced to kneel before him. A handful of foreign sailors were backing him up, crossbows at the ready. *Where did they come from?* They must have trekked in ahead of them to prepare this ambush, she realized, and Kalista cursed again. She should have expected this. Her eagerness to find this seer had made her reckless.

It looked like at least five of Ferros's newly arrived guards were down, but Vennix's four crew members were dead as well. The captain herself was bleeding, and one of her eyes was swollen shut.

Kalista glared at Ferros. She could kill him before he cut

Vennix's throat, but while it *would* be satisfying, it wouldn't stop his goons from dropping them with crossbow bolts.

"Kill the bastard!" Vennix snarled.

"Don't try it," said Ferros, tightening his grip on the knife. He drew blood, and Vennix hissed.

Kalista's gaze flicked again to the crossbows, gauging her chance of avoiding their bolts at this distance. It wasn't likely. "Fine," she spat.

"*Slowly*," Ferros urged.

Staring hatefully at him, Kalista slowly extended her arm to the side and dropped her beloved spear into the sinkhole. It instantly disappeared into the billowing mist. "Whatever you're being paid, it's not enough," she said.

Ferros shoved Vennix to the ground. "Bind her hands," he ordered, and one of his sailors hauled Vennix's arms back and swiftly tied her wrists together. "Hers too."

Two other sailors stalked warily toward Kalista. She scowled but didn't resist as they roughly twisted her arms behind her back and bound them with rope.

"What now, betrayer?" she asked as she was marched over beside Vennix and forced down to her knees.

"Betrayer? Ouch," said Ferros. "And for the record, no one's paying me. But I'm sure Camavor will be *very* keen to see the heir to the throne returned safely."

"You plan to hold me for ransom? All you will achieve is the butchery of every man, woman, and child in Oshra Va'Zaun. Do you really wish to be responsible for that?"

"You *are* a bloodthirsty lot, aren't you," said Ferros. "*Ransom* is an ugly word, in any language. You will be my *guest*. You'll be treated like the princess you are, and live in luxury in my fine city. All I want is for your king to open up trade to the Ferros clan. Then you can go home, if that is your wish."

"You are a fool, Ferros. This will not end well for you."

Ferros grinned. "We will see," he said. "You have already underestimated me once. I think perhaps you do so again."

Kalista traded a glance with Vennix.

"Sorry, princess," the captain said. "Took a few of 'em down, but I regret not managing to kill that silver-toothed bastard. At least then we wouldn't have to listen to this piss."

Kalista assessed the situation. She and Vennix were on their knees, hands tied. They were surrounded on three sides by Ferros's sailors, cutting off any attempt to escape...except over the edge of the cliff.

"*The pool is deep, and leads to the bay*," she breathed.

"What's that?" hissed Vennix.

"Something the seer told me," Kalista whispered.

She glanced up at Ferros, who was momentarily distracted, giving orders to one of his guards. She looked back at Vennix and gave a pointed nod toward the cliff. "Not scared of heights, are you?"

"Oh, you're not seriously—"

Kalista was already surging to her feet and sprinting for the sinkhole. It was awkward, running with her hands tied behind her back, but she was quick and had taken Ferros and his crew by surprise. There were shouts behind her, and a crossbow bolt hissed by her neck, missing her by less than a handspan.

Then she was at the edge of the sinkhole. Without pause, she leaped.

She twisted in the air, seeing Vennix a few steps behind her. The captain stumbled as a bolt took her in the shoulder, but she kept going and half leaped, half collapsed over the edge.

The cliff face streaked past Kalista in a blur as she fell. Suddenly she was in the cool spray of the waterfall and could see nothing. It was a curious sensation, and she wondered if this was what it felt like to fly.

Then she hit the water and plunged deep, the air driving

from her lungs. Bubbles and surging water surrounded her, blinding her, and she completely lost which way was up and which way down. She thrashed and kicked, and for a moment she was certain she was going to drown.

Then she paused, calming herself. The explosion of bubbles subsided, and she was able to take stock of her surroundings. She glimpsed dark, shadowy rocks below and could see the glint of moonlight above. She kicked toward that light, lungs burning, and finally surfaced, sucking in deep, shuddering breaths.

Vennix surfaced nearby, spluttering and laughing. "That was insane," she said.

"We're not out of this yet," said Kalista. She glanced at the bolt jutting from Vennix's shoulder. "You okay?"

Vennix shrugged, then winced. "Fine."

"Knife, on my hip. Quickly."

The two women, treading water, positioned themselves so Vennix could reach the blade with her bound hands.

"I think I've got it," she said.

"Don't drop it."

"I won't," said the captain. "Oh..."

"What? You didn't?"

"Nah, just joking," Vennix said. "Just give me...there!" She freed herself, then swiftly cut Kalista's bindings. "So, what now?"

"The seer said this pool leads out to the bay," Kalista said. "Will you be able to make it?"

"I won't slow you," said Vennix. "But first..."

She dove down into the depths. Even using just one arm, she moved effortlessly, her body rolling like a wave as both legs kicked together. Kalista stayed where she was, treading water. A minute passed, then another, and she was starting to worry when Vennix surfaced again.

"Here," she said, handing Kalista her spear.

"How did you...?"

"My eyes are keener than yours," said Vennix. "Now, come, I found the way out. And I think I spotted Jada."

Kalista dragged herself out of the water, spluttering and coughing. She crawled up onto the rocks, clinging to the jagged, sharp stone, even though it cut her fingers. A wave crashed over her with a resounding boom, but she clung on. Her grip was just loosening when Vennix grabbed her by the straps of her armor and hauled her out with surprising strength.

Safe at last, she lay on her back, gasping and staring at the dark water. Dozens of sharp fins were circling frantically where they'd exited.

"That was too close," she hissed.

"Now to get back to the ship."

They clambered over the rocks, heading for the narrow cove where they'd rowed ashore, crabs and tentacled things scurrying out of their way. Once on the sand, they ran swiftly, angling toward the lee of the cliffs where they'd dragged the boat. Ferros's boat was still there, so at least they'd beaten him back.

Moving as fast as they were able, they dragged their boat toward the water. "I hear them," growled Vennix, struggling to maneuver her side of the vessel with one arm.

Kalista could see the flames of torches in the jungle, heading toward them. There was a shout as Ferros and his crewmen saw them. She grunted with effort, hauling the boat until it finally slid into the water.

"Wait," she said. Kalista ran to the other boat, slid the oars free, and hurled them each as far out into the sea as she could. A great fanged maw reared out of the waves and crunched down on one of them, snapping it like tinder.

Eyes wide, she ran back to Vennix and clambered aboard.

"Let's go!" Kalista shouted, and the two of them pulled on the oars.

"I really hope you got what you needed from that seer," muttered Vennix.

"You sure you don't want to sink the bastard's ship?"

Kalista stared across the bay from the deck of the *Daggerhawk*. It was tempting, but she shook her head. "Not worth the risk," she said. "And Ferros's crew don't deserve to die just because of the greed of their master."

Vennix growled in pain as the crossbow bolt was wrenched free from her shoulder. "So this was all for nothing?" she said through gritted teeth.

"Seems that way," Kalista said bitterly. "The seer didn't give me any clear answers."

"So what now?"

Kalista sighed. "We return to Camavor."

She had failed.

Chapter Thirteen

The Eternal Ocean

"Ship ho!"

Kalista tore herself from her melancholy and pushed herself to her feet. She was soaked to the skin and chilled to the bone by the lashing rain, but despite the weather, she'd refused to go belowdecks. For hours she'd been staring listlessly out to sea, legs hanging over the edge of the ship. She squinted into the distance, shielding her eyes from the stinging sea spray, but could see nothing. Sheets of rain obscured the ocean, like great undulating curtains.

"Is she bearing on us?" Vennix shouted up to the lookout.

"No, Captain! I think... Yes, they're under attack!"

Kalista crossed the deck to join the captain. She could see something now: a vague, dark shadow glimpsed through the storm. It was far closer than she had expected, perhaps only a few hundred yards away. "Under attack from what?" she said.

Vennix swore under her breath. "Crimson warparty!" she hissed.

The rain parted, and Kalista saw *things* in the water around the vessel, as well as raiders climbing up its hull. The ship was listing dangerously to one side, and the thought of whatever could be causing that was unnerving.

"Crimson warparty?" questioned Kalista, but Vennix was already swinging away, shouting commands.

"Hard to port! Hard to port! Full sails! Get us away!"

"Hold that order!" bellowed Kalista. "Those people need our help!"

Vennix rounded on her. "*I* am the captain of this ship."

"And you are sworn to the crown!" Kalista shot back.

"They're already as good as dead!" Vennix snapped. "Crimson razorscales are vastayan hunters from the depths! We need to get away, *now*, or they'll claim us as well!"

Sea-green figures with long, serpentine tails were climbing up the hull of the stricken ship, weapons clasped in beaked maws. Their fins and crests were a vivid red. Others reared out of the ocean, hurling jagged obsidian harpoons, skewering sailors on deck. "They're being slaughtered!" Kalista said. "We have to help them!"

"It's too dangerous!" returned Vennix. "You don't understand! They're killers!"

"Where is your honor?" Kalista said, eyes flashing. "It shames us to do nothing!"

Vennix snarled and clenched her hands into fists. Her sailors were frozen, waiting to see the outcome of the confrontation between their captain and the princess of the royal blood. "Fine," she said. "But be it on your head."

Her face thunderous, she shouted new orders. Within moments the *Daggerhawk* turned toward the besieged vessel, while crew members gathered weapons. Some began to climb the rigging, bows and quivers of arrows slung across their backs, while others readied belaying pins and swords.

"Look for their leader," Vennix told Kalista. "Take out that one, and we may have a chance."

Along with a score of Camavoran sailors, Kalista swung across the gulf between the two vessels. She landed in a low crouch on the other ship's heaving deck.

A tall, gaunt crimson razorscale turned toward her, its mottled tail flicking around. Kalista was assailed by its rank stench of brine and rotting meat. The creature's spines and fins were pierced with dozens of corroded hooks and metal rings. Long strands of braided red kelp, threaded with bones, were tied around its wrists, ankles, and neck. Its pallid eyes blazed with feral intelligence, and it lashed at Kalista with its jagged obsidian harpoon.

She rolled beneath the blow, drawing her knife from its sheath. As she rose to one knee, she hacked into the back of the razorscale's leg. The creature roared in fury, seeking to skewer her. Again, Kalista rolled out of the way, this time rising alongside the ship's central mast. Another razorscale was impaled there, stuck to the mast by a spear she'd thrown from the deck of the *Daggerhawk*. She tore the weapon free and spun to turn aside another thrust from the enraged razorscale, now bleeding from its lower leg. Using her spear like a quarterstaff, Kalista struck the creature's head, then swept its legs out from under it. It hissed in anger as it went down, but she silenced it with a spear thrust.

There were at least a dozen razorscales on the deck, with more clambering aboard, thick nails digging into woodwork. A few were down, but most of the fallen were human. Arrows from the *Daggerhawk* sliced through the rain, striking a number of the vicious creatures, though killing only one. The others fought on, snarling and spitting.

A Camavoran sailor dropped his belaying pin as a barbed whip lashed out, wrapping around his neck. Before Kalista could aid the man, he was yanked into the surging ocean. The whip-wielding razorscale slithered onto the deck but met Kalista's spear.

"Come on, you salty bastards!" Captain Vennix bellowed

as she slashed around with her massive scimitar, Jada. She took down a raider with one savage strike and kicked its thrashing form overboard. Kalista met her gaze across the tumult, and the captain gave her a wild grin before hurling herself at her next enemy.

"Behind you!" came a shout.

Kalista spun just as a razorscale lunged at her from her blind side, spear flashing. A violet sphere of crackling energy hit the creature before it could strike, throwing it across the deck.

What in the name of the Ancestors?

She turned and saw a young man with purple runes burning within the flesh of his hands and forearms. He cried out in pain and dropped to his knees as the runes flared brightly, creeping farther up his arms. The deck beneath his hands blackened and smoked, then burst into violet flame.

An older, unarmed man in a robe stood behind him, berating him in a language she didn't understand. He wore a sigil around his neck, glowing brightly. He thrust an open hand toward the young man, and white light radiated from his palm. The runes instantly faded, and the flames were quenched, as if doused.

Kalista shouted a warning as a savage razorscale reared up behind the older man, thrusting a barbed harpoon toward his back, but she needn't have bothered. A blinding halo of light surrounded him, and the weapon and the raider wielding it were reduced to ash.

The ship lurched sharply to starboard. Scores of combatants on both sides went sliding across the deck. Kalista steadied herself, crouching low and grabbing hold of a railing, even as others tumbled past her. The ship tilted further, timbers groaning in protest. Kalista's eyes widened as she saw what was pulling the starboard side down.

A gigantic creature, perhaps half the length of the whole

ship, was hauling itself out of the ocean, water streaming off its leathery blue-green flesh. It had at least six limbs, and while the rearmost ones ended in giant flippers, the front pair were disturbingly humanlike. The monster's bloated face was dominated by a gigantic tooth-filled maw, each serrated fang as long as a dagger. Below its jaws were writhing tentacles, which probed the air, searching for prey. Two tiny, pallid eyes, pupils like pinpricks, glared down at the sailors scrambling desperately away from it. It screeched, spraying spittle and its sickening seaweed stench across the deck and exposing more tentacles down its gullet. Kalista's ears reverberated painfully at that keening wail, and fear tightened like a fist clenched around her heart.

A harness of chain and scaled leather was secured tightly around the monster's torso and neck, and a razorscale rider was crouched upon its shoulders. The raider hefted a jagged trident hung with totems and fetishes above its head and roared. It wore an impressive headdress of woven red kelp and bones, and its chest was tattooed with swirling patterns of glowing ink.

The leader.

For a moment longer, Kalista remained frozen, transfixed by fear. Then she snarled and broke into a run, angling directly for the titanic beast as it snatched up a sailor in its immense fist and slammed him flat against the deck. The razorscale leader leaned forward and placed its hand upon the monster's head, barking an order. A pulse of energy radiated from its palm, and the monster's eyes went blank. The rider snapped another order, leveling its trident at the robed older man, and the scaled behemoth turned toward him, making the ship lurch dangerously again.

Kalista dodged another stabbing blade and kept running, her eyes fixed on the leader. Vennix moved to give her support, dashing to cut down another raider, her massive two-handed scimitar hacking the creature from neck to sternum.

"Kill him!" Vennix shouted.

Kalista sprinted across the deck, unseen by the great beast or its rider, which were both intent on the robed man. The younger man with him stepped forward, ignoring the barked orders of his elder, wild energy crackling between his hands once more. Before he could unleash it, however, the behemoth swatted him aside, sending him through a banister and crashing down to the lower deck.

Kalista jumped onto a narrow railing, ran lightly along it, then leaped onto the back of the monster. Its hide was thick and encrusted with barnacles, giving her good purchase. She launched herself at the razorscale chieftain, spear clasped in both hands over her head.

The razorscale saw her too late. A swift pulse of energy made its massive steed whip around, but the raider was unable to avoid Kalista's spear tip, which plunged into its chest with force.

With its master slain, the immense beast went berserk. It screeched and thrashed, throwing Kalista from its back. It bit a razorscale clean in half, and its tail slammed an unfortunate Camavoran into the central mast. The man slumped to the deck, unmoving.

Grunting in pain, Kalista pushed herself up to one knee. The beast's eyes looked different now, narrowed and furious, rather than oddly blank, and it tore another razorscale apart with its giant humanoid hands. A hunting horn sounded, and the raiders fled, leaping overboard and disappearing into the depths. With a savage, ululating shriek of its own, the giant sea monster flopped across the deck, making the ship tilt alarmingly once again, before it slid into the water in pursuit of those who had enslaved it.

The battle was over.

"That was a good kill," said Vennix, as she helped Kalista to her feet.

Kalista looked around at the dead and injured littering the deck. "How many did we lose?"

"More than I'd have liked," said Vennix, "but less than I feared. We definitely came off better than this lot."

Kalista nodded. The besieged ship seemed to have lost more than half its crew. She took a deep breath, unsure if Vennix would resent her for forcing her hand to intervene with the stricken ship. "Captain," she began.

"It was the right decision," Vennix interrupted. "Coming to their aid, it was the right thing to do. It shames me that my first instinct was to do otherwise."

"Wanting to keep your crew alive is nothing to be ashamed of," said Kalista. She inclined her head toward the crew of the rescued ship. "Who are they?"

"I don't know," said Vennix in a low voice. "The ship is similar to Shuriman triremes in build, but those can't handle the open ocean. And these aren't desert folk. But I think we're about to find out."

She nodded toward the two men making their way toward them. Kalista recognized them from the battle.

"Greetings, friends!" boomed the older man. He spoke near perfect Camavoran, with just a hint of an accent. "And many thanks for your timely intervention!" He had the look of a scholar—with his gray robe, sharp eyes, analyzing expression, and neat, silver-streaked beard—yet he had the powerful build and tanned face of a soldier who spent most of his time outside. Kalista guessed he was of middling years. The sigil around his neck—shaped like overlapping triangles with a spherical stone in its center—was no longer glowing. "Truly, we would have been lost had you not come to our aid. I am in your debt."

"I am sorry we did not arrive sooner," said Kalista. "You

were hit hard, and many of your crew are now with their ancestors."

"It could have been considerably worse! But forgive my manners. Let me introduce myself," he said. "I am Seeker-Adept Tyrus. And this is my apprentice, Ryze."

Kalista glanced at the younger man, who she guessed was in his late teens. The sides of his head were shaved, and the hair down the center of his scalp was long and braided. He, too, wore a gray robe, though his hung open at the front, exposing his lean, tautly muscled, suntanned chest. He was clearly in some pain, though he tried to hide it, and there was a brash smile on his smooth-cheeked face. He was handsome, in a rakish way, and had the air of one who knew it too well.

"I am Kalista," she said, turning her attention back to Tyrus. "And this is the captain of the *Daggerhawk*, Vennix."

"It is an honor," said Tyrus, bowing his head.

"You speak our tongue fluently."

"I am a student of the world," he replied.

"But I do not recognize your accent. Where do you hail from, friend?"

"I was born in a small village to the northwest, called Ironwater."

"A place noted primarily for its...its...How do you say it? Its goats? Yes, *goats* is the right word," said Ryze. He, too, spoke Camavoran, though not with nearly the same fluency as his master. He flashed Kalista a grin, and Tyrus smiled dryly.

"Ah, the arrogance of youth," he said. "My apprentice likes the sound of his own voice a little too much, even when speaking a tongue he has not yet mastered. And he has little respect for his betters."

"Betters?" Ryze rolled his eyes. "I think—"

"Enough," snapped Tyrus. "Go report to the ship's surgeon. See what help you can be. I will join you shortly."

The apprentice stalked off, scowling and muttering under his breath in a harsh language Kalista did not understand.

Tyrus gave a weary sigh before addressing her again. "My apologies. He's an infuriating young man. Born with more talent in one finger than most of us have in our whole being, yet he's impulsive, feckless, and ill-disciplined."

"I know the type," Kalista said with a smirk. "He saved me from being run through, though."

"He shouldn't even be *using* those arts," said Tyrus, shaking his head. "He is able to draw in the raw essence of magic, but it's too much, too quickly. He lacks the knowledge of the runic forms to safely disperse that power, or channel it. And he does not have the discipline or responsibility to be *taught* such forms, not yet."

There was an anguished cry and raised voices from a little way off, and Kalista saw Ryze rushing to the side of a fallen sailor.

"Excuse me, please, I am needed," said Tyrus.

"Of course. We will stay and help," Kalista said. "We have some supplies, healing herbs and such."

"That would be appreciated," said Tyrus. "Again, I am in your debt." He bowed to her before taking his leave.

Kalista turned to find Vennix leaning over the side of the railing, frowning. "What is it, Captain?"

"What was it that seer told you back on the Serpent Isles? Follow the golden what?"

"She said the golden maiden would lead the way," said Kalista. "Why?"

Vennix pointed toward the bow, a wry smile curling her lips. Kalista looked.

"I don't see—" Her eyes widened. "Oh. Oh!" The ship's figurehead was a golden woman with a fierce demeanor, her arms fanning out behind her as she leaned out over the ocean, as if she were flying.

"Looks like you found your golden maiden, princess."

~

"You said you are from a town to the northwest," said Kalista. "Ironwater, was it?"

She was sitting belowdecks with Tyrus, supping on a meal of hearty soup and bread. The two of them ate alone, for Vennix had gone back to the *Daggerhawk*, and Tyrus's young apprentice was off on some menial task assigned by his master.

Tyrus smirked. "Calling it a town is giving it too much credit," he said. "Young Ryze was trying to embarrass me, but he's not wrong. Ironwater *is* rather barbarous."

"You don't seem uncivilized," said Kalista. "Far from it. You are scholars? Priests?"

"Priests? No, definitely not priests," said Tyrus, with a chuckle. He took a sip from a pewter flagon before continuing. "The only thing I put any faith in is the scientific arts. *Scholars* is a suitable term, though."

"And what are scholars doing braving the Eternal Ocean?"

"It is my belief that knowledge is the most precious resource in the world—far more valuable than gold—and I am committed to the gathering and preservation of it." Tyrus shrugged. "Sometimes that involves going places most scholars might otherwise avoid, and returning with artifacts and books worthy of further study."

"It sounds to me like you journey out into the world and take that which does not belong to you. You would make a fine Camavoran."

Tyrus smiled. "Camavor *does* possess a great many artifacts and books that my fellow scholars would dearly love to study," he admitted. "Though I would like to think my methods for attaining such things are somewhat less... aggressive."

Kalista laughed. "And where do you take this knowledge, good master Tyrus? Where are your 'fellow scholars'?"

"A place of little consequence in the larger scheme of things. It is a humble and insignificant place, really."

"A humble and insignificant place with enough wealth to send you around the world in considerable comfort, though," said Kalista. The plates they were dining off were of finely wrought porcelain, and the cutlery was ornate silver. Everything about the ship, the *Aureate Savant*, spoke of riches.

"Why does a minor fellowship of scholars interest a daughter of the royal bloodline of Camavor?" asked Tyrus. "Do you seek to join us? I am not sure you would find life among us as interesting as the delights of Alovédra. We are quite dull, I can assure you."

"You know who I am?"

"I would be a poor scholar if I did not," said Tyrus.

"Then let me be frank," said Kalista. "I do not believe your order is anything as humble as you suggest. I am on a quest to find the Blessed Isles."

Tyrus regarded Kalista with an impenetrable stare. "The Blessed Isles are a myth."

"We both know that is not true," said Kalista. "They are hidden within the mists at the heart of this ocean. We have tried unsuccessfully to penetrate them, but their magic turns us around, time and time again."

"Camavoran quests tend to end in blood and violence, from what I understand. Is it for conquest you seek those mythical islands?"

"No," said Kalista. "The questing culture of my homeland has long been corrupted, and I abhor how it is used to justify invasions. I seek the isles for a noble cause. The queen of Camavor lies dying. She was struck by a poisoned blade, a poison our best healers have been unable to halt. I need to find a cure. That is why I seek the Blessed Isles."

Tyrus patted his mouth with a silk napkin. "I wish I could help you," he said. "But it—"

"Please. I am *begging* you. My young uncle, the king, *adores* his queen. She is his life, and I fear what he will do should she succumb."

"He will do what we all must when we lose someone close to us. He will *mourn*."

"I fear he will do far more than that," Kalista said. "He will look for someone to blame, and he will unleash the might of Camavor upon them. Death and destruction will follow, and his rage and pain will not easily be slaked."

"That sounds like a threat. A way to coerce me to reveal anything I might know about your fantastical Blessed Isles."

Kalista sighed. "If you choose not to aid me, you have my word that I will speak none of this to another living soul. Viego will not be looking to attack an island of scholars in the middle of an ocean. His fury will turn upon Camavor's neighbors. And when they are no more, it will turn upon the people of his kingdom. And it will be my fault."

"Your fault?"

"I could have prevented it," said Kalista. "I *should* have prevented it, and my failure haunts me. Coming upon you was no accident! A single-horned seer told me it was written in the heavens that the golden maiden of the sea would lead me to the isles. That has to be your ship. I have never been one to put my faith in prophecies, but everything she said has come to pass. I believe I was meant to find you."

Tyrus frowned. "A single-horned seer? The Starchild?"

"She called herself Soraka. You have heard of her?"

He leaned back, rubbing his chin. "The being you describe appears in the legends of many cultures across the lands. You say you actually *met* her?"

"I did. And she guided me to you." Kalista took Tyrus's hands. "I swear on the Ancestors I will never reveal the truth of the isles. Imprison me forever if that is what you need to do, but please, if there is any way your scholars can help, do not deny me. I can grant you wealth, artifacts, ancient tomes. Knowledge that exists nowhere but in the libraries of Alové-dra. Whatever it takes. You said you were indebted to me. Help me, if you can. Please."

He said nothing for a long time. Kalista held his gaze, silently imploring him. Finally, he nodded. "I cannot make any promises," he said quietly, "but I believe your heart is true. I will take you."

Chapter Fourteen

Seeker-Adept Tyrus stood at the bow of the *Aureate Savant*, just behind its golden figurehead. He held aloft a faintly glowing sphere of pale stone, carved with intersecting lines. Kalista, watching from some way off, had seen him remove it from the sigil around his neck, and the white mist parted before it, allowing them clear passage.

The *Daggerhawk* remained outside the mist, for while Tyrus had agreed to take Kalista to the Blessed Isles, he had refused to guide the Camavoran ship through. Vennix had been uneasy about her going alone, but Kalista had little choice.

"You could have tried for a hundred years and never gotten anywhere near the isles without a waystone," said a voice.

Kalista turned to find Tyrus's young apprentice, Ryze, casually leaning against a railing.

"I'm glad I found you, then," she said, turning her attention back to Tyrus.

The ship slid through the still, glasslike water, the only sound the rhythmic dip of the thirty or so oars. Almost half the crew had been killed or seriously injured in the razorscale attack, yet they advanced at a decent speed regardless.

"The protective magic is old, and powerful," Ryze said. "It had to be, to allow the Fellowship of Light to continue its work without fear of raiders and invasion. The isles would be too tempting a target, otherwise."

Kalista was surprised he was offering up so much information, but realized he was showing off. Well, if this boastful young man wanted to tell her things that his master held back, she would let him.

"It's a fine defense," she said, watching the mist part around them. It was as if they moved through a tunnel, starting about a dozen yards before the ship's prow, and closing behind them. It was wide enough to encompass the width of the vessel, yet the ends of the oars were swallowed in mist. The slight motion of the deck was the only sign they were moving at all. "More effective than castle walls and armies. And no one can get through without one of those stones?"

"No one," confirmed Ryze.

"Does everyone on the Blessed Isles have one?" asked Kalista. "Do you?"

He glanced at her, and Kalista could see a hint of wariness in his eyes now. "No," he said. "Why would you want to know that?"

"Just curious," she remarked with a shrug, affecting nonchalance.

"I would like to visit Camavor one day," Ryze said, after a moment's silence. "My talents would be rightly prized and respected there. Not shackled, like under *his* supposed tutelage." He motioned at Tyrus with his chin. "Perhaps you could show me around."

"Perhaps," said Kalista.

"You fight well," Ryze said. "The way you move reminds me of the sword-maidens of my people, and there are no fiercer warriors in all the world."

"On the Blessed Isles?"

Ryze laughed at that. "No," he said. "No one there has the soul of a warrior. Not like you or me. No, I was born in a village called Khom, in an arid land to the north."

"And how did you come to be part of a coterie of scholars on the Blessed Isles, then?"

Ryze gave a shrug. "I outgrew Khom. It was too small for me. So I set out on my own." Kalista suspected there was more to the story, but didn't press him. "Made my own way for a year or two. Learned to fight, learned to hunt. Learned to take care of myself. I worked as a mercenary briefly, down in the sandlands. Was part of the Amber Hawks for a time. You've probably heard of them."

"I have not."

"Oh. Well, anyway, they didn't pay well, but I discovered I had a particular talent for getting into places I wasn't meant to be. And that was *far* more lucrative."

"You became a thief."

"I did what I had to, to get by," said Ryze. "Anyway, one day I noticed a new ship at the Bel'zhun docks. It wasn't local, and everything about it screamed money."

"Let me guess—it was the *Aureate Savant*."

Ryze grinned. "Tyrus found me in his quarters. I was backed in a corner, with nowhere to run. And that was the first time I manifested my talent." He lifted one clenched fist. Purple runes began to burn beneath his flesh. Then, with a furtive glance at Tyrus, he relaxed his hand, and the power dissipated. "Tyrus was impressed and took me under his wing. And when he left the desert lands, I went with him."

His expression soured.

"Things were good for a time. They said I was gifted, but I was considered a troublemaker."

"Can't imagine why," murmured Kalista, making Ryze smile again.

"I was excited when I became Tyrus's apprentice," he said. "He's one of the Seekers, see? While most of the Fellowship live dreary lives in Helia, Seekers get to travel the world, searching for items of power. I was going to see new places, and he promised to help develop my talent."

"And that didn't happen?"

"He's an overbearing tyrant," declared Ryze. "And he's taught me nothing. Wants me to focus on the theory of magic, and not anything of practical use, not until he deems me ready. I've been ready for years! He's just jealous that it comes so easy to me. He's able to *wield* magic but needs his sigil to draw power, whereas I need *nothing*. He's holding me back. Doesn't want me to eclipse him."

Kalista nodded along in sympathy, though inwardly she was rolling her eyes. She'd just about had her fill of entitled, talented young men.

"He just doesn't see my potential," he continued bitterly. "None of them do."

"You must know your way around the Blessed Isles, yes?"

"No one knows them better," he said. "When I was first there, I explored while the other students slept. I can get in and out of places restricted to the upper echelons of the inner circle without them ever knowing it."

"So you must know if the stories of the isles' life-giving magic are real?"

Ryze looked askance at her. "The Waters of Life? That's what you are seeking?"

"It is," said Kalista.

"I think you could save yourself some time and head back to Camavor now, then," he said, with a laugh. "The waters are nothing but a children's tale! Who knows how it started. Perhaps there was some old surgeon in the early days of the Fellowship who saved some lost sailor from drowning or something. Maybe they gave him a tonic, and the ignorant fool thought it was healing water. When he got home, he probably exaggerated the tale while in his cups at his local alehouse, and thus the story was born. I even heard a version of it that said the waters give eternal life. Ha! I think it might have been noticed if the old masters were living for hundreds of years."

"Maybe they *are* real, and you are just not yet entitled to that knowledge," said Kalista. "You are just an apprentice, after all."

Ryze scoffed. "If they were real, I would have found them by now. Whoever sent you on this mission is a fool."

Kalista's expression hardened. "Be careful what you say, apprentice."

"But they *are* a fool!" Ryze exclaimed, clearly not registering the change in Kalista's demeanor. "A fool, or someone with a perverse sense of humor. You sure being sent to find them wasn't a joke?"

Kalista looked at him without blinking. "Speak one more disrespectful word, and I will put you on the deck."

Ryze gave what he clearly thought was a playful, roguish smile, but Kalista did not find it endearing. "Who is the bigger fool?" he said, smirking. "The one who *gives* the order, or the one who *obeys* it?"

Kalista had a hold of his wrist in an instant, twisting it sharply. He cried out as he was forced to his knees, completely at her mercy. He sank lower to the deck in a vain attempt to escape her grip, but she did not relent.

"I gave you fair warning," she said. "So I'd say *you* are the fool."

She released him with a shove, and he stared at her angrily as he nursed his wrist. He looked ready to say something, then evidently thought better of it. Scowling, he swung away and was gone.

Kalista stood alone, watching him go. "Making friends, as always," she muttered.

Helia, the Blessed Isles

Warden-Prefect Erlok Grael sat at his desk, alone in his small, low-ceilinged cell, far beneath Helia.

Some wardens struggled with the enclosed spaces and ever-present darkness of the vaults. They found them oppressive, claustrophobic, maddening. Not Grael. The vaults were the only place he felt comfortable. Down here, he was in control.

Every inch of his cell was covered in drawings, maps, and annotations in his tiny, neat handwriting. Dozens of pieces of paper and open books were spread across the floor, his desk, his pallet. To anyone else, it would have looked chaotic, but there was an order here that made sense to Grael.

Central upon his desk was the ancient tome that had revealed to him the secret that lay at the heart of the Blessed Isles—the Well of Ages, the chamber that contained the legendary Waters of Life. It filled him with unbridled rage that the masters had kept this wonder for themselves.

Over the last weeks, he had worked obsessively, seeking a way into the Well of Ages. He knew it was beneath the Scintillant Tower, but the direct route was barred to him, for only the most senior masters were allowed there unaccompanied. He wouldn't get anywhere near the tower before being stopped and stripped of his rank and privileges.

Nevertheless, he suspected there must have once been a way to access the sacred waters from the vaults below the city. The tunnels spread everywhere, beneath every nook and cranny.

Many of the oldest tunnels were disused, or forgotten, while some had caved in and been buried in rubble in centuries past. Most of the collapses had been the result of accidents, but some tunnels had been intentionally brought down, their paths no longer needed or considered too perilous to leave intact.

Grael suspected that some of those older tunnels had once connected to the Well of Ages. From what he surmised, in the early days of the Fellowship, the waters had not been such a tightly guarded secret. In later years, when the masters decided the waters should be for them and them alone, they must have blocked the tunnels leading to the well. And so, Grael had been creating a vast map of the vaults, cross-referenced with the architectural drawings of the Well of Ages, hoping to uncover where these old tunnels were. His efforts had thus far been in vain... until now.

He held up a wafer-thin sheet of paper to the light of his lantern, peering closely. The sheet was largely transparent, and upon it he had drawn a bewildering array of tiny, interconnected dotted lines. He had created dozens of similar drawings, each for a different level of the vaults, each painstakingly drafted by collating the information from a dozen other maps. The dotted lines represented gutters or chimneys carved into the rock. Some were cut vertically, to allow food, water, and messages to be passed down from high above, or for smoke to safely exit the vaults. Others were made to channel rain and groundwater and direct them out to sea. Left to its own devices, such moisture would seep down into the vaults. Over years, that would cause untold damage to the precious artifacts and books. And so, a miraculous series of gutters, sluices, and channels had been devised. Most were barely large enough for a rat to navigate, but not all.

With delicate care, Grael moved to the center of the floor

and placed the overlay upon a map of a level of the vaults that lay close to the Well of Ages. On hands and knees, he traced the various dotted lines and at last found what he was looking for.

"There you are," he whispered, and a savage grin split his face.

Most of the lines made sense, running parallel or connecting vertically to vaults and corridors. But one was different. It connected to an old tunnel but went…nowhere. It cut directly into the large blank area of his maps, where no tunnels existed. That dead space was where the Well of Ages lay. And he had just found a way in.

Grael leaped to his feet with a bitter laugh of triumph and began stalking back and forth, quivering with excitement. His mind was blooming with violent thoughts of vengeance upon all who had dismissed and belittled him, all who had sought to keep him down.

He stopped his pacing. "One thing at a time," he told himself. He might have found a way to the Well of Ages, but there were other defenses and wards that would need to be bypassed.

His gaze was drawn to the small shelf above his bed. There lay the three-sided stone he had taken from the sigil of the long-dead master. A *keystone*, rarer and more tightly guarded than the most precious jewels. He retrieved it, then took a seat back at his desk. Flipping through the ancient tome, he came to the page that showed the plans for the great gilt doors guarding the Well of Ages. It had been a thrill to discover a drawing of a keystone matching the one now in his possession. Two rune locks sealed those doors. Two rune locks that each needed a master's keystone to be unlocked.

Grael had *one* keystone. Now he just needed to figure out how to get a second. Nevertheless, he didn't feel disheartened. He would get into the Well of Ages; he felt it in his bones.

And somehow, he would expose the masters for the deceitful hypocrites they were. He would *destroy* them.

The lantern upon Grael's desk spluttered and went out, but he made no move to relight it. He sat in the darkness, picturing the downfall of the masters.

It would be *glorious*.

Chapter Fifteen

Helia, the Blessed Isles

It took less than an hour to pass through the mists, though Kalista had no idea how far they had traveled—it could have been half a league, or it could have been hundreds.

The way opened before them, like a pair of immense, sheer curtains sliding aside, and there lay the legendary Blessed Isles, bathed in sunshine. Each isle was surrounded by dark cliffs, the tops carpeted in vibrant green. The larger islands were inhabited but not densely so. Kalista glimpsed geometric paddocks and walled fields among the white buildings dotting the land, along with carefully coppiced areas of woodland. Sheep and other livestock grazed, and people knelt along neat, perfectly arranged rows of crops or directed harnessed horned beasts to till the soil.

They rounded a headland, and a gleaming city was revealed. "Behold Helia!" declared Tyrus, pocketing the engraved pale sphere Ryze had called a waystone. "City of Knowledge and Learning!"

It spread as far as the eye could see, all white stone and golden ornamentation. Kalista saw towers, amphitheaters, and domed structures, each the size of an impressive palace anywhere else. Tiered, strictly ordered gardens were interspersed among the grand buildings, making Helia feel open, and far more planned than the Camavoran capital, which looked haphazard by comparison. Crossing the city were roads and arched bridges, arranged in perfect symmetry, forming neat quadrants and vectors. The geometry seemed to radiate meaning, yet its language was not one that Kalista understood. She could appreciate its precise design, but its higher purpose escaped her.

One tower, high upon a tiered terrace, loomed taller than any other. Tyrus saw her staring at it. "The Scintillant Tower," he remarked. "The seat of the council, and the beating heart of the city. That's where you'll be heard."

Kalista turned her attention to the docks. They were a series of concentric, curving wharfs that formed a broken ring squarely in the center of the harbor. Lighthouses marked the extremes of the docks, and scores of vessels were anchored around the perimeters. Larger ships—big triremes, for the most part—were positioned on the outside of the ring, while the inside was busy with smaller fishing boats and barges. Perfectly symmetrical bridges extended across the wharfs, and a pair of larger bridges connected to the city itself. It was truly a marvel of engineering, and Kalista could not fathom how it had been constructed if not by sorcery.

However, there was one thing about the city that struck her the most. *It's completely defenseless.* There were no towering walls, no fortifications, no portcullises, no killing grounds, no catapults or ballistae guarding the harbor. Kalista saw no sign of any military presence or warships. Assessing the city as a general, she knew it could be taken with a pitifully small armed force. She could invade it with a handful of ships and a few hundred good soldiers.

"It's a marvel, isn't it?" said Tyrus. "A shimmering haven in an otherwise bleak and dangerous world."

"I've never seen anywhere quite like it," said Kalista.

"Nor will you. Where else can people fully dedicate themselves to academic pursuits without fear of war and savagery?"

Kalista had no answer for that. *Surely, if anywhere can provide a cure for the queen, this is it.*

The *Aureate Savant* headed for the strange circular wharfs, gliding smoothly through the choppy waters. The ship was hailed by sailors on other vessels as they drew nearer, and laughter and friendly banter filled the air. A harbormaster directed them toward an open berth on the outside of the ring, and the *Aureate Savant* slowed as she approached. Her oars were hauled in and mooring ropes slung to waiting dockers, who deftly looped them around gleaming bollards. It was all done with a swift, well-drilled precision that appealed to Kalista's military background.

Curious onlookers craned their necks at Kalista as she stepped onto the solid stone wharf, and small groups of porters and fisherfolk pointed and stared.

"You don't get many outsiders, I'm guessing," said Kalista.

"Not often," Tyrus replied. "Oh, there are people here from cultures far and wide. Diversity of experience and voice creates diversity in thinking, after all. But no, newcomers are infrequent, and only those brought here by one such as me ever make it through the Hallowed Mist."

"Then I am honored you brought me here to plead my case," said Kalista.

The unloading process was swift and orderly. With a few final directives, Tyrus left his crew to finish the job and led Kalista along the interlinked, arcing wharfs and bridges to the city proper. Ryze slunk along behind them, looking surly. He had avoided Kalista since their altercation, which suited her just fine. Tyrus pointed out buildings and civic structures of note as they walked along the garden-lined streets and up grand marble steps. They followed a wide boulevard, passing lines of pillars, statues, and squares.

"This is Scholars' Way," noted Tyrus. "It rises from the docks straight up to the Scintillant Tower."

Kalista was raised in the royal palace of Alovédra, so she was used to luxury and wealth, but this entire *city* seemed to have the same level of opulence. Every building was resplendent with architectural detail. Every square had statues atop plinths, elaborate marble fountains, sculptures of golden eyes within triangular prisms, or ornate, carefully tended trees growing from marble cubes.

The people of Helia were no less impressive. While Tyrus's own robe was gray and humble, most of the citizens wore artfully tailored garments of vibrant hues, formed of dozens of overlapping pieces of fabric in geometric shapes and patterns similar to those that adorned the city. Many had donned head coverings that looked like unfurling flowers. Finely wrought pendants of gold, silver, stone, or bronze were worn proudly upon chests, their design complex and symmetrical.

"They mark which school of learning the wearer is attached to, and what rank of service they have attained," Tyrus explained.

Kalista was conscious that her spear was one of the few weapons in the city. She did see some guards, clad in white and wearing curiously blank, full-faced helms. They bore ornate halberds, which seemed more ceremonial than practical. More stares and whispers followed her, but she was well used to being in the public eye and did not let it bother her.

"I see no beggars," she observed. "No downtrodden. Are they elsewhere in the city and kept out of these districts?"

"You see none because there are none," said Tyrus. "We have the good fortune and means to ensure that none live in destitution, so why would we not help those who need it?"

"Why indeed?"

They climbed several sets of broad stairs, each rising to a higher section of the city. Finally, they approached an imposing archway—the Enlightenment Arch—guarded by more white-garbed sentries. Its stonework was inscribed with impossibly intricate geometric imagery. It clearly conveyed a wealth of information but only for those able to interpret it. Beyond it was a broad square, on the other side of which rose the Scintillant Tower.

Up close, the tower was even more impressive than it had appeared from a distance, grand even in a city of grandeur. It was easily twice the height of the palace in Alovédra. An immense golden eye, set within a series of overlapping triangles, was positioned centrally upon the building's spire, and a roaring waterfall emerged just below it, cascading down several stepped drops and into an angular pool.

"I will leave you here and go propose an audience for you with the council," said Tyrus. "I've sent word ahead for a room to be prepared for you. My apprentice will show you the way. We have no palaces, but I hope you will find everything to your satisfaction."

"My needs are few," said Kalista. "I had hoped my case would be heard immediately. I cannot linger. I have no way of knowing how long the queen has left." *Or if she even lives*, she thought, though she did not voice that fear.

"I will emphasize your need for haste, of course," assured Tyrus. "Bathe. Eat. Rest. I will send word as soon as I am able." He bowed and hurried past the guards at the archway.

"This way," said Ryze, not looking at her. He turned and began to stride away, not bothering to see if she followed.

They walked in silence, allowing Kalista to soak in the city without distraction. She saw young men and women seated in open-air amphitheaters, listening to older members of the Fellowship of Light, and parks where people played solemn games of strategy upon boards of marble. It was at once bustling, with scholars hurrying between the various buildings, and empty, with vast areas given over to wide squares and painstakingly manicured grassy spaces, with uniformly trimmed trees positioned at equidistant intervals.

The city was beautiful and ordered...yet something seemed to be missing. Something was lacking, some indefinable quality that stopped Helia from feeling lived-in or welcoming, even though many thousands of people made their homes here. It felt cold, for all the unblemished sunshine that bathed it. It was perfect, but soulless. Kalista could not find any fault to point to, but she wondered if *that* was the problem.

She knew well that people were not perfect, and a city should reflect its people. A city as precisely designed as this made her think there was something it wanted to hide. Some less pleasant side kept hidden from view.

Or maybe she was just cynical, having been surrounded by the viper pit of Camavoran politics since she was a child.

Ryze led her to her allotted quarters and left without further word. To say it was palatial was an understatement. Kalista walked through the various rooms, still feeling unnerved by how pristine and exact everything was. She found herself looking for faults—a crack in a wall, an uneven section of flooring—but found nothing.

An entire wing was dedicated to bathing, with three pools of different temperatures in three separate rooms. In another direction, there was a personal library with thousands of leather-bound books, and a sun-drenched balcony overlooking the city and the sea beyond. Beyond the bedroom itself—a cavernous chamber with a circular bed sunk into the floor—she found a garden terrace, filled with artfully maintained, marble-sided raised beds and a geometric fountain. Ivy and flowers cascaded down the exterior walls.

"Are all Helian homes like this?" Kalista asked a pale staff member as he poured her a glass of fruit-infused water. "Or is this just to impress visitors?"

The man smiled but clearly didn't understand her words, and he promptly bowed and took his leave.

She sipped the water but found it too sweet for her taste and put it aside. She bathed, luxuriating in the soothing waters, scented with oils and salts, and dried herself with warmed towels. Returning to her room, she found three sets of clothes laid out for her upon the bed, each of a different style. They were beautiful, made with fine silk and the softest cottons, and embroidered with symmetrical patterns. Nevertheless, she left them where they lay, choosing to dress in her well-worn armor and leathers. Those had been cleaned and oiled while she'd been bathing, which she found off-putting, though servants in the palace of Alovédra would have done the same thing. Even the long, black topknot of her helmet had been brushed out, removing the knots and crust of sea salt, and her tall leather boots had been polished. She was relieved, however, that her weapons had remained untouched.

A spread of food was waiting for her in the dining room: sweetmeats, cuts of beef and mutton, seafood, soup, baked vegetables, cheese, and sliced fruit, as well as a basket filled with an assortment of freshly baked breads. Kalista loaded up a plate, suddenly ravenous, and took it onto the balcony.

A sealed note was brought to her as she was finishing her third heaped plate. The seal depicted an eye upon a burning book. She broke it and unfolded the parchment, revealing precise, elegant handwriting. She read it quickly, then read it again, more slowly.

Tomorrow. She would meet the council tomorrow, accompanied by Tyrus. She released a breath. It all came down to this.

She prayed that the queen still yet lived.

Warden-Prefect Grael doused his lantern and cocked his head to one side. He stood in the pitch darkness, unmoving, listening patiently.

There. He heard it again. The unmistakable sound of footsteps, echoing faintly. This person was doing a good job of remaining quiet, but this was *his* realm. Anyone else might have missed the sound or passed it off as rats or an echo from the halls above, but he knew this underground labyrinth more than anyone. This was an *intruder.* And from the way they were trying to be stealthy, they *knew* they shouldn't be here. This was someone purposefully sneaking around, and that made them dangerous. They would know the ramifications of their actions if they were caught and would do whatever they could to ensure their infiltration remained undiscovered.

One option was for Grael to turn around and go back the way he'd come. He knew how sound traveled down here and could picture exactly where the intruder was, so it would be easy enough to steer clear of them. Nevertheless, Grael didn't even consider turning away, and not because of the oaths he'd sworn to guard these tunnels. He'd happily piss on those oaths. They counted for nothing. He'd been betrayed, over and over again, so why should he bother upholding them?

Grael made his way toward the sound of the interloper. *He* was the alpha predator down here. It was not for him to skulk around avoiding people. No, they would have been wise to have avoided *him*, but they had stumbled into his lair, and now they were his. A savage thrill filled Grael, and a cruel grin split his face. From a fold beneath his robes, he drew out his curved sickle. Whoever this intruder was, they would regret coming here.

Moving silently, Grael stalked through the darkness toward his unwitting prey.

Ryze paused, thinking he'd heard something in the distance.

Just a rat, he told himself, and continued through the twisting maze of the vaults, far beneath the Great Library. He closed the shutters of his lantern a little, however, so that its light was less visible, though he was confident he was alone, and even more confident in his own abilities in the unlikely situation that some pathetic Thresher did manage to stumble upon him.

It's all Tyrus's fault. He said Ryze didn't have enough control, that the runic magic coursing through his veins was dangerous. There had been a time when he thought his sorcerous talents would be nurtured by the Fellowship. How wrong he'd been. How was he ever to gain control if he wasn't allowed to practice? If he wasn't allowed to learn from the tomes of the great rune mages of the past? Ryze knew there were such tomes locked away down in the vaults. He'd gathered as much from reading between the lines of what Tyrus said, but his master had flat-out refused to put in the request to access those books for him. And so, here he was, forced to sneak around like a common thief.

Ryze grinned. He *was* a common thief, he reminded himself. Or at least had been once, before Tyrus had taken him under his wing and brought him through the mists to Helia.

It was like old times, breaking into places he wasn't supposed to be. He knelt by the next locked door he came upon, put down his lantern, and pulled out a rolled-up sheet of leather. He swiftly undid its ties and unrolled it, revealing his trusty picks. He'd made each of them himself, shaping and bending them to suit his needs. He inspected the heavy padlock on the door, then inserted a needle-like pick into the keyhole. It took only a moment to feel the pins and depress them in the right place. Holding the first pick steady, he inserted a second, feeling his way.

It wouldn't be easy to find the books he sought. He'd first come down here a year earlier and had been flabbergasted by the sheer scale of the vaults. He realized he could spend a lifetime searching and still not find what he was after...but it had turned into something of a game, a way to pass the time. A minor form of rebellion. Whenever he and Tyrus were in Helia, Ryze entered the vaults in the dead of night, exploring the depths. The risk only made it that much more fun.

There. There was an almost imperceptible click, and with a careful twist, the padlock slid open. Ryze lay the lock picks back onto the leather and rolled it up. Then he picked up his lantern, glanced up the corridor once more, and moved into the vault.

In another life, he would have stuffed his pockets with the golden artifacts in the sealed room, but he gave those trinkets barely a glance. The really good stuff was always locked up more securely. He spied a large chest near the rear wall and moved toward it.

"There you are," he said, as he ran his hands across its surface. He could feel the chest's arcane wards as a tingle beneath his fingertips, and he licked his lips in anticipation. That was a good sign. The wards were invisible to the naked eye, but he could feel them, like he could feel the pins in a lock beneath the pressure of his picks. He sensed that these wards were old and would require some time. He settled himself down onto his knees, rubbing his hands together.

He closed his eyes and began to work, his fingers tracing out the patterns of the wards. He pictured them, turning them around in his mind and identifying how to disable them. One by one, he unraveled the runic wards, and he heard a click as the latches on the chest snapped open. He grinned.

Then his heart lurched, and the hairs on the back of his neck stiffened. He heard the clink of chains, *right behind him*, and knew that what he'd heard before was no rat.

Eyes wide with panic, Ryze grabbed his lantern and swung it toward the door. A figure stood motionless within the room. It stared at him, a hideous grin plastered upon its pale face. With a cry, Ryze gathered his power, but before he could unleash it, the wraithlike figure surged forward.

Something struck him on the side of the head, and then the floor raced up to meet him.

Chapter Sixteen

"And so," finished Kalista, "I have come to request your aid, in the name of Viego Santiarul Molach vol Kalah Heigaari, king of Camavor, soul-bound to the blade Sanctity."

Having completed her formal request, Kalista stood at attention, her plumed helmet tucked under one arm and her head held high as she awaited an answer.

The Council of Helia loomed before her. There were seventeen masters in all, seated above her in a semicircular arc beneath the Scintillant Tower's immense golden dome. Some leaned forward upon the ornate railings of their lecterns, while others seemed entirely bored by the proceedings and were barely paying attention.

Kalista had thought Tyrus would be part of this council, but he had smiled at that and told her that he was merely a lowly adept, a good number of stations below the level of master. But he had accompanied her here and spoken to the council on her behalf, stating that he believed her intentions were pure and that she was a woman of honor. After speaking his piece, he had slipped into the shadows behind her.

Kalista stood alone now, bathed in light directed down upon her from a series of angled mirrors, while the council members were shadowed, making their exact expressions and features difficult to observe. One of the masters, designated as the Speaker—an aging man called Bartek, who had an unfortunate and striking resemblance to a toad—had asked her to articulate her request, and she had done so, in clear, direct statements, avoiding embellishment.

For long moments, she waited for a response. Several of the masters whispered among themselves, while a few stared down at her, as if in judgment. Those moments turned into minutes.

Kalista broke the silence. "The queen of Camavor lies dying of a poison unknown to our best healers and priests." She struggled to keep the frustration out of her voice. "If the stories of the Waters of Life hold any truth, and you are able to help her, I beg that you do."

Still there was no response. Kalista looked among the masters, confused. *Why do they not answer?* She glanced into the shadows behind her, seeking Tyrus, but she couldn't see him.

"Will none of you speak?" she said, turning back to the masters. "The Argent Throne would be forever in your debt, should you lend your aid. Camavor can be an ally to you."

Silence.

"Is it payment you want?" Kalista said, her patience fraying. "I am authorized to agree to whatever recompense your order would feel is appropriate. As I understand it, Camavor has a great many artifacts that your Fellowship has long coveted."

"The council does not respond to bribery, nor to threats, implied or otherwise, *Camavoran*," snapped one of the masters in the shadows. Kalista struggled to identify who it was.

"I offered neither threat nor bribe," she growled, shielding her eyes against the glare. "I have simply come to beg your help. I came in good faith."

This was met with yet more silence. Kalista's hands turned to fists, and she was just about to say something more, when the Speaker lifted his hand. "The council has heard your appeal, Princess Kalista of Camavor," he declared. "We will adjourn to discuss this matter. You will be summoned when we have an answer for you."

Kalista scowled. "What is there to discuss?" she asked. "You can either help, or let an innocent woman die! If you have the means to save our queen, please just tell me!"

"You will be summoned when we have an answer."

A bright light shone on him. His head was pounding, and his left eye was swollen shut. Had he fallen? He couldn't remember...

"Ah, there you are."

The voice was like a bucket of cold water thrown into Ryze's face, and he snapped to full consciousness. In horror, he realized his outstretched arms were affixed to the walls on either side with taut lengths of chain.

"Where am I?"

"In a cell, deep enough that you can scream your lungs out, and no one will ever hear it."

Ryze tried to squirm away from the blinding light. "Who are you?"

"I am the one who found you, delving into places you oughtn't. I am the one who holds your life in his hands."

Ryze squinted, trying to see past the glaring light to the speaker, but all he could make out was a vague shadow. He'd seen the man for an instant, though, before he was knocked out. He remembered his pallid, smiling face. But he had also seen the man's robes, and his keys, hanging from big iron rings. He was a warden.

"You're just a damn *Thresher*," Ryze spat.

The shadowy figure's outline went very still. There was violence in that stillness, a simmering rage that threatened to overflow. Ryze glared at the warden, refusing to give him the pleasure of seeing him afraid.

"Stop with all the theatrics and just hand me over to the custodians. Just get on with it!" he growled. "If they kick me out of the Fellowship, then so be it. At least then I won't have to deal with any more of their empty promises and nonsense."

The warden snickered behind the light. "What makes you think I have any intention of handing you over to the custodians?"

Ryze said nothing.

"Perhaps I would prefer to keep you here," he continued. "Perhaps I intend to *break* you. To make you suffer. To take you apart, slowly, piece by piece, until there's nothing left, and you beg for mercy."

Ryze swallowed heavily, trying to hide his fear but not confident that it was working.

"Does anyone even know you are down here?" the warden taunted.

Ryze could hear the cruel smile in his voice, and he faltered, his defiant expression dropping.

The warden laughed. It was a callous, hateful sound, full of bitterness and cruelty. "I think you are starting to realize the trouble you find yourself in," he said. "You swan around up there, full of your own self-importance, your own hypocrisy. You spit on us *Threshers*, but this is *my* domain. *Mine*. Here, all your wealth and influence and corruption count for nothing. Here, *I* decide what happens to those who violate my laws. Here, *I* am the powerful one. Here, *I* am king. And you came down here to steal from me."

The words were spat out in a long, breathless rant, burning with vitriol. In the silence that followed, Ryze could hear the warden breathing heavily.

"I'm not one of them," he said in a low voice. "I hate them as much as you do."

A bark of laughter met that statement. "I think not. You wear an apprentice's sigil on your chest. You are one of them, else they would never have let you wear that. You'd have been cast down here. Like me."

"You're wrong," Ryze snapped, letting his own bitterness bubble to the surface. "I don't come from privilege. Far from it. I come from nothing, and my master is determined to make sure I *stay* as nothing. He won't teach me, not anything important. He doesn't want me to eclipse him."

Silence. Then the lantern's shutters were turned, so that the light was not shining right in his eyes. Ryze blinked, the afterimage of the light still blinding, but he could now see who was holding him captive.

The warden was tall and gangly, his face pale. His eyes were impossibly cold, dead, and uncaring, like a shark's. In one hand, he held up a viciously curved blade, a sickle with an edge that looked worryingly sharp.

"Maybe you are telling the truth, maybe not," snarled the warden. "But it changes nothing."

There is something broken in this man. Ryze's fear tightened within him like a knot. Sucking in a breath, he drew power into his being, and his hands began to glow with wild purple energy. The magic burned within him, infusing him… but without his arms free, he was unable to form the runic shapes he needed to control it. Without that focus, the energy spluttered and faded, and was then gone.

"A rune mage?" the warden purred. "Now, that *is* interesting."

Ryze stared up at him. His vision was still colored by the

remnants of his fading magic, casting everything in tones of violet. "What do you mean?"

"Tell me, how did you unlock the chest? The one you'd opened when I found you? That chest was warded."

"The runic wards were not particularly powerful ones," Ryze said. "It wasn't difficult for me to unravel them."

"Interesting," the warden said again. He turned away from Ryze, pacing back and forth. He seemed to be having some kind of internal debate. Abruptly, he turned back to him. "Tell me, *who* is your master?"

"Seeker-Adept Tyrus."

"Tyrus of Hellesmor?"

"Yes."

The warden began to laugh. "Oh, this is too good," he said, shaking his head. "Tyrus, Tyrus, Tyrus."

"You know him?"

"He stole my position. *I* was the best of us, but they picked *him*. He was given everything, and I was thrown down here, to rot in the darkness."

Ryze met the Thresher's gaze. "He lured me into the Fellowship of Light with a promise to teach me. I have a rare gift, but I need to learn more runic forms to channel my power fully. He told me he would help, but he's taught me *nothing*. He denies me the knowledge I need, holding it over me to keep me in line. Says I am not yet ready for it. But how can I learn if I am taught *nothing*?"

"And you were down here seeking that knowledge, in defiance of Tyrus?"

Ryze looked at him squarely. "Yes."

The warden turned away again, stroking his chin. Ryze stayed quiet. After a moment, he turned back. "You could spend centuries scrounging through the vaults like a rat and never find what you seek. But *I* know where it is. I could get it for you."

"Why would you do that?"

The warden stared at Ryze with those unblinking, dead eyes. "How did you get down here? Those little tools of yours wouldn't have gotten you past the custodians, or the Warding Portals, or the Chamber of Echoes. How did you bypass them?"

"I've always been good at getting in and out of places I wasn't welcome."

The warden smiled, though it didn't reach his eyes. "I think there might be a way that we can help each other."

Kalista stalked back and forth in her room, like a caged animal.

"I understand your frustration," said Tyrus calmly, "but this is the way the council operates. They will argue and deliberate until they reach a unanimous decision."

Kalista glared at him. "It shouldn't be a decision that *needs* deliberation," she said. "You portray Helia as an enlightened society, but if helping a dying woman needs hours of debate, I think you might need to reassess your opinion."

Tyrus rubbed his eyes. "It has not generally been our way to interfere in the politics and affairs of the outside world," he said wearily. "Take no offense, but Camavor has historically been an aggressive and bellicose nation, and so the arrival of a Camavoran royal has caused some concern."

"I'm not a scout looking to find new lands to conquer," said

Kalista. "I would be willing to give any reassurance necessary as a sign of my good faith."

"I know," said Tyrus. "I believe you, which is why I brought you here. But there are many who feel I was wrong to do so."

Kalista paused in her pacing. "Will you face repercussions?"

"Possibly," Tyrus said, shrugging. "But if they sanction me, then so be it. I believe it was the right thing to do."

"You wouldn't have brought me here if you didn't think they could help," said Kalista. "The Waters of Life are real, aren't they? Can you not just give me a pitcher of it, and I'll be on my way? Isolde's life hangs in the balance!"

"I have faith that they will come to the right decision," said Tyrus. "It's frustrating, but we just need to be patient."

Kalista sighed. "I will try," she said. "Though sitting around and waiting does not sit well with me."

"That's understandable. You're a soldier and a general, a woman of action, and you've been searching for this cure without pause," said Tyrus. "Allow yourself this brief moment to rest. Read a book. Go for a walk. Whatever you need to pass the time. And hopefully the council will not deliberate too long."

"My grandfather always said there'd be plenty of time to rest once we're dead," Kalista said.

Tyrus grunted. "One could certainly not accuse the Lion of Camavor of being lazy," he said. "The man conquered what, thirteen independent nations across his lifetime?"

"Eighteen, technically," said Kalista, "if you count those who rebelled and were subsequently crushed."

"Quite a legacy for his heir to live up to," noted Tyrus. "But I digress. I will take my leave now, and see if I might sway some of the council members to your cause."

"Thank you, Tyrus," said Kalista. "You are a good man, and I appreciate the trust and belief you put in me."

"Thank me once your queen is saved."

Erlok Grael stood just inside the cell door, arms crossed, watching as Ryze worked.

He had not let the apprentice out of the cell, though he had freed him from his chains. Grael was wary of his prisoner attempting something foolish, but he had taken precautions.

"I have written a letter, which I have left prominently on my desk," he told the young man, before releasing him. "The letter identifies you by name and states that I apprehended you in the lower vaults, engaged in the theft of forbidden artifacts."

"Why?" Ryze said. "That's not what we agreed!"

Grael silenced him with a raised hand. "You do not know where my cell is located, but the custodians do. If you attempt anything when I release these chains, they will find that letter. And that will be the end for you. I know you say you don't care if you are kicked out of the Fellowship, but it is clear that is not true. Speak of any of this, or seek to betray me, and I will destroy you."

"That is really not necessary," Ryze said.

"Do this minor task for me, and I will deliver to you the knowledge you seek. And burn the letter."

True to his word, Ryze made no hostile moves after he was freed. And now the apprentice was sitting cross-legged on the floor, his eyes closed. Before him was a sealed strongbox. It was locked tight, though there was no traditional keyhole to release it. Instead, there was only an indentation for a master's keystone. Each of those stones was a skeleton key, able to open the rune locks that held Helia's most precious secrets—though exactly *which* locks they would open depended on the rank of the master. Grael had tested his own on this box and been pleased to find it worked.

Ryze had no such key. With his lips moving silently, his hands began to form a series of intricate patterns and shapes. A moment later, the lockbox clicked open. "Easy," he declared, cracking his knuckles in triumph.

"Impressive," said Grael. The boy was cocky and a braggart... but his ability to bypass runic wards was more than simply impressive. The warden's mind was whirling at the possibilities this presented, but he let none of that show.

"So what's all this about, then?" said Ryze. "You want me to open some runic lock that's giving you trouble? Bring it here, and I'll do it at once."

There was a seething part of Erlok Grael that was angry at needing this boy's help. That part of him would have preferred to keep him locked up down here in the dark, would have enjoyed seeing his defiant cockiness broken, giving way to panic, and fear, and terror. That part of him would have relished hearing him cry out in pain and despair as he—

"Warden?"

He tore himself away from his alluring daydream. "You said something?" he asked.

"The reward you promise—how do I know it will be worth it?"

Grael glared at him, then unhooked a leather scroll case from his belt and tossed it to him.

"What's this?"

"Open it."

The boy undid the clasp and drew out a rolled-up piece of parchment torn from a book. Frowning, he leaned in close, peering at the angular writing. "Icathian cuneiform," he murmured. He read a few lines, then paused, looking up at Grael in amazement. "Is this...?"

"Yes. It is."

Grael watched in silence as Ryze returned his attention to the page, swiftly tracing its lines with his finger, reading from right to left, as was common in that ancient text. After skimming half of it, he looked up again.

"This is what I've been looking for," he breathed.

"And I will give you the whole volume, once you have opened one particular lock for me."

Ryze grinned. "I think we have ourselves a deal. Now, where is this lock?"

Grael smiled his predator's smile. He had the boy, hooked like a fish on a line. "Tell me, Ryze," he said. "What do you know of the Well of Ages?"

Chapter Seventeen

The more time Kalista spent in Helia, the more she hated it.

It was undeniably beautiful, and she was sure there were those who would regard it as a utopia, but her feeling of it being soulless continued to solidify. The city seemed so sanitized, so vapid, so cold. It felt like a façade, a mask worn to hide the truth concealed beneath.

She quickly grew restless in the vast rooms she had been appointed. She had expected to wait a matter of hours for the council to make their decision, or even a day, but that day had passed, as had the next, with no word. On the third day, she'd received a note from Tyrus, telling her they had still not yet come to a decision.

On the fourth day, Kalista took up her spear and went exploring.

She found the extent of the Helians' hospitality after climbing an ornate staircase to an immense building that seemed to be some kind of museum. Her way was barred by the white-armored guards she had seen elsewhere. They said something to her, their tone consolatory yet firm, but she couldn't understand them.

Kalista assessed the pair of guards, confident she could take them, but she murmured an apology and backed away. All over the city, she found her path blocked as she tried to gain access to different structures and even certain gardens. Where she was allowed to go was tightly controlled, which only made her suspicions deepen.

She felt very alone. She missed the comradeship of the Host. She even missed Viego. She felt a twinge of guilt for not missing her betrothed, Grand Master Hecarim. She did miss Ledros, however, and the intensity of that feeling surprised her. Thinking of him was painful, for it brought back memories of the awkwardness between them in the early hours before her departure. It made her stomach queasy, so she quickly diverted her thoughts.

After hours of aimless wandering, Kalista found an isolated marble bench facing the ocean in one of the city's many parks and sat down. She stared toward the mist, halfway out to where the horizon would be on a clear day. It felt like the islands were surrounded by immense walls. Far from making her feel secure, it made her feel *trapped*.

Perhaps the masters will never *let me leave.* They clearly desired the existence of the isles to remain obscured in myth and legend, so it seemed logical that they wouldn't wish her to return to her homeland. She thought of Vennix beyond the mist aboard the *Daggerhawk*. The captain had said she could wait out there for two weeks before needing to head to a port for supplies. If the masters refused to allow her to leave, how long before Vennix realized she wasn't coming back?

She was so engrossed in her unpleasant thoughts that she didn't notice the approach of the petite, dark-skinned woman until she spoke.

"The mists are a marvel, are they not?" the woman said, her voice surprisingly deep and as smooth as velvet. "The magic within is ancient and not truly understood by anyone here, though the masters would never admit it." She wore loose dark robes edged in silver trim over tight black leggings, with a peaked cowl that encircled her angular face and shock of white hair. It would have been a severe look but for the woman's open expression, warm smile, and easy demeanor. "I hope you don't mind me interrupting. I often come out here to think and get away from all that," she added, gesturing back toward the city with a wave of her ring-covered fingers.

"Not at all. I needed to get away from *all that* myself," Kalista said, mirroring her gesture.

The woman laughed. "Helia can have that effect."

"Would you like to sit?" asked Kalista. Everyone in Helia was polite, but this woman was one of the few who seemed genuinely friendly. "My name is Kalista."

"Oh, I know who you are," her new companion said as she took a seat alongside her. "Gossip travels fast among academics. You are the Camavoran princess. The one who tried to get into the Great Library this morning!"

"I did?"

"Not even all the scholars in Helia can access the library. You could seek a writ of authorization from the masters, but they are rarely issued. Oh, and the Threshers have access, of course, but no one pays them any mind. It caused no small amount of amusement that you tried to walk in there, though!"

Kalista couldn't help smiling. The woman didn't make her feel like she was being made fun of, at least not in the cutting manner favored by the courtiers in Alovédra. "I'm...glad I could be a source of levity."

"I'm Artificer Jenda'kaya. It's a pleasure to meet you."

"It's a pleasure to meet you as well," Kalista replied.

"You spoke to the Council of Helia," Jenda'kaya said. "How did that go?"

"I asked a favor of them," said Kalista, "and four days later, I am still awaiting an answer."

"That's not surprising. They are a bunch of pompous asses. Insufferable, self-entitled, and petty."

Kalista snorted at her honesty.

"It's true!" Jenda'kaya insisted. "They protect their own interests above anything else. But to be fair, there are a few among them who are passably decent. I hope they will be able to sway the others to help you in whatever it is you have come to ask."

"I hope so, too." The pair sat in silence, watching the birds soaring on the updrafts. "What is it you do here?" Kalista asked. "You seem... different from the others."

"I will take that as a compliment," she said. "Most would describe me as an eccentric, if they are being kind, or a dangerous, rogue agitator, if being more pointed. I am an artificer-adept of the Sentinels."

"The Sentinels?"

"It's not as impressive as it sounds, at least not anymore."

"There are those in Camavor who consider me something of a *rogue agitator* as well," said Kalista. "Many of them, in fact. Most of the noble families and Knightly Orders regard me with suspicion."

"You're a princess, aren't you? Are they not required to throw rose petals before you walk and rejoice at your every word?"

There was a wicked gleam in Jenda'kaya's eyes, and Kalista laughed. "Not exactly," she said. "My views on certain things make them... nervous."

"Why?"

"Because I want to see change."

"Ah! There you go, then!" said Jenda'kaya, slapping her hand upon the bench's stone armrest. "The politics of Camavor and Helia don't sound all that different, to be honest, and it's probably the same the world over. Those with established power always see change as a threat to their position."

Kalista nodded. "But enough talk of politics," she said. "What sort of research do you do, if you don't mind me asking?"

Jenda'kaya leaned forward conspiratorially. "I make weapons," she whispered.

Now, *that* got Kalista's interest. But before she could learn more, a bell chimed in a nearby tower, and the artificer jumped to her feet like an excited child.

"I have to go!" Jenda'kaya cried. "I'm already late!"

She started running toward the main hub of the city. She was some thirty paces away when she paused and looked back at Kalista. "Would you like to see my work?" she called out.

"Yes! I would!"

"Meet me here at sunset tomorrow," Jenda'kaya shouted. "I should have the kinks in my latest creation worked out by then!"

"I hope I will have my answer and be on my way before then!" said Kalista. "But if not, I will be here!"

Two robed adepts were muttering and casting disapproving glances at them. Jenda'kaya rounded on them. "Oh, go hush yourselves, you boring old sods!" she snapped, with such ferocity that the scholars practically fled. She was still speaking Camavoran, which Kalista suspected was for her benefit. That was confirmed when the artificer gave her a final, mischievous grin, then ran off, holding up the hem of her black robes so she didn't trip.

Kalista watched her go, utterly bemused.

Grael stood in the shadows of the darkened square, waiting, seething. It was after midnight, and the air was still and cool. He didn't like being aboveground. After so many years down in the tight confines of the vaults, it made him uneasy without a low roof over his head.

"Where is he?" he hissed. Had the boy betrayed him? Was he wrong to have let him go free?

"I'm here," came a voice just to his left, startling him.

Grael turned, snarling, and had the speaker pressed up against a wall in an instant. He held him there for a second before registering that it was the apprentice, and he released him with a shove. "You're late," he growled.

"Had to wait for Tyrus to retire for the night." Ryze straightened his robe, glaring at him. "He's been getting suspicious."

Grael glanced around the square, eyes darting between shadows, looking to see if they were observed. Nothing. "Let's go," he hissed.

He led them around the back of the Great Library, silhouetted above them like some monolithic beast. It was a truly massive structure, as large as a palace, but that was only what was visible aboveground—the bulk of its true size lay underneath, in the warren of tunnels, vaults, hidden chambers, and caverns guarded by the Wardens of Thresholds. They went down an alley between two wings of the edifice, and down a narrow flight of curving stairs to a locked gate bearing the symbol of the wardens. He unlocked the gate, swung it open, ushered Ryze through, and locked it behind them.

"I can't believe it's all true," Ryze whispered. "The well, the Waters of Life. All of it."

"A truth the masters have long tried to bury and obfuscate. They concocted the tales of it being nothing but baseless rumor. A myth."

"Bastards!"

"Indeed. Now be silent. We are approaching the entrance."

He took them down a series of ever-narrower alleys and stairs, designed to be hidden from the footbridges and causeways above, allowing the wardens to scurry around below the feet of their betters without being seen. Finally, he led them to a heavily barred and locked door.

"Cover your face," ordered Grael.

Ryze pulled his hood down low, and the warden thumped his fist against the oaken door. A narrow window slid open, and bleary eyes peered out.

"Open," ordered Grael, lifting his prefect's emblem. The eyes shifted to Ryze. "My new warden," he continued. "Open, swiftly now, or I'll speak with the magister and recommend you for reassignment."

There was grumbling from within, but the bolts were thrown and the door creaked open. Grael swept past the custodians without a glance. Ryze hurried after him, keeping his head low.

A dozen different doors led into the labyrinth below, the lintel above each inscribed with a unique geometric symbol. This was but one of seven waystations before the entrances into the vaults used by the wardens. It was the smallest of them, and the least used, which was why Grael had chosen it.

He strode purposefully past several of the iron-bound doors before coming to the one he wanted. Grael licked his lips, feeling the gaze of the custodians on him, and flicked through the keys on one of his thick iron rings. His hands were sweating. He paused at one key, unsure, then kept looking. He'd found these keys secreted in Prefect Maksim's cell—keys Maksim should not have possessed. It had come as no surprise to him that his former prefect was corrupt. Maksim had been very forthcoming about all his sordid secrets after only a little of Grael's attention, chained down in the depths. He was down there still, though Grael doubted many would recognize the pathetic, shattered wreck now. And there he would remain, for his continued existence amused him.

"They're still watching," whispered Ryze. "Tell me you have the key."

"Be silent."

"One of them is heading this way."

Grael resisted the urge to look up. Instead, he returned to the first key he had paused on and thrust it into the lock. To his relief, it turned, and he pushed the door open. Narrow stairs dropped away to darkness beyond. Throwing a glare at the custodian drawing near, Grael lit his lantern from a nearby brazier in an unhurried manner, then led the way into the gloom. He slammed the door behind them with a resounding boom.

They could have reached their destination via the tunnels within Grael's purview, but it would have taken days to traverse that winding path, and it would have required them to cross through corridors that fell under the jurisdiction of a dozen other wardens and prefects. While his new position granted him considerably more power, wandering into other wardens' sections of the vaults would have elicited unwanted attention.

Of course, the most direct route to the Well of Ages was via the Scintillant Tower, but that way was out of the question, for it was jealously guarded. He'd need an army to storm it.

Down, and down, and down they went, deeper into the darkness. Grael had planned this route carefully. They still needed to pass through the jurisdictions of three wardens, but stumbling upon one of them was unlikely. He'd used the privilege of his rank to access the patrol schedules in these areas and taken them into consideration. Of course, that didn't account for the human factor—wardens often deviated from their official patrol routes—but it was the best that could be done. And if they did encounter a warden? Well, his blade would be ready.

"Come, boy," Grael snarled. "We have a long walk ahead of us."

Ryze couldn't judge the passage of time in the darkness beneath Helia, but it felt like they'd been walking for days.

He'd completely lost all sense of direction and was painfully aware that if the deranged warden chose to abandon him, he'd never find a way out. He'd be trapped down here for the rest of his life, wandering blindly, until he died of thirst and starvation, or inadvertently stepped over the edge of one of the impossibly deep shafts built into the maze of tunnels. Down some of those pits, he thought he heard a sound like distant waves crashing.

Anxiety gnawed at him. He'd always been rebellious, but this was taking things further than he ever had before. Should he have told Tyrus what this Warden-Prefect Grael was attempting? He'd considered it dozens of times since he'd made his bargain with him, but there was no way that was going to result in anything but his own banishment. Tyrus was a stickler for the rules, even if Grael didn't manage to see him expelled from the Fellowship for betraying him.

And besides, he shared the warden's outrage. Why should the masters hide something so wondrous from the rest of the Fellowship? Why should they be the only ones to benefit from it? Yet as much as he tried to convince himself of the nobility of this act of rebellion, he knew in his heart that the only reason he was going along with it was to get hold of the book Grael had promised him.

This is Tyrus's fault. If he'd just followed through on his promises and helped Ryze master his power, he wouldn't have ever sought this knowledge elsewhere.

Grael's lantern abruptly went out. The darkness was so absolute that Ryze couldn't even see his fingers waving before his eyes, and panic reared within him. He fumbled blindly, then bumped into the warden, who had gone still in front of him.

"Be still!" Grael breathed.

Ryze crouched in the dark, trying to quiet his breathing. They stayed there for what felt like an age, and he was about to say something when he heard a noise in the distance. It was an echoing, repetitive tapping, like wood on stone. It continued, getting steadily louder, and soon another sound joined it, in the same rhythm. *Footsteps.*

Grael's cold hand pushed him toward the side of the passage. Feeling with his hands, Ryze discovered a shallow alcove there, and he slipped into it, wincing as some gravel ground beneath his step. Grael himself didn't make a sound, moving as silently as a ghost. It was unnerving.

A few minutes passed, and Ryze slowly realized he could make out the silhouette of the warden in front of him, pressed flat against the side wall of the alcove. His heart began to thump faster as he realized what that meant: There was a light source nearby. The tapping and the footsteps got steadily louder. They were only a matter of yards from a three-way junction, and whoever was approaching was coming toward it.

The light got brighter, and the tapping and the footsteps grew painfully loud. Whoever it was reached the junction and stopped, their lantern shining down each corridor. Ryze pressed himself as flat as he could against the alcove wall, scarce daring to breathe. His heart was now hammering so thunderously, he felt certain the newcomer would hear it. If this warden came any farther down the corridor, they would be spotted instantly.

Ryze's eyes widened as Grael produced his sickle, evidently coming to the same conclusion. Ryze waved at him, mouthing

No! and shaking his head. The murderous warden's cold, dead eyes flicked toward him, then back toward the junction.

Killing a member of the Fellowship was not something Ryze had agreed to. He'd just decided he would leap out, shout a warning, and take whatever punishment would come his way, when the tap of wood on stone began again. Leaning out ever so slightly from the alcove, he saw the other warden, the hood of his robe up, walking away, having chosen to take another passage. The tapping came from a tall staff with a lantern atop it, and the man leaned upon it like a walking stick.

They stayed there, unmoving and silent, until once again Grael's silhouette was completely swallowed in darkness. Even then, they remained frozen in place, until the tapping of the warden's lantern-staff was long gone. Only then did Grael relight his lantern with a spark from his whetstone, and his sickle disappeared within the folds of his robes.

"You were going to kill that man," Ryze hissed.

"No, *we* were going to kill him," corrected Grael. "We are in this together, you and I."

That answer chilled Ryze. He already knew that Grael was dangerous, and dangerously unstable, but until that moment he hadn't really considered that he was this man's accomplice, and that whatever happened down here, he was a part of it. He had the urge to call the whole thing off, to abandon this fool's errand. But he'd seen the murderous glint in Grael's eyes. He'd *wanted* the other warden to come toward them. There was no way that Ryze was going to get out of this situation without giving Grael what he wanted.

And there was the matter of the book, of course. It was the key to unlocking his power. He *had* to have it.

And so, he swallowed his unease, and followed Warden-Prefect Grael deeper into the labyrinth.

Chapter Eighteen

"This is it," said Grael, coming to a halt.

They were halfway down a corridor that was largely indistinguishable from any other, though it had a shallow channel running down its center, with a trickle of water creeping along it. Similar gutters were not uncommon on the lower levels, and this was about as deep as Grael had ever ventured.

"Is that... is that the sacred waters?" Ryze asked.

Grael laughed at the idiotic question. "Drink it and find out," he sneered.

Ryze ignored Grael's mockery and looked around him, his skepticism obvious. "Are you sure this is the right place?"

Grael scowled. "Yes, I'm sure."

"All right, all right," said Ryze, under his breath.

"Hold this." Grael handed the apprentice his lantern. Then he turned to the wall, formed of thousands of precisely cut, interlocking stones, and felt along its surface, ignoring the dust and grime that soon coated his palms and fingertips. After long minutes, he stepped back, brow furrowed. "Stay here," he said. He snatched his lantern and stalked back to the last junction, muttering.

There he stopped, turned, and began pacing out his steps, counting as he went, though this time he consciously took shorter strides than normal. When he reached one hundred forty-four—a number considered potent in the arcane traditions of the Fellowship—he paused and turned to face the wall again. He was some twenty paces away from Ryze, and he impatiently ushered him over.

This time he found what he had been searching for. "Shorter steps."

"What?"

"The designer was short," Grael explained, grinning.

The warden pressed his cheek against the wall, looking along it with one eye closed. One of the stones protruded out farther than the others, almost imperceptibly. The imperfection was so minute that it would have been impossible to notice if he didn't know what he was looking for. Cautiously, he pressed the stone, and it retracted, just a little. There was a mechanical click, followed by a steady ticking sound that quickly increased in tempo.

"That doesn't sound good," said Ryze.

"There's a second switch," said Grael, calmly. "If it is not activated within the allocated time, an alarm will ring within the Scintillant Tower, and these tunnels will soon be flooded with custodians."

Ryze began looking around frantically, his eyes wild. "They can't find us down here! Where's the other switch?"

"Calm yourself," Grael said, even as the ticking reached a maddening staccato. Without hurrying, he took seven measured steps back along the corridor and turned to face the opposite wall. He counted the stones until he came to the one he sought. It really was ingenious, he thought, as he studied the nondescript stone. If he didn't already know where it was, there would have been no way he would have found it. The ticking was now an almost constant whirr.

"You don't know where it is, do you? We have to get out of here!" hissed Ryze.

Grael gave him a look, then pressed the stone. It sank

inward, and the ticking ceased. With a dull grinding sound, a small panel in the wall cracked open, down at ground level. "You need to learn to control your emotions," he said.

"You sound like Tyrus," Ryze muttered. "How'd you know where the switches were?"

"Never underestimate the power of research, boy."

"Now you *really* sound like Tyrus."

Ignoring him, Grael knelt and pushed on the panel, grunting with effort. It slid inward, then hinged up before it ground to a halt, halfway open. Positioning himself on the grimy floor, Grael reached in and shoved it upward. Ryze winced with each metallic squeal. Finally it was opened fully, revealing a dark rectangular hole. It was barely large enough for a person to squeeze through.

Ryze looked at it dubiously. "*This* is our way in?"

"This is *your* way in," corrected Grael, with a cruel smile.

"You're not coming?"

"Do you think I'd fit in there?"

The boy screwed up his face. "I'm not even sure I'll fit in there," he said.

"You will."

"And you're sure the custodians don't know about this entrance?"

"It's a sluice, built to drain off excess water in times of flooding, but it hasn't been used in over a century," said Grael.

"Doesn't mean it's not guarded on the other side."

"No, it doesn't," agreed Grael. "Which is another reason why *you* are going through, and not me."

"I don't know," said Ryze. "What if there's a blockage in it, or it's been bricked up?"

"There's only one way to find out. And going in there is the only way you get your precious book."

Ryze stared at the hole in the wall. It wasn't large enough for a person to crawl through on hands and knees—the apprentice was going to have to worm his way forward on his belly.

He cursed, then shrugged off the wide leather belt he wore diagonally across his chest, and his hooded surcoat, leaving his torso bare. He checked the contents of the leather satchel strapped to his hip alongside his empty waterskin, and tucked a small blade down the side of his boot. He picked up his compact bull's-eye lantern and knelt down before the tiny dark passage.

"One more thing," said Grael. From within his robes, he produced a rolled-up piece of soft leather. "You will need this."

Ryze unrolled the leather to reveal the keystone. "How in the name of all that's holy did you get *this*?"

"It doesn't matter how I got it. What matters is what it *does*," Grael said.

The apprentice shrugged and rolled it back in the leather before slipping it into his satchel.

"The upper levels are the most heavily guarded," he continued. "This way should bypass most of the custodians and wards and bring you out right below the Hall of Conjunction. The entrance to the Well of Ages should be obvious. There will be two locks. The keystone will open one. You will have to open the other yourself."

Ryze nodded. "Wait for me," he said. "Don't disappear."

"I'll be here. But if you're caught, you're on your own."

"So much for *in this together*," Ryze muttered as he lowered himself down to the hole. He ducked his head, swearing again. Both his shoulders scraped the sides as he slunk onto his belly and began to elbow his way into the darkness. With much grunting, scraping, and kicking, he made it deeper inside. It looked like he was being swallowed whole.

"Be swift, and be silent," Grael whispered into the tunnel. Then he reached in and grabbed the sluice hatch.

"No, don't close it!" hissed Ryze as the hatch began to groan, but Grael paid him no mind. With a final, mechanical click, he sealed the way back, leaving Ryze with no way to go but forward.

Panic welled in Ryze as he heard the sluice gate seal behind him, leaving him in absolute darkness. His breathing became shallow and quick, and he found himself wedged fast, unable to move forward or back—not that there was any way to *go* back now.

He tried to wriggle forward but achieved nothing. He was stuck, and he was going to die here, trapped in this claustrophobic tunnel, pinned beneath a mountain of rock. He could see nothing and had no idea if the exit was ten or a thousand yards distant. He wanted to shout, to beg Grael to open the door and pull him out, but he knew it would do no good. The Thresher bastard wouldn't help him, and if he started shouting, there'd likely be a very sharp blade waiting for him.

Tyrus's voice came to him then, a memory of a time when the adept had talked him down from a potentially fatal magical overload.

"I feel the sand beneath my hands," Ryze hissed, feeling a second wave of panic rising. "I feel the sand beneath my hands."

It had been during one of his early—and nearly lethal—attempts to use his magical ability. While Tyrus was sleeping, he had attempted to pull a small amount of magical energy into himself—enough to experiment with, but not enough to be truly dangerous—but that wellspring was quickly out of his control. He was flooded with raw magic, and it infused every fiber of his being. Burning from within and overloaded with power, he had risen off the ground, hot purple runes blazing within his flesh. He didn't have the knowledge of the runic forms to disperse that much power, or to channel it outward, and he would have been utterly consumed by it, left as a burnt-out husk, had not Tyrus woken and come to his aid. His master's voice had cut through the agony, like a soothing balm.

"*You're sitting cross-legged on sand. It's warm beneath you. Comforting. Soft. You feel the grains of sand beneath your hands. The sun is falling, giving way to dusk, but you can still feel its touch on your skin. You can hear birds calling on the wind, and smell the subtle aroma of desert blooms. What else can you feel? What else can you smell, and hear, and see?*"

"I feel the grains of sand beneath my hands. I smell bitter-root tea brewing in a pot over a fire," breathed Ryze. "I hear the crackle of burning twigs. I see the embers lifting into the sky, shifting from orange to purple to dark blue, like swirls of oil on water. I see the first stars. I feel the grains of sand beneath my hands."

And just as that simple thought exercise had once drawn him back from the brink of destruction, so it worked now. His breathing slowed; his heartbeat steadied. He was calm.

He began to wriggle forward.

The sluice tunnel was long and never broadened, but it was mercifully free of blockage or debris. He saw light up ahead and slowed his approach, moving as silently as possible. He squirmed on, but in horror, he saw that the exit was barred.

"No, no, no, no, no," he hissed. He scrambled forward faster, not caring if anybody heard him. He reached the end of the tunnel and wrapped his hands around the stone grating blocking his exit.

Peering out, he saw an expansive, circular room, its floor crisscrossed with arcane geometry. The marble panels lining the walls were replete with carved symbolism, and there was a large, spiraling staircase that descended into the center of the chamber, with cold, unnatural light spilling down from the level above. There was one other exit from the room—a giant archway, sealed by golden doors covered in yet more symbols and iconography.

Ryze was about to smash the stone grating loose when one of those gilt doors cracked open. He heard hushed voices, and a pair of robed masters emerged, flanked by white-armored custodians. All four wore hoods covering their features, and strain though he did, Ryze could not hear the words they said. The door clicked shut behind them. There was a mechanical whirr of cogs and levers, and runic wards around the lintel pulsed with blue light.

Still speaking in low tones, the masters and their guards climbed the spiraling stairs and were soon beyond Ryze's sight. A few moments later the entire stone staircase began to retract, folding in on itself and twisting as it rose. The stairs fit perfectly into the geometric blocks of the ceiling, slotting neatly into place like a fanned-out deck of cards being brought back together.

It was completely dark, and silent. Ryze gave it a few minutes, then inspected the stone grating by touch. It was one solid piece. He worked his fingers around it, probing at the flaking mortar. With considerable difficulty, he managed to retrieve the blade from his left boot and began to carve around the edge of the grate. It was slow, awkward work, and he got more than a bit of mortar in his eyes and mouth.

Once he'd finished, he took hold of the grate in one hand and positioned himself to strike at a corner with the meat of his palm. The tight confines made it difficult to put his full weight into it, but he struck as hard as he could and felt the grate budge. Encouraged, he struck it again, and again, and finally it came loose. He lowered it carefully to the floor and hauled himself out, stretching his back and rolling his neck. Then he lit his lantern with a single strike of his flint, keeping it shuttered so that its light was just a narrow beam.

He set the grate back in place and padded across the room toward the giant archway. The doors had no obvious handles or keyholes. Try as he might, he could not even find the crack between them, so masterful and precise was their construction. Geometric patterns covered every inch, the intersecting lines and shapes leading his gaze inward, to a symbol of a staring eye surrounded by flame. Ryze felt a tingling in the back of his head as he looked upon it—a sensation not unlike the feeling he had experienced with the keystone in hand. He felt drawn to the symbol, like it was pulling him inexorably toward it.

He placed his palm upon the blazing eye. A sudden jolt pulsed through him, making his breath catch in his throat, and he quickly pulled his hand back. There were a series of mechanical clicks, and an instant later, two triangular holes appeared in the golden doors, one to each side of the eye. They were the same size as the stone the warden had given him. He could see carved lines on their inner surfaces. The magnetic feeling was stronger, now drawing him toward the triangular keyholes.

Ryze swiftly retrieved the stone from his satchel and held it before the keyholes. It was tugged toward the left one, like a lodestone to iron. "Okay, okay," he breathed, and thrust the stone into it. It fit perfectly, and there was a pulse of blue energy that lit up the key as it locked into place.

The door remained sealed, of course. Grael had said he needed both keys.

Again he felt the strange pulling sensation, and his right hand moved toward that second keyhole, almost of its own accord. As he neared it, purple runes flared within his flesh, rippling along his hand and forearm. He pulled back in shock, and the runes faded.

Cautiously, he moved his hand back toward the hole, and again the runes burst to life within his flesh. This time he did not pull away. Closing his eyes, he began to move his hand around in the air above the keyhole, feeling the patterns of the runic lock. He quickly realized it was far more complex than anything he had seen before, almost overwhelmingly so. It was like a dozen locks in one, each one overlapping the other.

With a growl of frustration—and not a small amount of awe—Ryze pulled away from the lock once more. There was no way he could bypass this, at least not in any way he'd done before. He bit his lip, weighing his options. Again he felt the keyhole pulling at him. "What's the worst that could happen?" he muttered, and thrust his hand completely into the keyhole.

Nothing happened at first, and Ryze shook his head. *What did I expect?* Then something locked tightly around his wrist, and a force pulled his arm deeper into the hole. Agonizing pain seared him, and he was slammed against the door. He would have screamed, had the air not been driven from his lungs.

The pain was excruciating. It felt like his whole arm had been thrust into a brazier of glowing coals. He wilted, falling to one knee, but could not escape, for the door held him trapped. Purple runes flashed brightly up his shoulder, and the power within him roiled like an angry beast straining to be freed. Violet bled across everything he saw, and magical vapor seeped from his eyes, nose, and mouth. He'd felt this sensation only once before.

"I feel the grains of sand beneath my hands," he hissed. "I

feel the grains of sand beneath my hands." He clenched his eyes shut, trying to calm the rising thunder of magic, lest it rip him apart. His arm was still awash with agony. Sweat dripped down his body. "I feel the grains of sand beneath my hands!"

The pain lessened, just enough for him to gasp a breath, and the roar of magic within him quieted fractionally. He could *feel* the pattern within the keyhole, a pattern that wanted a match. The sensation was similar to what he had felt with other runic locks, but far, far more intense. With his eyes still clenched shut, he pictured the pattern of the interlocking knot of runes. They shifted and turned as he concentrated on them, slipped away from him, elusive and silken, but he pursued them. In a rush, the runic arrangement came into stark clarity, and it pulsed with a blue light.

It was much the same as picking a lock—find the pins that need to be triggered, squeeze them down, and move to the next.

With his free hand, he formed the first of the runes in the air, then unraveled it, and moved to the next. He did this with each one in turn, until they were all unlocked. With a final pulse of ethereal light, his arm was released.

He pulled it free, expecting to see his flesh charred to the bone, but it was completely unharmed. Runes were glowing beneath his skin—the same symbols he had visualized. They began to fade almost instantly, and he flexed his hand, still marveling that it was unscathed. The pain was gone as well, leaving nothing but its echo in the stiffness of his fingers.

There were a series of mechanical whirrs and clicks, and the doors swung open. White mist hung in the air within. Retrieving the keystone, Ryze walked cautiously into the chamber.

"The Well of Ages," he whispered.

It was more like a massive, opulent bathhouse than a well. The room stretched farther than Ryze's lantern could reach, and much of it was obscured by the thick mist, but what he saw was all white marble, gold, and arcane symbolism. Exquisitely carved columns rose into the fog, and steps all around the edge of the room gently dropped down into the pool. The water was perfectly clear and still, and only the lantern's reflection on its glasslike surface gave any indication of its presence.

Ryze walked to the edge of the pool, scarce daring to breathe. Kneeling on the step closest to the waters, he felt the white mist coiling around him, like ethereal tendrils. Knowing that he could be interrupted at any moment, he unhooked his empty waterskin from his side, pulled out the stopper—then paused.

It felt like a violation, taking the water from this sacred pool. But what were his alternatives? Return to the violent and dangerous warden empty-handed? Hand himself over to the custodians? Steeling himself, Ryze lowered the waterskin below the surface, sending ripples across the pool. The water was cool and felt perfectly mundane. He wondered if the stories of its life-giving magic were exaggerated. But if that were so, why hide it away from the world?

Waterskin filled, Ryze lifted it from the pool. He held it up before him, watching the water drip down the leather.

"Why not?" he said, with a smile, and raised it to his lips. He drank his fill, then wiped his mouth with the back of his hand. It was the purest-tasting water he had ever drunk, though if it had any properties beyond that, they were not immediately apparent. He refilled the waterskin and stoppered it, then secured it back on his hip.

Only then, as he stood to leave, did he notice the gentle illumination rising from the center of the pool. Ryze's brow furrowed. How had he not seen that before? He walked around the edge, trying to get a better look at that strange light, but it was just a little too distant, and just a little too submerged, to see clearly. But he *felt* the presence of the light source. It infused the waters and the mist itself. It infused the very air he breathed.

He peered down through the waters again, which were just now settling from the ripples he had caused. As the pool returned to stillness, his eyes locked onto something down there, something blindingly bright, and his heart lurched.

He felt it in his bones. It buzzed in the back of his mind. It whispered to his soul. This was something powerful and old. Something that had been old long before the rise of humanity. It was a *rune*, the notion coming to Ryze from nowhere, but he knew with utter certainty that it was true. It was a rune given physical form, one of the primordial forces that had wrought order from chaos.

And in that moment of wonder, Ryze felt the prickling sensation of someone watching him. He turned.

A shadowy figure stood on the edge of the pool, unmoving, only a few yards away. At first, Ryze thought its features were hidden within a dark cowl covering its face. Then he realized it *had* no features. Its face was blank, as shadowy as the rest of it, and yet he had no doubt that it saw him. He could feel its gaze crawling upon his skin. And in rising horror, he also realized he could see *through* it. This was not some being of flesh and blood.

This was a specter. A revenant. An echo of the past.

It pointed at him. The movement displaced the mist, and eerie greenish-blue light flickered around its arm. It took a step toward him, and more of its shape was outlined in that horrible, baleful light.

Ryze let out a cry of terror. Then he turned and fled. As he ran, he realized there were more murky figures standing around the periphery of the room. All were robed in shadows, their forms delineated by where the mist *wasn't*, and all had turned toward him, staring blankly.

He raced from the room, heart thundering, not bothering

to close the great golden doors as he sprinted directly for the sluice tunnel. He glanced back and saw the shadowy specter pass through the doorway. Its featureless face, glowing from within with flickering teal-colored balefire, snapped around to lock onto him.

Swearing, Ryze dropped his lantern. With a yell, he hurled the stone grate aside, then threw himself into the tunnel, uncaring of the scrapes and bruises he suffered in his haste. Breathing hard, he elbowed his way through, squirming and wriggling frantically.

He glanced over his shoulder, once. In the light of his abandoned lantern, he could see the empty room behind him, but nothing more.

Then a shadowy, faceless figure bent and looked down the tunnel toward him.

Ryze whipped his gaze forward, crawling as fast as he was able. It felt like it took an age, and he was certain he was going to feel the icy touch of a spectral hand around his ankle, but finally his head struck the sluice hatch. He hammered his fist against it. "Open it! Open it now!"

The hatch ground open, and Ryze scrambled out. Grael was there, grinning at him eagerly, like a cat with its prey. "You found it? You got it?"

Ryze ignored the warden's questions. "Seal it, quickly!" he barked. When Grael just blinked at him, Ryze swore and dropped to his bloodied knees to wrench the sluice gate shut.

"Answer me, boy!" The warden grabbed hold of Ryze and yanked him to his feet. "Did you find the Well of Ages?"

By way of answer, Ryze unclipped his waterskin and held it out before him in one shaking hand. "Take it," he whispered. "I'm done."

Chapter Nineteen

Kalista woke early, and sighed as awareness of her surroundings crashed down on her.

Another day in Helia. Another day waiting while the council deliberated. Another day that could mean the difference between saving Queen Isolde and her finally succumbing to poison.

Kalista hated knowing that her mission required the utmost urgency, but thus far she had been unable to hasten the masters' decision. And she hated that the bloodthirsty reputation of Camavor was making the masters suspicious of her intentions.

She had agreed to meet with the curious artificer, Jenda'kaya, at sunset, but there was a full day before then. If she sat around her suite until the evening, she knew she would only stew, so she put on her armor, took up her spear, and headed out in the predawn darkness.

Royalty she might be, but she was also a soldier and had risen before the sun for years. She couldn't help feeling some superiority over the soft academics of Helia, knowing they still slumbered. On the whole, there seemed to be no steel in them. They were lucky they had the white mist, otherwise they'd have been slaughtered by raiders long ago—probably by her ancestors.

She wandered the empty streets as the sky began to lighten

and found herself on the outskirts of Helia when the sun rose. It had been an unconscious decision, but she had no real desire to spend more time within the city itself. It felt too stifling, too controlled. The fresh air, trees, hedges, and lush open fields beyond the city were a much-needed respite.

The first person she saw was a herdsman, with a flock of odd-looking sheep with long, shaggy white wool, black faces and legs, and jutting horns protruding from their lower jaws. Those horns looked quite intimidating, but the beasts appeared docile, chomping on grass as the little bells around their necks chimed softly. The herdsman lifted a hand in greeting before leading his charges down to a stream with a few sharp whistles and barked encouragement from his hound.

Leaving the neatly paved white-stone road, she climbed over a low dry-stone wall using a wooden stile and followed a muddy track up a hillside to get a better sense of her surroundings. A child's swing hung from the bough of a lonely tree atop the hillock, which was afforded good views. Helia rose to the south, gleaming and majestic in the morning glow, while the sea glittered like shifting jewels to the west. The north and east were dominated by rolling, verdant hills, pastures, and pockets of woodland. A number of villages were visible, and thin lines of smoke rose from chimneys. A wagon drawn by a train of bullocks was making its slow, winding way along a road in the distance, and the tiny puffs of white dotted against green hillsides showed where other herds grazed.

The closest village wasn't far, tucked in a shadowed dell. It was small, consisting of perhaps a score of buildings, and she was impressed to see they weren't hovels. Each was built of pale stone and dark timber, and they shared many of the geometric designs and features of the grander structures in Helia. Even the little covered bridge leading into the village had been designed with care, formed of an intricate web of triangles and diamond shapes, its woodwork carved with symbols and intersecting lines. Farmers and villagers went about their business, their clothes bright splashes of color against the dark earth and green fields.

It spoke well of the society here that even the humble farming folk appeared to live comfortably and without any of the desperation so common among the poor people of other nations, Camavor included. Kalista had wondered if those outside Helia would be living like peasants while the pampered scholars in the city supped on wine and sweetmeats, but it seemed there was no hidden darkness, or at least none that she had yet glimpsed.

Of course, the isle was not perfect. It was obvious that politics and bureaucracy reigned supreme, as evidenced by the painfully slow deliberations of the council. But Kalista doubted there ever *could* be a truly perfect society. People were people.

She found herself wandering into a patch of woodland down the lee side of the hillock, stepping through a carpet of silvery ferns and tiny white and blue flowers. Delving deeper, she realized this wasn't a small wood at all but a part of a larger forest. The trees were massive, with gnarled trunks covered in moss and lichen, and great twisted roots that curled around ancient stones and crisscrossed over the way before her, as if trying to trip her. The sun didn't penetrate the distant canopy, keeping this little pocket of solitude locked in a dusklike gloaming. In the shadows beneath the boughs, she glimpsed tiny, flittering shapes that glowed faintly. Kalista couldn't tell what they were, for whenever she tried to get close, they darted away or disappeared altogether, but there was something about their playful movement that made her believe they were not simply insects. She thought she heard childish laughter on the breeze, but that could have been the rustling of leaves, or a trick of the wind.

The great trees creaked and groaned, as if they were speaking to one another. It felt like they were watching her. It wasn't a threatening feeling, nor was it a particularly welcoming one. It just *was*. On some instinctive level, Kalista knew this old forest had been here long before people arrived on the isles. Perhaps they, too, had felt its age and its magic, and that was why they left it wild and free. The age of it made her feel insignificant, in a good way—like all her worries were ephemeral, ultimately pointless, and all the jealousies, treacheries, and even wars of mortal beings were unimportant in the grand tapestry of the world. She felt a measure of comfort in knowing that just as this forest had been here before the arrival of humanity, so, too, would it remain long after they were gone.

Feeling a newfound sense of peace, Kalista reluctantly left the forest to return to Helia.

Glancing back, she thought she saw one of the trees move. It was a particularly twisted and ancient behemoth of the forest, full of life and covered in greenery, with a ring of saplings around it. She was almost certain it had shifted while her back was turned, and she could easily imagine a gnarled old face in the knots and swirls on its trunk.

She headed back toward the city, feeling calmer and more reflective than she had in many moons.

It was late afternoon by the time Kalista returned to the villa. She paused at her door, hearing a child's laughter. Rather than going directly to her empty rooms, she followed the joyful sound, weaving through corridors toward its source.

At last she came to a small courtyard, lined with arches and neatly planted bushes. Three young children—two frizzy-haired girls who looked like twins, and a younger boy—giggled and shrieked as they darted around, trying to evade a robed adult, who was lumbering around with his head down low. He held his hands up to either side of his forehead, like antlers, and harrumphed loudly as he stomped around, to the delight of the children scrambling out of his way. With much amusement, Kalista realized the man was Seeker-Adept Tyrus, and she folded her arms and leaned against an archway to watch.

It took a while for Tyrus to realize he had an audience. He straightened immediately, attempting to regain something of his usual stern demeanor. Kalista raised an eyebrow, and he coughed, looking quite sheepish.

"I, er, think that's enough elnuk hunting for today, children. Time to get back to your classes," he said, causing an eruption of disappointed cries and grumbles.

A pair of tutors came forward to begin the process of corralling the children. The twin girls scattered, screeching, as if it were part of a new game, while the little boy latched tenaciously onto Tyrus's leg.

"We'll play again soon, Tolu," Tyrus said, extricating himself with some difficulty. Once free, he made his way over to Kalista. "My carefully maintained aura of solemn gravitas is shattered, isn't it?"

"Oh, completely," confirmed Kalista. "But you do make a very convincing bull elnuk."

Tyrus offered her a small bow. "One does try one's best."

"Are they your children?"

"Oh goodness, no," said Tyrus, "although I do consider myself responsible for them. Sadly, they have all suffered tragedy in their short lives. There is no replacing the love of a parent, but here they will at least be taken care of and given a strong education. Still no word from the council?"

Kalista grimaced. "No. And I am losing my patience."

Tyrus nodded in understanding. "I am truly sorry they are taking so long. This was not what I had hoped for when I brought you to our shores. Will you join my apprentice and me for dinner this evening?"

"Thank you, but I cannot," said Kalista. "I have a prior

engagement. An adept of the Sentinels is going to show me some of her work."

"Oh, you met Jenda'kaya? Life is rarely dull around that one."

"She does seem...exuberant."

Tyrus made his goodbyes, promising to see what he could do about speeding up the council's deliberations, and left. Kalista lingered in the courtyard, watching as the orphans were rounded up by their patient caretakers and led off for dinner. One of the twins stuck her tongue out at her as she passed. Kalista reciprocated, making the child giggle.

She glanced up at the sky, which was starting to dim. She had just enough time to bathe and have a light meal before she needed to leave to meet the artificer. Still laughing at the vision of Tyrus pretending to be an elnuk, Kalista finally made her way back to her rooms.

It felt like something had followed him back from the darkness.

Returning to his room within Tyrus's suite, Ryze had been constantly looking behind him, expecting to see that faceless, shadowed shape ghosting his steps. He saw nothing but couldn't shake the feeling of being watched, of something malign lingering just outside his vision.

He had hoped daylight would eliminate the creeping sensation, but even when the sun was at its highest the next day, he could still see shadows lurking on his periphery. He could still feel that awful presence. He couldn't get the image of it leveling an accusatory finger at him out of his mind. Or the horrible, blank visage leaning down and looking toward him from the tunnel entrance.

"Can a soul linger after death?" he asked his master. He was meant to be reading a set of tomes Tyrus had given him—dull affairs, focused on the oral histories of the frozen northlands—but his mind kept returning to what he had seen.

Tyrus frowned. "What brought that on? I don't recall any of the founding arcano-historians speculating about the spirits of the dead."

"Just...just something I was thinking about."

"Concentrate on your readings, Ryze. You need to be more focused."

He tried but was largely unsuccessful. No sooner would he finish reading a paragraph than he had to go back and reread it, having not absorbed it at all. He watched the afternoon sun slip toward the horizon with rising dread. As the shadows lengthened, so, too, did the prickling sensation of being watched.

With no appetite, he prodded listlessly at the food on his plate over dinner. For his part, Tyrus barely seemed to notice. The adept was engrossed in a worn old tome, which he read through the tiny spectacles perched on the end of his nose while he ate.

There was a thunderous pounding on the suite's door, and Ryze started with a jolt. Tyrus glanced at him over the top of his glasses before returning his attention to his book. "See who that is, please," he said.

Ryze swallowed heavily and moved toward the door with trepidation, though he told himself he was being foolish. Whoever had knocked was a being of flesh and blood, not some malign spirit come to haunt him. But when he threw the door open, only to see the grinning figure of Warden-Prefect Grael, his fear spiked.

"Greetings, young apprentice," the warden said.

Ryze glanced back toward his master, then stepped out into the corridor and pulled the door closed behind him. "What are you doing here?" he hissed.

"I have something to show you. Something *very* interesting. And I need to give you your reward, as promised."

"You shouldn't have come here!"

There were footsteps approaching from inside the suite, and Grael's eyes narrowed. He stepped closer, too close for Ryze's comfort. The warden stank of dust and mold. "Make an excuse to leave, and meet me outside."

The door behind Ryze opened suddenly, and Tyrus stood there, frowning. "Warden?" he said. "Is there a problem?"

Ryze saw Grael's grin tighten into a rictus. "Tyrus," the warden said.

Tyrus's frown deepened, and he removed his spectacles. "Do I know you?"

"Once, long ago," said Grael, his smile now more of a grimace.

Seeing them together made the warden look all the more wretched. While Tyrus was robust, impeccably attired, and his features chiseled and suntanned, the warden was gaunt, his robes fraying, and his skin an unhealthy, pallid shade. Ryze shrank inwardly. The way the warden had described it, Tyrus had ruined his life. Did his master truly not even *recognize* him?

"Grael?" said Tyrus, narrowing his eyes. "Erlok Grael, is that you?"

"In the flesh."

"My, I don't think I have seen you since—"

"Since the Choosing," said Grael. "Since you were picked first, and I was thrown to the Thresholds."

"I..." stammered Tyrus. "Well, yes. The Choosing. That was a long time ago."

"Sometimes it feels like a lifetime," agreed Grael. "Other times it feels like yesterday. It seems you have done well for yourself." His eyes darted over Tyrus's shoulder, into his opulent suite.

Tyrus shifted awkwardly. "And you're a prefect, no less," he said, nodding toward the symbol hanging around the warden's neck.

"No less, and no more."

"What brings you here, Grael? Is there a problem?"

"All is perfectly splendid, Seeker-Adept," said Grael. "I simply knocked on the wrong door, is all. I will be on my way. I bid you both good night." His gaze lingered on Ryze for a moment. Then he turned and strode away.

"He was always a strange one," remarked Tyrus, before shrugging and going back inside.

Kalista met the artificer in the little park overlooking the bay, as agreed. Chatting nonstop, the diminutive woman led her into one of Helia's grand buildings.

A white-armored custodian tried to bar Kalista's progress, but Jenda'kaya leveled her finger at him and barked something that sounded rude, though Kalista could not understand her words. The custodian seemed instantly contrite but did not back down completely, gesturing at Kalista's spear. Jenda'kaya sighed and turned to her.

"I've vouched for you and he'll let you through, but not with your weapon."

Somewhat reluctantly, Kalista leaned her spear against the wall, and they made their way inside. They entered a vast antechamber, replete with marble and gold. Dozens of scholars hurried about, carrying books and scrolls as they made their way between the various corridors and staircases leading from the cavernous space.

"I tried to come in here once before, I think," remarked Kalista, staring around her. "I've been stopped from entering so many places, they've all started to blur together."

"The masters are not fond of strangers wandering Helia unaccompanied. But you're with me now," Jenda'kaya said with a wink.

On the way to the artificer's workspace, Kalista was taken on a swift tour of several of Helia's research institutions. She had thought the royal library of Alovédra was impossibly large, but its books would have fit into just a small section of any one of the libraries in this building alone. The sheer amount of contained knowledge was staggering.

"Library. Another library. And here we have...another library," the artificer said in a bored voice, waving vaguely at each in turn as she led them on. "You sensing a theme yet? Ah, here's something different. A scribe hall. Just one of many across Helia. Nothing terribly exciting."

Kalista's eyes widened, and she paused. In the whole palace of Camavor, there were perhaps a dozen scribes, but here there were easily a hundred, and this was just one hall of many. They were all busy at their individual desks, quills clinking on ink pots and nibs scratching on parchment, the sound like a plague of rats clawing at the walls.

"What are they transcribing?"

"Oh, you know," said Jenda'kaya, with a shrug. "Everything."

"What do you mean, *everything*?"

"One of the goals of the Keepers is for our libraries to have at least one transcribed copy of every known written work of value in the world."

"Is that...is that even possible? More are being written all the time, surely!"

"It's a logistical nightmare, but with enough scribes and translators, and enough Seekers like your friend Tyrus bringing in works both new and ancient, it should theoretically be possible. Of course, it will take many centuries."

"That's...ambitious."

"It's stupid, is what it is," said Jenda'kaya, turning and striding away. She was small, but Kalista had to work hard to keep up with her as she marched. "The Fellowship should be using its collective knowledge and wisdom for practical purposes, to do some good in the world, or give lost knowledge back to cultures that have forgotten it. But no, we endlessly gather and transcribe, then lock that knowledge away in our libraries and vaults, where no one outside the Fellowship will ever see it. It's infuriating. We have become an order obsessed with hoarding knowledge, and doing nothing with it."

"Your order definitely seems to like its books."

"Not just books. It loves its artifacts arcane and esoteric too, the stranger and more powerful the better. Those are all locked up down in the vaults, too. *Using* such items is greatly frowned upon, of course."

"What the nobles and knights of my people would give to be let loose down there," murmured Kalista.

"Oh, Camavor's lust for artifacts of power is well-known. It's likely the reason the council is taking so long to give you an answer," she mused. "I'm surprised Tyrus brought you here, to be honest. He must have taken quite the shine to you. Stirred up a right hornet's nest, he did. I'm actually rather impressed. Didn't think he had it in him."

"He seems like a good man."

"Suspiciously good, I'd say. Anyone that good has to be hiding something, right?" Jenda'kaya said, but there was a mischievous glint in her eye that made Kalista think she was joking. "But he's still a Seeker. They tend to view everyone outside the isles as children. That's essentially the attitude at the heart of the whole Fellowship, to be fair, so it's not all on the Seekers. It centers us as caretakers, while everyone else is running around and playing with dangerous toys they don't understand. Toys that might destroy them, or one another. Or all of us."

"What?" Kalista laughed. "That's...a little condescending, isn't it?"

"A little more than a little," said Jenda'kaya. "It's what Seekers like Tyrus are doing, gathering up all the magical artifacts they deem too powerful to be left out there unattended. They bring them here and lock them up, where they can do no harm. Me, I'd rather innovate and discover something new. But that is not the Fellowship's way. The Fellowship is obsessed with cataloging and gathering knowledge. But not furthering it."

"And is this whole building part of your group and its innovations?" she asked.

"I wish that it were! No, this building houses the Schools of Geo-Thaumaturgical Sciences, of which the Sentinels are just a tiny, now mostly overlooked part. We have a small, out-of-the-way wing of the lower subfloor to call our own, and sometimes I'm sure we only have that because they've forgotten about us."

The artificer led her down a series of grand marble staircases to the lower levels. There were noticeably fewer people down here, and the space felt like little more than storerooms.

"When the Fellowship was founded," Jenda'kaya continued, "the Sentinels were one of the most important chapters, proud and prestigious. Now we are regarded as largely irrelevant. So much so that it currently consists of me and four assistants." She laughed. "Most of Helia's masters would prefer to see the Sentinels shut down for good and our funding redirected elsewhere. But most of Helia's masters are idiots."

They arrived outside a door bearing an emblem that Kalista presumed belonged to the artificer's group, the Sentinels: a staring eye upon an open book. Anywhere else, it would have been a grand door, though among all the lavishness of Helia, it looked rather forgotten and insignificant.

"Here we go," the artificer said, throwing open the door with a flourish. "Welcome to my workshop!"

Kalista stared in open-mouthed awe. It was a bizarre combination of a blacksmith's forge, an alchemist's laboratory, and an armory. And whereas everywhere else in the city had been almost painfully structured, neat, and ordered, this room was utterly chaotic. A dormant furnace dominated one corner, replete with anvils, barrels, and an assortment of well-used blacksmith's tools, while elsewhere shelves overflowed with exotic, arcane apparatus, the purpose of which Kalista could only guess, along with curious vials and bottles of glowing liquids and crystals. Books, scrolls, and open volumes with drawings and notes scrawled on their pages were stacked upon bookcases, tables, and racks upon racks of weapons of every description.

A pair of robed acolytes looked up as Kalista and Jenda'kaya entered. One, a wide-shouldered man in a heavy leather apron and with burn scars across his forearms, gave them a curt nod and returned his attention to the devices he was assembling upon his workbench. The other, a slender, bookish young woman with a shaved head, gave them a smile.

"Evening, boss!" she said brightly, in flawless Camavoran. It shocked Kalista that so many people here spoke her native tongue.

"My lovely assistants, Piotr and Aayilah, working late as usual," said Jenda'kaya. "Go home! Be free! There's more to life than study and research, you know!"

"She says this, but I've caught her sleeping here more times than I can count," said Aayilah, speaking in mock-conspiratorial tones to Kalista.

"There's a saying among my birth tribe of a cooking pot and a kettle," rumbled Piotr, without looking up from his work, "but I do not know if it translates."

"The notion carries well enough," said Kalista with a grin.

"Oh shush, don't encourage them!" cried Jenda'kaya.

"You going to test the new one?" asked Aayilah.

"That's the plan."

Kalista found her gaze drifting to the wide assortment of weapons on display. There were swords and axes, polearms and crossbows, daggers, mauls, staves, and slings. There were more than a few that she could not even put a name to. It was an *armory.*

"There must be more weapons here than in the rest of Helia put together," Kalista murmured.

"Probably!" said Jenda'kaya. "Weapons are not something that my peers are very interested in, sadly. Here, let me show you something."

She handed Kalista a length of pale stone, carved into the form of a rhomboid, its ends angled sharply. It was about the length of her forearm, and geometric lines were carved into its sides. The edges were rounded and smooth, and she instantly had the impression this stone was old. *Very* old.

"This is what the first Sentinels used to defend Helia," Jenda'kaya said.

"They protected the isles with *stones*?"

Jenda'kaya snorted. "It does sound a little ridiculous when you put it like that, but these are *relic* stones. Ancient fragments created long before mortals walked this world." Her voice had taken on a solemn, almost reverential tone. "They're infused with spirit magic but are incredibly stable, as well as powerful. Oh, and also unfathomably rare."

"How do they function as weapons?" asked Kalista in confusion, still turning the strange stone over in her hands.

"These days, they generally don't. As I'm sure you are aware, being Camavoran, most magical artifacts do one thing, usually very well. They're tools, made for a specific purpose—heal someone, shoot bolts of lightning, protect you from harm. What makes relic stones different is that their utility is practically limitless. They're conduits, see. Essentially, they siphon magical energy from the spirit realm and store it in a stable form. That energy can then be used for a variety of purposes. You've seen them used to navigate through the Hallowed Mist, for instance. They also work as keys to some of Helia's most important vaults, and for myriad other mundane uses. They even provide the power source for Helia's lighthouses!"

Kalista frowned. "I'm sorry, you are losing me. You say the magic comes from the spirit realm. Do you mean the Halls of the Ancestors? Where we go when we leave this world?"

"There are many different names for it, but yes, they are essentially one and the same. Ours is the realm of the physical, while the spirit realm—which you call the Halls of the Ancestors—is formless, a place of the spirit and the soul. It is separated from our world by an intangible barrier, a veil, but it is all around us. The two realms overlap. And there is power in that other realm for those able to draw from it. That is the source of much of this world's magic, though it is often wild, and difficult to control. But not when it is stored in relic stones."

Kalista nodded. "I see."

As she spoke, Jenda'kaya was flipping through the pages of a heavy illuminated manuscript. She stopped on one page and turned the book around for Kalista to see. She drew her attention to one particular image showing a stylized depiction of a robed figure standing upon a rocky foreshore, holding forth a relic stone. A beam of light was projecting from it, burning up a ship filled with raiders waving axes and shields.

"The original Sentinels were said to be great warrior-mages," Jenda'kaya continued, "able to unleash the power in the stones in devastating fashion. But since mages are rare, even here on the Blessed Isles, I wanted to find a way that *anyone* could learn how to use these stones to defend Helia if necessary. After years of experimentation, we have finally done it."

Jenda'kaya withdrew the tome and headed for a weapon rack. After a moment, Kalista dragged her gaze away from the stone in her hands to find the artificer holding out a weapon unlike anything she had seen before. A rectangular relic stone was at its heart, bound in bands of gold forming geometric shapes. A handle had been fashioned at one end, like the pistol grip of a hand crossbow.

Kalista gave her the rhomboid stone in exchange for the weapon, admiring the exquisite craftsmanship. The metal-work appeared new, but this stone was just as worn and ancient as the other one.

Brow furrowed, she turned the weapon over a few times, studying it closely. Its primary purpose seemed to be as a ranged weapon, but it had no arms, like a crossbow would have, and there was nowhere for a bolt or arrow to slot. Nor did it have a trigger.

"How does it work?" she eventually asked.

"I'll show you," said Jenda'kaya, smiling.

The artificer led her into a different room, which was long and expansive, and largely empty. Aayilah followed.

"This should be fun," Jenda'kaya said.

The walls of this room, particularly the far one, were pitted and blackened in places. Splinters of stone were scattered across the floor. Numerous targets were set up at different marked intervals.

"Let's set you up over here," said Jenda'kaya.

She trotted over to a spot some twenty yards from where a battered iron breastplate hung from a wooden stand, while Aayilah leaned against a wall, folding her arms to watch. Kalista, still carrying the strange weapon, followed.

"Clasp it in your hand, yes, just like that, and use your other hand to support it here." Jenda'kaya adjusted Kalista's grip. "Now straighten this arm and look down the length of the stone, sighting on your target."

The artificer talked her through a dozen other small adjustments, altering her stance, getting her to relax her shoulders and bend her legs slightly. Kalista followed the instructions, still confused. "But there's no trigger," she said.

"It doesn't need one."

"So how does it work?"

"You have to *will* it to," Jenda'kaya said with a wicked grin.

Kalista frowned. "I don't understand."

"Focus on the target. Then ask the weapon to strike it."

Keeping the weapon locked on the iron breastplate, Kalista turned her head to look at the artificer. "You're making fun of me," she said.

"I'm not! I promise! Just give it a try!"

Kalista looked over at Jenda'kaya's assistant to see if this was some prank or ruse. The young woman gave her an encouraging nod. "It takes time to get it working, but it does work," she said.

Feeling foolish, Kalista looked down the length of the weapon toward the target. "Shoot!" she barked. Nothing happened.

Jenda'kaya laughed, but it was good-humored, not mocking. "You don't need to say it out loud," she said. "Try again!"

Kalista narrowed her eyes. She *willed* it to work... and still, nothing happened.

"Let me show you," said the artificer. She took the weapon and leveled it at the target. There was a sudden burst of light, like a lightning strike, and a hot, white beam shot forth from the stone tip, leaving geometric shapes in its wake. It slammed into the breastplate, lifting it and its stand off the ground. They clattered to the floor a dozen yards back, as if they had been kicked by an enraged warhorse. Kalista's eyes were wide with shock, and Jenda'kaya winked.

Kalista walked over to the smoking target and knelt by it. A hole she could fit her thumb in had been melted through the iron breastplate, and the metal was still warm to the touch.

"It was decided centuries ago that the Hallowed Mist provided enough protection to render the original Sentinels redundant, and thus the relic stones were turned to other uses," said Jenda'kaya, walking over to join Kalista. "I think that was shortsighted, and arrogant."

"A city could have the highest wall in the known world," remarked Kalista, "but it would still be worthwhile having some swords—and those who know how to wield them—at the ready. Just in case."

"Just in case," agreed Jenda'kaya.

Kalista stared at the potent weapon in the artificer's hands. The relic stone at its heart was glowing, most noticeably toward the end that the beam had shot from, though it faded after a few moments.

"It's pretty fun, right?" said Jenda'kaya.

"Let me try again," said Kalista.

Ryze followed Grael through the streets toward the Great Library without speaking. He kept casting sideways glances at the warden, wary of the rage simmering within him. In silence, they descended into the vaults.

All the while, Ryze sensed he was being followed by a presence in the dark. He stayed close to the warden and his flickering lantern, peering up every shadowed corridor and frequently checking behind him.

Finally they arrived at what Ryze presumed was Grael's cell. It was a horrid place. The walls were close, the roof low, and a bone-numbing chill hung in the air. It felt like somewhere you'd lock someone away if you wanted to forget they existed, a hateful oubliette. The contrast to Tyrus's lavish suite was painfully stark. *No wonder he has so much hate in him.*

Nevertheless, Ryze had no desire to linger any longer than necessary. He intended to get what he was owed, then get out of here, and if he never saw Erlok Grael again, he would not be upset.

He peered around, soaking in all the details: the hard pallet and its threadbare blanket, the chains and hooks and keys hung upon the walls, the tidy stacks of tomes upon rickety shelves, the line of lanterns by the door. A simple wooden desk occupied one corner, and books, sheaves of papers, inkpots, quills, and a rack of small bottles were neatly arranged upon a ledge behind it. He eyed the reddish-brown stains on the floor and the black mold creeping up the walls with unease. Everything about the room had an air of menace.

He jumped as Grael slammed the cell door and slid the bolts into place.

"What is it you wanted to show me?" Ryze said.

Grael waved one long, bony finger. "Something *most* interesting. Give me your hand."

"What?"

"Give me your hand!"

Gingerly, Ryze did as he was bid. Grael grabbed hold of his wrist and yanked him closer. In the same movement, the warden produced a knife and slashed it across Ryze's open palm before he could pull away.

Ryze cried out in shock and pain and tore himself free. The cut was deep, and blood was already dripping to the floor. Purple runes blazed within his skin, hot and dangerous, but the warden merely grinned.

"You're insane," Ryze hissed.

"Calm down," said Grael, setting down his knife. "Now come closer and give me your injured hand. This is where it gets interesting."

The warden turned his back, fiddling with a rack of tiny bottles on his desk. *I could strike him down right now, and there'd be nothing he could do about it.* Ryze was tempted... but he didn't. His hand dripping blood, he edged closer.

Grael glanced back at him. "You thought about trying to kill me just then, didn't you?" Ryze didn't answer, and the warden smirked. He had a small glass dropper containing clear liquid in his hand, holding it delicately.

"Is that the water?" Ryze growled. His hand was throbbing painfully.

"It is. Hold out your hand."

Ryze hesitated, and Grael sighed and started to turn away again. "Or don't. It doesn't really matter to me."

"Wait," said Ryze, and Grael turned back, a smug expression on his face. "Do it."

Ryze gingerly opened his hand. The warden held the dropper over it and let the liquid drip out. Ryze winced and closed his fingers reflexively.

"How long does it take?" he hissed.

"See for yourself," said Grael, handing him a cloth.

Ryze snatched it from him and wiped his hand free of blood. He stared at his palm in astonishment. All evidence of the cut was gone. "Why would they keep this a secret?" he breathed, clenching and unclenching his fist.

"Power," said Grael bitterly. "And control. The masters care only for themselves."

"There's got to be more to it than that. Suffering and disease could be ended, grievous injuries healed." Ryze frowned and lowered his voice. "This is what the princess is looking for."

"Princess? Whom do you speak of?"

"A Camavoran princess is the guest of my master," said Ryze. "She seeks a cure for her dying queen."

The warden blinked, digesting this information, and Ryze suddenly wished he had not spoken of Kalista at all.

"Curing ailments is far from the most interesting thing the water can do," said Grael, after a moment.

"What do you mean?"

"It was your glimpse of that dark shadow that got me thinking."

Ryze swallowed, not liking where this conversation was going. "I don't think that is something you should mess around with."

Grael made a dismissive sound and pulled open another drawer. He took out a dead rat, holding it up by its tail, and slapped it down on his desk with a wet thud. "I misjudged you at first, but we are similar, you and I. Both of us have been deceived. Both of us have had our true value overlooked."

Ryze couldn't take his eyes off the dead animal. Its paws

were curled upward, and its tiny pink tongue lolled out the side of its mouth.

"I can help you. I can give you everything that smug, insufferable master of yours has denied you. We can help each other," Grael said. "Now, watch closely."

He dripped water from the dropper onto the dead rat. Ryze drew closer, morbidly fascinated. At first nothing happened, but then there was a slight movement. It wasn't from the rat itself, though. Or rather, it wasn't from the rat's *body*. A shadow quivered around the vermin's corpse, followed by a flicker of green-blue light. Ryze's eyes widened in horror.

Grael leered. "Curious, is it not?"

Curious was not the word Ryze would have used. A shadowy version of the rat, as insubstantial as smoke and rimmed with balefire, tore free of the dead flesh. The spirit lifted its head, mouth working in a soundless scream, and twitched, seemingly in agony.

Ryze lurched backward. The ghostly rat gave a final, silent screech, jerking its head around spasmodically, then settled back into its corpse, and was gone.

"It seems to wear off quickly," said Grael. "But then I am only using a few drops."

Ryze backed up to the door, shaking his head. "I don't want any part of this," he said hoarsely.

Grael grinned, his smile reaching from ear to ear. It was the smile of a predator. "Too late for that, my young apprentice."

"I did what you wanted," said Ryze.

"The vaults are vast, and I can access all of them. Continue to help me, and you can have whatever you want."

"I just want what you promised."

"Don't be a fool. You said yourself the Waters of Life should not be a secret. Sickness and disease could be eradicated! Death itself could be overcome! Together, we could expose the masters' deception and hold them accountable!"

Ryze stared at him. Even now, Grael's eyes looked dead and cold. *He's lying.* The warden didn't want to make things better for anyone. He only wanted to take for himself what he felt he'd been wrongly denied, and to make all those who had ever crossed him suffer. *This* was where a lifetime of bitterness and nurtured, festering hatred led.

"We had a deal," Ryze said. "Give me what I was promised. You can do what you want, but I'll play no further part."

Grael scowled at him, then stalked across the room. He dragged his bookcase aside in one violent motion, sending dozens of books tumbling to the floor, then removed a section of the wall, revealing a hidden compartment. He pulled forth a leather-bound tome and tossed it to Ryze. "I am not like the others," the warden said. "*I* do not go back on my word."

Keeping an eye on Grael and clutching the tome under his arm, Ryze threw open the bolts to the door, one by one.

Grael licked his lips. "You are making a mistake."

"The only mistake I made was agreeing to any of this." Ryze threw the last bolt and swung the door wide.

"I can destroy you," the warden hissed.

"We can destroy each other," returned Ryze, snatching up one of the lanterns by the doorframe. "So we'll both remain silent."

He stepped out into the dark corridor. He was fairly confident he remembered the way back to the surface. Glancing back, he saw Grael staring hatefully at him.

"And for the record, we are *nothing* alike, you and I," Ryze said, as a parting shot. "They were right to send you down here to rot. It's where you belong."

Chapter Twenty

Breathing hard, Ryze dashed across the moonlit courtyard. He was thankful to be out of the cloying darkness of the vaults, but he was certain a presence had followed him. He felt it creeping behind him, getting closer and closer, but every time he looked, there was nothing there. Nevertheless, he sensed it getting nearer, and panic clutched at him.

He paused at the corner of the grand building dedicated to the Schools of Geo-Thaumaturgical Sciences, glancing back the way he'd come. The courtyard had a perfectly manicured lawn in it, crossed by five intersecting cobblestone paths. Archways leading into various faculty buildings enclosed the open area, darkness lurking beneath them. Ryze's eyes darted between the shadows, searching. He saw nothing untoward and forced his breathing to steady. He must be imagining it. Whatever that spirit had been down in the Well of Ages, it had remained there.

He turned to leave but pulled up short.

The restless shadow stood before him, blocking his path. It was the same as before, its shape robed and translucent, its features blank. It lifted a hand, limned by ghostly blue-green light, and pointed at him, condemning him. Then it stepped toward him.

Ryze staggered backward and ran.

Kalista and Jenda'kaya walked the darkened corridors side by side. She hadn't realized it had gotten so late, and she assured Jenda'kaya she did not need an escort back to her suite, but the artificer had insisted.

"I work late anyway," she had said. "A brisk walk before returning to my workshop will do me good."

They made their way through the silent halls and stepped outside. Kalista nodded to the guard on duty at the entrance and collected her spear from her. The city was quiet, with none of the raucous shouts and laughter that could be heard echoing across the rooftops of Alovédra at any hour of the night.

"If the council is still keeping you waiting, tomorrow I could show you some of the *other* relic weapons I have been working on," Jenda'kaya offered, as they continued through the shadowed streets.

"I would like that," said Kalista. "I still find it hard to believe you're the only one making these weapons. I would think the masters would be very interested in them."

"That's because you're Camavoran, and a soldier," said Jenda'kaya. "The masters don't see any purpose in my studies. They question why we need them when we have the Hallowed Mist."

"It is a most effective barrier," admitted Kalista. "But what happens if someone *does* get through it?"

"My point exactly. But it hasn't happened in all the centuries since the mist wall was raised, so they don't consider it a possibility."

"That seems foolish."

"I agree. But the military force needed to protect these isles is considered prohibitively expensive. Oh, the Fellowship has the funds, but no one would ever agree to spend them like that. We'd need ships, walls, fortresses, and lots of soldiers. It'd never happen. But my relic weapons could be the answer. A way that we could protect the isles *without* needing to fund an entire army. The Sentinels protected these isles once. We could do so again. I even have designs to create larger-scale weapons that could be mounted in towers overlooking the city, or aboard ships, or..." She gave a sigh. "But all that would require far more resources than I have at my disposal. And the masters would never allow it. They don't see the point, and..." Her voice trailed off as a figure came careening around a corner.

Kalista had her spear readied before she recognized him. "Ryze?" she said, lowering her weapon. Gone were all his bravado and swagger. He looked terrified.

"Run!" he yelped, sprinting toward them. "It's coming!"

"What's coming?" asked Kalista.

Ryze glanced back over his shoulder as he ran. "That!"

A shadow stepped around the corner behind Ryze, and Kalista lifted her spear once again. "Ancestors above," she breathed, as she realized she could see *through* it. It had the outline of a robed man, but its face was blank, and it strode forward with implacable determination. With every movement, eerie witchfire flickered, lighting the unnatural being from within.

Without hesitation, Kalista hurled her spear at the apparition. Her weapon struck the creature where its throat should have been, but then passed through it with a crackle of ethereal light and clattered against the wall. On the insubstantial being came, striding toward Kalista, who stared at it in numb shock.

"Let's go!" urged Ryze, tugging at her. "Move!"

A searing blast of light struck the revenant in its chest, ripping through its shadowy form. It reeled backward, arms and legs flailing. Half of its torso came apart, dissipating like smoke. As the blazing white light hit, the spirit's blank visage became that of an aged man, twisted in pain and surprise. It lasted only an instant, and was gone.

Nevertheless, the revenant was not destroyed. It moved swifter now, with invigorated purpose, even with the gaping, ragged hole through its chest. Artificer Jenda'kaya shot it again with a beam of light from her relic weapon, this time in the head.

For a split second Kalista saw that aged face again, wearing an expression that might have been relief. Then the shadowy apparition was blasted apart, its entire form collapsing into vapor that dissipated into nothingness.

Kalista looked at Jenda'kaya. The artificer was staring down at the glowing relic weapon in her hands, as surprised as everyone else.

"Huh," she said.

As the first rays of dawn banished the darkness, Kalista sat with Ryze and Jenda'kaya around the table in her suite, trying to understand what they had witnessed.

"So you really have no idea where it came from? Or why it was following you?" asked Kalista.

Ryze sighed and rubbed his eyes. "I do not know, my lady," he said. He was far more respectful now, she noted. The apprentice pushed himself to his feet, clutching a heavy leather tome. "I'm just thankful that I ran into you both. That weapon really did the trick."

They all looked at the relic weapon, lying on the table before them. The glow of its stone had long faded.

"I'm going to get some sleep before Tyrus wakes me for morning lessons." With a nod, he left, closing the suite door gently behind him.

Kalista rubbed her tired eyes. She could do with some sleep herself. "He knows more than he is letting on," she said.

"Oh, definitely," agreed the artificer. "And what was with that book? He was most elusive about it, and clutched it to him like a baby with its blanket."

"And you've never heard of anything like this happening before?"

"Spirits of the dead roaming the streets of Helia? Before last night, I would have laughed at the mere suggestion. No, this was a first, as far as I know. But who is to say if it could happen again?"

Before they could ponder, there was a rapping upon Kalista's door. A pair of custodians stood outside, and without a word, they handed her a note. She read swiftly.

"Finally!" she said.

"Good news?" asked Jenda'kaya.

"That is yet to be seen, but the council is ready to declare its decision."

"Moment of truth," said Jenda'kaya. "Good luck."

Kalista blinked as the council's decision sank in.

"You are refusing to save a dying woman?" she said, in a low, furious voice.

The seventeen masters stared down at her from the shadows of the cavernous audience chamber within the Scintillant Tower, impassive and unmoved. One spoke at last. "The so-called Waters of Life *do not exist.* We are sorry that you have been misled to believe otherwise."

"And it took this long to decide to tell me that?"

Another of the faceless masters answered. "That time was

necessary to determine if we felt we could be of any assistance to the queen of Camavor. Our decision is that we cannot. Had you brought the queen here, perhaps there might have been something that could be done, but we will never know."

Kalista's expression hardened. "How could I have brought the queen here?" she said through clenched teeth. "You have cut yourselves off from the world, content in your bubble of privilege."

"Well, *you* found your way here," yet another master remarked.

Kalista turned her gaze toward the speaker and took some meager pleasure that he looked hastily away. She scowled at the gathered masters. "You should all be ashamed of yourselves," she declared, which elicited a barrage of hisses and raised voices.

The din quieted as Elder Bartek lifted his hand. When he spoke, it was with a tone of finality. "The custodians will accompany you to your suite, and any aid you may require in preparing to leave will be given. Then you will be escorted to the docks, where a ship is waiting to take you through the Hallowed Mist. Contact has been made with your own vessel beyond, and it is expecting you forthwith. Your time in Helia has come to an end. You will not return. Our thoughts and hopes go with you for the swift recovery of your queen."

Kalista gave the council one final, dismissive glare, then turned and strode from the chamber.

Kalista marched toward the waiting ship, head held high, the long plume of her helmet streaming behind her. Four armored custodians accompanied her, two in front, two behind.

It hadn't taken her long to gather her belongings. Her gear was already packed and ready, along with her spear and short sword.

As she neared the curiously arcing docks, she heard a shout behind her. "Kalista!"

Glancing back, she saw Jenda'kaya running down the street toward her, waving her arms.

Kalista halted, forcing her armed escort to halt with her. She smiled as the artificer darted around the custodians and threw her arms around her. Kalista stood stiffly in the embrace, unused to such displays, and patted Jenda'kaya awkwardly on the back.

"I told you," said Jenda'kaya, finally releasing her. "Pompous asses. I'm sorry things turned out this way."

One of the custodians said something Kalista couldn't understand, and Jenda'kaya turned on him.

"Back off!" she snapped. "She will take as long as she wants!"

Kalista smiled. "I have known you only a short while, but I am privileged to name you a friend. I only wish I were able to know you for longer."

"The council's decree or no, I feel that we will meet again."

"If you ever get tired of this place, come to Alovédra. Your talents would be well regarded in Camavor."

"Maybe I will," said Jenda'kaya, with a pixie grin.

"Farewell, my friend."

Kalista was escorted to the same ship that had borne her to Helia, the *Aureate Savant*, and it seemed fitting that Tyrus himself was waiting for her on the deck.

For his part, the adept looked tired and disappointed. "I am so sorry, Lady Kalista," he said, surprising her by falling to one knee and bowing his head. "I truly believed bringing you here was the right course of action, and that the help you needed would be forthcoming. I would never have offered otherwise."

Kalista drew Tyrus back to his feet. "You have nothing to apologize for. I do not blame you for the council's decision. You brought me here in good faith, and I am grateful for that."

"You are gracious," said Tyrus.

"The masters of Helia are a secretive and suspicious coterie. They cannot cut themselves off from the rest of the world forever."

"I wish they had done more, but there is good reason for them to be wary of outsiders," said Tyrus. "Still, I am sorry that this all came to naught."

"You are a good man, Tyrus," said Kalista. "Perhaps we will meet again someday."

He smiled. "That would please me."

"Is your apprentice not joining us?" she asked, scanning the deck.

"He's running late, as usual. But he'll be here." Tyrus cleared his throat. "But before we set sail, there is someone who wishes to speak to you privately. He is waiting belowdecks."

Kalista frowned. "Who is it?"

Tyrus grimaced. "Someone I studied with, long ago. A Warden of Thresholds. A strange fellow, one I feel a certain pity for. He begged to be allowed to speak with you, and in truth, I feel somewhat obligated to indulge him. But I will ensure he doesn't hold you up for long."

"Why does he want to speak to me?"

"It seems he has some academic interest in Camavor." Tyrus looked abashed. "I would take it as a personal favor if you humored him. It would ease my conscience."

"Belowdecks?"

"Yes. He is waiting."

Still a little confused, Kalista made her way below. It took a moment for her eyes to adjust to the gloom. When they did, she saw a tall, gaunt figure dressed in gray robes waiting for her. He had chains around his waist and crossing his chest, and a vast assortment of keys hung from a number of large iron rings. He smiled, but it was not warm.

"Who are you?" she said, approaching cautiously.

"I am Erlok Grael, Warden-Prefect of Thresholds."

"A Thresher," said Kalista. "That's what they call you, isn't it?"

"Some call us that, yes." Grael's smile tightened. "I heard about your ill treatment by the masters. They are fools. And they lied to you."

From within his robe, the warden produced a small vial of liquid, perfectly clear.

"The Waters of Life *are* real," he said, handing it to Kalista. "I am sure the physicians and mages of Camavor will be able to verify the truth of that."

Kalista took the water, looking at it in awe.

"That is all I was able to bring you," said Grael. "Alas, it is unlikely to be enough to save your good queen. But I would like very much for your king to know that he has a friend and ally here in Helia. A friend and ally who will help him get all the water he needs."

Kalista gazed at the warden. His expression was unnerving. "How would that be possible?"

Grael brought forth something else from his robe: a small, circular stone, carved with intersecting lines. It was a waystone, just like the one Tyrus had used to part the mist.

"By that look, I take it you know what this is," he said.

"I do," said Kalista, instantly suspicious. "And from what I understand of Helia, this is not something a warden would normally have in their possession."

"We wardens are the true custodians of the isles. We hold the keys to all their secrets."

"Why would you give this to me?"

"Because I want to help."

Kalista didn't believe him. "What's in it for you?"

Grael's smile broadened. "I have no love for the council," he said, "but would be amenable to the patronage of the king of Camavor."

"And how do you imagine this will work?"

"Bring your dying queen here. Use the stone to find your way through the mist. The council will not be able to refuse your king, not when he arrives on their doorstep. And once the queen is cured, I want to leave with him. Yes, a position and title within the court of Camavor. That's the reward that I want."

Kalista reached out to take the waystone, but Grael pulled it away from her. She scowled. With a smirk, the warden tossed it to her, as if it meant little to him.

"Do not speak of this to Tyrus, or his apprentice," he said as he stalked past her to leave. "This will be our little secret. And I look forward to seeing you again soon." Chains clinking, the warden climbed the steps back onto the deck.

Moments later, she heard the shouts of sailors as they cast off their lines, and the ship set sail.

Kalista looked down at the vial of water and the waystone in her hands. This was what she had been searching for all this time, and yet a knot of uncertainty tightened within her. To go down this route was a betrayal of Tyrus, a man who had been nothing but kind to her. Going behind his back was deeply dishonorable, and not something she was at all comfortable even considering. But on the other hand, the queen's life was at stake. *How can I not take advantage of what might be Isolde's only chance?*

It was then that Tyrus came down to check on her. She swiftly pocketed the vial and the waystone, concealing them from his view.

"Is all well, my lady?"

"Everything is fine," she assured him.

Kalista stood on the deck of the *Daggerhawk*, watching as Tyrus and the *Aureate Savant* slipped back into the mist. It was like a veil came down. One moment the ship was there; then it was gone.

"Did you get what you came for, princess?" said Captain Vennix.

Kalista didn't answer immediately. She continued to stare into the impenetrable mist long after the ship had disappeared. She thought of the unsavory warden, and the things he had given her.

"Maybe," she said, finally.

"So where to next?"

"Home," Kalista said. "It's time to return to Camavor."

Part Three

A fool with power is a dangerous thing. And we live in a world overflowing with fools and power.

—Extract from "The Helian Primer of Light"

From the journal of Queen Isolde

I have but a few moments. I can only write when Viego leaves my side.

The Kindred of Death are near. I sense them, lurking on the periphery, waiting to claim me. I feel movement nearby where there should be none. Perhaps I am merely delusional with fever, but I swear I've heard the impatient padding of the Wolf circling my bed as I drift in and out of slumber. And once, I am sure of it, I saw a pale luminous form crouched on my windowsill—the Lamb, with her wolf's-head mask obscuring her ovine face.

And yet, while I want to live—oh, do I want to live!—I hold no fear of death. Why would I, for is it not said there is no pain or fear in the Beyond? There I will be reunited with the powerful women in my family I have heard so much about but never met in life—the aunts and great aunts who ruled our family as its protective and notoriously fierce matriarchs. It comforts me to know that when my own time comes, I will be one with them in the light.

So no, I do not fear what is to come for me... but I do fear for those I leave behind.

How fragile are the hopes and dreams of mortals! How delicately balanced are the paths of the future, so easily disrupted by chance and ill fortune. And how prideful of us to believe we can shape them to our liking. Such hubris!

To think that I, a simple peasant girl—no more than a seamstress—could aspire to change a kingdom! Oh how the Fates must have laughed, for I truly believed my union with Viego would usher in a new age for Camavor, one that would see an end to the greed-fueled slaughter and conquest it was built upon. And we are so close! But do I think he will continue down that noble road when I am gone? No, I fear not. He is too easily swayed by the machinations of those around him, too easily controlled by his own petty whims and impulses without my counsel. Ah, there it is again, my pride! But in truth, changing the direction of Camavor was always my dream, not his.

There is a gentleness in his heart, it is true—that was the part of him that I fell in love with—but I see less and less of that in him as time goes by. He has been too damaged by the venomous blend of cruelty, indifference, and privilege of his upbringing. It seems at times a war wages within him: On one side is an arrogant, entitled boy, angry that anything could exist in the world that he cannot own and control; on the other, a self-doubting, fearful young man, desperately seeking the love, respect, and approval of those who will never give it. I thought our love would help steer him out of that darkness. But it seems the Fates had other ideas.

Even before that fateful blade cut me, he was starting to look at me differently. I began to feel less like his partner and more like a prize. It seemed at times I represented something almost divine in nature to him, some ideal that no reality could ever live up to. He doted on me, lavished me with gifts and platitudes, swore he could never live without me—as he does now, even as I near the end—and told me I was perfect, but his eyes glossed over and his smile became fixed when I said things that did not align with his vision of who he wanted me to be.

He refuses to accept that I am slipping away, and I have seen how poorly he reacts when denied what he wants. I have a desperate, terrible fear of what will happen once I am gone. I worry that his rage and grief will lead Camavor down a far darker, more blood-soaked path than it already treads.

It is hard not to succumb to despair. What can I do? How can this be averted? All my hope now resides in dear Kalista. She is as wise as she is strong, as good-hearted as she is fierce. Viego would never admit it—to her least of all—but he yearns to prove himself worthy in her eyes. He often tells me stories of his childhood, and it was always Kalista who comforted him when he was hurt, or when he had a nightmare. Who else was there? His mother died giving birth to him, and his father neglected him right up until the end. Kalista was the only one who ever cared. It was she who gave him guidance and advice when he needed it, and the swift rebuke when he acted poorly. It is a shame she spent so much of his youth away on campaign—I cannot help but wonder if he would have been a better man had he spent more time with her, but that thought gains us nothing. One thing I know for certain: When I am no longer here, Kalista will be the only one who can guide him truly.

I am so tired, I can barely hold this quill steady. My eyes are as heavy as my heart. I feel the hot breath of the Wolf on my neck. It draws close. A part of me longs to give in, to allow it to take me, to move beyond pain and fear. But no. I must hold on as long as I am able. I owe it to all who will suffer Viego's wrath should he succumb to the madness I fear may claim him when I pass.

I must sleep.

Chapter Twenty-One

Alovédra, Camavor

"No black flags of mourning, no tolling bells," murmured Captain Vennix. "That's a good sign."

Kalista pocketed Isolde's journal and nodded. It *was* a good sign, and as the *Daggerhawk* slid toward the docks of Alovédra, Kalista's hope flared, though it did not dispel her anxiety. The queen had been on the verge of joining the Ancestors when she had left. It seemed only a miracle would have ensured that she still lived, and yet had she passed on, black flags would wave on the wind above the palace for a year and a day from her death.

It had been the height of summer when Kalista had first set out on her journey. Now the days were considerably shorter, yet from the sea, it looked as if little had changed in Alovédra in the time she'd been away.

That impression shifted dramatically once she stepped ashore.

There had always been beggars, drunks, and the destitute on the streets, but never in such large numbers as she saw now. There were entire encampments near the docks, with filthy blankets, rotten sails, and scraps of wood strung up and leaning against the buildings as meager protection from the elements. Dirty children ran about, hassling passersby for coin or food, and dead-eyed men and women stared out from beneath their wretched shanties. Most of the shops that she passed were closed, their doors and windows boarded up. The seedy dock taverns and bawdy houses seemed to be the only places that were still running in this district. Drunks, unconscious from the night before, were strewn across the roadway, forcing Kalista to step over them as she progressed toward the palace.

There was a heavy military presence in the city. The street leading from the docks was barricaded, carts and barrels forming a makeshift checkpoint. That checkpoint was guarded by her own soldiers of the Host, though it seemed as though they were acting under the command of the local watch. They were speaking to anyone trying to get by, and a mass of frustrated people were being held up, as well as a long line of wagons loaded with goods.

Shouts erupted as desperate citizens launched a sudden raid on an overburdened wagon, tossing stoppered urns and sacks of grain to others waiting below. A crate smashed to the road, scattering small boxes of dried figs, beans, and other delicacies, and people swarmed in like locusts, grabbing what they could before turning tail and fleeing into alleys and side streets as the guards charged after them. The swirl of frantic people passed around Kalista like surging water around a stone; they saw her armor and spear and didn't want to get close.

She saw a guard—not one of the Host, thank the Ancestors—beating a scrawny man to the ground. "Enough!" she barked, yanking the guard back by the scruff of his neck, giving the other man time to scramble away.

The guard rounded on her in fury. "How dare—" But he paled as he looked upon her, and he quickly lowered his gaze and backed off, bowing low. "My apologies, Highness."

A path to the blockade was hastily made for her, and her soldiers saluted sharply as she drew near. She recognized a junior sergeant.

"Sergeant Vivas, why is this blockade here?"

"King's orders, General," she replied. "Martial law is in effect."

Kalista frowned deeply. "But the queen, she lives?"

"I believe so, General. Can I provide you an escort to the palace? There has been violence in the streets. It would not be safe to travel without protection."

She accepted the sergeant's offer and was soon marching toward the palace with an entourage of twelve soldiers of the Host. What she saw along the way shocked her.

Virtually every home and business was boarded up, and more than a few had been gutted by fire. Smashed crates and barrels lay strewn across the streets, and packs of citizens, many armed with clubs, billhooks, and blades, roamed among the detritus, though they slunk away when they saw the soldiers coming.

"Has the city come under attack?" asked Kalista.

"No, General. The rioting started within the city. After the granaries were shut."

In grim silence, they marched on. Kalista was aghast to see that an execution platform had been erected outside the gates of the palace, overlooked by the weeping statue of the Revered Ancestor Cesca, Lady of Grief.

What madness is this?

She remembered this square being filled with cheering citizens when Viego walked from the Sanctum of Judgment in triumph, holding aloft the Blade of the King, Sanctity. Now it was an empty ruin, dominated by the black platform. By the look of the stains around the executioner's chopping block, it had seen much use. This was confirmed as she saw the grisly trophies arrayed along the top of the palace gates.

Once safely ensconced within the palace walls, she dismissed her entourage and strode purposefully across the grounds, ignoring the low bows and curtsies that preceded her and the whispers that rippled in her wake. She stormed up the wide steps into the palace proper. There were no guards at the doors to the throne room, so she pushed them open.

The chamber was empty. The gleaming throne stood like a weapon upon the raised dais, and Kalista's expression soured further. A figure moved in the shadows to her left, and she turned, leveling her spear.

"He's not here," said the king's advisor, Nunyo. He didn't seem particularly bothered about Kalista's spear, and she lowered it as he shuffled forward. "He hasn't left the royal wing since you've been gone."

Nunyo had always seemed old to her, but it looked like he had aged a decade in the time she had been away. He appeared tired, and deflated, and his back was even more hunched than usual.

"What's going on, Nunyo? The city is a war zone."

"The king is... distracted."

"But Isolde still lives, yes?"

The advisor sighed and rubbed a hand across his face. "I think you need to see for yourself."

Kalista's progress was barred long before she got to the royal chambers. The whole wing was sealed off, but to her surprise it was not palace guards who blocked her way but knights of the Iron Order.

They were massive figures, clad in heavy plate and gray tabards emblazoned with their iron fist iconography, and they stood with gauntleted hands resting nonchalantly upon the hilts of their blades.

"Stand aside," growled Kalista, staring up at the most senior of the knights.

The man looked down at her. "My orders are that no one passes."

"I am heir to the Argent Throne, granddaughter of the Lion of Camavor, and General of the Host," snarled Kalista. "This palace is my home. *Stand aside.*"

"I take my commands only from Grand Master Hecarim."

Kalista's grip tightened on her spear, but Nunyo stepped forward.

"And do you think your Grand Master will be pleased if you anger his betrothed?" he said, laying a hand on the knight's vambrace. "Let her pass. It is what the king *and* Lord Hecarim would want."

With surly reluctance, the knight stood aside. Kalista stalked by him without another glance.

"Since when does a Knightly Order control the palace? Aren't there laws against such things?" she said to Nunyo.

"There are, and Viego's flouting of them has caused chaos. There is open rebellion and bloodshed on the borders. And you've seen the state of Alovédra itself. It's madness out there."

"Rebellion?"

"The Taskaros region has seceded from the kingdom, declaring itself independent. Polemia is burning. The Knights of the Pale have torn up their oaths and besieged Draken Keep, reigniting blood feuds. I could go on."

"What of the Host?"

"They hold the walls of the capital, in case of attack. I am glad you have returned. Perhaps your presence can help restore sanity. Would that it had been sooner, though. Or if you had never left at all."

"I came back as soon as I could," said Kalista. "I believe I may have found a way for the queen to be saved."

The advisor made no reaction, remaining silent as they

headed toward the royal chambers. The rooms en route were uncharacteristically messy. Rugs were in unruly clumps and trampled with mud, chairs were knocked over, and wax from candles had melted over tables and ledges onto the floor. In one chamber, flies were feasting on the remnants of meals that had been left to rot. The reek of unemptied chamber pots suffused the air, making Kalista gag and cover her nose.

"Viego will allow no servants near him, fearing more assassins," Nunyo commented.

"He's dismissed all the palace's servants?"

"The *lucky* ones were dismissed."

Kalista thought of the heads arrayed outside the palace. "Ancestors above," she swore. "Has he gone completely mad?"

"That is not for me to say," said Nunyo, in a hushed voice. "But it would be wise for you to be wary. He is... unpredictable of late."

"Kalista! You're back!"

The doors to the royal bedchambers slammed wide, and Viego swept out. He was barefoot and wore only tight black trousers and an open black velvet robe, which trailed across the floor behind him. His long hair was disheveled, his skin pallid from lack of sunlight, and deep, dark rings surrounded his eyes, which were lit with intensity. He'd always been lean, but he looked positively gaunt now. Nevertheless, his smile was broad and winning, and he ran to Kalista and wrapped his arms around her.

He felt feverishly hot. "Thank the Ancestors you've returned," he breathed, holding her tight. "There are so few I can trust."

Over Viego's shoulder, she saw the immense figure of Ledros standing sentinel outside the royal chamber. Kalista's heart skipped a beat as she looked into his dark, soulful eyes, and she smiled nervously. He managed a slight smile and a nod in return.

She pulled back from Viego, eyeing him in concern. “Isolde?” she asked.

“Resting. But she holds on. She’s stronger than she seems, and she never gave up hope. Neither of us did.” Viego looked at her expectantly, eyebrows raised. “Well? Did you find the Blessed Isles?”

Kalista gave a nod. “I did,” she said, quietly.

“I knew you would!” cried Viego, raising his hands to the heavens. “I knew you’d save her! Come in, my love must hear of this wondrous news!”

He turned and bounded back through the doors, like an enthusiastic puppy. Neither Ledros nor Nunyo would meet Kalista’s gaze, however.

There is something terribly wrong here.

The stench hit her first. The room was heavy with incense, but even that could not disguise the sickly scent behind it. It was the stink of death.

“Come in, we’ll tell her together!” Viego beckoned to her, and she followed him to the bed, dread clenching tight within her.

Silk curtains obscured Isolde, but Kalista saw her outline, lying in repose.

“My love,” whispered Viego, drawing the silk aside, though she still couldn’t see within. “My love, wake up! I have wonderful news!”

Viego leaned forward and kissed the queen upon the forehead. He glanced at Kalista, shaking his head in wonder.

“She sleeps so soundly!” He turned back to his wife, gently stroking her cheek. “Perhaps we let her rest. We can tell her of your success later.”

Through a gap in the diaphanous curtains, Kalista noticed that Isolde was dressed in traditional Camavoran garb. That struck her as odd; the queen was proud of her heritage, and always preferred the flowing styles of her own land.

Kalista edged closer, easing aside the curtains, and at last looked down upon Isolde.

She was very, very dead.

Chapter Twenty-Two

Kalista stared down at the corpse and gave a despairing moan.

The queen's flesh was ashen and sunken, her lips blue turning to black. If Kalista had to guess, she had died recently, probably within the last week. Anguish and guilt shot through her. It felt like she'd been impaled. Had she arrived only days earlier, perhaps Isolde could have been saved. But there was no doubt that she was dead. Her chest did not rise and fall with her breath. And there was a stillness to her that was not present in even the deepest sleep.

Still, Kalista had to be sure. She reached out and gently put a finger to Isolde's throat.

"Don't wake her," murmured Viego.

Isolde's flesh was cold and unresponsive under her touch. There was no heartbeat.

"Oh, little uncle," Kalista breathed. "She is no longer with us. She's at peace. She's with the Ancestors now. We should draw the blood trident upon her head, that her passage to the Beyond is made smoother."

A myriad of emotions played out on Viego's face. He looked hurt, then confused, but that swiftly gave way to anger. He swatted Kalista's hand away from Isolde, scowling. "Get away from her," he snarled. "Why would you say something so hateful?"

Kalista backed off, raising her hands placatingly. "You're hurting, little uncle. But you need to let her go."

"You're just the same as the others. You're trying to come between us, to take her from me. I won't let you."

"Viego," said Kalista, hurting to see his pain and the toll his grief had taken. She moved closer, reaching out to him.

The cloying air within the bedchamber was suddenly charged, and the immense Blade of the King, Sanctity, materialized in Viego's hand. Kalista froze.

"*You won't take her from me*," he swore.

Nunyo was suddenly at Kalista's side, tugging her back toward the door. She had not even registered him entering the chamber. "You need to rest, my lord king," said the advisor. "It has been a wearying day."

Viego blinked and shook his head, as if he were coming out of a daydream. He looked at his blade in confusion. "Yes," he said finally, releasing his grip on it. The sword disappeared before it could strike the floor. "Yes, Nunyo, you are right. I am tired. I need rest. Ledros, will you watch over me as I sleep?"

"If that is your wish, lord king," said Ledros, from the shadows behind Kalista.

"Please," said Viego. "It would give me comfort."

Kalista placed a hand on Ledros's vambrace, looking up into his gentle, sad eyes. "We must speak, when you can." The big man nodded and placed one massive, gauntleted hand upon hers.

She glanced back at Viego as he sank to his knees alongside Isolde and laid his head on the bed. With a sigh, she allowed herself to be ushered from the room by Nunyo. The doors closed.

They walked back out through the chaotic mess of the royal wing. "When did she pass?" she asked in a low voice.

"It's hard to say, for the king stopped letting *anyone* inside the chamber, even the healers. But it couldn't have been more than a few weeks after you left. There was no way to contact you."

Kalista looked at the advisor in shock. "She's been dead that long? But she looks..."

"Mikael's Chalice," he explained. "It has slowed the decomposition."

"Ancestors," said Kalista. "This is a nightmare."

"It is." Nunyo sighed. "And it gets worse."

She stopped, feeling sick in the stomach. "What else has happened?"

Having dismissed the household guard, Nunyo swung open the heavy iron door to the palace's treasury and stood aside for Kalista.

Holding a burning brand aloft, she stepped within. It was a vast, cavernous space, though the ceilings were low and arched, much like the palace's sepulcher. Kalista had not been down here in years, and it took her a moment to realize the chamber seemed larger because it was mostly empty. When last she'd been here, each room was stacked floor to ceiling with chests and coffers. The wealth of Camavor had seemed endless, accumulated over hundreds of years of conquest, tributes, and taxation.

"He's spent it?" Kalista looked around her, aghast. "*All* of it?"

"Oh, it's worse than that," said Nunyo. "He's spent coin *we don't have.* Camavor is massively in debt. It will take decades to pay it back."

"But how is that even possible?" said Kalista, walking around the empty space.

"He's been throwing gold at any healer, magicker, priest, or alchemist to be found, desperate to find a miracle cure. And once word got out, a steady stream of them have been arriving at the palace gates every day, looking to get a part of that payout."

"Surely that couldn't account for all this," said Kalista, gesturing around her.

"He's sent offerings out to dozens of nations, begging for anything that might save his queen. It feels like every day a new ship or wagon train leaves here, piled high with wealth. Of course, many never reach their destination, taken by raiders, stolen by those sent to guard over them, or simply vanishing without a trace, and so he sends more to replace them. He's traded priceless heirlooms and artifacts that have been in your family for generations, for the empty promises of fakers and charlatans. Your family's legacy, gone in a matter of months."

"Could you not stop him?"

"I have counseled him as best I could," Nunyo said, lowering his head. "I fear if I had pressed harder, my life would be forfeit."

Kalista rubbed her eyes. "And the grain stores, why are they shut? People on the streets are starving."

"Reserved for the Host, city guard, and Knightly Orders, in case the capital is besieged. Oh, and there's also a famine. There's been no rain, and the fields are barren."

"This is a disaster."

"It is, my lady. The future of the kingdom teeters on a knife's edge."

"Where is Lord Hecarim? The Iron Order holds the palace, but I have not seen him. Is he helping maintain the peace in the city?"

"Your husband-to-be left a portion of his order here and marched the rest east, along with the Horns of Ebon and a few lesser orders."

"East?"

"He has sacked Port Takan, and last we heard was moving inland, toward the independent city-state of Alshalaya."

"What?" said Kalista, incredulous. "We need him here! Not off fighting meaningless wars! What is he thinking?"

"Oh, I agree, but he went on the king's command. Viego wants someone to blame. Port Takan was an obvious target. But it won't be his last, I fear."

Kalista sat down heavily on an empty coffer, thoroughly dejected.

She'd always wondered if those living at the tail end of a great civilization saw the cracks before it fell. Did they watch, helpless and full of dread, as it crumbled around them? Or were they oblivious to it, blinded by the minutiae and stresses of daily life? Did some live in denial, desperately trying to convince themselves things would get better? Did others attempt to forestall the inevitable, even if that effort was like trying to bail water from a boat that had already sunk?

Was that Camavor? Was the kingdom now in its death throes?

"I must leave you," said Nunyo. "There is a backlog of petitioners and claimants coming to the palace every day. Viego is in no state to hear them, but ignoring them only inflames the violence. I will hear what complaints and cases I can before sunset, even if there is little I can do. We shall speak after then."

After he was gone, Kalista buried her head in her hands and wept.

Two days after her arrival, Kalista was finally able to speak to Ledros.

She'd barely had time to breathe, spending her hours reading dispatches and reports and questioning Nunyo, trying to understand how the terrible state of things could even begin to be unraveled. Her immediate priorities were feeding the starving populations in the poorer quarters of the city and ending the violence in the streets... but neither problem was going to be solved quickly.

It was late, and she was standing alone atop the crenellated walls of the palace, gazing outward. Distant shouts and the clashing of weapons echoed up from the shrouded city, and fires blazed in several districts. Alovédra was tearing itself apart, and it was breaking her heart.

"General," he said, behind her, and she smiled. She'd missed his voice, at once deep and gentle. He moved surprisingly quietly for a man of his size.

She turned and looked up at him. His gaze was downcast, despite the fact that he was now a ranking noble. That he didn't look her in the eye was like a knife in her chest. She'd thought of him every day she was away, thinking of what she would say to him, but now that he was here in front of her, the words dried up.

"Ledros," she said, finally. "It's... good to see you."

"I am glad you returned safely, General," he rumbled, his posture awkwardly stiff, like he was on inspection.

"Look at me. Please."

He lifted his eyes, slowly, to meet hers, then looked down once more. Even that small glimpse showed the confusion, pain, and stress within him, however.

"Are you well?" she asked.

"I'm fine," he replied, automatically, but there was no conviction in his voice. "And you, General?"

"Fine," she said, turning to stare out across the city again. They stood in silence for long moments, until Kalista sighed and turned back toward him. "This is stupid."

Ledros frowned. "General?"

"This! Us! The way we are both acting! It's ridiculous."

His frown deepened, and he shuffled uncomfortably. She

took one of his giant gloved hands in hers. He went very still, and she closed her other hand over it, clasping tightly.

"You are my dearest friend and comrade," she said. "Perhaps things would be different if I were not of the royal family and sworn to another, but this is the world we live in. This is the way things are, as much as I might wish it otherwise."

Ledros's square features were as unreadable as stone.

Kalista sighed again and released Ledros's hand. In the gardens and courtyards below, she could see knights of the Iron Order joking among themselves, and her expression soured. "How long has the Iron Order controlled the palace?"

"Two days after you left," said Ledros.

"On Viego's order?"

He paused, then nodded.

"There is something you are not telling me," said Kalista. "Come now. You have always been terrible at hiding things from me."

Ledros's shoulders slumped. "It was Viego's order, but I believe the Grand Master took advantage of the king's distraction to get him to sign the writ."

Kalista gazed out to the horizon. "And now Lord Hecarim is sacking the cities of our allies," she said, bitterness tinging her words. "Did he manipulate Viego into that order as well?"

Ledros didn't answer... but that was a clear enough answer in itself.

"Wonderful," Kalista murmured.

"There is something else," Ledros said, somewhat reluctantly. "Something I feel you ought to know."

"What is it?"

"I have heard rumors," said Ledros. "Of how Lord Hecarim became Grand Master of the Iron Order."

Kalista frowned. "And what do these rumors suggest?"

"That he could have saved the previous Grand Master of

his order," said Ledros. "That he could have intervened to protect him. But he chose not to."

She blinked. "Hecarim left him to die?"

"It is what I have heard," rumbled Ledros, looking away, across the water.

"Where did you hear this? Is there any proof?"

Ledros continued to stare out over the battlements, his jaw set. "It is not hard to believe. The man will do anything to gain the power he craves. He is ruthless and has no morals." He turned and looked at her, holding her gaze for the first time since their conversation began. "You cannot marry him, Kal."

"You're telling me what I can and cannot do now?"

"I didn't mean it like that."

"Hecarim is ambitious and headstrong, but a *murderer*?" said Kalista dubiously.

"You are far too trusting!" snapped Ledros, shocking her. He'd never spoken to her like this before. "You see the best in people, but sometimes you are blind to the worst! Some people are just bad. *He* is one of them."

Ledros's chest was heaving, his massive hands were clenched, and his face was flushed red. He seemed to realize how inappropriate his outburst was, and he looked down.

"Is it for *my* benefit you want me to call off this wedding," said Kalista, her tone icy, "or your own?"

Ledros looked up at her, and she saw the anger and hurt in his eyes. "Do not trust him," he growled.

"Jealousy is an unattractive trait, Commander," Kalista said.

Without another word, she turned and walked away.

Kalista woke suddenly, her warrior's instincts firing, knowing that someone was in her room.

She was out of her bed in an instant, a short blade in hand.

Her heart was racing as she searched for the threat, her gaze finally settling on a dark shape sitting in the chair in the corner. "Ledros?"

She'd gone to bed cursing herself for how she'd acted. It would have been a blessing if he had come to her, so that she could set things right. But as the dark figure rose to his feet, she saw that he was not nearly large enough to be Ledros.

The figure stepped forward, and cold moonlight fell upon Viego's pale, narrow face. "I miss her, Kal. It's been so long since I heard her laugh. Since I saw her smile."

Kalista lowered her knife, sheathed it, and tossed it onto a table. She released a long breath, her heart still hammering in her chest like a war drum. "I'm sorry I wasn't here," she said. "I'm sorry I didn't get back in time."

"None of this feels real," said Viego, sitting down on the bed. He looked exhausted, drained and drawn, and his eyes stared blankly at the floor. "I wish she was here to help me."

Kalista sat down gently next to him. "I wish that, too. But I am here. I will help you through this. I promise."

"Everything's going wrong, Kal," he said, turning to look at her. There were tears glistening in his eyes. "I just want things to be like how they were. Before."

"I know, Viego," said Kalista, reaching for him. He leaned his head on her shoulder. "I'm so sorry."

They remained like that, clinging to each other in silent grief, for long minutes. It was Viego who finally broke the silence.

"But things will get better, won't they?" he said, pulling back and wiping at his eyes. "You found the Blessed Isles! She'll be restored, and everything will be like it was! You've saved her!"

"Viego," said Kalista, shaking her head. *For a moment there, he was coming back*. "It won't do any good. She's *gone*. Nothing can bring her back."

He seemed to retreat into himself, his expression hardening. "You pretend to care about my beautiful Isolde, but you don't, do you?" he hissed. "You're just like all the others. You want her gone."

"Ancestors, no. Listen to yourself," said Kalista, rising to her feet. "It's me! We are all the family we have left, you and I. I loved Isolde. She was the sister of my heart. And I love you. I just want to help you through this darkness."

Viego slowly pushed himself to his feet. Shadows fell across his face. "Tell me what you found. Tell me how to get through the mist."

Kalista thought of the waystone the warden had given her, along with the vial of water. Both were in a drawer in her dresser, but she resisted the urge to look in that direction and instead held Viego's gaze.

"I will not," she declared. "No good will come of it."

"Then you are useless to me," he said, turning his back on her. "Guards!"

Four hulking knights of the Iron Order entered the room. They surrounded her, hands resting on the pommels of their blades. They had the visors of their helms lowered, hiding their faces. Kalista hoped that was out of shame for what they were doing.

"Viego, please. Do not do this," she said.

"Take her," said Viego, still with his back turned. "Lock her in a cell."

Gauntleted hands grabbed her and she instinctively tensed, resisting them. Nonetheless, there were four of them and one of her, and she was powerless to stop herself from being dragged from the room. More knights of the Iron Order stood in the hallway.

"Search her room!" Viego shouted, following her out.

She squirmed and strained against her captors, searching desperately for Ledros, but he was nowhere to be seen. Even if he had been there, there was nothing he could have done—nor did he owe her anything, not after the way she had spoken to him.

All the fight drained out of her, and she allowed herself to be hauled away.

Chapter Twenty-Three

Matted black hair hung over Kalista's face, and she was lathered in sweat as she pushed herself through a grueling set of push-ups on the floor of her stinking cell.

She heard the squeal of hinges as the gate down the corridor swung open, as well as the clank of armored footsteps approaching, but she did not look up. Nor did she pause when the footsteps stopped just outside her cell. She assumed it was one of her jailers.

She slowly lowered herself to the floor, breathing in steadily, before explosively pressing back up with a sharp exhalation. Jagged stone dug into her knuckles, but she pushed on. She stopped only once she had counted two hundred repetitions. At last she sank to her knees, and then rose to her feet, facing away from the cell door, making whoever it was wait.

She wore a rough sackcloth gown, and she was filthy. Her hands and feet were blackened with dirt and grime, and her stomach growled like an angry bear. Still breathing heavily from exertion, she brushed her knotted hair from her face and took a sip of dirty water from a chipped ceramic cup, almost gagging on its foulness. Only once she had placed the cup back down did she turn to look upon her visitor.

Hecarim stood on the other side of the bars, a look of pity and anguish on his face. His armor was dented, and his dark gray tabard was torn and covered in road dust. He looked weary. He had a new scar on his face, cutting from the center of his forehead through one eyebrow and onto his cheek. His wavy dark hair was longer, and unwashed, and he sported an unruly beard. Yet even so, he seemed completely out of place in the wretchedness of their surroundings.

"You've been in here for *weeks*? This is insanity," he breathed. "My lady, are you... are you well?"

Kalista held herself tall, trying to maintain some dignity. "I am as you see me, my lord."

"He cannot keep you locked up down here," Hecarim said. "It is madness."

"The whole kingdom has descended into madness," commented Kalista. She tilted her head to one side and looked at Hecarim squarely. "And was your rampage against our allies a success? It seems someone almost took your eye."

Hecarim sighed and looked down. "You think it dishonorable that I led the attack to the east," he said. "I understand."

"Am I wrong?"

Hecarim did not answer. Instead, he dragged a chair over to her cell bars and sank down upon it with a weary grunt. Kalista remained standing, her back straight.

"I wish I had remained here," he said. "Things hadn't deteriorated quite so much before I left. There certainly wasn't open warfare in the streets."

"So why *did* you leave?"

"Viego insisted. But his reasons were not completely flawed. Word spread fast of the assassination attempt, and not striking back against *someone* was making us look weak in the eyes of our enemies *and* our allies. There have been increased raids against our southern borders, and several vassal provinces have collapsed into rebellion. We had to make a show of force."

"But the highlords of Port Takan were our allies. They had

nothing to gain from assassinating Viego!" Kalista snapped, pacing back and forth within her cell. Hecarim raised a warding hand.

"It doesn't matter if they were behind it or not. The king *believed* it was them, and so we had to act. After Siodona told him of his suspicions, there was no reasoning with Viego. My hand was forced."

Kalista ceased pacing and looked down at Hecarim in distaste. "You've always wanted to take Port Takan."

"I have," he admitted. "But not like this. They've been courted by Camavor and our enemies for decades now, and have gotten rich playing both sides. I have long believed they should be brought into the kingdom, and that doing so would strengthen Camavor."

"And fill the purse of the Iron Order," remarked Kalista. "But you didn't just subdue Takan. I understand you struck farther east, leaving the port city burning. The Ancestors alone know what other allies you've waged war upon in the meantime."

"Only those who had already turned away from us. Those with strong ties to Port Takan. I decided to crush them now, rather than have them gather their forces and march on our borders."

It was harsh, and callous, but Kalista could see the cold logic in it. The fortified towns and realms east of Port Takan were all in the pocket of the highlords. With the port city in ruin, they would be likely to sever their ties to Camavor.

"And I am sure you are aware of the financial situation," said Hecarim, lowering his voice. "Viego has drained the kingdom's coffers. Our enemies have grown rich off his foolishness. There is no coin to pay our soldiers. No coin to buy grain to feed our starving people. In crushing Takan and eastern regions, I have given us a small reprieve."

"And where is that wealth? Safe in the Iron Keep?"

"Better there than giving it to Viego to throw away." Hecarim scowled, standing up from his chair. "I have no intention of profiting from this miserable situation. I have already sent for grain shipments, and have ensured that your warriors of the Host have received the wages they are owed. We could not risk them abandoning their posts, not when they are needed most."

"The Host is loyal to the end," Kalista growled. "There are no deserters in their ranks."

"Desperate soldiers do desperate things," said Hecarim, shrugging. "But I did not come here to argue with you."

"Then why have you come?"

"You are my betrothed," Hecarim said, coming close to the bars that separated them. His expression was earnest. "I wanted to see you, to ensure that you were being well treated. I rode here as soon as I received word of your return. When I heard Viego had imprisoned you, I had pictured him locking you in your chambers. I had not imagined that his madness would see him throw you into the dungeon, after all you have done for him. It is intolerable."

"What *have* I done?" said Kalista, sitting down on the low stone shelf that served as her bed. She had tried to hold her despair at bay during these weeks of imprisonment, but it threatened to overwhelm her now. She felt so tired. "I abandoned the kingdom in a time of crisis, and for nothing. I should have been here."

"But you found them?" Hecarim leaned closer. "The Blessed Isles? They're actually real?"

"They're real, but it doesn't matter. It's too late. Isolde should have been entombed in the crypt before I ever set foot in Helia."

"Was it everything the stories say?"

Kalista looked up sharply, eyes narrowed. There was something in Hecarim's voice that made her on edge. A hunger she had not noticed before. "It doesn't matter," she said coldly. "I went to save the queen. I failed."

Hecarim leaned back, his expression full of regret and sadness. Kalista wondered if she had imagined the eagerness she'd sensed in him. She was weak with hunger and had been sleeping only fitfully, muddling her wits.

"You did all you could," said Hecarim. "The king owes you a debt of thanks. He'd be dead if it wasn't for you."

"Do not think too harshly of him," said Kalista. "Isolde was the best thing to happen to him, and her loss clearly broke something in him. But he will recover. He is a good man. He just needs to find his way out of the darkness."

Hecarim smiled. "He's left you down here to rot, and yet you defend him still."

"He is my family. He is all I have."

"You are as compassionate as you are fierce. I understand why the Host is so loyal to you." He turned to leave. "I will speak with the king. On my honor, I will convince him to release you."

Kalista remained deep in thought, her brow furrowed, long after he had left.

Outskirts of Helia, the Blessed Isles

Ryze sat cross-legged in a grassy glade, engrossed in the leather-bound tome in his hands. Dappled sunlight played across the yellowed pages as the breeze made the trees sway gently above.

He was just outside Helia, away from the prying eyes of his master, but he was not alone. The Sentinel artificer, Jenda'kaya, lay on her back in the grass a little way off, her eyes closed. Ryze enjoyed her company. And with the Camavoran princess Kalista gone, there was no one else to speak to about the apparition that had followed him. Jenda'kaya had no more understanding of what it was than he did, but it felt good just to talk to someone who had shared that experience. And having her relic weapons near gave him a measure of comfort. There had been more than one spirit haunting the Well of Ages, after all.

A butterfly landed on the page Ryze was reading. It slowly opened and closed its iridescent wings, antennae waving. He moved his finger underneath it, and it clung to him. He lifted it up and gently blew upon it. It took to the air, bobbing lazily, and Ryze returned to his reading, forefinger tracing the ancient cuneiform. Open on the ground beside him were two other books, which he was using to help him decipher some of the trickier phrases. Tyrus had been supportive of his sudden interest in the dead languages of Icathia and had given him those rare tomes to deepen his understanding.

Over the last weeks, Ryze had quietly dedicated himself to his studies. He completed the lessons and exercises assigned to him by Tyrus, while in private he learned all he could from this leather-bound volume of arcane runic magic. The horrific memory of the apparition coming after him still lingered, and he found that the best way to occupy his mind was to engross himself in his work.

Tyrus was puzzled by his sudden change in behavior, but the Seeker did not question him about it. Nor did he ask about why he spent time with the artificer.

"It's good to expose yourself to other forms of scholarship. I'm sure she is a fine mentor," was all he'd said.

Ryze glanced over at her, dozing in the grass, and grinned. He wasn't sure his master would approve of her methods.

Nevertheless, Tyrus seemed pleased that Ryze was finally taking his apprenticeship seriously. In truth, he was enjoying his studies now, something he'd never really felt previously.

And besides, with the book he'd gotten from Grael, he was finally beginning to gain some control over his power. That precious tome was not the work of a singular author but the combined experience of a dozen rune mages living centuries apart. There was so much more that could be achieved with mastery over runic forms than he had ever imagined. He'd barely scratched the surface. While he had been able to draw power into himself in the past, he hadn't known enough of runic magic to effectively *use* it. Despite what others might believe, he wasn't so arrogant to think he was anywhere near mastering this art, but he did have a better grasp of what he *did* know, and perhaps more importantly, what he *did not.*

Ryze reread one particular passage, lips moving as he formed the ancient words, pondering them. He then set the book aside and stood, centering himself, closing his eyes and taking a deep breath. He ran through the mental focusing exercise Tyrus had taught him. Then he took in another breath, only this time it was not just air that he breathed in—it was the raw stuff of magic. He didn't pull in too much, though it took some effort to stem the floodgates. Even the small amount he allowed in roared through his veins like molten fire.

Opening his eyes, he saw the magical energy glowing within him, revealing itself through his skin in a series of runes. Ryze smiled, exhilarated. The power did not overwhelm him. It was his to direct as he saw fit.

His eyes leaking arcane vapor, he turned his gaze toward a boulder. The energy in him roiled. It wanted to be released.

Still he did not give in to it. Breathing steadily, his lean muscles tense, Ryze traced a runic shape in the air. To complete the pattern, he stepped forward, thrusting both hands out, fists clenched.

The air wavered around his knuckles, and a burst of pale blue energy surged forward, leaving flickering, intricate runes in its wake. It struck the boulder with a resounding crack, and aetheric light rippled across its surface, dancing like lightning.

Ryze relaxed his arms, and the blazing glyphs within his flesh dimmed. He walked over to inspect the boulder and whistled through his teeth as he saw that it was neatly split down its center. Ribbons of acrid smoke rose from the two halves. They were cool to the touch, however, and his fingers tingled with the last vestiges of runic power as he ran them along the smooth, pale stone.

"I was trying to sleep."

Ryze glanced over at the artificer, who still lay with her eyes closed. "I thought you said you had some problems with your latest creation that needed to be worked out."

"Sleep is good for working out tricky problems," said Jenda'kaya. She sighed, reluctantly opened her eyes, and pushed herself up to a sitting position. She squinted at the sundered boulder. "You did that?"

Ryze puffed his chest out. "I did. Didn't even need one of your fancy relic weapons, either."

The artificer sniffed. "It's a start. Now, show me what else you can do."

Alovédra, Camavor

Kalista was washed and dressed in a clean shift when next Hecarim appeared outside her cell, two days after his last visit.

Earlier that day, a large basin of hot water had been delivered to her by her silent jailers, along with a bar of soap, scented oils, and a hairbrush. They'd brought her clean towels, fresh clothes, and a pair of simple sandals, and replaced her threadbare blanket with two new ones of thick wool.

She'd also been delivered a veritable feast upon a series of platters. As hungry as she was, she was careful not to gorge on it, knowing she'd only make herself ill, and so she ate sparingly and avoided the richer foods, as enticing as they were.

"I trust you are feeling more yourself now, my lady?" Hecarim said.

"Yes. I suppose I have you to thank for this?"

"Don't thank me yet. I have not managed to secure your release, but I can at least make you somewhat more comfortable."

"I appreciate the effort."

Hecarim leaned close to the bars, his gaze intense. "There is a way I can ensure that you will be released within the hour. Give him what he wants."

Kalista turned away. "It will do no good. Isolde is not coming back."

"He found the vial of water in your room," said Hecarim. "He's had it studied, and its healing properties have been proved. But he believes he needs more, far more, in order to save Isolde."

"She's dead!" snapped Kalista. "She could be *submerged* in the waters, and it wouldn't matter."

"He is still refusing to accept that she is gone," said Hecarim. "But perhaps he can be shaken out of this grief-induced madness."

"How?"

"We take him to the Blessed Isles," he said. Kalista made to argue, but he raised his hand. "Hear me out. We take him there and see what the masters have to say. I've spoken with priests and the king's physicians. With Nunyo as well. All agree that going there, and seeing for himself that nothing can be done for her, could bring him the closure he needs. It could dispel this insanity that grips him."

Kalista said nothing, furrowing her brow and chewing on her lip.

"If we do nothing, we both know Viego will drag the kingdom down with him," Hecarim continued. "Then *everyone* drowns. There are already vultures circling, waiting to pick Camavor's bones. This might be our only chance. It might be *his* only chance."

Kalista turned away, closing her eyes and pinching the bridge of her nose. The words of her grandfather came back to her, as clearly as the day they were uttered.

Promise me you will guide him. Counsel him. Control *him, if needed. Protect Camavor.*

She was suspicious of Hecarim's motives, but there was sense in his words. If nothing was done, Viego would likely lead Camavor to ruin. Ancestors, it was already well along the way. She recalled also her promise to Isolde, to help Viego come to terms with her passing.

Was Hecarim right? Was this the only way to shake him out of his delusion that his wife still lived?

Guilt and indecision clawed at her.

"Just think on it," said Hecarim, turning to leave, "that's all I ask. Whatever you decide, I will support."

Kalista knelt before the Argent Throne, like a penitent come to beg her king's forgiveness.

It had taken her two days to come to her decision. She was dressed in a clean, simple shift; her armor and weapons had still been denied her. Above her, Viego lounged on the great gleaming throne, his face pallid and drawn, his expression imperious. Sanctity rested upon his lap, and his long, slender hands, encrusted with rings, lay upon its blade like a threat.

Ledros stood to attention at his side, as unmoving as a statue, though his eyes revealed his pain in seeing Kalista forced to abase herself.

One step down from the throne stood Nunyo and Hecarim, the last of the advisors in whom the king had any trust. Both looked tense. Knights of the Iron Order stood around the perimeter of the audience chamber.

"You have something to say to me?" said Viego, testing the edge of Sanctity with his thumb.

Kalista resisted the urge to spit a curse and storm from the room. She glanced over at Hecarim, who gave her an almost imperceptible nod.

"I will take you there, my lord king," she said, finally. "I will guide you to the Blessed Isles."

Viego surged to his feet, dismissing Sanctity and smiling broadly. "I knew you would!" he declared. "You have always been my most dependable and beloved friend and ally. You are my older sister in all ways but name, and I love you dearly. You have no idea how much it pained me to treat you as you forced me to do. Yet I knew you would not turn your back on me, or my beloved Isolde. Stand, stand, please."

Kalista pushed herself to her feet as Viego snapped his fingers at Nunyo.

"We have so much to do!" Viego cried. "Prepare the ships, and a bier to bear my darling love. We must lose no more time. We leave on the evening tide."

"I have one request, however," said Kalista.

"Anything, anything!"

"I am concerned the Helians may not take favorably to a Camavoran armada arriving on their shore. They will be terrified, and I worry that may hamper the masters' willingness to lend their aid to fair Isolde."

Viego nodded, considering. Hecarim's brow had risen in alarm, and he was mouthing something to Kalista over Viego's shoulder, but she continued on.

"I suggest a single ship, and an honor guard chosen from the best soldiers within the Host. I will handpick them myself."

"The king trusts the Iron Order above all others," interjected Hecarim. "We are the finest fighting force in Camavor. No one can protect him better."

"Those are my conditions, Viego," said Kalista. "The Iron Order does not come with us."

"This is outrageous," snarled Hecarim. "My lord, think of the queen! Who would you have guard her? Your finest knights or lowborn rabble?"

"It will be as you suggest, Kal," said Viego, ignoring Hecarim's entreaty. "One ship, and the Host as my honor guard."

"My lord..." Hecarim growled, his face now an ugly shade of red.

"I have made up my mind," snapped Viego.

Hecarim glared balefully at Kalista, then turned and strode from the room.

"Now, let us prepare!" Viego clapped his hands. "We sail for the Blessed Isles!"

Chapter Twenty-Four

Kalista stood at attention on the docks, waiting for the king's arrival.

"Heard you had a nice little respite in a private room below the palace," murmured Captain Vennix. "That's one way to say thank you, I guess."

"He's lost his wife," replied Kalista. "He is not himself."

"I'd say he's lost a bit more than his queen."

Kalista glanced at the vastayan captain sharply.

"And here's our benevolent ruler now." Vennix nodded toward where the king was approaching, farther along the dock. He rode next to the queen's golden litter, which was carried by a team of indentured servants. "And everyone is just meant to pretend she's alive in there, I take it," she added. "Oh, this is going to work out just fine."

"Hush," hissed Kalista, glancing around to see if anyone else had heard the captain. "Are you looking to get yourself executed?"

Kalista forced a neutral expression onto her face as the procession headed toward the waiting ship. Hecarim led the way, astride his massive armored warhorse, accompanied by fifty knights, all resplendent in dark armor and slate-gray tabards. They surrounded Viego and the golden litter. Thankfully, the curtains were closed, saving the crowd from seeing the corpse of their queen.

Viego himself rode a tall white stallion. He was lavishly dressed in regal purples and blues and wore his golden, tri-pointed crown upon his brow. The onlookers, hungry, desperate, and angry, watched in silence. Viego seemed completely unaware of their mood, smiling broadly and gracing them with a wave. It was painful to watch, and Kalista winced inwardly. She prayed that there would be a city to return to, once all this madness was done.

Ledros rode stiffly beside Viego on a giant, placid draft horse. It was probably the only beast capable of bearing his weight. As far as Kalista was aware, he'd never sat in a saddle in his life, and he looked terrified, his face drawn as he clung to the saddle horn. Nunyo was there, too, shuffling along behind the procession.

Hecarim stared at her coldly as he reined his snorting and stamping steed before her. She looked up at him, head held high and back straight, refusing to be intimidated by the massive beast.

"My lord," she said.

"Lady Kalista," he replied, with the slightest nod of the head.

The procession came to a halt, and Ledros half slid, half fell from the saddle. Kalista gave a small laugh under her breath, though she regained her composure immediately, seeing Hecarim's eyes narrow.

The Grand Master of the Iron Order stepped out of his stirrups, sliding to the stone dock with natural grace. He ushered a young squire forward. "See that my chest is stowed safely on board," he ordered, barely taking his gaze from Kalista.

She stiffened. "The king agreed that the Iron Order would not be coming with us."

"I am coming not as a knight of the Iron Order but as a dear companion and friend to the king. And to accompany and protect my devoted wife-to-be, of course."

Kalista made no reaction, but the knuckles of the hand holding her spear went white. What game was he playing? She felt this was all part of some larger plan, but for the life of her, she did not see it, and that made her nervous.

"Unless there is a reason you do not *want* your betrothed to travel with you?" Hecarim said.

She took a measured breath, calming the fury within her. "Of course not," she said, her tone icy.

Captain Vennix glanced between them, then turned to cross the boarding ramp onto the *Daggerhawk*. "Yeah, this is going to work out great," she muttered.

The Eternal Ocean

They set sail as the shadows of twilight drew in. Kalista stood alone, watching as her homeland slipped toward the horizon, and melancholy settled upon her like a shroud. When last she set out for Helia, she was full of trepidation and doubt, but also a desperate hope. She felt none of that hope now, just deep, unsettled anxiety and dread.

She watched until Camavor was lost to sight, then turned away.

The rear deck had been taken over by the queen's covered litter, and spare sails had been rigged up around it to give additional privacy and protection from the wind, rain, and salt spray.

"The queen is too ill to be moved from her bed," Viego had said.

From where she now stood at the stern of the *Daggerhawk*, she could hear Viego's voice within that overwrought litter, though she couldn't decipher the words.

She gave the litter a wide berth, nodding to the soldiers of the Host standing at attention around its perimeter. Ledros guarded the front, his immense tower shield on his left arm, and his right hand resting on the pommel of his sword. Kalista altered her course to take her by him.

"Whom does he speak with?" she asked quietly.

"No one has entered, General," Ledros replied. It skirted the question, but it confirmed her suspicions.

"He speaks to her as if she is alive," Kalista said. "Does he still do this often?"

"Sometimes, General," said Ledros.

She sighed, both at the answer and at Ledros's formality. A wall had been raised between them...and it was her fault.

"I'm sorry," she said, in a low voice, "for the way I acted. It wasn't fair of me."

"There is nothing to apologize for," Ledros said, looking uncomfortable. "I spoke out of turn. It was not my place. It will not happen again, General."

An awkward silence descended between them. If anything, things felt worse now than before, and she could tell from the stiffness of his pose and the set of his jaw that Ledros felt it, too. He saluted, which felt like a dismissal. Her face burning, Kalista saluted back and walked away.

The mist towered before the *Daggerhawk* like an unscalable cliff.

"Fascinating," breathed Viego, gazing in awe.

He stood alongside Kalista at the prow of the ship, the shouts and chatter of the sailors and soldiers having drawn him out from the queen's covered litter. It was one of only a handful of times he had been seen on deck during the weeks-long voyage.

The days had dragged, and Kalista felt as taut as a wire.

The stilted awkwardness between her and Ledros remained, and they had not spoken further during the journey. Nor was there any warmth between her and Hecarim. Most of the time she kept to herself. Even Vennix seemed tense.

As they drew nearer the mist, Viego's expression was one of childish wonder, banishing the fevered, haunted look he had borne since Kalista had returned. He *almost* looked like his old self.

"And you say that without the stone, the mist will divert us and spit us back out?" he said.

Kalista nodded. "We tried for days. The captain even strung up the ship's wheel with ropes, to be sure our course did not deviate. Even then, we were turned completely around."

Viego shook his head. "It's an astonishing defense. Unless, of course, you have its key. Can I see it?"

Kalista pulled out the pale, spherical waystone, and after a brief hesitation she handed it over.

"It seems such an innocuous thing," murmured Viego, turning it over in his long fingers. "How did you get it, again?"

"I was given it by someone hoping to ingratiate himself into your favor."

"If it works, they can have anything they want," said Viego.

"He seemed an undesirable sort. Made my skin crawl."

"Unpleasant *and* seeking favor. Sounds like Camavoran court life would fit him like a glove," he said, laughing.

Kalista smiled. "It's good to see you laugh. You seem better today."

"And why shouldn't I? We are so close! Now, show me how this stone works. Nunyo, come see this!"

Kalista took back the relic stone, anxiety churning within her. She had no idea if this was going to work.

The sheer bank of white mist loomed before them, now less than an arrow's flight away. Captain Vennix roared orders, and the *Daggerhawk*'s last sails were furled, though it continued to glide on. Another shout, and oars were extended. Silence descended as the crew awaited their captain's word, and everyone else held their breath in anticipation.

"Princess? You ready?" called Vennix.

Kalista lifted her hand in acknowledgment, glancing back to meet Vennix's eyes. She nodded to the vastayan captain, who bellowed out to her crew. "At the catch!"

As one, the blade of every oar dipped into the water.

"And *heave*!"

The *Daggerhawk* pulled smoothly toward the mist, powering forward with each rhythmic stroke. Kalista stared at the approaching wall and took a deep breath to steady herself.

"Camor, guide me," she whispered. "Please work." She lifted the waystone high, just as she had seen Tyrus do. But as the *Daggerhawk*'s prow met the wall of mist, it did not part. The ship slipped through until it was completely engulfed. All sound within was muffled, and the sea was instantly calm and lake-like.

"Is it working?" asked Viego.

"It...does not seem so, my king," murmured Nunyo.

Kalista ignored them, holding the stone up even higher. "Come on!" she muttered.

"Well, this is rather anticlimactic. I'm going to make sure Isolde is not unnerved by the mist. I'm sure you will not let us down, Kal," declared Viego. He turned and strode away, leaving just Nunyo as her audience.

On the *Daggerhawk* continued, and still nothing happened. Approaching bootsteps sounded sharply on the deck behind her.

"Princess?" said Vennix, leaning in close. "Do we have a problem?"

"Maybe," admitted Kalista.

"How will the king react if this doesn't work?"

"Badly."

The captain nodded, whiskers quivering. “Wonderful,” she said. “Just wonderful. You ever think things would have been better if we had never returned to Camavor at all? We could be at that little Buhru clam bar right now, watching the sunset and sinking a few. No? Just me?”

“Just you,” said Kalista, angrily thrusting the relic stone into the air, to no good effect.

“Well, good luck with that rock,” said Vennix. “I’ll go get my crew ready for... whatever happens next.”

Kalista was left alone again with Nunyo. She glanced back along the deck. Sailors and soldiers watched her expectantly. She turned again toward the white void ahead.

She remembered the artificer, Jenda’kaya, trying to help her fire the relic weapon.

Focus on the target. Then ask the weapon to strike it.

That weapon had a relic stone as its heart, so it stood to reason that coaxing this one to work would require a similar focus.

“Okay, you can do this,” she whispered. “Focus on the mist, and ask the stone to part it.”

Of course, she hadn’t been able to get the weapon to fire... She shook her head to dislodge that thought.

“Could I be of any assistance?” offered Nunyo, from nearby. “I do have a certain affinity with such artifacts.”

Kalista glanced at him. His eyes were lit with curiosity and interest as he peered at the stone. “Let me try once more,” she said.

“Of course!” he said, bowing and backing off.

“Focus on the mist,” Kalista muttered as she turned back toward it.

She concentrated on the blankness before her, lifting the stone up high once again. It felt perfectly smooth in her hand. And did her skin tingle slightly beneath it? Or did she imagine that?

"Now part it, you bastard thing!" she snarled.

A pulse from the stone ran down her arm, and the mist parted like a tunnel opening before the *Daggerhawk*. There was a cheer from the crew, and the ship slid through. Kalista lowered the stone, staring in wonder.

Vennix appeared at her side again and slapped Kalista on the back, hard enough to knock her forward a step. The captain was stronger than she looked...and she already looked strong.

"How'd you do it?" Vennix said.

"I swore at it."

Vennix shrugged. "Whatever works, I guess."

Chapter Twenty-Five

The Blessed Isles

It was a few hours before dawn when the *Daggerhawk* emerged from the mist. They left the blanketing shroud suddenly, as if a curtain had been whipped aside, revealing the islands beyond. Captain Vennix consulted with Kalista, getting her bearings, then called for the oars to be retracted and for sails to be unfurled now that the unnatural stillness of the mist was behind them.

On a darker night they might have slipped in unseen, but the silver moon hung low in the cloudless sky, casting its radiance across the shimmering water. As the Camavoran ship cut between several smaller islets, beacons lit up atop rocky peninsulas, first one, then a long string of them. They might have been a warning, but they were also a guide, leading the Camavorans to Helia.

As they rounded the final headland, bells echoed across the sea, and they saw the glimmering city ahead. The beam from the port's giant lighthouse swept across them, bathing them in its white light, then locking onto the *Daggerhawk*, spotlighting the ship against the dark water.

As they drew nearer, they could hear shouts and make out robed individuals running along the moonlit streets.

"It's beautiful," said Viego, standing on the edge of his queen's litter and gazing toward Helia.

"And no defenses at all," commented Hecarim. His back was to Kalista, but she glared at him as he shook his head at the Helians' foolishness. Not for the first time, she was relieved the Iron Order was not with them.

"They will help my queen, won't they?" Viego asked, his expression pleading. "I cannot lose her, Kal."

Kalista was conscious of the stillness of all those within earshot. None were looking at the king or her, but they were listening.

"If it is in their power to help, I believe they will," she said. "But regardless of the outcome, you will *never* lose her. When we pass on, we join the Revered Ancestors. And even while we live, our loved ones are never truly gone while we honor their memory."

"If she passes over, I will join her," said Viego in an empty voice.

"Speak not of such things!" hissed Kalista, looking at him in alarm. "That is not what Isolde would want!"

Viego's face was grim. "I am nothing without her," he murmured. "I could not bear the thought of living on alone."

Kalista reached out and took Viego's hands in her own, leaning close to him. "You will never be alone," she said.

He smiled, and a portion of his gloom lifted. "Loyal Kal," he said. "Niece by blood, mentor and protective sister in heart." His smile faded, and his eyes became vague, like water clouded by silt. "She loved you, you know."

"I loved her, too," breathed Kalista. Her heart hurt, but there was hope there as well, hope that Viego was finally coming to accept that Isolde was gone.

He looked down, and his shoulders slumped. "I am failing, aren't I?" he whispered. "I'm failing everyone. You, Father, Camavor. I'm failing *her*."

"You have the blood of kings in you, Viego," Kalista said fiercely. "You are soul-bound to the Blade of the King! Sanctity *chose* you. The sword recognized the strength within you, even if you do not see it. There will be pain, and grief, but you will emerge from this unbroken. Camavor will be forged anew."

Viego looked into her eyes and nodded slowly.

"Be strong," said Kalista. "For Isolde."

"I will try."

The *Daggerhawk* slid like a knife through the darkness, toward the arcing docks of Helia. The city was brightly lit, and bells and shouts of alarm echoed across the water to greet them. Robed adepts and students spilled onto the streets. Some ran in terror, arms loaded with books and precious scrolls, while others simply gawped at the approaching ship.

The *Daggerhawk*'s sails had been furled as they entered the harbor, and oars were deployed, slowing their approach toward one of the larger outer docks. Custodians ran onto the pier, heavy armor clanking, long, spiked halberds clasped in their gauntleted hands. Their white tabards glowed in the cold light emitted by the flameless lanterns atop the docks' pylons.

Kalista wondered if those guardians had ever faced a real fighting force before. She doubted it. The worst they had run up against was probably nothing more serious than drunken students and feuding schools of learning. Nevertheless, they presented a solid wall, their polearms lowered like spears, as the *Daggerhawk* drew nearer.

"Easy," growled Kalista, feeling the tension in her handpicked warriors. "We defend the king if it comes to that, but we have not come to fight. Be calm. Offer no threat."

"Oars in!" roared Vennix. Her crew responded instantly, leaving the *Daggerhawk* to glide the rest of the way.

"You said they had no soldiers," commented Hecarim.

"These are *not* soldiers," Kalista said, not even deigning to look at him. "And I said they had no *army*."

Hecarim fell into brooding silence, and Kalista cast a nervous glance toward Viego. The young king stood imperiously upon the steps of his queen's bier, staring down his nose at the custodians gathering before them. Ledros was one step below him, hand on his sword hilt. Kalista prayed that Viego's unpredictability wouldn't inflame an already tense situation.

Half a dozen of Vennix's crew stood ready with ropes, warily eyeing the spiked tips of the custodians' halberds. In one smooth movement, the guardians took three steps back, giving the sailors room, though still they hesitated.

"What are you waiting for, a kiss of welcome?" snapped Vennix. "Get over there and secure those ropes!"

Fearing their captain's wrath, the sailors leaped over the gap between ship and pier, and ropes were thrown over and wrapped swiftly around heavy iron bollards. The *Daggerhawk*'s momentum was slowed until it rested alongside the stone dock.

A red-faced figure that Kalista recognized as Elder Bartek climbed atop a cargo box behind the line of custodians, granting him a view of the *Daggerhawk*'s crew and passengers. He looked as much like a toad as ever, even dressed in golden-edged robes, and he glared at them with barely disguised contempt. Kalista recognized several other masters in the gathered crowd.

"State your purpose here, Camavorans!" Elder Bartek bellowed. "And declare how it was you breached the Hallowed Mist!"

"Do not make demands of us, *scholar*!" barked Hecarim. From his mouth, the term sounded like an insult, and the hand clenched around the hilt of his blade made it a threat. Kalista rolled her eyes and swore under her breath.

Nunyo placed a placating hand on Hecarim's arm, gently pushing him aside. "Greetings, masters of Helia!" the advisor called out. "I present to you King Viego Santiarul Molach vol Kalah Heigaari! He who bears the Blade of the King, Sanctity! Heir of the Lion, Lord of the East, and victor of the Scouring Plains!"

Silence met the grandiose introduction. Kalista scanned the Helians. The custodians' expressions were hard, while Bartek looked unimpressed. But on the faces of others, she saw concern or outright fear.

Viego rose, and all eyes turned toward him. Kalista tensed, knowing this could go badly very quickly, depending on Viego's state of mind.

"Good masters!" he called out, opening his arms and casting a winning smile across those gathered on the dock. "I come before you to humbly beg your counsel, for it is renowned across the known world!"

Kalista relaxed a little. Viego's earlier doubts and darkness seemed gone, and he appeared rational and humble. She prayed it would hold.

"Please, good masters! My queen lies stricken with poison! Help her, I beg of you! Do this, and I swear on the Revered Ancestors that we shall depart and never return. Camavor will be forever in your debt. But please, by all that is good and holy, have mercy on my innocent, beloved queen."

There were mutterings among the masters, and Elder Bartek scowled as he saw Kalista. He leveled an accusatory finger at her. "We extended our hospitality and courtesy to you, Princess Kalista of Camavor, and this is how you repay us, appearing on our shores with armed soldiers?" he growled. "We considered your request and gave you our answer, yet you return in violation of the Council of Helia's order! You have no honor! And we do not deal with those who have shown us bad faith."

She winced. Everything he said was true, and shame burned within her. She took a deep breath. "The council told me that had I brought the queen here, you might have been able to help her," she said. "Now I am here, with the queen. Will you truly deny us? Have you no mercy in your hearts?"

"The council has already made its decision!" spat Bartek. "And I ask again: How is it that you made your way back through the mists? What Camavoran sorcery or trickery is this?"

"No sorcery," said Kalista. "No trickery. I used this." There were mutters and whispers as she held aloft the waystone. "It was given to me by one of your own number."

Bartek's jowls jiggled with indignation. "*Tyrus*," he snarled. "He will be banished for this outrage!"

"I did not receive this from Seeker-Adept Tyrus," Kalista declared. "He is blameless and had no part in my return."

"In the name of the Council of Helia, I demand that you hand over that waystone immediately," said Bartek.

"This waystone has served its purpose," said Kalista. "I give it back freely."

"No," said Viego.

She turned. Viego was staring at the stone. "Viego," she said in a low voice. "We have no further need of it."

"No, I think we will hold on to it for now," stated Viego. "Give it to Nunyo, Kal."

"You test our patience, Camavorans," growled Elder Bartek.

The old advisor shuffled over to Kalista's side.

"What is he doing?" Kalista hissed.

Nunyo gave an apologetic shrug. "He's... being Viego."

"Give it to him, Kal," ordered Viego.

All eyes were on her, but Kalista made no immediate move to hand it to Nunyo.

"I assure you, good master," Viego said, appealing to

Bartek but speaking loudly enough that all could hear him. "The stone will be returned as soon as you look upon my stricken queen. Please, I give you my word, sworn on the souls of the Revered Ancestors." He glanced back at Kalista. "Kal, please, give it to Nunyo."

Uncomfortable but not wanting to publicly go against Viego, she reluctantly handed it over. Nunyo took it from her, then walked over to give it to Viego.

"For safekeeping," Viego said, putting the waystone into a pocket.

"You seek to *extort* the Fellowship of Light now?" Elder Bartek scoffed.

"No! I seek your mercy!" Viego said. "Just look upon her, please, and assess if there is any help you could grant her." He lowered himself to his knees and lifted his hands in supplication.

Kalista's eyes widened, and Hecarim bristled. Even the stoic soldiers of the Host glanced at one another in shock.

"In all of Camavor's long and proud history, no king has ever knelt," said Viego. "But I do so now, and I beg you, not as a king, but as a man—please, help my wife. Help my beautiful Isolde."

The custodians shuffled, and whispers spread through the masters, adepts, and students. More of them had crept down onto the docks while they'd been speaking, and a crowd of hundreds was now gathered.

"Help them!" came a woman's cry. "Have a heart!"

Kalista recognized the voice and scanned the crowd for its owner. Her gaze settled on the artificer, Jenda'kaya. Her shock of white hair was unmistakable, and she winked at Kalista as their eyes locked.

Her cry was taken up by others, until shouts on all sides urged the masters to lend their aid. Bartek scowled and stepped down from his box—or was hauled down, Kalista wasn't sure which. A different master took his place, one wearing an iridescent eyeshade and an extravagantly tall hat hung with geometric symbols. She was in her twilight years, her hair long since given over to gray and her face deeply wrinkled. The deep lines around her eyes showed that she had spent a good portion of her life smiling. She raised a delicate, ring-encrusted hand for quiet.

"Greetings, King Viego. I am Hierarch Malgurza, and your humility and earnestness do you credit," she said. "Please rise. No one should ever need prostrate themselves in Helia, least of all a king."

Viego stood, his head held high.

"Ours is not a nation ruled by a single voice," Malgurza said. "We must adjourn to gather the council. But I promise you, we will return before the sun reaches its zenith. Is that agreeable, noble king?"

"It is," said Viego with an imperious nod.

"As a show of good faith, I would ask that you stay aboard your ship until then," Malgurza said. "But we will ensure that refreshments are brought to you, so as to make you as comfortable as possible."

"Thank you, gracious lady," said Viego. "It will be as you request."

The masters departed, and the white-armored custodians stood to attention, lifting their weapons so that their points were up, rather than leveled at the Camavorans. Fully half their number turned and marched toward the city, while those who remained pulled back some distance. They were still vigilant, but it eased the tension.

Some onlookers lingered, chatting in small clusters, but most of them wandered off, returning to their beds or to gossip with neighbors. Jenda'kaya waved enthusiastically at Kalista and disappeared into the predawn darkness.

"Who was *that* magnificent epitome of womanhood?" said Vennix, sliding up beside Kalista.

"A friend."

"You holding out on me, princess? You need to introduce me to friends like that, all right?"

Kalista smiled. "If I get the chance, I most assuredly will."

The dawn was just starting to brighten the sky. Kalista doubted she would be able to quiet her anxious mind, but she'd been awake most of the night and needed rest.

"I'm going to turn in for a few hours," she said. "Wake me if anything happens."

Kalista only realized how tired she was as she approached her cabin. She had intended to go there directly but had been sidetracked checking in with her soldiers, calming their nerves, and ensuring that they were settled and fed. Her hammock called to her, but as she opened her cabin door, she found Hecarim and the hunched figure of Nunyo deep in conversation within. They fell silent as Kalista entered and closed the door behind her.

"What is this?" she asked warily.

"Necessary," answered Hecarim. Nunyo, for his part, looked conflicted.

"Explain," said Kalista, folding her arms.

"It grieves me, but I believe it is time to discuss possible contingencies," said Nunyo.

"Contingencies?"

"In case Viego reacts poorly to whatever comes next. In case he becomes completely incapable of ruling. In case this endeavor does not go as planned, and he does not come to accept that the queen is gone."

"He will," said Kalista.

"But we need to make plans in case he does not," growled Hecarim.

"This was *your* idea," she snapped. "Are you now so quick to abandon your king?"

"I don't think any of us can truly predict how he will react," said Nunyo. "You've seen the state of Camavor, my lady. The kingdom desperately needs leadership. It will not survive another year like this. It will fall and be forgotten in the annals of history. All that your ancestors built will be as dust."

Kalista tried to rein in her anger, for she knew that what the advisor said was true. Planning for the worst was the logical thing to do. "What do you suggest?" she asked, defeated.

"Ideally, he abandons his delusion," said Nunyo. "We return home, and he rules, as he is meant to. It is likely many duties will fall to you, until he is able to once again bear the burden of running the kingdom. But if he refuses to accept the truth, we may need to...pacify him."

"Lock him in one of the cabins for the journey home, perhaps," said Hecarim. "Stop him from doing anything destructive, to himself or anyone else."

"And if he is still not fit to rule once we return to Alovédra?"

"Then *you* rule," stated Hecarim.

"You are the heir to the throne," said Nunyo. "You have the Host's undying loyalty, and the common people love you."

"And you have the Iron Order," Hecarim added.

"You are wise, and you are a born leader," Nunyo said. "I know you will not shirk what needs to be done."

"There is a word for what you are proposing," said Kalista, coldly. "And it is *treason*."

"Would you truly stand by and watch him destroy everything?" asked Hecarim. "Centuries of legacy, shattered by one unstable monarch."

"It pains me to even contemplate this, my lady," said Nunyo. "But we must. I am loyal to the *kingdom* before any one individual. I am loyal to its people. To your ancestors. To the memory of your grandfather."

"But not to your king?"

"Not if he would see everything ruined."

"The king *is* Camavor," Kalista asserted. It was a maxim she had heard often repeated when her grandfather had ruled, but now it sounded hollow.

"Then it is already lost," said Nunyo, bowing his head.

Hecarim looked downcast, and he shuffled uncomfortably. "I wish there were another way," he said. "But if there is, I cannot see it."

"It would be one of the few times a king has been forcibly removed from the Argent Throne," Kalista said. "I would be a usurper. And I truly have no wish to rule."

"That would, perhaps, make you the *best* choice to rule," said Nunyo, softly. "You could save Camavor."

Kalista turned away, pressing her palms hard against her eyes.

"With the grace of the Ancestors, none of this will ever come to pass," said Nunyo. "You know him best, my lady. Perhaps our worries are unnecessary. Perhaps he *will* break out of his madness."

"He will," Kalista said, her back still turned to them. "He *must*."

"I pray to the Ancestors you are right."

"And if he does not, I will be there at your side," said Hecarim, reaching out for her hand, "to support you as your husband, however I can. To help you rule."

Kalista pulled back, out of Hecarim's reach. There was something in his voice that didn't sit right. Something that came across as false. Perhaps it was his earnestness. It felt feigned to her. She gave him a frank look, as if seeing him for the first time.

Yes, there was something in his eyes. He tried to hide it, but there was an eagerness there, a lust for power she had glimpsed before but overlooked, thinking it mere ambition. She saw now that his ambition was far larger than she had ever considered.

"You want to be king," she breathed. "How did I not see this before?"

"I want what is best for Camavor," said Hecarim, shaking his head.

"I've been a fool," Kalista said, softly.

"My lady..." cautioned Nunyo.

"Viego *will* be himself again," said Kalista. "And in time, he will wed anew. He will have many heirs, and you, Lord Hecarim, will never get anywhere close to the Argent Throne."

Hecarim's expression hardened. "You do me a disservice, lady."

Nunyo raised his hands. "Please, calm yourselves, before anyone says anything they may regret," he said, but Kalista was not to be silenced.

"*You* did Camavor a disservice when you started ransacking it like a corpse, long before it was dead," she hissed.

Nunyo wilted, as if knowing that things had gone beyond a point of no return. Hecarim stared at Kalista in stunned silence before his expression turned thunderous.

"Without the Iron Order, Camavor is *already* a corpse," he growled.

"Your actions when it was at its weakest will not be forgotten," Kalista said.

"When we are wed—"

She laughed. "We will *not* be wed!" she snapped. "I will not marry a man such as you, not now, not ever. I was a fool to have agreed to it in the first place."

"Because of the lowborn wretch serving as the king's champion? Your *lover*?" snarled Hecarim. "Oh yes, I know about you two."

Kalista raised an eyebrow. "My *lover*?" she scoffed. "My lord, you need better spies if that is what they are feeding you. Ledros has never been my lover, though he is twice the man you could ever hope to be."

"I should have left you to rot in the dungeon."

"Ah, but without me on your arm, you would not have a claim to the throne. I see why you wanted to bring our union forward. You wanted to make your claim official. And now, you never will." Kalista opened the door behind her, though she did not turn her back on the furious Grand Master.

"You are as mad as the king!" Hecarim snapped, his fists clenched.

"At long last the real Hecarim reveals himself," said Kalista. "Warriors of the Host! To me!"

Within the space of a few heartbeats, she was surrounded by her soldiers, all with spears leveled at Hecarim. He stared at them in undisguised loathing.

"You impudent fools dare raise weapons against *me*?" he snarled, hand on his sword hilt. "I'll see you all hang!"

"No, you won't," said Kalista. She addressed her soldiers. "Take him."

They edged forward. Hecarim licked his lips. He was a consummate swordsman and was likely judging if he could fight his way out.

"Don't be a fool, Lord Hecarim," said Nunyo, from behind him.

Hecarim's face twisted, like he was tasting something foul. He relinquished his grip on his sword hilt and held his hands out to the side to show that he was unarmed. Four soldiers stepped forward and grabbed him. He was a tall man, strong and heavily armored, and though he resisted, their hold was tight.

"I wanted to see the good in you," Kalista said. "I knew you were ambitious, yes, and arrogant, but I wanted to believe that you were an honorable man at heart. I see now that you are not. You have betrayed your king, you have betrayed me, and you have betrayed Camavor."

Nunyo edged toward the door, skirting the cluster of

soldiers, and approached Kalista, looking shamefaced. She ushered him aside as Hecarim was taken into the corridor.

"I beg your forgiveness, Highness," said Nunyo. "I felt it right to discuss contingencies, but I must admit I did not realize the depths of Lord Hecarim's ambitions. I fear he has manipulated me, and that I have failed the Argent Throne in not seeing it until now."

"You are not the only one he fooled," said Kalista.

"What will you do with him?"

Before she could answer, there was a shout from up on deck, and one of the Host ducked her head down the stairs. "The masters return, General!" she called.

Kalista regarded the soldiers holding Hecarim. "Lock him in there," she ordered, nodding toward her cabin. "Post guards on the door. We will deal with him later."

Chapter Twenty-Six

Escorted by white-armored custodians, a deputation from the Fellowship of Light was approaching along the pier when Kalista and Nunyo climbed up from belowdecks. Two of them were masters, their rank evident by the richness of their garb, the ridiculousness of their hats, and the intricate golden symbols hanging upon their chests. As they drew closer, Kalista recognized them as Hierarch Malgurza and Elder Bartek. The others appeared to be a mix of healers, adepts, high-ranking officials, and priests, though one of them looked notably ominous, garbed in a long, black hooded robe and bearing a tall staff.

Kalista noted that the brawny figure of Tyrus was among them, his expression stern, and she felt a stab of guilt.

As she moved toward the king, Vennix sidled up next to her. "Problem with the husband-to-be, princess?" the captain asked out of the corner of her mouth.

"I've realized he's a treacherous swine," murmured Kalista. "So I've called off our betrothal and locked him in a cabin."

"Nice," said Vennix, nodding approvingly.

Kalista took her place by Viego, who was standing on the edge of the queen's curtained palanquin to greet the Helians. Ledros was in front of the king, while soldiers of the Host stood at attention in a line along the edge of the ship, facing the newcomers.

She leaned forward and placed a hand on Ledros's pauldron. "When this is done, we must talk, you and I," she whispered in his ear. "I've been a fool."

Ledros tensed at the warmth of her breath but gave a short nod, still facing forward. She straightened his long cloak, smoothing it flat and letting her hand linger a moment longer than was proper. Nunyo cleared his throat, and Ledros reddened. It made Kalista smile to see this giant of a man blushing like a boy at his first kiss.

"What were you whispering about?" asked Viego, his gaze locked on the approaching masters.

"Something I should have admitted to myself long ago," replied Kalista. Viego grunted and did not probe further.

The procession halted on the dock, and Hierarch Malgurza stepped forward to address the Camavorans. "Greetings, lord king," she said with a low bow, speaking over the line of the Host. "We come with the council's decision."

Thankfully, it appeared Malgurza was the designated communicator, for Bartek remained in sullen silence, arms folded across his chest.

"Your entreaty has been discussed," Malgurza continued, "and it has been decided that the Fellowship wishes to aid your queen, if it is in our power to do so."

"Wondrous news!" exclaimed Viego, clapping his hands and stepping down off the queen's litter. He moved swiftly to the edge of the ship, squeezing through the soldiers of the Host. "Extend a ramp! Hurry up now!"

The sailors looked to their captain, who in turn looked to Kalista. She gave a curt nod. Instantly, her soldiers parted, and sailors slid a boarding ramp forward, bridging the gap between the ship and the dock.

Viego stepped onto it and reached out a hand to Malgurza. "Please, let me help you across! Come, come!"

The kindly woman accepted the king's hand and allowed

him to help her step lightly onto the deck of the *Daggerhawk*. "I have with me our finest physicians, adepts of the schools of chirurgy and arcano-medicine," Malgurza said, "and other learned folk who may be of assistance, including an expert in the field of toxicants."

"In what?" said Viego.

"Poisons," said Kalista.

"The lady has it," said the hierarch, with a nod to Kalista.

"And who is this grim figure?" asked Viego, indicating the black-robed individual who accompanied the masters. "He has the look of a gravedigger."

Viego had never been one to censor his thoughts, but Kalista had to admit the observation was apt. Upon closer inspection, she noticed that his staff of office was shaped like a shovel. He was short but powerfully built, and around his neck he wore a vial of clear liquid. As if feeling her gaze on it, the man tucked it beneath his robe.

"One of the Brethren of the Dusk," the old woman said. "Few understand the liminal boundary between this life and the next better. Do not be put off by his macabre appearance. They are sweethearts, really. And distill the best spiced liqueur in the known world."

Viego smiled and ushered Hierarch Malgurza and her companions forward. He hurried in front of them, leading the way to the golden litter. "My beloved queen is resting at present," he said. "I would ask that you take pains not to disturb her. Her health is very frail."

Kalista and Nunyo traded a glance. This was the pivotal moment.

"They will be thorough but respectful and gentle, you have my word," Malgurza said.

"Perhaps just one at a time?" said Viego. "So as not to crowd her?"

"Of course." Malgurza bowed her head.

"Who will be first? You?" Viego asked of a robed physician with two pairs of armless crystal spectacles on his nose. "Come, then!"

With a nod, the man followed Viego up the stairs of the litter. Kalista edged up a step as well, putting her near in case she was needed—she had no idea how Viego was going to react to whatever happened next. Nunyo, too, stepped closer, wringing his hands nervously.

Viego held open the curtain, and the physician stepped inside, stooping beneath the king's arm. The curtain was then dropped, leaving the two of them alone with the queen. The *body* of the queen, Kalista reminded herself.

For a moment there was silence. Then came the sound of muffled voices, which quickly rose in pitch. The curtain was thrown aside, and the physician stomped out.

"Is this a kind of sick Camavoran joke?" he barked over his shoulder, removing both pairs of spectacles with a pinch of his fingers. "She's dead, man! And has been for some time!"

"Dead?" exclaimed Elder Bartek, his expression one of alarm. "What is the meaning of this?"

"Are you certain?" breathed Hierarch Malgurza, her face paling.

Kalista could understand why they would be outraged, but Malgurza looked almost *afraid*. Was her fear borne out of what Viego might do if they could not help? Or was there something more?

"Oh, I am certain," said the physician. "See for yourself." He whipped the curtain aside so that all could see within.

Viego was kneeling beside the bed, holding the hand of the queen's corpse. And it was obvious to everyone she *was* a corpse, even from a distance. Despite the power of Mikael's Chalice, her skin had turned a foul gray color, and the flesh had begun to emaciate, shrinking upon her skeleton. Kalista saw the queen's blank-eyed doll—what had Isolde called it? Gwen?—propped up against the pillow next to her head. Viego was stroking its hand and whispering to it as if it were Isolde.

"Ancestors above," Kalista breathed.

There was an audible intake of breath from the gathered Helians, who looked aghast. Shouldering the physician aside, Kalista snapped the curtain closed, but the damage had been done. The king's madness had been exposed for all to see. At least he seemed relatively calm, though it was only a small mercy.

"Why did you come back?" asked Tyrus, looking up at Kalista in bewilderment from nearby. "What did you hope to gain?"

"We hoped it would help him finally accept the truth," she said.

"Well, it is clear there is nothing we can do," said Hierarch Malgurza. She still looked fearful, but she was trying to hide it. "I am sorry. All that can be done is to bury her, and to grieve. I hope the king will come to accept this, in time."

"As do I," said Kalista. "Thank you."

Malgurza leaned forward and lowered her voice. "Please, if you truly have no ill will toward the people of these isles, make your king leave, and do it swiftly. No good will come of lingering. And I must insist that the waystone you used to get here be handed over immediately."

Kalista glanced at the curtained litter, where Viego was doting on the corpse of Isolde.

"I will ensure that it is returned," she said, "though perhaps now is not the right moment. He needs to grieve. He will be more amenable later. But I give you my word, it will be done."

The hierarch hesitated, clearly uneasy, but gave a reluctant sigh. "Fine. But we cannot allow you to leave with it still in your possession. Be sure to relinquish it before you depart."

With those words, the hierarch bowed her head and turned to leave with her entourage.

Tyrus gave Kalista one last, disappointed look, and she lowered her eyes, unable to hold his gaze. He walked off with the others, shoulders slumped.

One of them lingered, however: the grim monk, his face shadowed by his hood. "In Camavoran speech I am not... fluent?" he said, his words heavily accented. "Death is not feared among my... Among my..."

"Your holy order?" offered Kalista. "Your brethren?"

"*Brethren*," the monk said, as if testing the shape of the word. "Yes, that is the right term. Death is a part of life, just as is birth. Not to be feared. But sometimes it is hard to let loved ones go. I could help your king, perhaps?"

Kalista shrugged and ducked behind the curtain. Viego had his head resting on Isolde's lifeless shoulder, his eyes wide and staring.

"Viego? There is another who would like to see her," Kalista said. "Or would you prefer them to leave now?"

"They can approach," Viego said, his voice devoid of emotion.

Kalista ushered the black-robed figure inside. He approached Viego and Isolde, moving with calm and measured assurance. She lingered on the periphery, watching as the monk touched the queen's forehead, then her cheek. He moved his hands above her body, then pulled back his hood. He had a boyish face and a kindly smile, which seemed at odds with his morbid appearance.

"She is... at peace," he assured Viego, speaking gently in his halting Camavoran. "Beyond pain. Beyond suffering. She is in the light. She *is* the light." He tilted his head sideward, as if listening to something no one else could hear, and he laughed. "She says she... misses someone. Gwen? A close friend, or sister, I think?"

Kalista's eyes widened in surprise, and she felt the hairs on the back of her neck rise up. Viego's gaze was drawn away from Isolde, and he stared up at the black-robed figure, his expression a piteous mixture of wonder and horror.

"She's really gone, then?" In that moment he sounded just like the sad little boy Kalista remembered from childhood.

The monk gave a slow nod, a sympathetic smile on his face. "At peace."

Viego buried his face in his hands and began to sob. The monk placed a comforting hand on the king's shoulder, then turned to leave. He gave Kalista a nod as he walked by her, pulling up his hood once more.

"Thank you," she said.

After he left, Kalista sat with Viego, putting her arms around him. They didn't speak. They didn't need to.

Finally, he mourned his lost wife.

The afternoon shadows were lengthening when Kalista finally emerged from the golden palanquin.

The docks had been cleared of onlookers, leaving just a detachment of custodians lingering nearby, watching to ensure that the Camavorans did not try to come ashore.

Vennix was barking orders, and her crew scurried about the ship, making it ready to sail once more.

"How is he?" asked Nunyo, appearing at Kalista's side.

"Grieving, finally," she said. "He seems to have accepted that she is gone, at long last."

"Ancestors be praised."

In the darkness below Helia, Erlok Grael heard the bells ringing. The sound reached down into the vaults, echoing along the labyrinthine, empty corridors, reverberating through the cells and claustrophobic chambers where treasures and secrets were locked away.

Grael looked up from the piles of books and astronomical charts spread across his room. Without Ryze and his runic magic, he had spent the last weeks making plans to get into the Well of Ages without the apprentice's help. But the sound of the bells drew him away from his studies. It led him to the surface, and he crept, blinking, into the moonlit predawn morning.

Clusters of adepts and students were chattering and gossiping. Grael stalked through the press of bodies. He found his way into the tiered Gardens of the Sublime Arithmetic, crunching across gravel as he headed toward one of the low stone walls. From there, he was able to gain a view over the harbor below. He saw the approaching many-sailed ship, illuminated by the mighty beam of the largest of the Helian lighthouses. Grael smiled broadly in recognition. There was only one nation that sailed ships of that design.

His smile faltered as he scanned the ocean. There was only a single ship. Where were the others? Where were the vaunted warships of Camavor? Where were its armies? Still, even a single ship of bloodthirsty Camavoran killers would be enough. The masters would refuse their demands, of course, and bloodshed would surely follow. Helia was completely unprepared. *Vulnerable.*

He hurried through the streets, heart thumping in excitement. They had come! They had breached the mists, as he had planned. Everything was starting to fall into place.

He lingered near the dock, his hood drawn over his face, waiting for his moment. He watched as the custodians blocked the outsiders' progress, and then as the porcine figure of Bartek—the same hated master who had condemned him to the Thresholds so long ago—loudly demanded answers. Grael's breath quickened as he realized that the Camavoran king himself was aboard the ship.

"Do it," Grael urged, as Bartek goaded them. Everyone knew Camavorans were a bellicose people, quick to anger and quick to attack, and he could barely contain his eagerness to see the blood of the masters spilled.

And yet, to his surprise and disappointment, the Camavorans did not rise to the bait. Bartek was yanked unceremoniously from his box and replaced by the hierarch of Esoteric Geometry, that scheming harpy, Malgurza.

He watched them speak, and he watched the masters depart, and still he watched and waited. The sun rose, painfully bright, but he resisted the urge to slink back into the comforting darkness below the city. There were far too many custodians to allow him to get close to the ship, and so he kept waiting.

His opportunity came in the hours after the masters had returned and left again, as the Camavorans appeared to be preparing to depart.

The ship's crew scurried like ants, and Grael's good humor shattered. This was not how he had imagined things would turn out. This was not how it was meant to be.

There were still dozens of custodians near the ship, but he couldn't wait any longer.

He was challenged as he stepped onto the dock. Two helmed custodians barred his way.

"Step aside," Grael snarled. "I have business with the Camavorans."

"What business? And on whose authority?"

He lifted up his sigil. "I am a warden-prefect, and I come on the order of the Magister of Thresholds."

"This is the first I've heard of it," said one of the custodians. "Go back and get a writ of authority, if you want to get by."

"There is no time, fool," he snapped. "They will have sailed before I am halfway back. The magister will be furious. But if you insist, then let me take your name to her, so she knows who it was who countermanded her explicit order."

"Oh, just let him past," rumbled the second custodian. "The magister's a right vicious one. She'd see us docked a month's pay and condemned to vault duty, if we are lucky. It's not worth it, not over a Thresher."

Grael bristled at the casual insult but did not offer a retort. The custodian would pay, as they all would. And if all went as he hoped, they would pay today.

"Fine, go through, Thresher," said the first custodian, stepping aside. "But I don't want any trouble. See that you are gone long before the Camavorans set sail."

Grael swept by them and stalked over to where the outsiders' ship was moored. None of the other custodians stopped him. Few of them even gave him a glance.

At last, he came to the Camavoran ship. He stopped on the edge of the pier.

"I would speak with the king," he declared, his voice booming.

Chapter Twenty-Seven

Kalista warily eyed the gaunt, pallid warden standing on the dock.

She cursed under her breath, then leaped lightly across the gap onto the wharf. "We are leaving," she hissed as she hurried toward him. "Nothing can be done for our queen, not even here. But I thank you for your aid. Though your masters were not best pleased you gave us the waystone."

"They are *not* my masters," stated Grael. "I wish to speak with your king."

"So you said. That will not be possible."

"I cannot stay in Helia, not after aiding you!" he snarled. "I told you I wanted a place in the court of Camavor."

"You did say that," agreed Kalista. "But I did not agree to any such thing. We are done here. We have achieved what we came to do."

Grael grabbed Kalista's arm and pulled her to him, showing his teeth. "I gave you what you wanted," he hissed, "and have not received anything in return. I would speak with the king!"

"Let her go, or things will go badly for you," rumbled a deep, booming voice behind her. Neither of them had noticed the approach of Ledros.

"What are you going to do?" Grael sneered up at Ledros. "Break the peace and cut me down?"

"I wouldn't need to," he growled. "You'd be dead before I even drew my blade."

Only then did the sallow-faced warden register Kalista's short blade pressing against his ribs. He glanced down at it mockingly and released her, and the two of them stepped apart. His gaze darted between her and Ledros, then across to the *Daggerhawk*.

"I wish to speak with the king!" he bellowed.

"Be quiet, you fool!" hissed Kalista.

"I wish to speak with the king! It is a matter of grave importance!"

Kalista cursed as she saw the curtains of the litter sweep aside and Viego emerge.

"What is going on?" he asked.

"Gracious king!" Grael called out, with a slight bow. "I have vital information for you, information that you will want to hear!"

Kalista curled her lip in disgust at how swiftly his tone had shifted from angry to ingratiating. It reminded her of Hecarim.

"Who is this?" said Viego.

"He is a snake," snapped Kalista. Not taking her eyes off the warden, she turned her head slightly to address Ledros. "Get him out of here."

The big man moved toward Grael, but the warden backed away, desperately appealing to Viego.

"My king! You only got through the mist because of me! You must hear me!"

"Wait," said Viego, and Ledros froze. "Bring him over here. I would hear what he has to say."

The warden grinned at Kalista. Scowling, she followed as he hurried across a ramp onto the *Daggerhawk*. He approached the king, bowing and scraping in a servile manner that made Kalista's scowl only deepen.

Viego stood on the top step of his queen's golden litter, arms folded across his chest. "Speak, then," he ordered.

"It was I who delivered you the waystone, great king! It was I who gifted you the vial of healing water, taken from the Well of Ages!"

Viego glanced at Kalista. "Does he speak the truth?"

"He did give me the water, and the stone, yes," said Kalista, begrudgingly. "But—"

Before she could finish her thought, the warden interrupted, speaking over her. "The masters are lying to you, great king!" Grael said, in a rush. "Even now, they clutch their secrets to their bosom, desperate to hide them. But *I* know the truth."

"What truth?" said Viego.

"There is a way to bring your queen back," said Grael. "Even from beyond the veil of death."

"Do not listen to him!" cried Kalista. "He speaks falsehoods! Let us leave, now, Viego! Let us go home, and mourn Isolde as she should be mourned!"

"Let him speak," urged Nunyo. Kalista looked at the advisor in shock, but he avoided her gaze.

"Is it true?" whispered Viego. "Can she come back to me?"

"I have no need to lie, no matter what the princess says," said the warden. "The truth is so much more damning. Did not my gift of the waystone allow you to come here? I am a *friend*, great king. All I want is to help you, and for you and your beloved to be reunited."

Viego stared at him without blinking. Dark, deluded hope had rekindled within him, and Kalista despaired.

"How?" he asked.

Grael smiled his shark's smile and pointed toward the grandest and largest of the buildings in Helia, where Kalista had met the council. "Beneath that tower lies the Well of Ages," he said. "Bring the queen to the well, and she will be restored to you. I promise you. And I can guide you there."

"This is madness, Viego!" Kalista pleaded.

They were inside the curtained litter, and Viego was lifting up the corpse of Isolde in his arms.

"She deserves a proper burial!" she cried. "Do not dishonor her like this, please!"

"If there is a chance, I will take it," said Viego.

"There *is* no chance! The warden is manipulating you for his own benefit, I guarantee. He's a liar!"

Viego paused. "I could never live with myself if I didn't at least try."

"Please, Viego," said Kalista, grabbing hold of his arm. "Don't do this."

He looked down at her restraining hand, then into her eyes. "I must."

He pulled away from her and walked out into the afternoon light, bearing the corpse of his wife. Carefully, he stepped down from the golden litter. The warden leered.

Viego looked around him, ignoring the horrified stares of soldiers and sailors on the deck. "Where is Grand Master Hecarim?"

"He is, ah, *indisposed*, my lord," said Nunyo.

Viego frowned, then shrugged and turned to the grinning warden. "Lead the way," the king said.

Grael bowed and walked off the *Daggerhawk*, and he followed.

"What do we do?" asked Ledros.

"You are the king's protector," said Nunyo. "It is your duty to go where he does."

There were shouts on the dock, and the custodians roused themselves. Still Ledros hesitated, looking to Kalista, as did the soldiers of the Host. Her mind was racing, her emotions churning. They had been so close to leaving, to finally putting all of this behind them.

Protect Viego. Protect Camavor.

She sighed. "We can't let him go alone," she said reluctantly. "He's still our king."

She shouted orders, and more boarding ramps were extended onto the dock. The fifty soldiers of the Host marched across.

"Double time," she called. "Form up around the king!" The Host encircled the king and the warden, Kalista at their fore. Ledros took up his place in front of Viego, and Nunyo shuffled half a step behind.

The custodians upon the docks were heavily outnumbered. The Camavorans must have seemed an intimidating force, marching in lockstep, each soldier bearing a black shield and spear, their bronze helmets obscuring their faces. Anyone looking upon them would have thought they were marching to war.

"We want no bloodshed!" Kalista bellowed, as much to her own soldiers as to the custodians and any observers watching. "We are here on a mission of peace!"

A handful of custodians stood in their path, halberds leveled.

"We go through them, whether they stand aside or not," declared Viego. Kalista cursed, and Grael hissed in laughter.

"This is insanity," she breathed. Even when Viego was at his worst, she had always believed he would see reason eventually. Had she been wrong the whole time?

All she could do was ensure that this did not turn any uglier, and pray that Viego regained his senses.

"Give ground, Helians," she warned, in a loud voice. "We are advancing into the city, but we offer no threat. Escort us, but do not try to stop us."

"Good little guard dog," taunted the warden.

Kalista turned, breaking rank, and slammed her fist squarely into the sneering man's face. He staggered back, clutching at his shattered nose.

"Kal," said Viego, reprovingly.

"You will regret that," the warden snarled.

"Maybe, Warden Grael," said Kalista. "But it was worth it."

She quickly rejoined the front rank. With relief, she saw that the custodians had wisely fallen back before them. The Camavorans marched off the stone docks onto the island proper. Locals dashed out of the way as they headed deeper into the city, straight toward the Scintillant Tower, the dominating edifice the warden claimed housed the Well of Ages. The custodians escorting them had fanned out around them, ensuring that the road was clear.

A large crowd had gathered, following in the wake of the Camavorans, though they kept a wary distance. Kalista eyed the mass of people uneasily, praying that nothing would happen to spark violence. Their mood didn't seem hostile, though, for which she was thankful.

On they marched, led unerringly by the warden. The wide promenade was called Scholars' Way, Kalista recalled, and it cut through the heart of Helia. It rose steadily toward the distant Scintillant Tower, positioned atop a plateau at the highest point in the city.

Halfway to their destination, they came to a wide set of pale marble stairs that led to a higher tier. A line of custodians stood on the lowest step, and just above them was a gathering of robed masters. In their center was Hierarch Malgurza. Gone was her friendly demeanor.

With a renewed pang of guilt and shame, Kalista saw that Seeker-Adept Tyrus was among the Helians. His expression was stony, but she could feel the anger and betrayal radiating from him. His eyes widened in alarm as he saw Grael striding alongside Viego.

The custodians escorting the Camavorans hurried to join their comrades, forming an additional rank in front of the others. They were of similar number to the soldiers of the Host now. Nevertheless, Kalista did not think they would be any real match for her soldiers, though she hoped that instinct would not be tested.

"You will go no farther," said Malgurza. "We told you there could be no help for your queen. There is nothing here for you! Go back to your ship and depart these lands, never to return!"

"She's lying. She doesn't want to share the bounty of the blessed water," hissed the warden. "She seeks to keep its secrets for herself!"

"Let me pass," said Viego. "I am taking my wife to the Well of Ages."

"What do you know of the Well of Ages?" asked the hierarch. She turned her gaze on Kalista, and her eyes narrowed. "You *were* a spy, then, sent ahead to scout the way. We should never have let you set foot on these lands!"

Kalista's face burned with shame. "It wasn't like that," she declared, but it sounded weak even to her own ears. It *was* her fault that Viego was here.

"It was discovered that an intruder managed to get into the Well of Ages during your stay with us. Some within the council suspected you had something to do with it, which is partly why your request for aid was refused. I myself argued *against* that, believing you were innocent, but it seems you had me fooled."

Kalista shook her head. "I don't know what you are speaking of. I had nothing to do with it." The hierarch was no longer listening to her, however.

"And who is that with you?" said Malgurza, squinting past Kalista, toward the warden. "A Thresher? I see you've worked your influence even among our own. It makes sense now. Allying yourself with one of the wardens to bypass the well's defenses was clever. We should have expected nothing less from a Camavoran!"

The warden straightened. "You call me a Thresher as an insult, you self-serving harpy, but *you* are the one who condemned me to that life, so long ago."

"You are a deluded fool, Erlok Grael," said Tyrus. "And I was a fool for feeling sorry for you."

"I am what you made me," declared the warden. "And all that happens now is on your heads."

"We should have banished you years ago," said Malgurza. "It was only out of pity that you were not expelled as a student. I see now that was a mistake."

"Let. Me. Pass," Viego growled through gritted teeth. The tone of his voice made Kalista tense. She knew him well enough to know how close he was to losing control.

"Viego, no, please," she breathed.

"You have no notion of the consequences of what you are attempting," the hierarch said. "The power of the Well of Ages is not to be trifled with. We cannot let you pass."

"She lies," commented the warden.

"I speak the truth," said Malgurza. "And I would lay down my own life before I let you put everyone in the city at risk."

"So be it," said Viego. He turned to Kalista. "Kill them."

No one moved, stunned at the magnitude of the order.

Kalista looked at Viego in horror. "Viego, enough! This is not who you are! Let us turn around and forget this folly."

The king's face darkened. "They bring this on themselves. My father would have them slaughtered without giving it a second thought. And *his* soldiers would obey him."

"The Lion of Camavor would have no part in this," snapped Kalista. "He was brutal, but he was not a fool."

Viego glowered at her. "Soldiers of Camavor," he said, holding her gaze. "*Kill. Them.*"

"*Hold*," she countermanded.

She was drawing a line in the sand, a line that she should have drawn long ago. She saw now what Viego was, what he had become.

The custodians shifted nervously, and she could feel the uncertainty in her soldiers.

"I am your *king*," snarled Viego, glancing among the helmed warriors, "and I've given you an order! March forward and kill them!"

"They take their orders from me, Viego, not you," said Kalista.

Viego seethed. "Ledros..."

"I am your protector, lord king," he rumbled, "and I am duty-bound to kill any who threaten your life. But I see no such threats here."

"I am surrounded by traitors!" Viego cried. "Fine! I'll do it myself."

He turned toward two of the Host. "You two! Bear your queen. And if any harm comes to her, I will have your heads."

The pair of soldiers dutifully took Isolde's body in their arms. Viego stalked toward the masters and their guards, Sanctity materializing in his hands. The rest of the Host stepped hastily out of his path, lowering their eyes in deference, and the custodians tightened their ranks, halberds brought to bear.

"No," said Kalista, stepping in front of him.

"Get out of my way, Kal."

"No," she repeated. "I will not let you do this."

"I have no wish to see you harmed. But I will cut you down if I need to."

"Don't do this, Viego!" she pleaded. "Turn away from this madness while you still can! I beg of you!"

It seemed like there was a war raging within Viego. His expression shifted between anger, and pain, and fear, and regret. He'd stopped his advance but still held Sanctity at the ready.

"Please, Kal," he said, in a quiet voice. "Help me. I have to do this. Don't make me kill you."

"I am not *making* you do anything," replied Kalista. "But I will not stand aside and let you slaughter innocent people."

"I had hoped it would not come to this," sighed Viego. "But on your head be it."

Kalista tensed, lifting her spear, but Viego didn't come toward her. Instead, he pulled something from his pocket and handed it to Nunyo, who was hovering close.

"Do it," he said, giving his advisor a nod.

"About time, my lord king," Nunyo said.

Kalista's eyes widened as she saw what it was Viego had handed him: *the waystone*. Dread tightened within her.

"Nunyo? What are you doing?" she said.

The old man glanced at her. "What's best for Camavor," he said. Then he turned away, facing the harbor and the wall of mist in the distance.

Only then did Kalista realize his intent. The betrayal was like a knife in the heart.

"Ancestors above, no!" she cried. But before she could make a move to stop him, Viego leveled Sanctity at her.

She watched, powerless, as Nunyo's mouth moved in an intoned whisper, and his eyes began to glow. Then he stepped toward the sea and thrust the waystone up high, just as he had seen her do aboard the *Daggerhawk*.

And in the distance, the immense wall of mist parted.

This was not the small opening to allow a single ship to pass through; a massive gap ripped open, from the sea to the sky. And out from that gap sailed a score of warships, ships that must have been waiting just beyond the mist for this moment.

Camavoran warships.

“What have you done?” breathed Kalista.

“You forced me to this, Kal,” Viego said. “You wouldn’t obey, and now the Iron Order will be unleashed.”

Chapter Twenty-Eight

It was the Iron Order in its entirety—almost a thousand knights—and they came to kill and plunder. Once unleashed, they would show no mercy.

There were wails of alarm, and people scattered in panic as bells tolled across the city.

"Soldiers of the Host!" Kalista roared. "Shield formation!"

The Host responded without hesitation, forming up around Kalista in tight ranks.

"I should never have expected loyalty from lowborn scum," snarled Viego.

He glanced at the only two of the Host remaining with him, still bearing Isolde in their arms. It was clear they wanted to join their brethren but didn't wish to set the queen upon the ground to do it.

"Take your treasonous hands off her," he hissed, dismissing Sanctity.

Viego took Isolde's body from them, and they rushed to join their comrades. He turned his gaze on Ledros.

"And you, Commander Ledros? I raised you from nothing, gave you a title, lands, and a future. Will you, too, spit on your sacred oaths and abandon me?"

Ledros stared down at the king, his expression unreadable. He said nothing, and without salute or bow, he turned his back on Viego and walked to join Kalista. Now only Nunyo and the viciously smiling warden remained at his side, facing the spears of Kalista's Host.

"You are traitors, all of you!" Viego screamed. "And I will see you all dead before the day is out."

"By your actions today, you have damned yourself, Viego," Kalista said. "You've betrayed your oaths, betrayed the Argent Throne, and betrayed the people of Camavor. You've betrayed your father and yourself. You will not be welcomed in the Halls of the Revered Ancestors. You will find no peace, in this life or the next. But above all, you have betrayed the memory of Isolde."

"*All I do* is out of love for her."

Kalista shook her head in disgust. "If she could see you now, she would *despise* you."

"No," whispered Viego. He looked down at Isolde's lifeless body, then back at Kalista. She could see in his eyes that he knew she spoke the truth, but he had gone too far to stop now. "No, you're wrong." He backed away from the wall of armed soldiers, his eyes wild. "You're wrong!"

With a final, frantic glance around him, he turned and hurried away, back down Scholars' Way toward the docks. Nunyo shuffled after him, and with a mocking bow, the warden followed.

"Do we go after them?" asked Ledros.

"No," said Kalista, "let him go."

She turned toward Malgurza, who was frozen in horror, staring at the approaching ships. "You have to evacuate Helia!" she shouted to the hierarch over the din. "The city cannot withstand them, and they will kill everyone they find!"

The old woman shook her head. "We cannot stand aside. There is too much at stake."

"Then you will die!" Kalista returned hotly.

"If it costs our lives to protect the Well of Ages, then so be it," replied Malgurza, though her eyes revealed her fear.

Kalista swore at the hierarch's folly. "Your deaths will protect nothing! They will *achieve* nothing! It is time to run."

"If your king does as he intends, it may not matter if we run or not! The power at the heart of the Well of Ages is unstable. *Dangerous.* He has to be stopped. We have *no option* but to stand against him."

Kalista frowned and approached Malgurza. "What do you mean, dangerous?" she said, her voice low.

"There is a magical artifact deep beneath the tower, something of such power that it makes everything else in the vaults look like children's toys. It is this artifact that gives the waters their magic."

"I thought the waters were not real."

Malgurza gave her a look. "A necessary deception. For there is a flaw in this ancient relic, one discovered hundreds of years ago. It is *unstable.* That is why we hid it away, and why we tried to convince the world it was a myth. Not well enough, clearly. It's dangerous. And it is imperative that it be protected."

"And what will happen if Viego gains access to it?"

"Maybe nothing. But maybe something catastrophic."

Kalista felt suddenly chilled. "How bad?" she asked, her voice little more than a whisper.

"Imagine a dry forest where there's been no rain for years. Then imagine the devastation that could be caused by a single lightning strike. It *might* do nothing. But the likelihood of it burning the whole forest to the ground is high. Helia is that forest."

Kalista turned away, swearing under her breath. The Camavoran ships were approaching fast, and she swore again.

Her mind was racing, but she turned her thoughts toward the layout of the city and the likely advance routes of the Iron Order once they landed. While most of the ships were heading for the main port of Helia, others were veering off toward nearby islands. A few appeared to be striking toward coves outside Helia, clearly intending to attack from different angles, ravaging the countryside and running down those fleeing the city.

"If you will not run, then pull back to your tower," she said finally. "It is the most defensible point in the city. Barricade yourselves within."

"And what are you going to do, Camavoran?" said Malgurza. "Join the plundering?"

Kalista's expression was hard. "I will stand against them. I will hold them as long as I can."

This choice was death for her, of that she had no doubt. But if she was to perish, then she would at least make her sacrifice mean something.

Craning her neck, she saw Seeker-Adept Tyrus through the frightened crowd. "Tyrus!" she called, trying to make herself heard over the panic. "Tyrus!"

He turned toward her, and his expression darkened. It was obvious he blamed her for this situation. *And he is right to.* But she had to ensure that at least some people escaped the wrath of the Iron Order and whatever else might come of Viego's insanity.

"Helia cannot hold!" she shouted. "Save your wards! Get the children out of the city!"

Tyrus glared at her, then nodded and began running toward his villa.

Her heart thumping, Kalista ordered the Host to turn and commence the final climb up to the Scintillant Tower.

The afternoon light was waning as the Iron Order commenced its rampage through the streets of Helia, burning, slaughtering, and pillaging. Normally it would take hours for a military force to disembark and organize itself for an assault of this scale, but with virtually no opposition, the Iron Order attacked quickly, striking out in small groups as they landed. As Kalista reached the Scintillant Tower and ensured that the masters were secured inside, screams and smoke rose from the city below.

The broad square before the tower was a grandiose space, intended to emphasize the greatness, opulence, and power of the ruling council. It was a vast expanse of marble, surrounded on four sides by columns and pale stone buildings. Long pools of water—fed by small waterfalls powered by some unseen arcane mechanisms—ran along either side of the main approach, which was framed by a line of identical trees, all designed to draw the eye toward the Scintillant Tower at the far end.

Set atop the highest tier of the city, the square had a single main entrance. The thoroughfare of Scholars' Way funneled those approaching the tower beneath a large archway, which was the most defensible location. An enemy could only come at you from one direction, and the narrowing of the archway ensured that you couldn't be easily surrounded. And so, it was there that Kalista would stand with Ledros and her fifty soldiers of the Host.

"And there are no other ways into this square?" she asked the most senior of the white-armored custodians. She had been relieved to discover he spoke Camavoran.

"Not that an armed force of any significance could take," the custodian said.

Kalista narrowed her eyes. "But there *are* other ways?"

"Just one." The custodian pointed to the northern end of the square. "An entrance to the vaults, seldom used. The way is locked, and narrow enough that you'd have to approach in single file."

"Show me."

Kalista left Ledros to oversee the Host and hurried across

the square with the custodian. It was as the man described. A locked gate of ornate wrought iron barred the path to a narrow set of stairs that descended some fifteen feet below the square to what looked like a solid stone wall.

"That's a door?"

"It is, General. Only a master's keystone can open it."

Kalista frowned. The Iron Order were not known for their subtlety, preferring to sweep their enemies before them in a massed charge, but she could not leave a possible avenue of attack undefended…particularly with that warden, Grael, at Viego's side. If enemies came up there, they would be free to attack the tower, or hit the Host in the rear.

"My soldiers and I will hold the archway, but I do not have the numbers to spare anyone to guard this gate," she said. "I have no authority over you, but if the enemy breaks through us, the tower *will* fall."

"We will gladly hold this position, General," the custodian said without hesitation. "On our lives, none will pass us by."

Kalista gave him a nod. "You do your order proud, soldier."

The custodian stood taller at the praise, and he saluted her, slamming his fist into his chest. She returned the salute and made her way back across the square to the Host.

"Will they hold?" asked Ledros quietly, glancing toward the custodians.

"The main thrust of the Iron Order will come here," said Kalista. "I don't expect that an attack will come from that angle, but if it does, the custodians should be able to deal with it."

"And if they can't?"

"Then we'll be surrounded."

Screams and roars of the dying and their killers echoed ever louder from the lower tiers of the city. With swift orders, Kalista readied her soldiers. They filled the narrow archway in tight lines, ten soldiers wide and five ranks deep.

They didn't have long to wait.

A wave of Helian citizens raced toward the archway. They panicked when they saw Camavorans blocking the route to the tower, but Kalista barked a command and the Host split, opening up a corridor through their midst.

"Hurry!" she called, ushering them through. Still, many were wary and unwilling to approach the mass of armed soldiers, until one among them urged them on.

Artificer Jenda'kaya was shouting as she ran forward. At her encouragement, the terrified citizens began to stream through the gap. The artificer herself joined Kalista.

"They are here," said Ledros, calmly.

Kalista saw the first of the Iron Order appear. There were only a handful of them, a breakaway group that had charged ahead, eager for spoils and bloodshed. They surged forward, their heavily armored warhorses snorting and foaming at the mouth, cutting down stragglers with sword and mace.

"Quickly!" shouted Kalista, urging more people through.

"We have to close the formation," said Ledros.

"A few more," hissed Kalista. "You too, artificer. You need to get to safety."

"I'll stand with you," Jenda'kaya said, drawing her relic weapon from within her robes. To Kalista's surprise, she also drew out a second, a pair to the first, though it was subtly different—slim and elegant where the other was more brutal.

"You've been busy," Kalista said.

"You should see what else I've made," Jenda'kaya said. "Back in the workshop."

"General," warned Ledros.

Kalista looked up to see the Iron Order rampaging ever closer. Still, there were easily a hundred innocent people between the knights and the archway—she couldn't in good conscience close the formation and leave them to die.

Narrowing her eyes, she gauged the distance to the lead

knight. Then she took a few steps forward and hurled her spear, throwing all her strength behind it.

It arced high, a perfect throw. It descended fast, hissing through the air, and took the knight between breastplate and helmet. His steed reared, hooves flailing, and the armored man fell, dead before he hit the ground.

"Spear," ordered Kalista, holding out her hand. A soldier passed her another, and she darted forward to hurl it. It flew straight and struck a second knight with enough force to punch through his breastplate and throw him from his saddle.

Three more knights continued on. One of them leveled his sword at Kalista and gave a shout, and all three of them spurred their steeds into a charge.

"Spear!" she commanded.

The next knight managed to get his shield up just in time. Nevertheless, the spear pierced both it and the knight's arm, and he pulled out of the charge, roaring in pain.

The other two kept coming, bearing down on Kalista.

The first was struck by two searing blasts of light from Jenda'kaya's weapons. The beams cored through the knight's chest, and his horse reared in fear, kicking and bucking.

The second was met by the immense figure of Ledros, interposing himself in front of Kalista. He swung his giant kite shield, slamming the warhorse aside. It fell heavily, crashing to the marble flagstones. Before the knight could disentangle himself from the saddle and his frantic steed, Ledros loomed over him. One heavy strike, and the knight was still. The warhorse found its footing and ran off, still bearing its dead rider.

"Get through, all of you!" shouted Kalista, and the remaining citizens ran beneath the archway. Once they were all past, she ordered her soldiers to re-form their ranks, forming a wall of spears and shields.

The wounded knight tore the spear out of his arm and hurled it aside.

"Spear?" asked Ledros. Kalista shook her head.

"Tell your honorless master that we are here!" she bellowed at the last knight. "Tell him we are waiting for him if he wishes to face real soldiers, rather than simply butcher unarmed civilians like a coward!"

The wounded knight glared at her, then wheeled his horse and galloped back the way he had come.

Kalista watched him go. "May this buy time for some of the citizens of this doomed city to escape."

"Let them come, then," said Ledros. "We'll kill them together."

The artificer, Jenda'kaya, lingered nearby, looking watchfully down the approach to the archway with her relic weapons in hand.

"Now it is time for you to go," Kalista said to her.

"I can help hold them," the artificer protested.

"There will be no holding them, not indefinitely," she said, her voice low. "They are too many, and we are too few. The city *will* fall."

"Then I will stand with you until the end."

Kalista glanced at the Helians who had made it through their lines, now milling in the courtyard behind her. There was nowhere for them to go. She shook her head.

"No, Jenda'kaya. Your weapons cannot fall into Camavoran hands. They are too powerful."

Jenda'kaya looked conflicted. "I am a Sentinel, and this is my home. It is my duty to stand and fight."

"Dying here with us will not protect your home," said Kalista in a quiet voice. "A good general knows when a fight cannot be won, and when the best option is to retreat. It will hurt, but you'll be alive. Alive, you can gather your strength and find those you trust to wield your weapons. Then come back and reclaim this city when the time is right. As long as one ember burns, darkness can always be banished. Stay alive, and *keep that ember of hope burning.*"

The artificer looked distraught. “Where would we even go?”

“To the docks,” said Kalista. “Make for the ship I came here on, the *Daggerhawk*. The captain, Vennix, is a good woman. She can be trusted. She will help you.”

“I can’t just leave you here to die!”

“You have to,” said Kalista. “I’ll hold them here as long as I am able, and stop them from getting into the tower. It should give you the time you need. Now go!”

The artificer looked like she was about to argue.

“Go!” Kalista shouted. “If I am to die here, then at least give my death a purpose!”

Jenda’kaya stared at her. For once her perennial smile was absent. Then she nodded. “Goodbye, Lady Kalista. May your ancestors welcome you as the hero you are. And thank you.”

Kalista rejoined Ledros in the formation’s front rank as the artificer called to the other Helians, swiftly organizing them. In a matter of moments, Jenda’kaya had them moving, and with a final wave to Kalista, she led the citizens out of sight.

“How long do you think it will be?” Ledros asked.

“Not long,” Kalista replied.

Chapter Twenty-Nine

"Here they come," rumbled Ledros.

A column of knights appeared, all wearing the slate-gray tabards of the Iron Order. They filled the wide boulevard of Scholars' Way, heading toward the towering Enlightenment Arch, where Kalista and her soldiers waited.

Grand Master Hecarim rode a black warhorse at the head of his knights. He came to a halt some fifty paces away, and the entire column stopped with him. Even from this distance, his contempt for those who faced him was obvious.

Bedecked in heavy plate, their immense snorting steeds clad in steel and mail, the Iron Order were giants compared to the lightly armored warriors of the Host. The soldiers around Kalista wore hardened leather cuirasses, bronze helms, and bronze greaves over their lower legs, but their arms and thighs were unprotected. Each carried a tall oval shield, a long spear, and a short sword strapped at their waist, but those seemed simple and lightweight next to the armored bulk of the Iron Order. The Host had been honed into an exceptionally disciplined fighting force under Kalista's guidance, but the aristocratic Iron Order was the best of the Knightly Orders, with the finest blades and armor money could buy.

The Host had never faced any of the Knightly Orders before, not even in training, for noble-born knights would not deign to lower themselves in such a way. Even in war, the lines drawn between the nobility and the lowborn were upheld.

Until today.

But in Ledros, the Host had a giant of its own. Clad in the heavy plate and mail afforded him by his newfound rank, he was half a head taller than even the largest knight of the Iron Order, and his presence gave his fellow soldiers strength.

Nevertheless, there was unease in the ranks, and Kalista stepped out and turned her back on the Iron Order to address her soldiers. The knights were not yet ready to charge. She had a few moments.

"They are just people of flesh and blood, nothing more!" she declared, walking along the front rank. "They will face us and they will die by our spears, just like every other foe we have faced and beaten! They do not fear us yet, but they will, and we will use their arrogance against them!"

Every eye was on her. These fifty were the best of the Host, the most loyal and battle-hardened of her army. All were veterans who had fought at her side for years. They would not let her down.

"They are no better than any of you, for all their finery and wealth," she continued. "They are weak, for they have never had to fight for their place. They've been given everything on a silver platter, every privilege, every honor, where you've had to fight for everything, every day of your lives. And that makes you stronger than they can *ever* be."

Kalista's gaze flicked from eye to eye.

"I am from that privileged world. It would be hypocritical to pretend otherwise. Everything I have was given to me. I never had to work for it, and I never had to fear where my next meal was coming from. The difference between them and me is I *see* you. I *know* you. I've fought at your side and bled with you. I know your worth, as soldiers and as men and women. Hear me now," she roared, her voice rising to a crescendo, "and by the Ancestors, know I speak the truth when I say you are better than all of them! They fight for greed. We fight for honor! And today you will teach them to fear you! Today, we will kill every damn noble bastard who tries to come through here, making them pay in blood for every step they take!"

The Host lifted their spears in salute and roared their approval. None was louder than Ledros, who stood in their center, his heavy sword raised high.

Kalista turned and rejoined the ranks.

Down the road, the Iron Order were finally ready to attack. And with a dismissive gesture, Hecarim sent a hundred knights forward.

"He doesn't even come to face us himself," snarled Ledros.

"He will come," Kalista replied. "When we break all those he sends against us, shame and fury will bring him to us. And then we'll kill him too. The Revered Ancestors will hunt him and his treacherous order of oath breakers in the afterlife. He will never know peace."

There was a blast of a horn, and the Iron Order surged forward, urging their warhorses into a gallop.

"For the general!" bellowed Ledros, and the cry was echoed by fifty voices.

The wall of horse and metal roared toward them, as unstoppable as an avalanche, yet the Host faced it without faltering. Nevertheless, it would have been wrong to think they felt no fear. Kalista felt it herself, making her breath come short and sharp, and her heart hammer. Her palms were sweaty and her mouth was as dry as a desert. Bravery, she knew, was not the absence of fear; it was doing what needed to be done, *despite* being afraid.

The narrow frontage beneath the arch forced the knights' formation to contract, ensuring that they could not lap around the smaller force, nor come at them from an angle. When the knights were no more than twenty paces away, Kalista gave her order.

"Now!" she roared, dropping into a low crouch and setting her spear, stamping her back foot onto its base to keep it secure. The entire front rank did likewise, as did the rank behind, and the third, presenting a three-tiered wall of jutting spears.

The fourth rank hurled their spears over the first three ranks, straight into the charging knights. Horses screamed and reared, and knights dropped from their saddles. Other knights trampled over the fallen, and their steeds tripped and fell.

It was a disjointed and uneven line that reached the Host, and many warhorses balked, turning and bucking to avoid the wall of spears before them. Others, driven forward by fear and the weight of numbers behind them, plowed onward.

Kalista rammed her spear up under the chin of a knight, even as Ledros hacked another from the saddle with a brutal blow of his sword.

Knights thrown to the ground by panicked warhorses were efficiently dispatched by Kalista's soldiers. More than a few of the Host fell, crushed beneath flailing hooves and falling horses, or felled by blades. But in the compact space, each knight faced three or four lowborn foot soldiers, and they were brought down, one by one.

The knights' strength was in their speed and the power of their charge, but in the tight confines beneath the Enlightenment Arch, both were blunted. The Host had held against the knights' attack, and the battle now swung in their favor.

No matter how many battles Kalista was involved in, the deafening sound, the claustrophobic crush, the stink, and the sheer horror of killing were still shocking, almost overwhelming. There was little that could be done to prepare for it. Truthfully, she would have been disturbed if she had ever become numb to it.

The Iron Order had lost all momentum and were faltering, and with a shouted order, Kalista intensified the pressure against them. With a heave, the Host stepped forward, thrusting with their spears. The knights were forced back, and their warhorses began to panic as they came up against those behind them pushing forward.

Ledros hacked down everything that came near him, his heavy blows cleaving through armor, flesh, and bone, and every desperate strike against him was smashed aside by his immense shield. Kalista's spear haft was slick with blood, but her grip didn't falter as she killed and killed again.

Kalista tore her spear from a fallen knight and found that a space had opened up before her. Without pause, she hurled her weapon with a grunt, dropping another enemy before snatching up another spear from the lifeless fingers of a fallen comrade. As yet another was cut down by Ledros, the knights' resolve shattered.

The battle became a desperate scramble, then butchery, as the surviving knights tried to wheel their steeds around. Trapped between the unforgiving, methodical soldiers of the Host and their own brethren, the knights were brought down without mercy.

In moments the whole formation of knights was in a rout, and scores were slain by the vengeful soldiers surging after them. Kalista shouted an order, and the Host halted before they left the confines below the Enlightenment Arch. Had they ventured into the open space beyond, it would have been a simple matter for Hecarim to have them surrounded and massacred. It wouldn't have surprised her if that had been the Grand Master's plan all along. Many among the nobility believed that lowborn soldiers were ill-disciplined and impossible to control. Kalista was pleased to prove otherwise.

Ledros wiped sweat from his brow, beaming. "That was a

victory for the ages!" he boomed. "We may yet fall, but none who hears of this will ever look down upon the Host again."

The soldiers of the Host were smiling and laughing, reveling in what they had achieved. Kalista was deeply proud, and while she didn't feel the same elation—she knew this victory would be fleeting—she pushed her exhaustion aside and forced a smile of her own. *Let them have this moment.*

"They were arrogant, and underestimated us," she said in a quiet voice, so that only Ledros could hear. "It won't happen again."

"I know." Ledros grinned. "But this is still a moment to savor."

Wearily, she turned her gaze over the killing ground, toward Hecarim. He sat motionless in the saddle, features hidden beneath his helmet, but his stiff body language spoke volumes. He was simmering with anger and burning with shame. *Good.* An angry commander took risks and made foolish decisions. And with every moment she and the Host resisted, it gave more time for the Helians to escape.

Corpses of knights, lowborn soldiers, and horses littered the shadowed space beneath the Enlightenment Arch, and the smooth stone underfoot was slick with blood. *That is going to be a problem.* But there was little to be done about it, and it was as hazardous to the enemy as it was to her own soldiers.

Keeping a wary eye on the Iron Order, Kalista commanded the archway cleared of bodies. Those of the Host were hastily carried back inside the square and lined up in neat rows. A tri-pointed smear of blood was daubed between their eyes, to hasten their passing to the Beyond and ensure that they were recognized and welcomed by the Revered Ancestors. Of the injured, all but those bearing the most grievous wounds stayed in the line, determined to fight to the last.

The bodies of fallen knights and their steeds were shoved

forward, forming a makeshift barrier against further assaults by the Iron Order.

"The king is here," said Ledros in a low voice.

Kalista looked across the open space between the two forces. There was Viego, still with Isolde cradled in his arms. The warden lurked at his side, whispering poison in his ear. The king was furious, and he snapped at Hecarim. His words didn't carry to the Host, but his intent was obvious.

He wanted all who stood in his way slaughtered. *Now.*

"Wait!" hissed Ryze, peering around the corner of the building.

Behind him, Tyrus crouched in the shadows of the alley with the three orphaned children under his care. Ryze shrank out of sight as a pair of knights thundered past. He waited until they disappeared around the next corner, then glanced back at Tyrus. The seeker-adept had the little boy, Tolu, in his arms, while the twin girls, Abi and Karli, were just behind him. All three children were silent and pale, their eyes wide.

"We need to go now," Ryze said.

Tyrus nodded. "Ready, children? Let's go! Swiftly now!"

Ryze ran in front, watchful for danger. It was chaos. Statues had been toppled, their heads hacked from their shoulders, and wagons and carts were overturned. A book bindery was ablaze, burning fiercely from within, filling the air with ash and smoke. Screams and shouts echoed through the street, along with the awful sound of men laughing.

There were bodies as well, fallen where they had been cut down. Ryze tried not to let his gaze linger on them. Glancing back, he saw Tyrus doing his best to shield the children from the sight, but it was next to impossible.

One of the twins froze, staring at the corpse of a woman. Ryze's heart lurched. He heard hoofbeats approaching through the smoke and hissed to Tyrus. "More coming! Quickly!"

Tyrus knelt by the girl and gently closed the dead woman's eyes. Ryze couldn't hear what his master whispered to the girl, but she nodded, wiping at her tears, and took Tyrus's hand.

"Down here!" Ryze urged, waving them toward another alley cutting between the streets.

He stood at the alley entrance, ensuring that none were left behind. A pair of horsemen appeared in the distance, cantering down the street, laughing and joking. Ryze could see golden artifacts bulging from their saddlebags and blood splattered across their tabards. His hands turned to fists.

"This is not the time, Ryze," Tyrus said, at his shoulder.

Swallowing his anger, he nodded and ducked into the alley behind the others. "Should we head into the vaults beneath the city?" he asked. "We could hide down there for months without being found."

Tyrus shook his head. "Starvation or thirst would take us, even if they didn't root us out," he said, so that only Ryze could hear. "No, we need to get out of the city. We will cut northward, into the Scribes' Quarter. The streets are narrower there. It will be easier to remain unseen. From there, we break north, toward the Old Woods."

"There's a lot of open ground to cover before we make the tree line," said Ryze.

Tyrus nodded. "We will have to wait for nightfall."

Ryze looked up at the sky. It was still at least two hours until then. "We'll need to find somewhere to lay low."

"It's not safe here," said Tyrus. "We're too close to the main thoroughfare."

As if to emphasize his point, there was a shout from the street they'd just abandoned.

"Search the buildings!" barked a harsh voice, speaking Camavoran. "Kill everyone you find!"

"Let's move," Tyrus said.

Ryze took the lead once more, guiding the group through the destruction of Helia.

Guilt stalked him like a creeping specter. If he hadn't aided the psychotic warden in gaining access to the Well of Ages, would the Camavorans have returned? He felt certain the answer was no.

After a fraught half hour, they found themselves in the Scribes' Quarter. It appeared they were behind the main force of the enemy. The streets bore evidence of violence, with doors caved in and fires burning, but they saw no sign of Camavorans. Broken glass crunched beneath Ryze's boots as he glanced inside an abandoned storefront. It had been ransacked, with boxes and tables overturned and smashed.

"Looks as good as anywhere else," said Tyrus.

"It's already been ransacked, so it should be safe, if we're quiet and unseen," Ryze said.

Tyrus nodded and ushered the group inside. "We'll shelter here until nightfall," he told them. "It'll be safer to move about after dark."

Having barricaded the door, Ryze took up watch, positioning himself so that he could peer out the shuttered window. Tyrus found some food in a back kitchen, and after the children had eaten their fill and settled down, he came and sat by Ryze. He handed his apprentice a hunk of bread, and the two of them shared a block of cheese, slicing it with a small knife.

"Do you really think Kalista betrayed us?" Ryze said, chewing on the tough bread.

Tyrus sighed. "No," he said at last. "I fear she was manipulated, but I believe she was only doing what she thought was right."

"How did they get the mist to part?"

"I saw one among them use a waystone in a way I didn't even know was possible," he said. "He opened the mist like a curtain, allowing their entire armada to sail through."

"A waystone? But how would they have gotten hold of one?"

Tyrus sighed deeply and looked down, his shoulders slumping. "Just before Kalista left, I allowed that warden, Grael, to speak with her. You remember him? The strange fellow who mistakenly knocked on my door? Though I wonder now if it was a mistake at all."

At mention of Grael, Ryze tensed up, but he remained silent.

"All I can surmise is that he managed to find a waystone somewhere down in the vaults," continued Tyrus, "and that he gave it to Lady Kalista. What a fool I am for letting him speak with her! I always knew he was an odd one, but I never imagined he'd scheme to destroy everything we have built here in Helia. All of this may be my fault."

Tyrus hung his head in despair. Ryze had never seen him like this, and he wasn't sure how to respond. His own shame and guilt hung heavy upon him, and for a moment he almost confessed his own mistakes...but he couldn't bring himself to do it. They sat there in silence for a time, each pondering his own failings.

"If what you guess is true," Ryze said, breaking the silence, "then the blame lies with the *warden*, not with you." Even to his own ears, it sounded hollow. Was he merely trying to assuage his own guilt?

"Perhaps," Tyrus said. "And it was certainly hubris that we never considered the mist would fail us. The Sentinels long warned of such a thing and urged us to be prepared. We did not listen."

"Were they—" Ryze fell silent as he heard footsteps outside, coming closer, glass crunching under heavy boots.

"You're imagining things," said a gravelly voice. The language was instantly recognizable as Camavoran, and Ryze shrank away from the window.

"I'm telling you, I heard voices," said a second voice. "Everyone's as rich as kings here. If there are survivors, they'll have gold."

"This is a waste of time. Come on, you heard the Iron Harbinger's horn! The Grand Master calls!"

The footsteps went past the window, and Ryze and Tyrus remained motionless, scarce daring to breathe.

There was silence...

Then the door was kicked in.

Grael grinned as another wave of knights charged toward the tight knot of Camavoran foot soldiers gathered beneath the Enlightenment Arch. His grin widened as a dozen knights fell, dropped by hurled spears.

He didn't care that Kalista and her soldiers were mounting a desperate defense of the masters, nor even that they seemed to be getting the better of the knights once again. He reveled in the mayhem and the chaos, the panic and the confusion. The screams of the dying were the sweetest of music to him, and it made him laugh that the terrified masters within the tower could hear that death, knowing that their own end was near.

The defense couldn't last, yet it held strong. They were fighting off this latest assault as effectively as they had the others. In fact, this wave seemed even more disastrous for the Iron Order, for the infantry's grim wall impeded their path, while providing a measure of defense for the foot soldiers.

Grael watched the giant of a man who had come to Kalista's defense on the docks cleave knights left and right, hacking like a butcher at his slab, and he saw the lithe figure of Kalista weave through the combat like a dancer, impaling enemies with every spear thrust.

Again the charge faltered, horses slipping and panicking, and more knights were dragged down from their saddles and stabbed to death on the ground as their mounts fled. The Camavoran king roared in fury, spittle flying from his mouth.

"I don't care if your order bleeds to the last, just clear the way!" he screamed at the leader of his knights, Hecarim. "Send them all in!"

Grael tittered, amused by the madness of the foreign king. He was spiraling rapidly, but that suited the warden fine.

For his part, the Grand Master looked equally angry, his face flushed red beneath his helmet. The entrance to the archway was strewn with so many bodies that another cavalry charge would be futile. He slid from his saddle and angrily threw his reins to his squire, barking orders. The other knights followed his lead, dismounting and seeing their horses led away. With his cruelly bladed glaive clasped in both hands, Hecarim ordered the advance, determined to bring an end to things once and for all.

The king seemed determined to fight as well, ordering two nearby knights to bear his queen. Grael's grin faltered. A massive, shimmering blade materialized in Viego's hands, appearing out of nowhere, and his grin turned into a frown. This did not fit with his plan. If the king fought, then he might fall. No, he needed him alive...at least until his soldiers cleared the way to the Well of Ages.

"There is another way into the square, lord king," Grael hissed. "A way less well protected than this one."

"What?" said Viego, head snapping in his direction. "Why did you not say so before?"

Grael shrugged. "I did not think your knights would be held by that rabble."

"Tell me of this other way," Viego said, and the warden's grin crept back onto his face.

Chapter Thirty

"They come again," said Ledros. "This will be the final push."

His armor was heavily dented and breached in several places, the chain links beneath shorn. He was splattered with blood—most of it his enemies', but not all—and his chest was heaving.

Kalista knew she looked little better. She had suffered a raft of injuries, but the rush of battle and the threat of impending death were keeping the worst of her pain at bay.

The knights had dismounted and were now trudging toward their line. It seemed Hecarim had finally tired of waiting and was throwing forward the entirety of his order—one overwhelming hammer blow to sunder their ranks. The Host had fought well, but it was now only a matter of how long they could last.

For centuries the Knightly Orders had looked down upon the infantry, regarding fighting on horseback as the way a true noble waged war. It pleased Kalista to see the Iron Order forced to meet her lowborn soldiers on an even footing.

Nevertheless, Ledros was right. The end had come.

She prayed that she had bought Jenda'kaya, Tyrus, and the seeker-adept's wards enough time to escape.

"See! I told you I heard something!"

A pair of knights stalked through the sundered doorframe, weapons in hand. They were massive figures, each easily a head taller than Ryze and perhaps twice his weight, and clad in heavy armor. Neither wore a helmet, and they grinned through thick beards as they advanced.

"Get behind me, Ryze," said Tyrus. "Protect the children."

Ryze made no move to do as his master bade, and when one of the knights lunged forward, sword stabbing, he thrust out a hand with a shout, swiftly forming a runic shape.

"No!"

Violet runes pulsed beneath Ryze's flesh, and a glowing column of energy appeared around the knight, enclosing him within. The warrior's sword ricocheted off the barrier with a bright burst of purple-blue light, and tiny runes flickered at the point of impact before fading.

It was the first time Ryze had managed to cast a runic prison, so he was almost as surprised as Tyrus, who turned and looked at him in wonder. Ryze grinned and gave him a shrug.

"Sorcery!" the knight snarled. He tried to shoulder his way through the runic barrier, but again there was a burst of energy, and he was forced back, his armor scorched and smoking.

The second Camavoran roared and swung at Ryze with his heavy sword. He dodged, then swayed to the side as the return stroke came at his neck.

"Close your eyes, children!" shouted Tyrus.

Ryze knew what was coming and shut his eyes as well. The Camavorans, not understanding Tyrus's speech, did not. A blinding white light flashed, and the knight attacking Ryze staggered backward, clearly blinded.

"Move!" shouted Tyrus, urging everyone out through the back door. Scooping up little Tolu, he led the way out onto the street.

Ryze was last to leave. He was just wondering how long his runic prison would last, when it flickered and failed. The knight snarled and launched himself forward, but Ryze upended a small table into him, giving him enough time to run.

It was closing in on sunset outside, the sky lit with brilliant hues, painting the streets in vivid red. It should have been beautiful, but tonight it seemed full of foreboding and menace.

"Run!" shouted Ryze.

Grael strode onward, lantern held aloft, leading the Camavoran king and a score of dismounted knights through the darkness beneath Scholars' Square. The way was narrow and twisting, and he was almost disappointed that they had encountered no resistance thus far.

Two of the knights bore the dead queen. Grael knew there was no returning her to life, not how the fool wanted, but it suited him for the king to believe otherwise. With these warriors at his side, no one could stop him from reaching the Well of Ages. Of course, he knew the masters would *try*, however, and he relished the thought of the bloodshed that would follow.

"How much farther?" demanded the Camavoran king, directly behind him.

"Not far," Grael said, not bothering to turn to look at him.

"I dislike being down here, scuttling like vermin."

Grael bit back his retort. It would not do to antagonize the arrogant king. He needed him, at least for now.

"A necessary discomfort, lord king."

They rounded a corner and came upon what seemed to be a dead end. The stone wall before them was carved with geometric symbols, but it appeared solid.

"What is this?" snarled Viego. "You *have* been this way before, haven't you?"

"I have not," stated Grael. "Only the masters are allowed to use this route."

"Then why did you bring us this way, you fool?"

Now Grael did turn to look at the king, and while his gaze was cold and blank, inside he was raging. Oh, how he wished he had this one chained in the depths so he could take him apart, piece by piece. His screams would be delectable.

The warden forced a smile. "I know all the hidden ways beneath Helia, even if I have not walked them," he said. "And I do not need to be a master to access the way. Fear not, my king. This is the door we seek."

He turned and traced a finger along one of the lines carved into the wall, studying the patterns. The line intersected with another, then several more, but at last he found what he was searching for. Where four lines met, he tapped the stone, and a small aperture slid open.

"Be ready," he said over his shoulder. "It is likely this way will be guarded."

He pushed the master's keystone into place, and the wall opened silently. Fresh air rushed in, along with the distant sounds of battle. A narrow set of stone steps was revealed, rising to ground level. With a grind of hidden mechanisms, the heavy wrought-iron gate atop the stairway swung open, prompting shouts of alarm. Grael grinned.

White-armored custodians appeared at the top of the stairs, halberds at the ready. Grael's grin widened. Too long had the custodians made him feel powerless and weak. Now they would be slaughtered.

"They seek to deny you," he hissed at Viego. "They want to keep the secrets of the waters to themselves. They could save your queen, but out of spite and jealousy, they choose not to. They *laugh* at your misfortune."

"And they will suffer for it," vowed the king, summoning his blade.

Grael stepped back and swept his arm forward. "After you."

Viego stared up the stairs, his red-rimmed eyes full of pain and anger, then glanced back at the knights clustering in the tunnel behind him. "Clear the way."

The knights edged past their king and began to climb, single file. They lifted their shields high, wary of their enemies' long polearms. As they came into range, the custodians thrust at them, but most of their strikes crashed against shields. A few got past, and the hooks behind the halberds' axe blades were used to good effect, dragging a shield down and yanking the knight off-balance. The first few knights were swiftly slain, but then the Iron Order were pushing up into the defenders, and custodians began to die.

They made the top of the stairs, clambering over the fallen. Viego and Grael followed, along with the knights bearing Isolde. A custodian on the ground, blood spitting from his lips, grasped at Grael's leg as he passed.

"Help me, brother," he gurgled.

Grael held his curved sickle before the dying man, savoring his confusion and fear. "This is what you deserve," he whispered. "You and all the others."

The man tried to fend him off, but he could do nothing as Grael slowly ended him.

When he was done, Grael looked up to see that the knights had pushed the custodians back enough to gain a foothold above. With the way clear, Viego surged up the stairs and stepped out onto the square. Grael hurried up behind him.

The Camavoran king strode into the fight, shoving several knights out of his way. A few of the surviving custodians turned on him, lunging with their halberds. Grael hissed, expecting the arrogant young monarch to be skewered, but Viego simply let out a sharp bark in a strange language, making a chopping motion with one hand. An invisible force smashed into the custodians, deflecting their weapons as they speared toward him. Grael startled in shock. He had not known the mad king had such power, and realized he would have to proceed with great caution.

No longer in the confines of the stairway, Viego now had room to swing his immense blade. Dropping to one knee, he slashed it through one of his attackers before sidestepping neatly, ripping his sword free as he spun and slaying his second attacker with a savage blow.

Grael watched in fascination as the two custodians wasted away from the inside, as if all life had been sucked out of them. In seconds, they were nothing more than dried husks.

The last remaining custodians backed away, their eyes wide with fear. The Iron Order surged forward, hacking and stabbing. The guardians were quickly surrounded and slain, and through the mayhem, Viego strode across the square. The Camavoran infantry still held the Enlightenment Arch, battling hard against the Iron Order, but he ignored them. His gaze was locked on the great golden doors of the Scintillant Tower.

"It will be barred from the inside," said Grael, stalking at Viego's side. "We might need—"

With a wordless roar, Viego thrust an outstretched hand toward the doors. They crumpled inward as if struck by a battering ram, ripping out great chunks of masonry, and the heavy bar holding them shut snapped like a twig. The doors smashed to the floor inside the tower with a resounding crash, revealing a handful of startled masters and custodians, blinking in shock.

The king surged through the sundered doorway, his terrible sword singing mournfully as it sliced through the air. Three custodians and a master were cut down, their flesh withering before they even hit the ground. The others fled.

Viego turned back toward his knights, his eyes lit with baleful light. "You two, bring the queen," he ordered. "The rest of you, go kill the traitors."

The knights seemed more than happy to depart. They saluted sharply and ran toward the fight beneath the arch, approaching the foot soldiers in the rear of their formation. The pair bearing the queen traded uneasy glances but did as he commanded, following the king inside the tower.

"Lead the way, warden," Viego said.

The end was near, but Kalista was determined to resist the Iron Order until her last breath.

At her side, Ledros roared like a wounded bear, killing every knight that came within reach. His sword hacked through mail and flesh alike, and pommel strikes and backhanded blows with the rim of his great shield crushed plate and bones. Gaping rents had been gouged in his plate armor and the chain underneath, and he was bleeding from sword thrusts and axe strikes, but he did not falter. He killed and killed and killed, an unstoppable behemoth of war, even as his own lifeblood flowed.

A sword stabbed through a crack in his armor, lodging between two ribs. With a bellow, Ledros spun and rammed his elbow into the swordsman's face, then rammed his blade through him. Ledros kicked him forcefully in the breastplate, freeing his blade and bringing down two other knights behind him.

Kalista danced forward, killing both knights with swift spear thrusts. Another knight swung at her, and she took the blow on the haft of her spear before dropping to one knee and sweeping the warrior's legs. He clattered to the ground with a curse, then fell silent as Ledros's blade hacked him almost in two.

Where Ledros fought with brute force, Kalista fought with speed, precision, and perfect form. The other soldiers of the Host had bronze shields, but her defense was more than capable without one; she wielded her spear with exquisite skill, deflecting and turning aside everything that came at her.

She caught an overhead sword stroke with her spear, then slammed its steel butt into the side of her attacker's helm. As he staggered, she stepped lightly forward and struck again, the butt of her spear driving into his throat, crushing his windpipe. A spiked mace swung at her, and she deftly turned her spear around it, pulling the weapon wide of its mark and the knight wielding it off-balance. She slashed the blade of her spear across the back of the knight's knee as he stumbled, then finished him with a precise strike that slid through the vision slit of his full-face helm.

Her soldiers fought bravely, standing toe-to-toe with their more armored, highborn enemies, doing their general proud. Their spears gave them significantly farther reach, and Kalista had trained them well.

More knights fell before the ruthless, disciplined spear thrusts of the Host...and yet the Iron Order had numbers on their side. There were less than a score of soldiers of the Host remaining, and each who fell left a gap in their formation, yet there were always more knights pushing forward, blades hungry for blood.

The Host had lost ground as well, pushed back step by bloody step until they were in the open square behind the archway. The knights could now use their greater numbers more effectively and began to surround them.

There was a shout from the rear, and Kalista cursed as she saw knights running across the open courtyard behind her soldiers.

"Rear rank! About-face!" she bellowed, even as she slew another knight. She almost lost her grip on her spear as the knights behind him surged forward with renewed vigor, determined to finally end the Host's resistance.

Risking another glance behind her, she saw Viego striding toward the Scintillant Tower. *Ancestors!*

"We have to stop him!" Kalista hissed.

"You go," growled Ledros, dispatching yet another of the Iron Order with a devastating blow. "We will hold them here."

Before Kalista could even consider that, a figure loomed before her.

Hecarim.

Chapter Thirty-One

Ryze, Tyrus, and the frightened children crouched behind a low wall. They were on the outskirts of Helia, looking out across the fields toward the Old Woods. The tree line was tantalizingly close, but a dozen knights were positioned atop the hill between them and the safety of the woodlands, grim silhouettes against the setting sun, watching.

"Think we can get past them?" asked Ryze.

Before Tyrus could answer, a handful of Helians broke from cover some distance eastward, sprinting desperately toward the woods. Like hounds drawn to the scent of prey, three knights wheeled their steeds and galloped to intercept them. They covered the ground with shocking speed, crouched low in the saddle, hooves churning up great clods of earth. Without slowing, they leaped over the walls separating the fields and lowered their spears.

"They're not even going to get close," breathed Ryze, horrified.

"Don't watch, children," said Tyrus, putting his arms around the youngsters, drawing them close.

Screams echoed across the open ground as the knights plowed through the distant Helians. Those who survived the first charge scattered, but the Camavorans simply wheeled and galloped after each fleeing man and woman. They were methodical and merciless, and when they were done, they laughed, and cantered back to join the other knights and take up their vigil once more.

"I think that answers your question," said Tyrus.

Ryze nodded. "We could perhaps wait until night?"

Tyrus shook his head. "It's too open here. I think we'll need to find another way out of the city. Helia is lost."

"The south gates, perhaps?"

"They're too far," said Tyrus. "And the children are exhausted."

Ryze furrowed his brow as he considered their options.

"I'm sorry, Ryze," said Tyrus, abruptly.

Ryze looked at him, confused by this unexpected apology. "For what?"

"I've been too hard on you," Tyrus said. "Kept things from you. I know you've been frustrated that I haven't helped harness your innate power."

"It's fine," said Ryze, feeling a pang of guilt. He was very conscious of the heavy leather-bound book strapped to his belt. So far, Tyrus had not inquired after it. "You were just looking out for me. I get that now."

"It's *not* fine," said Tyrus. "I was trying to protect you, but I've gone about it all wrong, and for that I am sorry. You are capable of far more than I've given you credit for, I can see that now. We get through this, and I promise you, things will be different."

"Well, I haven't exactly been the easiest apprentice," said Ryze, looking away. "We get through this, maybe we can both be better. Start anew."

Tyrus nodded. "But first, we need to get out of the city."

"What about the docks?" said Ryze, cocking his head to the side.

"Explain your reasoning."

"I figure most of the enemy are pushing deeper into the city, or out here looking for stragglers. We're already behind their main force. There's probably not much of a rear guard, for what's to threaten them? We're not far from the harbor. I say we sneak down there, find a boat, and get out that way."

Tyrus stroked his short beard. "It's not a bad idea," he said.

"Really?" said Ryze.

Tyrus nodded. "Let's do it."

Grael strode through the Scintillant Tower at Viego's side, while the two knights bearing the dead queen hurried along behind them. He laughed as masters ran before them in panic. He felt like a king. There was no one to deny him what he sought. All their privilege and entitlement, all their wealth and connections, counted for nothing. None of their pathetic rules to keep the likes of him out of their exclusive little club meant anything now. *He* was the one with the power. Now they would grovel before *him*.

They came to a giant door, guarded by a pair of ornately armored custodians, ceremonial blades lowered.

"By ancient decree, none but the masters of the Fellowship may enter," one of them intoned.

"*We* are your masters now," hissed Grael.

"Our oaths are our lives," said the other guard.

"What are they saying?" snapped Viego, not understanding their speech.

"That they will die before they stand aside."

"Then death is what they shall have."

They were slain an instant later, crushed against the door by the power of Viego's sorcery, their armor crumpled like paper.

Grael thrust the door open, striding brazenly into the most sacred inner sanctum of the tower.

Everything was marble and gold. The vaulted ceilings soared overhead, so high they were lost in shadow, and the arches around the edges of the room each contained a gleaming golden sigil. Blue-green arcane light flickered in sconces set into the walls and the pillars, lighting the gaggle of masters cowering within. They looked pathetic, clustered together and trembling like a herd of nervous sheep. Two more custodians stood before the masters, but there was no way these poor shepherds would be able to stand against these wolves.

"This is an affront and an abomination!" declared one of the masters, clearly terrified but standing defiant regardless. "Turn aside now! Do not do this, lord king! Whatever twisted promises that vile spider at your side has spun, they are lies!"

Grael smiled when he recognized the speaker.

"Hierarch Malgurza," he said, his grin a promise of suffering. "I was hoping to find you here."

"You are a repulsive worm, Erlok Grael," snapped Malgurza. "You were not fit to step inside this hallowed sanctum fifteen years ago, and you are far from fit now. You're a disgrace, a hateful little man who was never able to accept his own failings."

"And yet when the sun goes down, I'll still be here, victorious, and you'll be lying dead on the floor. No one will remember you."

"Enough talk," snapped Viego, stepping forward with Sanctity readied, clearly intent on cutting Malgurza and the others down.

"Hold," barked Grael, abandoning his sycophantic deference to the king.

Viego spun toward him, his long hair whipping. His eyes were wild with madness and fury. "How dare—"

"You *need* me," Grael returned, spitting the words out. "You cannot get to the Well of Ages without me." Viego seemed about to skewer him anyway, and Grael softened his tone. "Patience, great king. Your queen will be returned to you. But we need to handle this correctly."

Viego glanced at his lifeless wife borne by the two knights behind them, then nodded curtly. "Just be quick about it," he said haughtily. "Whatever you need from these wretches, get it and let's be on our way."

Grael gave him a mocking bow and turned back to Malgurza. "I see you have a keystone around your neck," he said to her. "I'll be taking that now."

The older woman reached up, unconsciously touching the triangular stone set into her sigil of office.

"Oh yes, I know what it is, and what it opens." Grael laughed. "It must feel terrible to know that it was, in the end, *you* who provided me the final key to the Well of Ages."

"It will not help you."

"Because I need two of them? Yes, I know that as well."

Malgurza could not hide her surprise, but she recovered quickly. "You may take mine, but you will never find a second keystone."

"I already have one."

She narrowed her eyes. "You lie."

"A master disappeared more than a hundred years ago, a master bearing the same sigil you wear. You fools believed that he left the isles and was lost to history, perhaps in a shipwreck. But he never left these shores."

"Elder Holdon," whispered the hierarch.

"Elder Holdon." Grael nodded. Unable to resist the

opportunity to gloat, he pulled out his keystone for Malgurza to see. "Amazing what doors one of these opens. Did you know they can even access the Seeker Vault?"

"That's where you got the waystone you gave to the Camavorans."

"Very good," Grael said. "It's almost like you masters have been given *too* much power, no? Now...give me your keystone."

"I will not."

Grael smiled. "I was hoping you would say that."

He hurled his sickle, and the cruel blade embedded deep into Hierarch Malgurza's chest with a horrible thud. The elderly woman gaped down at it, uncomprehending, before toppling to the floor.

Grael turned toward the remaining masters, his eyes cold and dead. "*Now* you can kill them, great king," he said.

Hecarim bellowed in fury as he swung his curve-bladed glaive.

Kalista ducked beneath the lethal swing, and the blade cleaved into a nearby knight's neck, hacking deep. She stabbed up with her spear, but the Grand Master slapped it away with the haft of his weapon and followed with a thrust of his own that she barely avoided.

"Listen to me!" Kalista snarled, before he could strike again. "Viego must be stopped!"

Hecarim scoffed, and attacked. Kalista deflected the blow,

but the power of the strike left her hands ringing. Nevertheless, she struck back, twice, hitting him in the chest and the gorget. It didn't cause any real harm, but it did knock Hecarim back a step, buying her a moment's respite.

"Hecarim, *listen*!" she hissed. "If Viego gets to the Well of Ages, it could lead to disaster! He cannot be allowed to go ahead with what he plans!"

"I don't *care* what he intends to do. And you speak of disaster?" Hecarim laughed. "Look around you! Disaster has already come. This city has fallen!"

He came at her again, thrusting his glaive, but she swayed aside and struck at him in return, stabbing at his face. He turned at the last moment, and the blow hit his helmet, snapping his head back.

"Don't be a fool! You won't be spared what Viego could unleash!"

"Did the masters of this isle tell you that?" Hecarim shook his head, laughing. "And you believed them?"

With a roar, he surged forward to drive her to the ground.

But then Ledros was there, at her side. He smashed into Hecarim with his massive shield, throwing the Grand Master off-balance. Ledros's sword sliced the air, and Hecarim barely avoided it, scrambling desperately out of the way.

"Face me, coward!" he bellowed, aiming a heavy downward blow at Hecarim's head.

The Grand Master thrust the sword aside with a deft flick of his glaive and riposted toward Ledros's face. The big man turned his head away, but the cruel blade sliced his neck.

"Lowborn bastard!" snarled Hecarim. "You think to challenge *me*?"

Ledros roared and slammed his shield into Hecarim, forcing him farther away from Kalista. But he had exposed himself by stepping out of the line, and she fought desperately to keep the other knights from attacking him from the flank. She deflected a thrust aimed at his blind side and leaped high, stepping off the back of a fallen warrior to plunge her spear down into the knight's neck.

Trying to buy himself some room, Hecarim swung his glaive around wildly. Ledros took the blow on his shield, which was wrenched out of shape, and struck back, a powerful, rage-fueled blow that Hecarim parried desperately.

A knight lunged at Ledros from the side, but Kalista saw it coming and struck first, landing a killing blow. She yanked her weapon free, and the knight fell, but she cried out as she saw Hecarim ram his glaive into Ledros's torso.

The big man shook off his sundered shield and grabbed the haft of Hecarim's glaive. Hecarim struggled to free it, but the weapon might as well have been stuck in stone. With a devastating strike, Ledros brought his sword down upon Hecarim's shoulder. The Grand Master twisted away from the full force of the blow, but it buckled his armor, finding flesh.

Hecarim roared in pain and fell to his knees. With a grimace, Ledros pulled the Grand Master's glaive out of him, and threw it aside.

"Die knowing it was a lowborn bastard who bested you," he said, lifting his sword high.

"Down! Down!" hissed Ryze, ducking behind an overturned wagon. Tyrus and the children followed suit, crouching low.

"What is it?" whispered Tyrus. "Enemies?"

Ryze pressed a finger to his lips for silence, and a moment later they could hear several individuals approaching at pace, boots clomping. He sucked in a breath, gathering power, and glowing runes appeared within his forearms as his fists clenched.

He half expected his master to try to stop him, but Tyrus simply gave him a nod and mouthed, *Be careful.*

The footsteps came closer, and Ryze leaped out from behind the wagon, ready to unleash... but he pulled up short when he came face-to-face with a small, fierce, white-haired woman aiming a relic weapon at him.

"Not being followed by any wandering spirit today, I hope, apprentice?" asked Artificer Jenda'kaya with a grin as she lowered her weapon.

"Wandering spirit?" said Tyrus, stepping out from behind the wagon.

"Don't worry about it," said Ryze, with a slight shake of his head at the artificer.

Jenda'kaya nodded to Tyrus in greeting, then saw the children with him, and her sardonic smile faltered. She lowered herself to their eye level and spoke to them earnestly. "I'm guessing I have you three to thank for keeping Tyrus and Ryze safe." The little boy, Tolu, nodded seriously. "Good work, young sentinels. Keep it up."

There were two assistants with the artificer: a big man in a leather apron, whom Jenda'kaya introduced as Piotr, and Aayilah, a slender woman with a shaved head. She had what appeared to be a wrapped bow over her shoulders, while Piotr had what looked like a stone-headed sledgehammer across his. They also had a heavy chest of dark wood bound with silver, evidently lugging it along between the three of them. Jenda'kaya looked ready for a long journey, with a bulging satchel over one shoulder and a long leather case strapped across her back.

"Best we stick together," said Ryze. "We're heading to the docks."

"Us too," said Jenda'kaya. "Lady Kalista said the captain of her ship could be trusted. I figured a Camavoran ship might get out without being sunk."

Ryze nodded. "Didn't think of taking a Camavoran ship. That's a good idea."

"Is the lady with you, then?" asked Tyrus, searching behind Jenda'kaya and her assistants.

The artificer sighed. "No," she said, her voice quiet and full of regret. "She's making a stand against the other Camavorans at the Enlightenment Arch. Drawing them to her. It's only thanks to her that we've gotten this far."

Ryze looked at the Sentinel, not immediately comprehending what she was saying.

"She's sacrificing herself to save us," said Tyrus grimly, and Ryze cursed under his breath. He turned away, fists clenching, feeling helpless and even more impressed with Kalista than he already had been. He dearly wished he had not made such a bad impression with her. Too late now, he thought with regret.

"She's a fool," said Jenda'kaya, "but a better and more noble woman I have yet to meet. But come, the way is clear. We must make haste."

The Well of Ages was deep beneath the Scintillant Tower. The route was guarded by the most senior and trusted custodians, but none were a match for the foreign king, who slaughtered them with contemptuous ease, his awesome and terrible blade cutting them down and draining their life essence.

"I have read of your sword but thought the tales exaggerated," Grael mused, as they descended through the lower sublevels beneath the tower, stepping over the emaciated corpses of the latest of the blade's victims. "*Soulrender*, I have heard it called."

"That name is a curse," replied Viego, his voice strangely devoid of emotion, "spoken only by enemies of the Argent Throne. This is the Blade of the King, Sanctity. It is the most precious holy relic of my kingdom. Every Camavoran monarch since the first has been soul-bound to it."

"What does it mean to be soul-bound to the blade?"

"Sanctity was not forged by human hands, nor even on this mortal plane. It exists only in the Halls of the Ancestors—the Camavoran afterlife—unless summoned forth by one soul-bound to it."

"And when you die, is your soul then trapped?"

"No. The binding is broken the moment the wielder dies." Viego glanced over at him, and his eyes narrowed. "Why are you so interested?"

"Merely curious, great king," said Grael.

"How much farther is the water?"

"Not far. But the Well of Ages is protected by more than just guardians of flesh and bone," said Grael. "There are three locks that we will need to open in order to access the waters."

"You have the keys for these locks, yes?"

"I do, in here," said Grael, tapping first the pockets of his robe, then the side of his head. "And here."

They stepped down into a wide, cavernous space, ringed with tall columns. Every surface was of marble and gold, and painstakingly carved with bewilderingly complex geometric symbols.

"Behold the Hall of Conjunction," declared Grael.

Even in a city of wealth and opulence, this room was something special. Every angle, every column, and every golden line drew the gaze toward the soaring, domed ceiling. Tens of thousands of glowing pinpricks of light glimmered upon the inside of the dark expanse—a perfect map of the night sky, showing all the stars, constellations, and heavenly bodies as they appeared at that exact moment above the Blessed Isles. Though it was nigh impossible to see with the naked eye, the twinkling lights shifted ever so slowly, precisely tracking the movement of every star. As they gazed up, a shooting star sliced across one portion of the dome.

"Nothing of its kind exists anywhere else in the known world," said Grael, speaking quietly. "And no outsider has ever been privileged enough to have set eyes on it before now. You are the first, good king."

He did not add that *he* had never seen it before, either. All that Grael knew of this place he had gleaned from the notes, scribbles, and blueprints he'd found in the sealed vaults beneath the Great Library.

There were no more stairs down from here, or at least none that were immediately obvious. The room was dominated by a large circular dais, raised just above the surrounding geometric patterns cut into the stone. To anyone without the knowledge of what lay below, this was as deep as the sublevels went.

"And where is the water?" said Viego.

"Deeper still," said Grael.

"Deeper?" The king looked around in confusion. "But how do we get there?"

"The conjunction will lead us," said Grael, pointing upward and enjoying the feeling of control that the secret knowledge gave him.

Viego followed his gaze, staring up at the spectacle of the stars. "I see no conjunction."

"No," agreed Grael. "Nor would it help us if there were one! No, the key is the *precise* conjunction that occurred directly above the Blessed Isles on the eve this hall was completed, and there will be no such astral occurrence for another ten thousand years. The construction of this hall was timed with masterful precision."

A flash of frustration sparked in the Camavoran king's already unstable eyes. "I do not have ten thousand years to wait," he snarled. "If you can open the way, do it. *Now.*"

Grael glanced at Viego's keen blade, and he nodded, bowing his head low. "Of course, my king."

He moved to a column that had a niche carved into it. Set horizontally within were parallel brass rods, each with a score of pearl beads strung upon it. The beads could slide left and right, allowing them to be set at specific intervals along the hundreds of tiny notches carved into the rods.

Grael began arranging them in a precise pattern. "The vision we see above is the map of the heavens as they currently are," he said as he worked. Satisfied, he stepped back.

A heartbeat later, a silver-white glow appeared at the edge of the central, circular dais, right where several intersecting lines converged nearest the column. Nodding, Grael then moved to a second column, which housed a similar array of rods and beads, and rearranged them as well.

"But in order for the radiance of alignments to be unlocked, we must roll back time, to that one specific moment centuries past."

A second light began to shine on the edge of the circle, at another point of convergence.

Grael moved to five more columns, causing more lights to glow in the floor. At the eighth and final column, he moved a score of beads, then paused.

"And in the light of the conjunction shall the path be opened," he breathed. He pushed the final bead into place.

The heavens in the dome began to move, slowly at first, then faster and faster. The moon and the stars rose and fell from west to east as time was reversed. Soon they were moving so swiftly they were a blur of light, forming solid lines streaking overhead. After a time, everything started to slow, and then all perceivable movement stopped. The heavens showed constellations that had not been seen for hundreds of years. And directly overhead the silver moon hung, surrounded by eight perfectly equidistant stars.

Those eight stars gleamed brightly, and the light of the full moon shone down upon the circular dais below, framed by eight matching lights. A ninth and final light began to glow in the center of the room, and a myriad of runes and arcane symbols became visible, shimmering and glowing across the floor.

"Watch your footing, lord king," suggested Grael, with an obsequious bow.

No sooner had he spoken than the floor shifted.

"Drop her and your lives are forfeit," Viego snarled at the pair of knights holding his queen as, with a grinding of stone, the entire floor, all the way out to the columns, started to sink.

It was revealed that each of the summoned lights was cast by a slender pentagonal pillar, which rose like growing stalks as the floor fell away around them. The pillar in the center was the largest, an eight-sided formation that rotated like an unfurling flower as it rose. Rays of light now shone between each of the pillars, forming an intricate web of interconnecting beams above Grael and the Camavorans as they descended with the floor.

When they had sunk twice a person's height, the outermost sections of the floor stopped moving, forming a series of stepped tiers, while the rest of the floor continued to sink. It was an astonishing feat of arcane construction. When the floor was intact, the stones fit together so seamlessly that anyone running their fingers across them would have been unable to discern that they were so many separate pieces.

The door was suddenly thrown wide, and a handful of custodians ran in. Behind them, leaning heavily on one of the guardians, was Hierarch Malgurza. The elderly woman was pale, and the wrappings of her hastily bandaged chest were soaked with red.

Grael snorted in amusement. "Don't you know when to die?"

"Do not do this!" Malgurza rasped, looking down at them as they continued to descend. "The dead cannot be brought back! Our earliest founders tried, and it leads only to poor souls becoming trapped on this side of the veil! Do not subject your wife to that horror!"

Viego stared up at her, distrust and bitterness oozing from his expression. "You seek only to keep it for yourself! I will not listen to your falsehoods!"

The hierarch winced, and it was clear she would have fallen had she not been propped up. "You toy with things far beyond your understanding," she said hoarsely. "I beg of you. The rune is dangerously unstable! If you do as you intend, it could be catastrophic!"

"Rune? What rune?" hissed Viego.

"She seeks to turn us aside with misdirection and falsehoods," Grael hissed. "The masters will protect their secrets however they can!"

"The rune is the source," said Malgurza, addressing Viego. "It is what gives the waters their power."

"I care nothing for the risk," declared Viego, though Grael noted that the knights with them were looking suddenly unsure. "All that matters is that Isolde is returned to me."

"Folly!" gasped the hierarch. With a gesture, she directed the custodians forward. "Stop him!"

They fanned out around the room and dropped down the first tier, armor clanking. As the lowermost platform continued to sink deeper, Viego turned on the spot, his immense blade tracking their movements.

At last, the descent ceased. Grael gestured for the others to remain back, for the innermost circle began to move, petals of stone sliding across one another and dropping down in a smooth, turning corkscrew, forming a spiraling staircase.

"We must hurry," urged Grael.

The custodians were close now, just a few tiers above them. They were wary of Viego's blade, however, having seen what it had done to their comrades.

"Quickly," Grael said, descending the final staircase.

"Give me my wife." Viego's sword blinked out of existence, and he gently took the queen from the knights. "Hold them off," he said to them, then followed Grael downward.

The two knights drew axe and sword as the custodians advanced once more, emboldened now that Sanctity was no longer present.

As weapons clashed above them, Grael and Viego hurried down the spiral staircase into the final chamber, a vast circular room, with bas-relief symbols around its exterior. It was just as the boy, Ryze, had described. He noted the small stone grate where the apprentice had entered, then switched his attention to the giant golden doors—the last barrier standing between him and the Well of Ages.

There were shouts and grunts of pain up above, and one of the knights tumbled down the stairs with a crash. He lay still at the bottom, though whether it was the fall or the custodians' halberds that had killed him, Grael neither knew nor cared.

After a moment, several custodians descended into the chamber, blood splattered upon their white tabards.

"I will need a moment to open the doors," Grael said.

Viego laid his corpse-bride down upon the floor, and his immense blade appeared in his hands once more. With a gesture, he hauled a custodian toward him, then ran him through.

Grael hissed in appreciation and padded over to the giant golden doors. Engraved at their center was a staring eye surrounded by flames, and he felt a tingle as he placed his hand upon it. There was the sound of turning clockwork, and a pair of triangular holes snapped open.

Licking his lips, his heart beating fast, Grael pushed the keystones into place. The doors opened, and white mist rolled out to greet him.

The Waters of Life were *his*.

Chapter Thirty-Two

Ledros loomed over Hecarim, his sword held above him like an executioner's blade.

"*Wait*," ordered Kalista.

He froze. "Why?"

Kalista knew it was taking all of Ledros's will to obey her order. On the ground, Hecarim's gaze flicked between her and his would-be killer, perhaps sensing an unexpected chance to live. Soldiers on both sides paused to see how this situation played out.

"With him alive, we may avert *complete* disaster," said Kalista, stepping forward and putting a hand on Ledros's shoulder. She felt him trembling with fury. "Above all else, Viego must be stopped."

"This honorless bastard deserves death." The words were spoken through clenched teeth.

"He does," agreed Kalista. "But there is more at stake."

"Listen to your general, soldier," said Hecarim, a smile in his voice.

In that moment, Kalista almost killed him herself, and she felt Ledros tense.

"Hold," she hissed, as much to herself as to the giant commander.

"Knights of the Iron Order!" Hecarim bellowed, from the ground. "Stand down! Cease fighting!"

The battle slowly came to a halt, as other knights took up the cry and stepped back. There were only nine warriors of the Host still standing. The Iron Order had them completely surrounded, but Kalista noted with pride that far more knights littered the ground than her own soldiers.

Finally, Ledros grudgingly lowered his blade. Grunting in pain, Hecarim pushed himself up onto one elbow, beginning to rise, but Kalista halted him, pressing her spear tip to his throat. "No," she said.

Hecarim swallowed, eyeing the spear, and sank back down to the ground. "What is it you propose?" he asked. "You may have me at your mercy, but you are surrounded. Kill me, and you and all your soldiers die. You are not exactly in the strongest of bargaining positions."

"I'd go gladly to my grave knowing I took you with me," growled Ledros. He hefted his sword once again, and the Grand Master flinched.

Kalista stepped in front of Ledros, pushing him back behind her, though she still kept her spear tip at Hecarim's neck. She looked down at the Grand Master, her lip curling. "I hold the only thing you care about—your own wretched life. I'd say I have a *very* strong bargaining position."

Hecarim stared at her coldly. "What do you want?"

"I have to go after Viego. You live, and in return, your knights let us pass."

Hecarim laughed. "That's it?"

"That's it. He has to be stopped."

"We could have removed him as a problem before it came to this," said Hecarim. "But your honor would not allow it. Remember?"

"He went too far," Kalista breathed, but Hecarim's words cut her. She *could* have avoided all of this.

"Oh, I'd say he went too far *long* ago, but you refused to see it." He waved a hand dismissively. "But fine, fine! Go do what you need to do! The Iron Order will not stop you."

"His tongue is forked," snarled Ledros. "We cannot trust him."

Hecarim rolled his eyes. "Hear my words, knights of the Iron Order!" he bellowed. "Let it be known that Kalista vol Kalah Heigaari and these brave soldiers of Camavor are under my protection! Any who harm them will face the iron judgment and be executed for betrayal of their oaths! Let them pass."

Kalista stared at him.

"I really don't care if the last of your soldiers live or die," explained Hecarim, "but I *do* care that *I* live to see another day. I have ambitions that have yet to come to fruition."

"A coward to the end," Ledros growled. He looked at Kalista. "Let me kill him. We will all die willingly for you, General." His statement was met with muttered agreement from the surviving members of the Host.

"Not a coward," Hecarim corrected. "Just not a fool."

Kalista narrowed her eyes. "What guarantee can you give me that you will not rescind your order as soon as there is no blade hovering over your neck?"

"Ancestors above, I am not a savage, Kalista. I don't want to see you *killed*," he said, then smiled. "I want us to be *wed*."

"Really?" scoffed Kalista. "After all this?"

"Like I said, I have ambitions. You are a woman of your word; give me your oath you will honor our betrothal after all this is done."

Kalista's laughter turned into a scowl. "Why would I do that?"

"As assurance of your safety." Hecarim's smile widened. "It wouldn't make much sense for me to kill the one who would make me a king, would it?"

"Kal," said Ledros. "Don't listen to him."

"And what of my soldiers?" asked Kalista.

"If it will sway you, I will let your soldiers walk free. Even this one," he said with a glance at Ledros. "They've done you proud. *More* than proud. Fought a damn sight better than I would have ever expected. Once you deal with Viego, I'll let them go, unharmed. But *you* will come with me, and we will rule Camavor together."

"Don't do this," Ledros begged.

Kalista turned to look up into his eyes. She hated Hecarim, hated him with every fiber of her being, but she understood him. It was power that he wanted, and marriage to her would give him that. He'd do anything to secure it—and that gave her something to bargain with.

She placed a loving hand on Ledros's arm. "If there is even a chance to save you, I have to take it," said Kalista. "You have to understand that."

It broke her heart to know they would not be together, but it would be worth it to know she could protect him.

"I'd rather die!"

"You are the best of men, Ledros. Never let anyone make you think otherwise," Kalista said.

"This is all very touching, but time is running short," said Hecarim. "Viego went into that tower quite some time ago. Who knows how far he has already gotten?"

Kalista risked a glance at the tower, with its demolished doors. Slowly, she lifted her spear away from Hecarim, who scrambled backward and pushed himself to his feet, grunting in pain. He snatched up his glaive as a squire rushed forward with his horse.

Kalista stepped toward him as he hauled himself into the saddle, the effort making him wince. "I agree to your terms," she said.

"Kal, you can't—" said Ledros, behind her, his voice full of angst. Then he grunted, and the ground shook a heartbeat later.

She turned to see the giant warrior on his knees. "*No*," she breathed.

Only now did she realize the true extent of his injuries. She dropped her spear and stepped close, pressing her hand to the wound just below his chest as she eased him to the ground. Hecarim's glaive had struck deep. Hot blood pumped through her fingers, and she stared at it in horror.

"You can't die. You can't!"

"Kalista..." breathed Ledros, his face pale.

She held his face in her hands. The life in his eyes was already fading, like the brightness of the sun obscured by clouds. She pressed her lips to his, tears running down her cheeks. It was their first kiss...and their last.

"It wasn't to be for us in this lifetime," Ledros whispered.

Kalista sobbed. "But we will be together in the next. Wait for me in the Halls of the Ancestors."

Ledros's eyes tried to focus on something over her shoulder. "*Kal!*" he cried, struggling to rise.

She felt a presence then, and heard the sound of a steed's hooves on the stones behind her. She rose and started to turn...

Hecarim's glaive rammed into her back, and the blade punched out through her chest.

"You really are *far* too trusting, Kalista," Hecarim said. His voice seemed strangely muted, like she was hearing it underwater. "My knights will swear we wed while crossing the Eternal Ocean, before you were *tragically* cut down by the wicked masters of Helia. I avenged you, of course."

She blinked, staring down at the blade protruding from her chest. It took her a moment to realize what had been done.

He'd betrayed her. Of course he'd betrayed her. And now she was dying.

She tried to speak, but the searing pain hit her then, and she gasped and dropped to her knees.

Her vision wavered, and she saw figures around her, bathed in glowing light. *The Revered Ancestors. They have come to meet me.* She tried to tell them she was not ready, that there were still things she needed to do, that Viego needed to be stopped, and Ledros needed to be protected... but she couldn't muster the energy.

One of the numinous figures placed a hand upon her, and all her pain disappeared. Everything was becoming indistinct, and she felt suddenly tired, so tired. Her eyes began to close. She could rest now.

Then she remembered everything, and her eyes shot open once more.

"*Betrayer,*" she breathed, the word a curse and an accusation.

This would not be the end, she swore. *I will not go peacefully into the Beyond. I will find a way to make him pay.*

Her strength finally gave out, and she collapsed to the ground. Ledros stared at her, blinking, fighting to retain consciousness. Then he roared in fury, denial, and grief. His eyes blazed with renewed vigor, and he surged to his feet, sword still clutched in his hand.

Hecarim struggled to pull his weapon free, then gave up, releasing it and hauling his warhorse's head away from Ledros's rampage. The giant swung at him, but Hecarim rode out of reach.

"Kill him! Kill them all!" Hecarim bellowed, and the Iron Order closed in.

Kalista watched from the ground, breathing her last, unable to rise. She saw Ledros in a frenzy, killing with impunity, desperate to carve his way to Hecarim, but the Grand Master was gone.

Finally, Ledros fell, pierced by dozens of blades, and Kalista's eyes glazed over in death.

It was over.

Once the last of the custodians fell to Sanctity, Viego went back and gently gathered up his dead wife in his arms, but Grael paid him little attention. The warden-prefect walked slowly through the doors into that final chamber housing the Well of Ages, his eyes wide.

He felt like he knew this space intimately, having spent so many hours poring over its ancient designs. But seeing it now was something else entirely.

His gaze was instantly drawn to the water. It glowed with pale light, emanating from a source at the bottom of the well. Whatever it was, it was too deep and too bright to see it clearly, but it hardly mattered. *He had won.*

With a victorious cackle, he dashed forward and dropped to his knees, greedily scooping up handfuls of the glowing water and drinking it in great, heaping gulps. This was what the masters had kept from him, hiding it for themselves. But now they were dead, and all of this was his.

It was then that he noticed the shades standing around the pool, about a dozen of them. They were motionless, watching him impassively. For his part, Viego appeared not to notice them at all, nor the power and promise of the source of the water's light. The mad king seemed completely lost in his own delusions.

Viego was staring down at his dead wife with an adoring smile, though the woman's face was an unhealthy shade of gray, and her flesh had begun to rot. Grael didn't know what it was the king saw, but it was not anything close to reality.

"Can you feel the sun, my darling?" the king whispered. "Is

not its warmth wondrous? Come back to me, and we can live together forever, in the sun's light."

Grael shook his head and resisted the urge to laugh at the king's delusion. The only light here was the ethereal glow given off by the waters.

Bearing the queen in his arms, Viego walked into the pool. His back was to Grael, and his sword was still impaled within the withered body of the well's last defender. Now was the time to strike.

Grael clutched the handle of his sickle. It would be so easy. All he had to do was step forward and bury its blade in the back of the king's skull. There was no one to stop him, and Viego's usefulness had passed. And besides... he didn't imagine the king would be best pleased once he realized the queen wasn't coming back, at least not how he was imagining.

And yet Grael stayed his hand, morbidly curious. He'd seen what a few drops of the sacred waters did to the corpse of a rat. What would they do when a human corpse was submerged? He was certain things wouldn't turn out how the king hoped, but he *wanted* to see what would happen.

Ripples radiated outward as Viego stepped farther into the pool and lowered his wife into it. His face was full of reverence as he gently released her. She floated on her back, her pale hair spreading out like a fan over the water, which shimmered with iridescence around her.

Grael edged closer, watching with keen interest.

A bright light flickered in the depths of the pool, like clouds lit from within during a storm. The queen's body rapidly began to sink, as if being pulled down by a great weight. The corpse plunged deeper and deeper, but that was not what made Grael's breath catch in his throat. The body had sunk, but a shadowy form remained floating atop the water.

It was an ethereal replica of the queen, perfect in every detail, utterly motionless.

Her eyes flicked open.

The queen's shade stared into the darkness above her, unblinking, her eyes leaking pale light. Then she rose from the water. No ripples radiated out around her as she moved, nor did any water drip from her.

"My love," breathed Viego.

She glanced around her, down at her shadowy arms, then at her own rotting corpse, lying on the bottom of the pool. The light down there had grown dim once more, fading into darkness. When the specter looked back at Viego, her visage was wrenched in horror, revulsion, and panic.

"*What have you done?*" she said. Her voice was hollow and sepulchral, like it was coming from far away.

"I have saved you, my darling," Viego said, stepping toward her. "I have brought you back to me!"

"*Send me back*," the spirit begged, shaking her head. "*Send me back!*"

"You are alive, my love! All will be well now!"

"*Send me back!*" she cried, covering her face with her hands. "*I was one with the light! I was at peace!*"

"Now we can be together, forever and always!" said Viego, wading toward her, holding his arms wide.

The spirit stared through her fingers. She looked at Viego, approaching with a loving smile on his face, then glanced at Grael. Her eyes were full of rage, and the warden staggered back beneath the force of will behind them. She returned her attention to Viego and rose above him.

She floated up high, staring balefully down at her husband, who was looking up in rapture, as if she were some divine apparition. Fury radiated from her in palpable waves. Her dress and hair flowed languidly around her, as if she were still submerged. Grael edged farther away, but Viego was still lost in his delusions, holding his arms out to her as if yearning for her embrace.

She moved in a wild blur, whipping past Viego and streaking through the air toward Grael, her eyes trailing blue-green witchfire. Grael cried out in shock as he felt her pass *through* him, and an icy coldness clutched his heart, making him gasp. It was like plunging into a frigid, ice-covered lake. He couldn't breathe. He couldn't feel anything.

The blur that was the queen's spirit whipped around the chamber, passing over the custodian's corpse, still impaled by Sanctity, and swung back out over the pool of sacred water. She returned to where she had started, looming over Viego, and Grael was finally able to suck in a breath, still chilled from the spirit's passage. Only then did he realize the queen now held the massive Blade of the King in her spectral hands.

"Come to me, my love!" cried Viego, oblivious to the danger she presented.

She did as the king asked.

Her face twisted in rage, the spectral queen hurtled forward and impaled the king upon the length of his own sword. The point of the blade slid out his back, and she drove it on until the crossguard pressed against his chest.

Only now did the king's expression falter, his beatific smile turning to shock.

Viego's blood ran into the water, and a sudden flurry of blinding flashes came from the depths. Sparking energy danced across the surface of the pool, and Grael jolted backward. He remembered Malgurza's dire warning, and in alarm he realized the old harpy might have been speaking the truth.

Viego's flesh withered before his eyes, the king's life and spirit drained by the immense blade. At the same time, the water flared even brighter, its magic working to heal him. The king's face was twisted in torment as the sword and the water worked to destroy and restore him in one endless, agonizing loop.

The waters began to darken and roil around Viego's

shuddering body. Black mist seeped from the king's fatal wound, bleeding out of him in writhing tendrils. The waters were now as turbulent as a raging sea, even as the strobing light in the depths flickered and flashed erratically, getting brighter and brighter.

Grael stood transfixed as the specter lifted Viego into the air. Blood pooled upon the surface of the sacred water, like oil. The white mist roiled and twisted like a living thing, recoiling from the pair, locked together in their deathly embrace.

"*You never loved me*," hissed the ghostly vision of the queen, her snarling face close to Viego's. "*Had you cared for me at all, you would have let me go!*"

Viego's expression shattered like a broken vase, her words causing far more harm than the sword that killed him ever could.

With a screech of pure fury, Isolde dove, angling the sword downward and driving the king down with it. They hit the water hard and she continued driving deeper, toward the source of the now wildly flashing light at the bottom.

Darkness trailed behind him, leaking from his fatal wound, corrupting the waters further.

The stone chamber of the Well of Ages cracked and groaned with a force that must have made the entire city of Helia shudder.

Dread washed over Grael. Something catastrophic was about to happen. He turned and ran.

Ruination was unleashed.

Chapter Thirty-Three

The Well of Ages was consumed in blinding light.

Erlok Grael was halfway up the spiraling staircase when the blast wave hit him with the force of a hurricane. He screamed as he was obliterated, but nothing could be heard above the roar of the ruination.

The blast radiated in all directions, shattering rock and stone. It smashed through every sublevel of the Scintillant Tower, and the living souls cowering within were instantly killed, their bodies consumed in the maelstrom.

Giant chunks of the tower hurtled high over the city before falling with devastating effect. Boulder-sized rocks and masonry smashed through libraries and homes, bouncing and ricocheting down streets, causing carnage and panic. They ripped through immaculate golden domes and shattered centuries-old stained-glass windows. They crushed pillars to splinters and brought buildings crashing to the ground, killing everyone within. Stone smashed upon the docks and into the bay, sinking ships and killing indiscriminately, sending up great plumes of water.

The square before the tower rippled like a pond into which a brick was thrown. Knights of the Iron Order and those few living soldiers of the Host looked on in horror as the shock wave hurtled over them, obliterating them in a heartbeat.

Ledros lay pierced by a score of blades, his broken sword nearby. The last of his lifeblood was leaving him. He didn't register the screaming wave of destruction coming toward him; he saw only Kalista, lying unmoving beside him, her eyes blank and staring. He reached for her and closed the armored fingers of his gauntlet around her pale, lifeless hand.

"I will see you in the Halls of the Ancestors, my love," he breathed.

The blast swept over him, rendering him to nothingness.

The old advisor to the throne, Nunyo, saw it coming as he shuffled toward the docks.

"Damnation," he said with a resigned sigh. He clenched his eyes tight as the wave of devastation overtook him.

"We're almost there!" Ryze shouted over his shoulder.

They were only one terrace above the docks now. One narrow set of stairs to navigate—a far more direct route from their current position than using Scholars' Way—and a few streets, and they would be there.

While he waited for the others to catch up, he scanned the docks for the *Daggerhawk* but could not pick it out among the flotilla of other Camavoran ships anchored there. Curiously, he saw one of the foreign ships sailing *out* of the harbor, striking toward the protective wall of the Hallowed Mist, though it was too far distant to tell if that was the ship he sought.

Before he could voice this discovery, however, a searing flash of light filled the sky. Ryze swore, momentarily blinded. The light was swiftly followed by a roaring boom a heartbeat later, the sound making the buildings and the ground violently shake.

"Gods, what have they done?" breathed Tyrus, and Ryze saw genuine fear in his master's eyes, something he couldn't recall ever seeing before.

Then the terrace rippled like water, cracking and ripping up flagstones. The buildings around them groaned and great cracks appeared in their stonework, and Ryze staggered, grasping at a nearby railing to keep his footing upon stone that was suddenly far less steady than the deck of a ship in a storm. Tyrus dropped to one knee, still holding little Tolu in his arms, and the twins, Abi and Karli, cried out as they were knocked from their feet. Jenda'kaya and her assistants, Piotr and Aayilah, dropped their heavy chest and got low to the ground, looking around in alarm.

Ryze helped the twins up, making sure they were unhurt. His gaze was drawn back the way they had come, and his eyes widened.

He should have been able to see the Scintillant Tower above them, rising in the distance—it was visible from almost everywhere in the city—but it was...gone. In its place was a storm of blue-green energy, roaring outward at colossal speed. Ryze knew instantly that they would never make it to the docks before it reached them.

The others, it seemed, came quickly to the same conclusion, for none of them made any move to run. They stood transfixed by the awful spectacle as the wave of devastation screamed toward them, engulfing everything in its path.

"What did this?" Ryze whispered, but even as he spoke, he felt certain it had something to do with that ancient rune in physical form hidden in the Well of Ages. Shame tightened within him like a hangman's noose.

A handful of knights appeared, galloping hard down Scholars' Way in a vain attempt to flee the rapidly closing explosion, their steeds frothing at the mouth. The one in front was the leader of those knights, Ryze recognized, and his massive steed ran like the wind. Still, it was not enough to escape.

The wall of painfully bright light, crackling with green and blue energy, surged across the city. Buildings splintered before it, like ice shattered by a mallet. In a few heartbeats it overtook the Camavoran knights, and they were lost within it. Their leader roared in defiance as he tried to outrun it, but he, too, was consumed.

It screamed onward, coming straight toward them at impossible speed, annihilating everything in its path.

"Get close to me!" barked Tyrus. "All of you! Quickly now! You too, Ryze!"

They all surrounded him, packing in tight. Tyrus held Tolu close, shielding the boy from the vision of the onrushing devastation, while the twins clutched at his robes. Jenda'kaya dropped to her haunches, putting her arms around the girls and turning away, clenching her eyes shut. Piotr wrapped Aayilah in his burn-scarred arms.

Ryze himself didn't look away. If this was the moment of his death, he would meet it with defiance.

He roared as the blast began to wash over them. Just as it hit, a blinding white light surrounded them, and Ryze could see nothing. There was a deafening noise, like ten thousand souls screaming in agony and horror. Then the sound faded, as did the blinding light.

Ryze turned to Tyrus—the last of the light was dissipating from him, and the sigil around his neck was glowing.

They lived! The wall of eerie light had passed over them.

But around them, the city was in ruin. Not a single building remained standing, as far as the eye could see—everything was leveled and reduced to rubble. Ryze had no doubt that they were the only living souls left in the city.

Looking down to the harbor, he saw that the ships there had suffered a similar fate as Helia itself. They'd been smashed like twigs, masts and hulls shattered. That blast wave continued to surge out across the harbor, though it was clearly weakening. He saw it wash over the distant Camavoran warship, almost capsizing it, but the storm's power was waning, and the ship remained afloat.

"Is it over?" breathed Jenda'kaya.

The last vestiges of the magical explosion reached the edge of the Hallowed Mist, upon the horizon. Blue-green light flashed, like eerie, ethereal lightning within a cloud bank, and the wall turned an ugly, bruised gray, like gathering storm clouds.

"I don't think so," Ryze said.

The Hallowed Mist grew darker still, becoming heavy with threat. Crackling, forked arcs of energy continued to flash within it. It was soon as black as ink—and then the entire mist wall collapsed.

The distant ship disappeared from sight, obscured by the dark mist, still flashing with ethereal light.

"Is that getting *closer*?" asked Jenda'kaya.

It was.

Black mist, darker than a moonless night, was now hurtling toward them. It moved with an unnerving, undulating motion, tendrils reaching out before it, as if the roiling mass were some eyeless, ravenous beast.

Ryze glanced at his master. "Can you do that again?"

Tyrus shook his head. His face was drawn and gray, and he was breathing heavily. "The shield exhausted my sigil," he gasped. "It will take time to replenish."

It became apparent that the power of the black mist was not the same as the blast wave that had shattered stone and flesh alike, though it was no less terrifying.

As it writhed back across the harbor, engulfing the ships and docks farther out, it seemed to reverse the damage the blast had caused. Masts and ruptured hulls were remade, and immense chunks of stone were lifted up, to be returned from whence they had come...but imperfectly. Buildings down by the docks, shattered moments before, were re-formed, their stonework frozen in the very moment of their destruction. Chunks of masonry hung in midair, surrounded by blue-green light, caught in stasis a fraction of a second after the initial wave had hit. The trees that had once lined the terraces returned as ethereal, ghostly copies, transparent leaves blowing in a wind that no longer existed.

"Down!" shouted Jenda'kaya, pulling the twins to her and crouching behind the heavy chest as the black mist rushed toward them.

Covering his eyes, as if facing a screaming sandstorm, Ryze braced himself, ducking down alongside the artificer.

The black mist rolled over them, and it was like being plunged into freezing water. He gasped as all the warmth was sucked from his body. It felt as though icy talons clutched at his heart, at his soul, and he dropped to his knees in shock. Maddening whispers and distant screams came at him from every direction, and despair and despondency pushed down upon him, pressing him into the ground. He clenched his eyes shut and moaned. All he wanted to do was sink into the darkness. For this to be over.

A hand pulled him to his feet, dragging him out of his misery, and he opened his eyes to see Jenda'kaya's worried face before him.

He blinked, looking around him. The city was now swathed in the darkness of the black mist, making it impossible to see more than a few hundred yards. Tyrus and the others glanced around them in shock and horror, clearly all suffering the same experience that he was. The children were wide-eyed and pale.

The city had been restored, in a fashion, but there was an

unnerving wrongness to it. Helia had returned, but everything was twisted and contorted, as if in pain.

In a brief gap in the black mist, Ryze glimpsed the great Scintillant Tower looming over the city, imperfectly re-formed. Part of its lower levels remained frozen in the process of detonating outward, so the majority of the tower had no support beneath its weight, but it did not topple. It hung in the air above the city, unmoving, while black mist coiled around it.

"We're not alone," Jenda'kaya warned.

Ryze lowered his gaze. Several figures were appearing from the buildings. Not all the citizenry had been killed by the marauding Camavorans; many had hidden themselves away and were now emerging from their concealment. It was clear, however, that it wasn't just buildings that had been macabrely restored.

These figures were not living beings but ghostly shades, their insubstantial forms hazy and indistinct. Ryze had seen their like before, haunting the Well of Ages, and his blood turned to ice in his veins.

Some of these wraiths were aware of their new, horrific existence, screaming and railing against their fate, while others seemed confused and lost, or oblivious to the changes that had been wrought upon them.

"Something is very wrong here," murmured Tyrus.

"You think?" remarked Ryze.

"The veil between realms must have been torn asunder," continued Tyrus, ignoring his apprentice's sarcasm. "Or the souls of the dead somehow ripped across from the spirit realm. This is not good."

"This is *damnation*," breathed Jenda'kaya. "It must be every soul in the city. Perhaps every soul across all the isles."

For the most part, the spirits ignored them, or had not yet noticed them, but Ryze saw that the Camavoran knights that had been blasted to nothingness had also returned. They were a ways off, partially obscured by the coiling dark mist, but Ryze could see that their leader had become a terrifying blend of man and beast, his human form fused with his warhorse. His hooves tore up the ground as he swung his helmeted head from side to side, taking stock of his new unlife.

His gaze locked onto Ryze, perhaps sensing his attention, and cold, glowing green light spilled from within his helm. The monstrous behemoth began to stalk toward him, eyes burning with pale fire. His flesh was insubstantial, but there remained a heavy physicality to him, for he was clad in weighty, dark plate, and his weapon was very real.

"We need to go!" Ryze barked.

"You think any ships survived that?" asked Jenda'kaya.

Ryze didn't think it likely, but there was no time to think of a different plan. "Quickly, down the stairs!"

Like a hound unable to resist the call to the hunt, the monstrous amalgamation of man and warhorse began to canter, then gallop as Ryze ushered the others down the stairs.

"Faster!" Ryze urged. Halfway down, he risked a glance back. Nothing. *Surely that creature can't follow us down these steep, narrow steps. Right?*

They reached the bottom of the stairs and raced into a small square with an ornamental fountain at its center. Partly shattered statues stood in the fountain, corrupted black water spilling from their mouths. As one, they turned their heads toward the newcomers, eyes glowing with fell light.

"Keep moving!" shouted Ryze, taking up the lead once more and angling toward a narrow side alley he knew led to the docks.

Just as they were entering the alley, there was an almighty crash behind them.

"Oh gods," wailed the assistant Aayilah, and Ryze glanced back to see that the monstrous knight had leaped into the square, blazing hooves sending out a spiderweb of cracks where he landed. He saw them and surged forward in pursuit, leveling his massive glaive at them.

Jenda'kaya drew one of her relic weapons and sent a blast of pure light at the beast. It hit squarely, blasting a hole clear through his armored torso, but he did not come apart as the spirit that had followed Ryze back from the Well of Ages had done, nor did it slow his charge. Roaring, he came at them with renewed fury.

They ran.

The alley twisted and turned. In the tight confines, the monstrous knight was hampered. He slammed into the alley walls as he turned a corner too fast, dislodging bricks, and his hooves skidded on the smooth flagstones, but it was still clear he was going to run them down. Another blast from Jenda'kaya brightened the darkness, but the shot was taken in haste, and it lanced past the knight's head, missing him by less than a hand's breadth.

"Through here!" Ryze shouted, shouldering open the rear door of a storefront.

The door was narrow, and he didn't think the knight would be able to fit through. It opened into a cartographer's office, one that Ryze had been sent to multiple times over the years to acquire maps for Tyrus, and he knew the front entrance would get them ever nearer the docks.

The shade of the old mapmaker himself sat at his angled desk, but having been obliterated and then returned to unlife, he was almost unrecognizable to Ryze. His body was gone, and his form was now little more than curls of twisting parchment and maps, held together in the rough shape of a man by dark mist and glowing energy. The cartographer still clutched the elaborately feathered quill that he had always used in life, and he was scrawling manically on a stretched sheet of vellum.

Last through the door was Jenda'kaya. She unleashed a

blast from her relic weapon behind her, then slammed the door shut. The others hurriedly overturned a bookcase to block the doorway, but they all backed off as hooves smashed into the door from outside.

"That won't hold," said Tyrus.

"Out the front! Quickly!" barked Ryze.

The phantom cartographer looked up as the group barged through his office, crunching on broken glass, stamping upon scattered maps, and knocking things over in their rush. Enraged at this desecration, he reared up with a hollow, furious howl, parchment limbs unfurling and whipping out like striking snakes.

One wrapped around Aayilah's throat, the other binding tight around one of Tyrus's arms. The Sentinel's assistant dropped to her knees, eyes bulging as she gasped for air, but she was released when a heavy sledgehammer blow smashed the ghostly cartographer apart in a detonation of bright white light. Ryze gazed at the glowing weapon in the hands of Piotr and gave the burly assistant a quick nod of respect as Jenda'kaya helped Aayilah up.

The door behind them gave way, collapsing inward with the snapping of wood. The massive knight tried to smash his way inside, but he was too large, and with a snarl of fury he spun away and galloped off down the alley to find a different way around.

"We're close!" called Ryze, and he led them on their frantic way, bursting out the front door. They were on the waterfront now, and the docks were just before them. They sprinted on, but Ryze's momentum slowed as they drew near.

"Why are you slowing?" huffed Tyrus, but then he, too, saw what Ryze was looking at and came to a halt.

The docked ships had all been blasted to splinters, then partially re-formed by whatever foul magic had been unleashed across the isles, but they were now twisted, haunted wrecks.

Their figureheads gazed around them, snapping and snarling, and the shadowy spirits of sailors stood upon their decks, staring balefully toward the last living souls in the city.

"It was worth a try, lad," said Tyrus, putting a hand on Ryze's shoulder.

Erlok Grael gazed down at his remade, spectral hands in wonder, marveling at their glowing translucency, and how they now ended in wicked, knifelike talons.

He looked around him, and a wide, predatory grin split his horrific visage. He no longer resembled the man he had been. His face was skeletal, his eyes burned with balefire, and his teeth were as numerous and sharp as a shark's. The darkness of his soul was now reflected in his outward appearance.

The Well of Ages had been remade around him, though the secretive space now writhed with black mist. Curiosity driving him on, he glided back through the doors to the pool where the Camavoran king had been slain. The pure, healing waters were now a corrupted black sludge, the surface slick and reflective like an oil spill. Of the king's and the queen's spirits, he saw nothing. And whatever the light had been at the bottom of the pool, it was now gone.

Ascending through the levels of the Scintillant Tower, enjoying the spectacle of each new wonder, Grael came across a gluttonous spirit wearing the raiment of an elder.

"*Bartek*," he said, grinning widely.

"Grael?" The spirit quivered, wringing his hands. "Is... is that you?"

"Yes," said Grael, brandishing his sickle and drifting forward. "It is."

The spirit of the master wailed in fear, his jaw distending impossibly wide. He tried desperately to flee, but Grael was on him in an instant, his sickle finding its mark. He lifted Bartek off his feet, savoring the fear and pain coming off the spirit in waves. After a moment of agony, the master's form dissipated, then coalesced into a glowing sphere of light.

"Interesting," Grael hissed. The quivering ball of light still appeared to be in pain, and the warden smiled. He drew the sphere slowly off his blade, relishing how it pulsed and dilated in distress.

He sheathed his sickle, and at a gesture, a twisted, dark lantern materialized in his hand. It was similar to the one he had borne in life, but its frame was made of bone. He shoved the sphere of light into the lantern, which began to glow brightly.

Peering closely at the lantern, he saw Bartek's soul trapped within, thrashing about in panic.

"*Very* interesting," he said.

Lifting his gaze, he saw other frightened spirits, other masters fleeing from him, and his predatory smile widened yet further. Now *he* had the power. And in this new state, he could inflict as much pain and torture on those who had ever dared cross him as he wanted, without fear of repercussion. And he had an eternity to do it.

For years they had all looked down upon him. *Just a Thresher*, they had sneered. They had made him what he was, and now they would suffer the consequences of their arrogance and petty cruelty. "Erlok Grael is dead," he hissed. "Now there is just *Thresh*."

He began to laugh.

"Yes," Thresh said. "This will do nicely..."

The spirits of the dead were gathering in the black mist. *Hundreds* of them. They leered at Ryze and the others, eyes burning with pale fire. Some bared teeth, snarling, while others prowled back and forth within the darkness, like wolves beyond the firelight, awaiting the signal to attack.

There were spirits among the pack that were less threatening, yet perhaps more piteous. These lingered on the periphery, their expressions distraught, pulling at their faces and wispy, ethereal hair. Some cried for aid, while others beckoned, urging the living to come to them. Ryze recognized a few of them, and his horror redoubled as some called to him by name, begging him to help them attain peace.

"Don't listen to them," cautioned Tyrus. "They are not the people we once knew. Not anymore."

Little Tolu was still in his arms, and the twins clung to his robes.

"More are arriving," warned Artificer Jenda'kaya. She was holding two of her relic weapons: the elegant ranged one he'd seen her use before, and a sweeping blade with a relic stone set into its hilt. Her two assistants were similarly armed, Piotr with his massive relic hammer, Aayilah with a gleaming white bow with a relic stone at its heart. That bow had no string, but Ryze had no doubt of its capabilities. He was very happy to have the artificer and her weapons with them, having already seen their effectiveness.

"It may be that they are drawn to our life essence," posited Tyrus. "Like leeches to blood."

"That analogy feels a little *too* apt," noted Jenda'kaya.

A spirit launched itself through the mist, reaching for them with arms outstretched. It barely looked human, its jaw distending far more than it should, and its fingers ended in raking talons. The blinding beam of burning hot light from Jenda'kaya's relic weapon tore through it, and it screamed piteously as it came apart like smoke before a strong wind. Another hurtled toward them and was obliterated by the relic bow.

Ryze's hands formed a runic symbol in the air before he punched his fists toward another charging wraith. A surge of purple energy trailing runic shapes blasted outward, and the spirit writhed as it dissipated into oily black vapor.

There was a grunted curse from nearby. Ryze turned to see two shadowy spirits dragging Piotr toward the black mist. He flailed around him with his hammer, smashing one of them to smoke, but others lunged forward to grab hold of him. Jenda'kaya destroyed one, and the others were banished as Aayilah's bow flared.

The screams of the twins, Abi and Karli, drew his attention. Another snarling spirit, its face dripping like molten wax, had surged forward and grabbed Tyrus from the side, yanking him off-balance.

"Master!" cried Ryze, but before he could act, Tyrus placed an open hand upon the ghostly forehead of the phantom that grasped him, and sparks crackled from his fingertips. The spirit's head was lit up from within by a bright burst, and it collapsed into dark smoke.

More phantoms lunged at him, but Ryze tore them apart with a blast of runic power.

They formed a circle, back to back, with the children cowering in the center. The spirits were now wary of them and had pulled back, for a moment at least.

"We need to figure a way out of this mist," said Ryze. "Their numbers are only growing."

Ryze saw the looks traded between his master and the

artificer. They didn't think any of them were going to survive, but he refused to give in. He prided himself on being able to get into—and out of—places he shouldn't have any business being. This was no different.

"Wait," he breathed, remembering what he had glimpsed out in the harbor. With a quick glance around him, he clambered up onto the marble plinth of a nearby statue to give himself a better view out to sea.

"What are you looking for?" asked Tyrus.

"There!" Ryze cried, pointing. Even through the black mist, he could just glimpse the distant Camavoran ship, heading for open water.

"Lady Kalista bought us this chance with her life," he said. "We can't give up now."

Tyrus frowned. "You want to swim there?"

"No," said Ryze. "I want you to trust me."

He dropped off the plinth and began flicking through his leather-bound book of runic sorcery, frantically searching for the page he needed. He found it and gave the Icathian cuneiform a quick scan.

"What is *that*?" hissed Tyrus, giving the book a double take, while still keeping a wary eye on the gathering spirits. "Ryze, where did you get that?"

Ryze waved off the question, eyes still flicking across the page. "I'll tell you later. I can do this. I *think* I can do this."

"Whatever you're going to do, do it fast," urged Jenda'kaya. "Look!"

The giant, nightmarish blend of knight and horse was galloping out of the mist toward them.

He charged through the maelstrom of lesser spirits, sweeping them aside with his glaive and trampling others. Jenda'kaya and Aayilah sent searing beams of light into him, but he did not slow. Ryze summoned a runic prison, but the monstrous knight smashed through it, hooves flailing.

Piotr stepped in front, hefting his massive hammer. It was a noble—if reckless—act.

Unable to resist this clear challenge, the knight angled his charge toward the assistant, hefting his glaive high.

Piotr stood firm before the charging behemoth, waiting until the last moment to strike. His hammer blow slammed into the side of the beast in a burst of light, but even as it hit home, the knight slashed his glaive around him, cutting through Piotr.

The knight stumbled, knocked aside, skidding and sliding on the cobblestones.

Piotr was down, and Ryze could tell at a glance he wouldn't be getting up. The blow had been a mortal one. He wasn't yet dead, though, and as he struggled to rise, he was set upon by a handful of ravenous wraiths, who dragged him back into the darkness.

Aayilah cried out and made to go after him, but Jenda'kaya stopped her.

"He's gone, Aayilah. He's gone."

Ryze glanced around him. The hulking knight had righted himself, and while Piotr's blow had clearly injured him, he had not been destroyed. Ryze didn't think any of them would survive a second charge.

"Master?"

"Do it, Ryze," barked Tyrus.

Ryze drew more power into him than he'd ever done before, and violet runes burned hot within his flesh.

"*I feel the soil beneath my hands*," he muttered, moving his hands and arms to swiftly create a runic form in the air.

A circle of runes appeared around them, spinning softly, and Ryze felt the energy struggling to overpower him.

"I feel the soil beneath my hands!" he roared, and the circle was complete.

The black mist closed on them, and the giant knight charged, glaive swinging to cut them down... but they were no longer there.

A circle of burning pale runes appeared on the heaving deck of the *Daggerhawk*, eliciting new shouts of alarm.

"What now?" said Captain Vennix, spinning around, her long, curving, two-handed scimitar already in her hands.

She'd watched in mute horror as Helia was consumed, and she was still shaken by the horrific, crawling sensation of the black mist as the white wall had darkened and collapsed atop the *Daggerhawk*. Being surrounded by the white mist had felt invigorating, the magic within it making her vastayan heritage sing, but the touch of the corrupted darker version was vile. It felt like her soul was being drawn from her.

A small group of figures materialized within the runic circle, shimmering energy dancing around them. At first they were insubstantial, like spirits, and Vennix and her crew readied their weapons. Then the light began to fade, and the figures became more solid. She saw a cluster of young children in the center of the group and lowered her blade.

"It worked!" exclaimed a lean young man, collapsing to his knees. He seemed utterly drained. Fading runes glowed within his flesh. Vennix recognized him as the student of the older man whom Kalista had traveled with to the isles on her first visit.

That older man knelt and put an arm around his young apprentice. "You did well, my boy," he said.

"That's sweet, but you're not out of trouble yet," snapped Vennix. "Look!"

Spectral knights of the Iron Order were galloping across

the harbor toward them, borne aloft within a surging mass of black mist. In their lead, riding with furious intent, was their Grand Master, Hecarim, though he was now a monstrous hybrid of man and steed. Their eyes burned with witchlight, and their blazing hooves never touched the surface of the choppy water.

Vennix had seen many things in her years sailing the Twelve Seas, but dead knights and horses charging over the ocean was not one of them. The very *wrongness* of it filled her with horror, but she wasn't going to let her crew see how unnerved she was.

"Be ready to repel boarders!" Vennix roared, and her crew leaped to the starboard side of the ship, drawing swords and hefting belaying pins. "Let's show these bastards they'd have been better staying dead!"

"Your weapons will be useless against them!" shouted one of the newcomers. It was the petite dark-skinned woman she had seen in the crowd earlier that day. Her shock of white hair looked like molten silver.

"Then what do you suggest?"

As if in answer, the woman leveled a small, elegant weapon at the charging ethereal knights and let loose a beam of pure light. It lanced across the dark open water and caused one of the knights to dissipate in a blinding corona. The others leaned low over their snorting steeds, urging them faster. At her side, a woman with a shaved head pointed a strange bow at the incoming spirits, and the two of them blasted white light into the charging enemy.

"You have more of those weapons?" shouted Vennix.

The white-haired woman fired another beam into the oncoming wraiths, then hurriedly unhooked the long leather case strapped across her back and tossed it to Vennix. "Here!"

Vennix tore open the case and drew out a long weapon, unlike anything she had seen before. It was akin to some kind of giant crossbow, though there was no trigger, no string, and no bolts for it, and her skin tingled as she took it in her hands.

"It takes training and time to attune," said the white-haired woman. "You won't be able to fire it, but the magic of the stones should at least make it an effective club."

Vennix hefted the weapon to her shoulder. She thought of how Kalista had used the waystone to part the mist, and judged that this weapon was likely operated by a similar method.

"Shoot, you bastard!" she shouted, and a torrent of light erupted from the tip of the weapon, consuming one of the knights.

The three women stood together, their weapons blazing. The knights charged on through the storm of fire, until their Grand Master, snarling in fury and pain, finally swung away. He had been struck a dozen or more times, leaving gaping rents in his dark armor, and only a few of his comrades remained. The black mist itself recoiled at the blinding display, and Vennix's crew cheered as the last of the spectral knights retreated back toward the darkness-enshrouded isles.

The white-haired woman looked at her in wide-eyed surprise, lowering her weapon. "Most people take months to get even a spark from these weapons, if they can do it at all..." she breathed.

Vennix winked at her. "What can I say?" she said. "I'm not most people."

"It would seem not," said the woman, appraising her with interest. "Lady Kalista said you were a good woman. I will add *intriguing* to that description."

Vennix made a mental note to thank Kalista...but she had a horrible feeling that wasn't going to be possible.

"She escaped too, right?" she asked, already fearing she knew the answer. "Perhaps a different way?"

The grim expressions on the faces of the survivors gave Vennix her answer.

"She sacrificed herself so that we might escape," said the burly older man, Tyrus. "She drew the Iron Order to her. It was the only reason we made it out."

Vennix hung her head, feeling like someone had just punched her hard in the gut. "That does sound like something she'd do, the noble damned fool," she muttered. "I take it you're the only ones left?"

"We believe so," said Tyrus.

Vennix wiped away a tear, but the floodgates were opening. "Well, you better bloody well make sure you're worthy of her sacrifice."

Betrayer...

Kalista's eyes snapped open. She pushed herself to her feet, groaning with remembered pain, and stared down at the black blade jutting from her chest.

Betrayer...

Gritting her teeth, she yanked the glaive out with a squeal of tortured metal and dropped it to the ground. A ghostly, glowing mirror image of that weapon still protruded from her chest, and Kalista stared at it, uncomprehending. She tried to tear it free, but her hand passed straight through it. In horror, she saw that her arm was glowing and translucent, as insubstantial as smoke, and that her fingers were now elongated and ended in talons.

If she still had been able to draw breath, it would have caught in her throat as she looked down at herself. Her armor and weapons were whole, though they were blackened and cracked, as if they'd been through a fire. But of her flesh, there was nothing.

"*Kalista*," echoed a voice. It sounded at once close by and far away.

She turned to see a giant revenant looming before her. Its armor was black and riven with battle damage, and its transparent body glowed through the cracks. It held a broken sword in one fist, a spectral point showing what the blade had looked like before it snapped.

Kalista peered at the ghostly visage beneath the dark helm, and her eyes widened in horror.

"Ledros?" she whispered.

"Yes, my love," he rumbled, and her pain and grief were almost unimaginable. Gone was the proud, strong, loyal man she had loved. Now there was just this broken wraith, a vile mockery of the noble warrior she had known in life.

She turned away and took in the vision of the shattered city.

All fifty soldiers of the Host who had fought and died beneath the Enlightenment Arch stood before her in serried ranks, awaiting her command. That they, too, were trapped here made her despair. They were only here because of her. She had damned them all.

"Please let this be a dream," Kalista wailed.

"It is a nightmare," said Ledros. "But it is real."

Black mist coiled and writhed around them, like a living, breathing creature.

Betrayer...

"Who said that?" snapped Kalista, whipping around.

"I heard nothing."

Kalista turned back to Ledros, her brow furrowed. "We

are dead, then," she said. It was a statement, not a question. "This is all there is."

Ledros nodded. "But this is not the Halls of the Revered Ancestors."

"I remember a warm light," said Kalista. "There were voices within it, and they were welcoming me, but I was dragged away. Then I woke to damnation."

"Whatever was done here, we will undo it. And then we can rest, together, as we were meant to."

Betrayer.

Kalista narrowed her eyes. "*Viego*," she hissed, finally realizing. "*He* did this."

Betrayer.

Righteous anger and fury flooded her, drowning out everything else, all sense of grief and pity and loss and pain.

Ledros brought forth the necklace he had tried to give her before, back in Alovédra. "Here," he said, holding it out to her. "It is a symbol of my love, and it holds true even after death."

Kalista barely even registered what he was doing. Her entire being was quivering with rage.

Betrayer.

Her life had been *defined* by betrayal. Viego. Hecarim. As she thought of those two names, a pair of ghostly spears appeared in her back, protruding like spines. The pain was intense as they materialized, making her hiss, but she welcomed it. The pain merely strengthened her resolve, keeping the memory of those betrayals keen and sharp.

Those two were her chief betrayers, but they were far from the only ones. Nunyo Necrit. Rhazu Ferros. Erlok Grael. And the others. She remembered every betrayal she'd suffered through her life, however slight, and each one filled her with fury, and bitterness. Her nobility had made her a fool, betrayed over and over again.

More spears manifested in her back.

"What is happening to you?" whispered Ledros.

Kalista didn't answer. Nothing existed except the need to revenge herself upon all who had wronged her.

"*Betrayers, all of them*," she said.

"Don't give in to it," Ledros said. "Stay with me!"

A gap appeared in the mist, revealing a handful of baleful revenants with glowing eyes. They were seated in the saddles of armor-clad, spectral beasts that might have once been horses but now seemed far more predatory, with smoke billowing from their nostrils and tusk-like teeth jutting from their mouths.

"The Iron Order," growled Ledros, stepping forward, hefting his blade and shield.

Kalista glowered at the ghostly knights prowling at the edge of the mist, her eyes blazing and leaking witchlight.

"*Betrayers*..." she hissed.

Hatred burned within her like a fire. A glowing, ethereal spear was in her hand, though she didn't remember it being there moments before.

"Stay with me, Kal! We will fight them together," someone said nearby, but she didn't recognize who it was. It didn't matter anymore. Nothing else existed but vengeance. Without hesitation, she darted forward and hurled her spear.

The ghostly weapon took one of the Iron Order in the neck, throwing the spirit out of the saddle. The other knights wheeled their snarling steeds and charged. The Host lowered their spears as one, and a new spear materialized in Kalista's hands.

"Death to all betrayers!" she cried.

Ryze watched the shattered ruin of Helia receding from the ship, shrouded in black mist. That same malignant gloom now lay across all of the isles.

He shuddered to think how many had been killed. How many souls were now trapped within that hellish darkness?

We are the only ones who got away.

Remorse, guilt, and shame weighed heavily upon Ryze. The full horror of what had just happened had not yet sunk in. Above all, he felt utterly, utterly drained. And he knew he would never be the same.

The twisted warden had said he saw himself in Ryze, and it haunted him. His words would have been easy to dismiss had there been no truth in them. Ryze had seen what he might become if he gave in to bitterness and selfishness. But there were far bigger things at stake in the world than his own petty concerns—he saw that now—and he swore to never again be driven by ambition.

"What happens now?" he pondered.

He didn't realize anyone was in earshot until Jenda'kaya answered. "We do what the captain said. We make sure Kalista's sacrifice was worth it."

Ryze glanced over at her. She and her last remaining assistant had secured their relic weapons in their cases, but she had one of them out and was turning it over in her hands, as if seeing it for the first time.

"But how?" Ryze said.

"I think each of us will have to figure that out for ourselves," said the artificer.

"What will *you* do?"

"I'm not sure yet," Jenda'kaya said with a shrug. "But these weapons hurt the spirits pretty good. I could do worse than making more, training up new Sentinels to use them, and coming back here to end all this."

Ryze looked back toward Helia. Even from this distance, hundreds of spirits were visible, standing statue-still on the shore, watching them sail away on the *Daggerhawk*. That was only a fraction of their number, he knew. It seemed an impossible task.

"You're going to need a lot of Sentinels," he remarked.

"Got to start somewhere."

She left Ryze to his morose thoughts, and he stood staring back until the islands were completely obscured by black mist.

For millennia they had been known as the Blessed Isles, but that name no longer fit, in Ryze's mind. Now they were something altogether different.

"*The Shadow Isles*," he murmured.

Then he turned and walked away.

Epilogue

Thirty Years Later

I ache. I am weary in my bones. I do not see well anymore, and my hand cramps as I write these words. Any beauty I may have once possessed has long since faded... yet Vennix remains at my side, loyal till the end.

I have begged her to go. I don't want her memories of me to be as this aged, feeble wreck. I want her to remember the good times...and oh, did we have many of those! She, of course, is largely unchanged—her vastayan heritage sees to that. She remains as strong-willed, fierce, and full of life and love as ever.

Tyrus turned his back on the cause long ago, taking Ryze with him, claiming there were larger things at stake than the isles. He was right, of course...The Rune Wars saw untold millions killed. Entire nations destroyed in the blink of an eye. And none of that would have happened had Helia not fallen.

Over the years since the Ruination, I have tried to end the isles' curse. How could I not? All those souls, trapped for eternity, unable to move on. They deserve peace, none more than Kalista, who remains lost in there somewhere.

How many incursions into the Black Mist have I led now? I have lost count. And each journey back to the isles has cost me. Each day spent there is a year stolen from one's life, but we have recovered a good number of relic stones, which I've since worked into new weapons.

We have even managed to claim some artifacts from the vaults that are just too dangerous to be left unprotected. I dread to think of how many others have been stolen by enterprising scavengers.

My task to undo the horror unleashed by the Ruination remains unfulfilled…but even now there is hope. Kalista's selflessness gave us that. I can rest knowing that her sacrifice was not in vain, for there are others who will take up the fight. I have recruited and trained them as best I could, arming them with weapons to banish that darkness. Most of this growing coterie of new Sentinels never saw the Blessed Isles as they were, but they will not rest until the curse is ended. I know they will do what needs to be done.

Already they have proved themselves time and again, and saved countless lives. Years ago, the Black Mist began to surge beyond the borders of the isles, claiming the souls of all who perish within its grasp. But where it strikes, my Sentinels resist it.

Our new outpost nears completion. Here new Sentinels will be trained and inducted into our ways; here all of our collective knowledge and our relic weapons will be stored. It is also here that I pen this journal, and here that I will end my days.

All may be dark right now, but there is still an ember of hope.

And one day soon, that ember will become a flame, and the darkness will finally be banished.

Sentinel-Artificer Jenda'kaya

Acknowledgments

Writing a novel can be challenging under the best circumstances...and the best circumstances these were not! There was a lot going on during the writing of this book, and for a while there I was genuinely unsure if it was going to get done. But it did, largely thanks to the help of the folks listed here.

First, there's no practical way this book would have been completed without the help of my parents-in-law, Trish and Gary Wilson. Your help during a difficult time was invaluable.

Big thanks must also go to Cate Gary, my editor, who has been a great partner in crime, supporter, and ally during every step of this book.

I'd also like to thank the rest of the Books team at Riot—William Camacho, Greg Noll, Mike Rozycki, Morgan Ling, Ariel Lawrence, Ghiyom Turmel, Roderick Pio Roda, Stephanie Lippitt, and Glenn Sardelli. Also from Riot, Bridget O'Neill, Michelle Mauk, and Greg Ghielmetti for their art direction, sourcing, and icons, respectively, and Dan Moore for localization. And much appreciation goes to Paula Allen, whose consultation helped make this book possible.

Thanks as well to my editor at Orbit, Bradley Englert, and to Lauren Panepinto for her art direction.

To Graham McNeill: Your feedback was—as ever—invaluable. I also had great feedback on the manuscript from Molly Mahan, Ian St. Martin, Laurie Goulding, and Michael

Wieske. Thank you, all. You made this book significantly better than it otherwise would have been.

Of course, huge thanks to Brandon and Marc, Riot's founders, for getting this world off the ground to begin with, and allowing folks like me to play within it.

And also thanks to Larry Ray, who did the original concept art of Kalista back in the day, and to Kudos, the art studio behind the novel's interior illustrations.

Most of all, I'd like to thank all the *League of Legends* players and fans. You're awesome, and you're the reason we get to keep telling stories in Runeterra. Thank you.

Meet the Author

Riot Games

Hailing from Sydney, Australia, ANTHONY REYNOLDS developed a passion for gaming early. This passion led him to pursue a career in games and writing, and he's had innumerable stories, games, novels, and audio dramas published over a span of more than twenty years. He started playing *League of Legends* in Season Two (playing Shaco, badly), and joined Riot Games in 2014. After years living abroad in the UK and the US, he now resides back home in Sydney near the beach with his wife, Beth; their daughter, Maya, and son, Avery; and their lovable idiot of a cat called Thor.

antreynolds.com
Twitter: @_AntReynolds_

Find out more about Anthony Reynolds and other Orbit authors by registering for the free monthly newsletter at orbitbooks.net.

Kalista

Viego

Erlok Grael

Ryze

Hecarim

Jenda'kaya

Vennix

Soraka

orbit